FROZEN
SUMMER

Ian Austin

Acknowledgement

For Sallie who's supported my journey, lit the way, held my hand and occasionally kicked my backside too. If anybody is responsible for me being an author it's she. Sallie's 2014 painting Forbidden Love has been the cover image inspiration for the Dan Calder trilogy. The painting shows three characters and I've always seen Calder as a different one of those characters in each of the books. The cover of Frozen Summer shows the painting with its original colours and finally reveals two of the characters with their red hearts.

Sal, no amount of love and grateful thanks will ever be enough. X.

MY STORY

CHAPTER FOURTEEN

DAN CALDER'S AUTOBIOGRAPHY, THE MISSING CHAPTER

The shiniest of golden rules associated with a UC's conduct when involved in a test-purchase operation—and there's a fair few—is you never compromise your professional integrity or the integrity of the operation by taking drugs. Never.

I was a successful UC (undercover) for a long time and once or twice when things got tight, I managed to get out in one piece somehow, usually by saying I was buying for a terminally ill relative and having a complete backup story to go with it.

The opportunity to get away and do something different was always one of the best aspects of the job. I often thought if you were bored then you must be doing something wrong. Working for T-7 meant that the word 'boring' might as well be done away with.

I did UC work with them, Special Branch, other regional forces and my own force to a lesser degree for six or seven years before I was tasked with running as the UC operative in a major test-purchase operation to identify drug dealers in Mapperley. I'd done similar smaller scale jobs a hundred times before and I was comfortable in the role. This one was slightly different and therefore even more interesting as it was set up to last between six and eight weeks, not the usual long weekend. Also, I would remain in character 24/7 and only have limited contact with my handler.

I was a reliable UC and up to the task. At that time in my life, the less contact with the real world the better as far as I was concerned.

My handler was a local detective involved in the greater investigation of which my role was just a part. His name was Ed Weston; he looked like a fatter Rod Stewart after a particularly rough night and had some of the worst psoriasis I've ever seen. We had not met before and I could tell we were never going to be best friends, although I was going to be putting a hell of a lot of my trust in him for the duration of the operation. Ce'st la vie.

In the first two weeks I sat in a load of disgusting pubs, cafés, houses, and flats building up associations and trust with the lower end of the food chain before the chance to get to some of the major players materialised. In that time, I bought a shop full of cannabis mostly off the street and some harder stuff too with my marked bank notes and reported back to Ed on an irregular basis. On the days I didn't see him I made a log entry of what I'd done for evidential purposes and dropped those T-7 entries in our dead letter box for collection.

A dead letter box is a prearranged secure point for items to be left and collected. Ours was a metal fence post outside a disused petrol station; it had a false fascia plate we could remove to conceal then retrieve our correspondences.

As activities became more exciting and I got closer to the people we were more interested in, the contact with Ed lessened, but that was fine; I felt I was in control; my constant risk analysis was always acceptable to me and the bosses. After five weeks I was so fully immersed in the local scene that my regular places no longer went silent whenever I walked in and I could score whatever I wanted without raising eyebrows. In the week before it all went wrong, I started to push my acquaintances for more, explaining I was developing a small network of my own who I could supply to; this readily explained why I had cash with me most days.

In previous chapters I've talked about other undercover jobs, so I won't waste any more time on this one because up to now it was no different.

One day I met a new associate. I watched as he spent over an hour with the same pint glass in front of him. I made my approach and bought him another. His name was John Trew. A few days later he introduced me to another new 'friend' called Stan who took me to an address I hadn't visited before: 22 Powton Road. Stan wasn't his real name, that was Craig, but he got his nickname because of his surname, Matthews, after the footballer.

At first, I thought this house was just another horrible hole, but I soon realised it was the Mecca I'd been searching for. Inside it was dark and dirty but there was a lot more activity here than any other house I'd been taken to up to then. Stan didn't stay for long. He said hi to a few people in the hallway and then told me he needed to go. One guy was clearly running the place and a group of lieutenants buzzed around him like bees, waiting to be sent out on deliveries or returning with handfuls of cash. Mobile phones were also in constant use everywhere by all these whispering characters who together resembled the cast of a cheap scare attraction.

Cannabis smoke filled the main downstairs room like a stinking fog, and I saw heroin, or its methadone substitute being injected into skinny bruised arms by at least three individuals who soon descended into their personal abyss. This surprised me as injecting is far more dangerous than smoking. I'd seen it before but not so openly in what was a virtually public area. Heroin was in great supply here; it was the first time I saw so much available in one place.

I dropped myself into a lounge chair which offered no comfort at all; its ancient springs pushed into my body and forced me to sit with my weight to one side. I soon realised it was damp too, as my grubby jeans soaked up whatever it was that wet the chair before. I tried not to think too hard about the source.

I didn't talk and pretended not to look around either, although I tried my best to count numbers and commit the features of the captain to memory in my own way of comparing him to someone famous and then detailing the differences. He was like a twenty-year-old version of the guitarist in U2, not the Edge, the other one, a bit skinnier and taller, but facially just like him. His hair was a number one or two buzz cut which dripped down into sideburns, then a manicured beard, being so short all I could say was it was a brown colour. No glasses, no obvious marks, scars, or tattoos. He wore generic dirty blue jeans and matching jacket but he did have on an expensive looking wristwatch on his right wrist, a Tissot, black face, black leather strap, yellow numbers, yellow hands, the second hand was red and it was broken and stuck between the 4 and 5. The thing with describing someone or something is to find what is unique, if you can. You'll always remember he was a white male, or she was about five foot eight inches tall so don't clutter up your mental picture with that. Find the scar on his middle finger or her mole under her chin. Favourite items of jewellery are good too—they will always be around after the clothes have been changed and the hair cut or grown out; hopefully to be remembered by other switched-on police colleagues. I remember thinking, this was all good and I really believed I was finally getting somewhere. I liked the watch especially because he chose to wear it even though the second hand was broken. But it didn't tie in with his clothes and that made me wonder if the watch was wrong or if it was the clothes that were a disguise of sorts.

After a while the smell of the place stopped making me want to puke and I found I was more alert and on edge than at any time in weeks. I contemplated getting up and moving around to see what else was going on but as I was about to climb out of the uncomfortable seat two figures appeared from the kitchen, so I stayed put. I was so taken by the nearer person that my memory of the person behind her has faded to nothing as I'm writing this.

She couldn't have been older than seventeen I guessed, and she looked like a reject from the Annie musical due to her unbelievably wastrel-like appearance. She wore a combination of aged black and street grime from the ground up; work boots with non-matching laces, skin-tight jeans with torn knees and a vest covered by a faux fur jacket several sizes too big for her which weighed her down as if she was carrying a bear on her back. The only hint of another colour was from a once red bandana screwed around her wrist, so it resembled a misplaced Boy Scout's neckerchief, and a small cloth badge badly sewn onto the breast pocket of her jacket. I could make out a cartoon sun with a face pattern repeated all over the bandana and an animal skull on the badge. I was conscious not to stare but felt sure my look was enough for me to remember them in the future. The pallid skin of her face was a mixture of grey tones into which her eyes were set but mostly hidden by a greasy fringe. I would never forget them, either.

This was Zoe, but I shouldn't get too far ahead of myself.

She held something in one of her tiny hands; as she crept nearer, I saw it was a can of cheap supermarket cider which she frequently put to her lips and tilted back. When she got to me, she crumpled to the floor so her back was against the arm of my chair and her knees were concertinaed in front of her like a giant insect. I just ignored her.

The captain continued to orchestrate the movements of the minions around him and it became clear he was responding to requests from others by phone and then sending the drugs out to order. I surmised this method minimised the need to carry large quantities on the streets and it explained why on some days I had trouble in getting gear on street corners or in the disreputable pubs that had become my regular daytime haunts before today.

It took a while before anybody gained enough interest or curiosity to talk to me which suited me fine; the longer I could stay there just absorbing information without having to do any more than look disinterested the better, and meant the less I needed to do on my character.

"You buying?"

I acknowledged the male who looked like a teenage George Best with an orange Mohawk and a small crescent mark on his right cheek.

"Yeah, smack, but I need a good deal and no fake shit."

"How much have you got?" Mohawk asked.

There's a certain art in getting the right combination of desperation for your drugs and paranoia about getting screwed over for your last remaining few pounds that I could always get perfect. Don't ask me why. Maybe it just means I could have made a good addict in another life but in any event, I wasn't fazed.

"Have you got it or is it one of these?" I indicated vaguely around the room with a dirty finger.

"You want it or not? Twenty-five."

"Okay, yeah I want it."

Mohawk knew I did.

"Let's see your coin," he blustered, rubbing filthy fingers together.

I fished in my jeans pocket and brought out three of the dirty ten-pound notes I was issued at the start of the week, all marked and recorded by one of the T-7 admin team from a warm, comfortable office. Holding them deliberately so tight it made my knuckles white I showed just enough of them for Mohawk to be sure.

"I got thirty, so I need five back right, five back yeah?"

I wanted to convey nervousness at the prospect of parting with my money. Mohawk seemed happy enough; with an upward twitch of the jaw as an acknowledgement he crossed the room to where the captain sat, apparently paying no attention to me whatsoever. Mohawk's back concealed whatever exchange there was between them and a minute later he was in front of me again.

For a split second I thought everything was okay and then I knew somehow it wasn't. Something in the way Mohawk glanced at me before focusing on me properly was my first alert and I immediately started to think of my escape routes, my cover stories, my options if they failed. My second alert and confirmation was the feeling against my left leg of something tensing. Zoe had not moved from her mantis-like position, but she too was now aware of a change in the atmosphere as if she were a bird knowing rain was on the way five minutes before it arrived.

Over Mohawk's shoulder I could make out movements that were more deliberate than all the ones I had witnessed up to that point, but I stayed put and hoped things would work out. I wanted Mohawk to ask to see the money again and want me to hand it over before he released the wrap of powdered misery to me; anything else at all and I was in the shit.

"Who did you come with?" he asked, *trying to sound non-chalant.*

Oh fuck, *I thought.*

As I considered what to say and do next a small voice pierced all the other ambient noises around the room.

"I need something Vic, please?"

So, Mohawk was Vic. His attention drifted down to Zoe.

"No money, no shit," he said curtly.

Zoe slowly stretched out her skinny legs and big boots and lifted herself to a bending position and then put both hands on my thighs.

"Please Vic, just this once?"

"Fuck you, Summer. I said who did you come with?" he said, looking at me again.

By this time the girl he called Summer, who I now know to be Zoe, was sitting on my lap although she was so light, I could hardly feel her. When she looked into my eyes with hers, they conveyed a message of such desperate urgency my heart stopped for a long moment.

"Here?" she said.

"Here?" It sounded like a question at the time and still does to this day when I think back. So why I took Zoe's warm can of cider from her at that moment I can't explain. Her eyes never left mine as I held the can in my hand momentarily before lifting it to my dry mouth.

"It's for us," she said.

Whether that was to Vic about the smack I wanted or to me about the cider will remain a mystery forever because that's where it all ends. Remember what I said about the golden rule?

I don't know what happened next because all recollection of the subsequent events has been wiped from my mind. I can only relay what happened when I woke up the next morning.

I was aware of many things even before I was properly awake. The smell of age and dirt associated with the run-down house mixed with residual cannabis hung in the air and it was strong but still couldn't compete with the sweet, acidy, and unmistakable stench of human vomit that felt like it was burning the inside of my throat and nostrils. I could still feel the springs of the worn-out chair from the evening before sticking into my backside but above all else my ears buzzed with the sound of flies which were obviously attracted by the free regurgitated meal close by.

I slowly opened my eyes to see I was virtually lying in the chair, having slipped down overnight. The job dictated I wasn't carrying anything on me other than the marked bank notes, so I wasn't concerned about checking for things like a wallet or ID.

The reason I was still in the chair and had not slipped down to the floor completely was an obstruction which stopped my straightened legs and feet from sliding across the threadbare carpet. Zoe's head was at an unnatural angle, which resulted in the rest of her body appearing to coil around the side of the chair at my feet. Her eyes were open wide and staring directly at me as if she had been lying there for hours, waiting for me to wake up and see her. It was my brown boots wedged into her neck and shoulder that had kept me in place.

The puddle of sick was on the other side of the chair and for some reason I can remember every detail about it. It was bright green, and I mean bright like new grass, and had a very smooth consistency apart from a few grains of rice. I will never forget it for as long as I live.

My whole body ached with a particular brand of discomfort I had never experienced before. It was the pain of the morning after a drug-filled night. I always prided myself on the way I was able to exercise control over all my senses and so this wholly new sensation consumed me with dread and panic. When I first tried to move, my bones felt brittle and old. As I reached down to touch her, I already knew she was dead. Her body radiated cold before my fingers met the skin of her neck. When I touched her, she was dry too. I could see some bruising on her neck and nose and there was also some dried blood on her jeans in the area of her groin. I turned away; I didn't want to see any more and I dreaded the thought of remembering it, which was usually my best ability.

The flies continued to circle and feed. The sight of them behaving normally, just doing what flies do, lacking respect for the young girl suddenly filled me with an angry energy. I swung wildly at them, with no hope of making the slightest contact, until I was worn out.

As some sense of reason returned to my frazzled brain, I began wracking it for any memory of the last twelve hours that could shed some light on what had happened. Zoe was there before I was; she came from the kitchen when I arrived and sat with her back against the arm of my chair. The open can was in her hands already. How could I have been so fucking stupid?

Whatever else happened, I had no clue. All I knew was the previous evening wasn't filed in my head as it should have been; it was if it didn't happen, or rather, had happened to someone else. Reality quickly dawned on me; I frantically dragged my sleeves up to reveal bare forearms and studied both for puncture and tourniquet marks. I was relieved to see that they appeared unmolested.

Work with T-7 necessitated some risk and the ability to operate unsupervised; I'd gone to Powton Road the day before without reporting it to Ed. I had been working on this job for almost two months and in the last three to four weeks the clandestine meets, purchases, and sundry deals became more and more regular as I was accepted into the greater group and got closer to the main dealers. The previous night was just another of several I wanted to complete before leaving it to my handler and others to use all the intelligence and evidence I obtained to arrest, prosecute, and convict, but it had obviously gone very wrong.

In the years which have now passed since I decided to leave poor Zoe there to the flies, I've mentally re-visited the scene on a thousand occasions, each time hoping but not believing I could remember what really happened. At that time on that morning, although I thought I was being rational I know now it was the worst decision I ever made, probably influenced by whatever poisons remained in my body after I drank Zoe's cider and then snorted, smoked, or otherwise consumed whatever it was I did.

Then, as now, I can't believe I was responsible for her death. Then, as now, I can't discount the possibility I was.

A few hours later it was far too late anyway. During active operations I always painted my fingertips and palms with a mixture of clear nail polish and baby oil to prevent leaving fingerprints; after I made my hands dirty no one could tell. With enough clarity of thought to check myself and Zoe for traces of a sexual connection between us, I was relieved to see we both appeared clear in that regard, so I knew I could walk away from the house leaving no forensic link from her to me.

Later that day my duty report submitted on official T-7 documents stated I was at another address the previous evening and had then gone back to my own flat (for the purposes of the job) before midnight.

If it was ever known I took an illegal substance my under-cover career would've been over. I know what you're thinking but let me explain. At the time I prized work above everything else, I somehow legitimised the decision I made to save my sorry arse. The moment I deposited the log into the dead letter box my fate was sealed, and the rest of my life would be contaminated by the lie.

Zoe's body was discovered a few days later by a new band of druggies who saw the vacant address as ideal for their needs un-til her stiffened body swiftly convinced them otherwise. I carried on with the job for another ten days during which time the whole area became so overcrowded with police my usefulness dwindled to zero as the dealers evacuated the area faster than an Olympic sprinter. My sleep was filled with visions of stinking bright green and I spent a couple of days unsuccessfully trying to dis-cover what drug induced such an abnormality.

I then returned to Garstone to resume my normal duties. Normal! What a joke. In those ten days and in the weeks which followed, I ran the full gamut of emotions over what happened to Zoe and my actions; every time I relived the evening at Powton Road I cursed my stupidity, cowardice, and plain bad luck. Then, as now, all I really remembered with certainty was she called herself Summer that night. It wasn't unusual for people in and around the drug scene to use an alias. What made it all the more tragic was the news that Summers was Zoe's real surname.

Months later the inquest found she died as a result of stran-gulation, although she also sustained an unusual wound or gash on the upper left leg with an object similar to a large skewer, resulting in blood loss, but not enough to kill her. In the weeks after I went back to Garstone, I deliberately tried not to investigate or even enquire about the matter for fear of drawing attention to myself.

I was interviewed by one of the Major Incident Team detectives assigned to the job as my undercover duties in the area were made known to them. I answered a few questions by saying I knew nothing and pointed them to my T-7 logs to show I didn't go to the address that night.

So, there you have it. What does what happened make me? I wish someone could explain it because I don't know. But then again, as nobody in the whole world knows what I was a part of at 22 Powton Road, Mapperley, there doesn't seem much chance of that, does there?

Rest in peace Zoe, I'm sorry.

CHAPTER ONE

November 2018

"Finished, come and look," Dan called from the top of the stairs.

"About time, we're coming."

The instructions accompanying the flat-pack box stated the whole operation should be completed with consummate ease in just a few minutes, so how it was that it took him almost two sweat-filled hours to assemble Bradley's first bed was completely beyond him.

Tara appeared in the doorway holding Bradley against her hip, and with Jet in close attendance too.

"Down, you know better." Dan growled causing Jet to turn on his hairy heels and make a rapid descent.

"Oh, grumpy Daddy." Tara giggled and Bradley looked as if he would burst into tears, but his mother's laugh quickly transformed his face into a beaming smile.

Tara gave the junior bed a good look over and seemed satisfied. "Hey, it looks great. What do you think, Baba?"

Bradley was nearly nine months old and at least nine more away from using the new bed but they heard somewhere it's good for babies to become familiar with their new bed before they made the transition from the cot, so the latest piece of his room's furniture was made up in readiness.

He was far more interested in sucking on Tara's hair than the bed.

"Time for a coffee," Dan said, pecking his son on the forehead and then repeating the action on Tara.

Tara groaned playfully and lifted Bradley up with both hands.

"Here, I'll do that, and you take him. He's getting too heavy for me."

"Come on then Baba, let's go," Dan said, taking Bradley from her and nuzzling his face into his son's tummy, causing a gurgle of delight.

They had come a long way in a short space of time.

When Dan got back from his trip to England the year before he and Tara thought for a time their relationship may not survive. His guilty admission about Zoe Summers and Powton Road tested them to the absolute limit; he failed to see how Tara could live with him and be in love with him given the knowledge he might have killed another human being. Her love and support plus Dan's eventual willingness to seek help in the form of some very confidential counselling started to rebuild the bridge between them, but it took another human being, Bradley, to finally mend them properly. From then on, every new day was a step forward along the path of resolution.

Tara was hurt and confused as Dan confided in her the details of chapter fourteen over a long holiday weekend. The slowly delivered bombshell of how something so vital in his life could be kept from her was by far the worst of the whole episode and she initially responded badly, not least because even if they were to separate, her being pregnant with Bradley would irrevocably bind them together forever.

The situation finally came to a head months later, just before Christmas. They were getting ready to go out when a stupid disagreement over a TV news item curtailed their plans and almost ended a lot more.

He said, "I could kill these people sometimes. Their reporting stuff like this is jeopardising soldiers' lives."

"They have to report the news. I think we've a right to know what the major governments are doing," she responded.

Both innocent remarks started a short but violent burst of argument and counter-argument, which soon got off topic, culminating in Dan's foolish comment.

"So, you really do think I'm capable then?"

Tara bit back, "Oh no not all that again. Of course, I don't believe you killed that poor girl. The trouble is you think you might have and until you can come to terms with that or realise what I know to be true we'll be going over and over this every time we read a newspaper or watch the bloody TV. Jim is all but convinced too, so why don't you just give me, and more importantly, yourself a break because I've just about had enough of it and you."

"Enough of me? What does that mean?"

"What do you think? You're the detective."

At that point Tara grabbed at her stomach as a shooting pain like lightning bent her in half and she yelled out in anguish. Dan dived to the floor where she was holding her belly and panting through agonised tears.

"Tara, what is it?"

"I don't know."

"You need to go to the hospital. Can you just hold on while I call an ambulance?"

"Hurry please," she cried. "Dan, help me, I'm scared."

Dan was scared too; Tara's pregnancy had been troublesome throughout and she was under doctor's orders to take things easy. Fifteen minutes later, as the ambulance backed off their driveway, there was only one thing on their minds. Tara was admitted to Auckland Hospital for observation and after her sedative took effect, Dan went home.

As Tara spent an incident free night in hospital, Dan spent the whole night wide awake thinking about his life's priorities. He was a very different character when he went back in to collect her. The thought of anything happening to her or the baby because of something he said or did was unconscionable.

"Darling, I promise you I will never get like that again and if I ever do you have my permission to lock me in a box and throw away the key."

From that moment on he wasn't only as good as his word but ten times better. He updated her regularly on the developments he was making on the research she'd nicknamed 'Frozen Summer' because of the length of time it had been a cold case.

The coffee aroma as he entered the kitchen made Dan's smile widen.

"Oh, Mummy's got the good stuff out. You don't know what you're missing, Baba."

Bradley smiled and blew saliva bubbles, which Dan wiped away with a tissue. They were never without at least one tissue in a pocket or up a sleeve and often found them turned to mush in the washing machine.

"I've made some biscuits too, so you boys sit down and I'll bring them over," she said without turning to face them.

Dan sat on the long sofa and dandled Bradley on his knees until Tara brought the tray over. She put it down on their coffee table, which now displayed a healthy number of marks and scars, including Dan's small ink heart he placed there before he went off to England last year and which he secretly recoloured occasionally to maintain its vibrancy.

Tara poured their two cups but left them on the tray.

"I've got something to tell you," she said, leaning back.

Dan grinned. "The good coffee and home-made biscuits, I should have guessed. Okay tell me, what have we bought?"

Tara punched him playfully on the arm. "Actually, you're sort of right. I was looking at the flights to London yesterday." Dan's mouth dropped open. While they talked about it happening one day, *the* one day had never been discussed. Tara continued before he could respond. "And I called Jim and Gwen last night while you were at the pub with Paul. They said we can come whenever now he's better again. What do you think?"

When Bradley started to whine, Dan realised he had stopped jiggling his legs—Tara's sudden disclosure momentarily affecting his thoughts and actions.

"Wow, this is all a bit sudden," Dan said finally, resuming the rhythmic leg movement which brought the smile back to Bradley's face.

"Well from what we know, and you do have quite a bit now to start with, Jim is certain he can cope. So, the question is, if not now, when?"

Dan's research into Zoe Summer's death comprised all he read and worked on relating to the files Jim Allen gave him in Nottingham Hospital. After he'd got home from that trip, explained about Zoe, and Jim's suggestions for solving the mystery of her death, Tara was initially abhorred by the notion, but she quickly became a convert to Jim's thinking, much more so even than Dan in the early months.

"He's right," she said one day while Dan was miserably poring over the reams of paperwork in his office. "Let's end it once and for all, then we can get on with our lives."

"And if it's bad news?" In those days he was still a confirmed pessimist.

"It won't be."

"But if it is?" he protested.

Tara groaned. "You're impossible, Dan."

And the conversation ended for another few days until they went over the same ground again.

Now that things were so much better, their conversations were altogether different too.

Dan turned serious. "Really? You're happy to come and bring Bradley with us?"

"Yes, absolutely."

"You know I've secretly been itching to get over there."

"Dan, it's hardly a secret. I think we should take a few days, starting now, to get things sorted and go. If it takes a week, fine. If it takes a month, so be it." Tara touched Bradley's cheeks. "Come on you've been through enough. Let's finish this."

He kissed her gently on the hand and cuddled Bradley closer to him. "Okay."

"I'll make some arrangements," Tara said.

Dan leant forward and picked up their coffees. Handing Tara's to her, their eyes met.

They quickly changed the subject.

The following morning Dan went to his regular counselling meeting while Tara took Bradley to his specialist's appointment. He first met Toby McCallister from the Coping with Grief Network because Toby counselled Tara's brother Neil until his untimely death. After the episode with Katrina Mallinder was over, Dan went to Toby himself but at that time only disclosed a fraction of his feelings and none of them to do with Zoe Summers. It took a while before Dan was completely comfortable to talk about his childhood but when he finally broke the shackles, the years of secrecy, mistrust, and guilt that suffocated him loosened; he was able to speak freely and felt exponentially better.

The break from meeting Toby when he returned to England to assist Nick and the Hetherington family knocked him back for a while after he returned home. It was two full months before he called Toby again. Talking about the Frozen Summer project with Tara or Jim was one thing but opening up to Toby was very hard, notwithstanding the respect and trust Dan had for his young confidante.

After exchanging hello, how are yous, they got down to business, both ever mindful that in order for their continuing discussions to work for Dan it could never be anything else; they were friendly but would never be friends.

"So, you were saying Bradley's condition contributed to yours and Tara's improvements when we last saw each other?" Toby started.

"Yes, strength through adversity is a great bond builder for us. I think we both appreciate it more because of the trials we've experienced separately and together."

"Good, do you need to add more?"

"No, we cope better with him because of it."

Toby jotted a few words in his book. "So, what else is new?"

"Quite a lot as it happens. We've decided now is the time to go back to England."

"Oh really, so you and your friend Jim can look into the death of Zoe Summers?"

"Yes, what do you think?"

When Dan first told Toby about Zoe about the possible extent of his involvement in her death, a necessary conversation ensued regarding what Toby might be obliged to do if he ever got to the stage where he suspected Dan was culpable. The matter remained unresolved.

"To know is always better than to hope or to be unsure. Knowing something you would rather be different, well that's another dilemma altogether," Toby said.

Dan nodded. He liked the way Toby made him give his own answers to the questions he posed. "Well I need to know, if possible, and I'll only be able to say if I'd prefer it to be different once I do know."

"Yes."

"So, I do know enough already to say I'll be happier than I am today even if I would rather the situation was different. Tara and Jim are sure, but I think they base that on what they want."

Toby nodded this time. "That's natural."

"Yes, of course. I'm really very concerned how they'll react to bad news though. I can live with whatever we find out, but Tara's life especially will never be the same, Bradley's too, come to that, if he has to grow up without a father because I'm in prison."

"So, you still think if you find out you did have a hand in her death you will report the facts to the authorities?"

"I have to. Wouldn't you? I couldn't live with myself otherwise and I'd be sure to destroy my closest relationships in the fallout."

Toby ignored the question. "When do you plan to go?"

"Tara's saying within the next two weeks."

"And you're all going?"

"Yes, I decided no more secrets a while ago, remember?"

A previous discussion prompted Dan's decision not to keep anything from Tara in the future. Toby had argued it was the person telling small lies or keeping the little secrets who was far more dangerous to themselves and others. His work with convicted criminals led to the theory which he described to Dan during the early days of their meetings.

Dan recalled the conversation.

"Let's say you've committed a serious offence, or you tell a lie to keep your job," Toby had said. "There's an immediately obvious reason to keep it to yourself, to avoid the consequences in the first instance and to keep your job in the second. It's reasonable to see the provocation. Now take the type of person who constantly tells small lies or keeps innocuous things secret from people they're close to even though there would be no real adverse consequences. What does that say about them?"

Dan had thought for some time. "I can see misplaced insecurity issues, but I can't see how they're somehow less preferable."

"Consider this," Toby continued. "A person compelled to lie or maintain a secret because the ramifications of not doing so are so serious or the person who has no compunction about lying and keeping secrets faced with nil pressure?"

Dan caught on quickly. "Oh, I see. We're talking about the unknown capabilities of that person. If one is prepared to do that over a minor issue, then what might the same person be capable of in extreme circumstances?"

Toby looked pleased. "I found in my studies the profiles of the two groups were entirely different. You've also studied people throughout your career, so you tell me, what do you make of your finding?"

Dan was amused by what was so apparent now but eluded him completely for over twenty-five years of police work. He found no fault with Toby's logic but still placed a caveat on his own thoughts when he answered. "The argument is compelling if we take it on face value and don't consider individuals, only groups. A person prepared to lie and maintain secrets for no good reason must have the propensity to tell bigger lies and keep bigger secrets in relation to the stakes."

Toby raised an eyebrow as if to say well, that's something to think about and Dan considered this new information.

That was then, when nothing concrete was decided. Now there was an immediacy to the conversation.

"You'll need a strategy" Toby prompted.

"A strategy?" Dan replied.

"A map of what you will do depending on what you discover. Depressives find that having one helps when it all hits the fan. Knowing you can set into motion certain actions when you can't think straight can be a pressure release."

Dan liked the idea and didn't mind the depressives tag. "In the job we called it an operation order. Information, intention, method, administration, and communications. Admittedly up until now I've not considered an op order for the whole trip, but I've been thinking about them if I have to follow somebody or perform certain covert acts."

"What do you think? Is it something which might help?"

"Yes, definitely."

"I expect you will also find if you do make a plan it will clarify some of your objectives."

"No, Toby, that's the one thing it won't do. My objectives are as plain and simple now as they've been from day one when Jim convinced me this was the only way."

They talked until 11:58 a.m. when an electronic bell sounded the end of the meeting. At that moment the discussion they were part way through stopped, as it always did, and both men sat back and closed their eyes. Two minutes of personal reflection followed until another bell sounded. Stopping mid-discussion meant there was always a ready place to begin the next meeting, therefore negating false silences or a pressure to find something new to talk about each time.

"Thanks Toby, I'll see you next week."

They shook hands on another concluded business meeting and Dan left.

When he got home Tara and Bradley were already back from Bradley's doctor date.

"Hello. How was it?" Dan asked.

"Good, well, the same as before. No better or worse. I said about going overseas and he was fine with that especially as he has been attack free for close to ten weeks now."

Jet sat between them listening to the conversation and receiving attention from them both. Since Bradley was a month old, they knew there was a problem as he cried non-stop for the whole week, but despite several hospital visits and specialist appointments, they were no closer to knowing the cause. The most recent best guess was he was suffering from a stomach or bowel problem which occasionally manifested itself with searing pain causing him to howl like a wolf cub until it subsided. When it did strike, he would curl into a tight ball and try not to let anybody touch his abdominal area.

At the time, Doctor Best Guess said Bradley's organs were normal and he hoped it was something to simply grow out of.

Thanks for nothing, Dan replied at the time.

"Is he in bed now?"

"Yes, I put him down when we got home. I stopped at the travel agents as well to see if there were any deals, but I think it doesn't make much difference if we do it online ourselves. Shall we do it now while it's quiet?"

A few minutes later they sat in Dan's office looking at the computer screen. A dozen airlines described a range of flights from Auckland to London, but they wanted one which departed in the early evening, hoping that Bradley would sleep for a big chunk of the first leg.

"What about this one? It leaves later than we ideally want but the stop-over and the second flight are good for us," Tara said, pointing to an Emirates Airline's schedule.

Dan looked encouraged. "Fine by me. Can we go business class with him?"

Tara grinned. "I'm sure we can, but I'll check. Shall I go ahead and book it if they do?"

The hours of reading Zoe Summers' files and subsequent note taking, the weeks of self-examination, and the months of uncertainty were now at an end. If Dan answered in the affirmative, then the full implications of what they might discover could transform their lives forever. Therefore, he hesitated.

"Dan?"

"Sorry, yes you know I love you both, right? Yes, let's book it."

CHAPTER TWO

The only issue with being away for an unknown amount of time was Jet; putting him in kennels was an absolute no. They agreed before taking him on that he was a part of the family and they would look after him accordingly. Rather than let him go to one of the several volunteers who offered to take him for the duration, they preferred to find somebody who could stay in their home where his surroundings would be familiar even if the occupants were not at first. The situation resolved itself when they were able to secure a house-sitter who could dedicate enough time to his needs but also look after the place. The sister of Tara's business partner was moving to Auckland from Christchurch; in the aftermath of the two catastrophic earthquakes in 2010 and 2011 she still didn't feel completely safe years afterwards. Christine was a perfect fit as she worked from home and had a pet dog of her own before the two big shakes; it disappeared when the second hit and was never found. She was due to come up and was already actively looking for a house to rent. The timing couldn't have been better.

The prospect of being in England so close to Christmas was exciting for Tara. She visited the UK years before when travelling and working her way through Europe after finishing university, and three years ago when Dan brought her over at the time of Katrina Mallinder's trial.

The day they arrived was one of those quintessentially English winter days. The sky was patchwork of greys, the air promised yet continually failed to deliver rain, and the temperature hovered somewhere between comfortably cold and cold enough to make people complain. Tara was tired as she spent the entire time with one eye on Bradley, who slept for the first leg of the journey but stubbornly remained awake for the second and became progressively grumpier until another big spoonful of Calpol finally got him off to sleep twenty minutes before they were due to land.

When they found their hire car in the vast ocean of vehicles behind the main terminal, they spent several minutes loading the bags and getting Bradley settled in the space-age baby seat. By this time Tara's mood was as dark as the sky and her patience maxed out.

"How long till we get there?" she asked, expecting a number in reply which would undoubtedly make her even more miserable.

Dan tried to help with the baby during both flights, but it was clear right from the outset Bradley just wanted his mother. Dan didn't endear himself to Tara by offering a limp smile or shoulder shrug on more than one occasion in explanation for a failed attempt to give her a few minutes rest as he handed the crying Bradley back. In reality, it was all part of travelling long distances with an infant, but as they'd discovered, parenthood was the one thing nobody ever taught you.

"It could be up to four hours. Let's hope he sleeps in the car," Dan answered.

Tara groaned as Bradley filled his lungs for another crying episode at being put down. Ten minutes later they were clear of the car park and on the motorway heading west and south. Mercifully, Bradley was sound asleep before they were out of the car park.

"Better?" Dan asked shooting her a glance.

Tara rested her hand on his left thigh as the car reached cruising speed to match the flow of traffic.

"Much," she said, turning the radio up slightly and closing her eyes as Simon and Garfunkel serenaded them. "Are you going to be okay driving?"

"Yes fine, I'm back in a comfort zone again. We shouldn't need to stop for fuel and it's motorway for most of the way. Why don't you close your eyes too?"

He adjusted the rear-view mirror so he could see Bradley in it and still maintain a decent enough look at the traffic behind them. He felt happy the two most important people in the world were safe and hoped their dreams were better than his. On the seat next to Bradley he caught sight of his briefcase, the same one he'd had since transferring from the surveillance team to Garstone a lifetime ago; inside were documents relating to Zoe Summers. Their current destination of Salcombe on the Devon coast would be the beginning of a new chapter in his book. In his more positive dreams, it might be the last, but it was a long way from being written yet.

From the beginning of the M4 motorway it was exactly 100 miles before a deviation was needed at the Junction 20 exit where they joined the M5. With Tara and Bradley sleeping, Dan took the time to divide his attention between the road and the journey's end, which would mean meeting up with ex-Detective Chief Superintendent James Allen once more.

Their professional relationship had been poisonous to say the least when Dan worked under Allen's supervision at Garstone, and at the time he left the police, he regarded Jim more than partly responsible for his demise. When he returned to England to help Nick and Amber Hetherington, his initial feelings towards Jim remained as hard and fast as ever, until the truth emerged and he finally realised how wrong he had been about his old boss and how he alone was responsible for his own suffering consequently. When Teddy Parker savagely attacked Jim, beating him close to death, Dan literally saved his life by getting medical assistance just in time. Subsequently shared periods at the hospital ranging from brief moments to whole days in each other's company formed a new bond of friendship and mutual respect as close and deep as any blood oath. In all honesty, to both it felt more like father and son.

Dan went home to Auckland long before Jim was discharged but they stayed in regular contact afterwards. When Jim and Gwen moved down to Salcombe in Devon, Dan and Tara had a rose bush called New Beginnings delivered as a moving in present. Later, they sent flowers to Gwen for her birthday and a copy of the first family photo of them with Bradley. Gwen said the picture was the single biggest thing that encouraged Jim to get better as quickly as he could. Their own son Bradley had disappeared somewhere in South Africa many years before, and Bradley Calder was a reminder of happier times.

Now Jim was as fit and well as he was ever going to be, he and Gwen had insisted every time they spoke that Dan, Tara, and Bradley must stay with them when they came over, and not just because Jim was going to try and help Dan regarding Zoe Summers. Dan missed his private conversations with Jim and felt their comradeship was like one of the missing pieces of his life's puzzle.

The late afternoon traffic was heavy as workers escaped London for the weekend; the hired Ford never got above sixty-five, meaning the turn off to the southbound lanes of the M5 didn't arrive for the best part of two hours. By that time Dan needed a break to stretch his legs and switch off his brain for a few minutes; the combination of air travel from Auckland and his thought-filled drive was taking its toll. He could still remember a hundred different motorway services from his days on the surveillance team and training courses; there was another one a couple of junctions ahead.

When he pulled into the sodium light-filled car park and stopped, Tara woke but Bradley didn't stir.

"Hey, are we here?" she said sleepily.

It was cold, dark, and uninviting outside.

"Sorry no, only a little over halfway but I needed a break. Do you want to stay here while I go to the toilet? Do you want anything?" Dan replied, brushing some rogue hair away from her face.

Tara placed her hands on top of his and held them there against her cheek. "Sorry I was so tired."

"No problem. The little monster gave you a hard time on the plane. I'll go and get some water inside and then we'll get going again. The worst part is over. Hopefully we can be at their house by eight."

Dan got out and immediately felt the winter chill through his thin knit sweater. In the times he came back to the UK from New Zealand he was convinced the sky was lower and the atmosphere more oppressive. He involuntarily hunched his shoulders as he walked towards the artificially bright entrance.

Tara had woken and changed Bradley by the time Dan got back. Seeing his daddy appear back in the car made him chuckle and blow more bubbles, which Tara dabbed away. Dan settled again and refastened his seat belt. The Ford purred into life and they glided out of the car park on the final leg of their journey.

In Salcombe Jim and Gwen Allen were expecting their visitors at any time after six; Gwen spent the whole of the day washing towels and baking bread, cakes, and biscuits. Dan and his family were their first proper visitors and they were looking forward to seeing them for a raft of reasons. To have a baby around again would be a joy since they had no children to give them grand-children and they felt a connection to Bradley from the second Dan told them he and Tara decided on that name. They knew Tara through Skype, but this would be the first time they would all meet in the flesh. To have Dan around them again was the most poignant of all.

"What time is it?" Gwen asked.

Jim raised his bushy eyebrows. "About ten minutes since you last asked, love. Have you forgotten I bought you a watch two years ago?"

"Admit it. You're just as excited as me to see them," she teased.

The old detective was. The long road from death's door to being able to sit upright in a wheelchair and be pushed out of the hospital was only the first part of his recovery. The subsequent months of physiotherapy, return visits, and endless courses of medication took a heavy toll. Though he would admit it to no one, the emotional scars were as fresh and raw as ever.

The only very good thing was the way the force treated him in the aftermath and the way he was able to retire with all his benefits intact. He felt no remorse in taking up all the support they offered before, during, and after. The day he and Gwen moved down to Salcombe closed that chapter of their lives and he was genuinely content to now be living the quiet life in the southerly corner of the West Country, surrounded by his new rose gardens and in the company of the woman who'd been with him through thick and thin. His relationship with Dan was the one great bonus in his life he would never have dreamt of before, and for that he could be grateful for the beating and the injuries. Enduring the pain of losing their son, he rationalised, was worth enduring a whole lot more to discover another.

The word *son* was one he used often when talking to younger subordinates throughout his career, picked up from his own father and other males of the same generation. While he genuinely meant it to be a sign of friendliness and affection then, its meaning with Dan transcended all that. It was the word which first got them talking to each other like normal people after years of animosity, it was the word which alerted Dan to his desperate situation the night of the attack, and it was the word which best described his feelings towards him now. Gwen was right as usual—he couldn't wait to see Dan again.

Tara remained awake for the remainder of the journey, although Bradley fell asleep again as soon as the car left the services. She and Dan chatted about anything and everything as they continued southwards to Salcombe, but it was another hour and a half before they saw the first distance road sign and another half hour before they turned off the A381 Main Road into Beadon Road.

"Finally," Dan sighed. "Beadon Hill Cottages, on the left along here somewhere."

After a hundred metres they saw a new sign mounted in a stone pillar indicating the private road and as they turned in, the tarmac starburst in four directions leading to the driveways numbered 1 to 4. Dan drove into number 1 and pulled up outside the cedar clad barn conversion, which seemed to be illuminated by every light in the house being on, flooding the front courtyard through large windows.

Before they could get out and stretch their weary limbs, the house door opened; Jim and Gwen appeared with smiles as bright as the lights. Dan got out and met them halfway; Gwen threw her arms around him and planted a warm kiss on his cheek.

"Gwenny give the boy some air." Jim laughed. "Hello son, it's good to see you."

They stood for a moment a step apart with beaming smiles before Dan extended his hand. Jim took it warmly, pulling him into another, manlier hug with their spare arms. To Dan it felt like coming home. When they released each other, he turned back towards the car.

"This is Tara."

"And this is Bradley," Tara said, holding the drowsy baby so the Allens could get a good view.

"Welcome, welcome," Jim said, still with his arm around Dan's shoulder.

Bradley shyly buried his face into Tara's chest while Gwen cooed around him and gave Tara an equally affectionate kiss.

"Oh, he's a darling! We've been so looking forward to you coming, haven't we Jim? Let's get you all inside in the warm."

Dan headed back to the car.

"I'll get the bags. Travelling with him means we've so much stuff."

"Here let me help," Jim said, following.

Gwen stopped and barked a happy order at her husband. "Nothing too heavy, remember what the doctor said."

When Dan opened the boot Jim's eyebrows shot up again. "You weren't kidding, were you?"

They shared a laugh as Dan heaved the first case out. "Tara has planned for every eventuality and natural disaster." He pulled several more bags and suitcases out of the boot, deliberately handing a couple of the smaller ones to Jim. "Okay that's it."

It took two trips to get all the cases inside but when Jim closed the front door behind them Dan immediately felt the familiar wave of English central heating rush to surround him.

Jim shook his shoulders again. "It's good to see you. Drink?"

"Music to my ears, lead the way."

Gwen had Tara and Bradley settled in the spacious lounge and was already busy re-telling some of the moving day stories.

"Oh, here they are. Jim, I was just telling Tara about the trouble we had getting the furniture in here." Without giving him the opportunity to reply she continued. "Look at this little boy. He's going to be a real heartbreaker. Is he talking yet?"

Tara stood and held up Bradley again who was now wide awake and seemingly enjoying all the attention. "He's been making sounds for a while but no real words."

"May I?" Jim asked, taking the baby from Tara and holding him as if it was the most natural thing in the world. "There we are, you're a bonny boy," he said as Bradley gave him a wet, gummy smile and thrust a whole fist into his mouth.

"He's normally a bit doubtful with new faces," Dan said.

Jim replied without taking his eyes away. "No, we're going to be great friends aren't we, Bradley."

Gwen was sitting on the sofa next to Dan; she quietly touched his knee, expressing her thanks for them coming and her hopes for a brighter future. Bradley managed another five minutes before he wanted his mother back again, and shortly afterwards Gwen showed Tara the way to their room so they could put Bradley down for the night. Alone in the lounge for the first time, Dan and Jim sat in comfortable quiet, listening to the radio playing a classical concert. Dan closed his eyes and could easily have fallen asleep there and then, but Jim's voice forced them open again.

"You have a wonderful family; you must be happy."

"Yes, I really am. What about you? Down in this part of the world and no more job."

"Honestly it took no time at all to adjust. Perhaps if I got to retirement as originally planned it might have been different, but we came down here on a long weekend and this was the first house we saw. In no time at all we sold and were packing up the house in Tinsley. There has not been a single day when I've missed all we left behind."

There was no need for Dan to query what it all meant or for Jim to explain it further; each allowed their mind to travel back in time sharing the same private thoughts.

Dan was holding his cup in both hands, allowing the heat to radiate through him as the aroma of the coffee wafted up. He contemplated a safer topic, roaming the walls with his eyes. "I can see it's a conversion, but they've done a great job to make it feel modern and homely all at the same time."

Jim smiled. "No need to get up now but I'll show you around later. Yes, this is our last move and it will do us just fine. Wait until you see the gardens in the daylight tomorrow and you'll see why I'm really as happy as a pig in—"

"Jim no! Not in front of visitors," Gwen said, preventing him from finishing his description as she and Tara returned.

Tara giggled. "Don't mind us. I'm sure your house can't be as colourful as ours at times."

Five minutes later they all were able to sit and relax properly for the first time and catch up with some of the latest family news.

"Gwen's got us in a lovely room and Baba has his larger travel cot made up in the walk-in wardrobe. It's perfect," Tara said, resting her head against Dan's shoulder and stifling a yawn.

"Oh, it's nothing, but he'll be able to sleep through when you go up and you can still turn the lights on if you need to. Are you hungry? I've made a fish pie."

"Mm sounds lovely. Dan's always hungry," Tara replied.

Dan felt his stomach rumble. "Sounds great, thanks Gwen. We brought a few bottles of New Zealand with us."

"Come on then, let's eat. Before Tara falls asleep," Jim pronounced.

The dining room was more formal but no less comfortable and the relaxed air continued throughout the meal. They were able to find enough to talk about without Jim and Dan thinking to approach the prime reason for the visit, although everybody knew it would be weighing heavily on their minds. The challenges to come could hold off one more night.

By ten Tara couldn't wait any longer for bed; hugging Gwen and thanking her and Jim for their hospitality she excused herself.

"I'll follow you up in a minute," Dan said as she got up from the table.

Jim touched his wife's hand. "That was lovely. If you want to go up, I can tidy all these things."

"I just wanted to say how great it is to see you both again," Dan said.

"You too, son."

"Are you as fit and well as you look?"

Jim was still covering Gwen's hand with his; it wasn't lost on Dan when he closed his fingers around hers in an involuntary action.

"I'm not twenty-one anymore whereas at the beginning of last year I still thought I was. The doctors are pleased with my progress and Gwen here keeps an eye on me too."

She managed to squeeze out a smile for Dan's benefit; Jim had cleverly avoided actually answering the question.

"Okay well I think I'll take your advice and head on up too. I hope Bradley doesn't wake you during the night."

Within the hour the household was quiet as they all slept.

CHAPTER THREE

When Dan opened his eyes, he was already aware of being alone in the bed and sensed that Bradley wasn't in his cot. He had no idea of the time; the thick curtains concealed whatever light there was outside.

When he pulled back the curtains he was surprised by the view. Jim's gardens gave way to a thick ribbon of dark green fir trees and in the distance, a spectacular view of Salcombe Harbour and the rooftops of the town to the left. As they arrived after dark, he didn't realise how high above the town the house was, or its orientation; now he could tell it was in a prime location.

After showering he found his case underneath all Tara and Bradley's luggage, put on some casual clothes and headed downstairs.

"Well, good afternoon," Tara said, turning from the kitchen sink as he walked in.

The big wall clock confirmed she wasn't joking, albeit only by five minutes.

"Sorry, I had no idea."

"That's alright. When Bradley woke up in the night you didn't even stir and this morning I was wide awake at six, so I got up. As I was getting dressed, he woke up as well. We've done all sorts while you've been snoring your head off."

"Where is he?" Dan could count on the fingers of one hand the amount of times Bradley had been out of Tara's sight since he was born.

"Gwen and Jim have taken him for a walk into town. They're so lovely; they can't get enough of him."

"I guess they feel connected in a way."

"I know, I think it's great. He has no grandparents, so they might be the closest he ever has, and he could do a lot worse."

"Listen to you, you sound like you want to adopt them." Dan grinned.

"Well while you were sleeping, they've been telling me all about moving down here from Nottingham, what their plans are and how much they've been looking forward to seeing you again. They showed me all around the house—wait till you see his rose gardens! I would adopt them if I could. Here, coffee," she said, passing Dan a steaming mug.

They chatted at the big pine table until the sounds of Jim, Gwen, and Bradley returning stopped them. Bradley's cheeks were as rosy as any children's book character even though he was wrapped from head to toe; he was clearly delighted to see his parents again and gurgled noisily as Gwen took off his outer layers and passed him back to Tara.

"Sleep well, Dan?" Jim asked, unbuttoning his heavy coat.

"Too good. I've only been up a little while. What a great view you've got from upstairs."

"The views sold us on the house the minute we walked in," Gwen said. "Although it has to be said Jim did his homework before we came down to see this place and others. You had your gardens mapped out in your head already, didn't you?"

Jim dropped onto one of the wooden chairs as if the walk robbed him of a good deal of his energy.

"No use if I couldn't have grown my roses; I was just saving time. Is there any coffee left, Tara? I'm allowed one in the morning and another either in the afternoon or evening."

Dan wanted to know more as Jim was a little evasive the previous night. "Are you still on the strict diet?"

"Strict everything, son. Food, drink, exercise, even the amount of driving I can do in one go. You name it, I'm under orders about it."

Gwen rested a hand on his shoulder. "It's all helping though, isn't it? Honestly Dan, you wouldn't believe how much better he's been in the last few months. I suppose now is as good a time as any to tell you, whatever he says, you can't let him over-do things."

"Gwenny love, don't go on," Jim began.

She ignored her husband's irritated look. "I mean it Dan. He's still only half as strong as he used to be."

Dan looked between them and Tara, wishing he had not broached the subject at all until Bradley came to his rescue by calling out for some attention. Dan was glad to give it.

Later in the afternoon Jim gave Dan the full tour of the house and gardens. The house was deceptively large. Jim finished in his office, which was lined on three sides with bookcases and shelves but still seemed light and airy. He gleefully remembered to mention his desk with its broken drawer locks that Dan and Nick broke into the year before.

"Still makes me smile every time I see it. By the way I've never told Gwen so…"

Dan puffed out his chest in a show of mock defiance. "Enough said. Well for the record I'm still not sorry we did it. You deserved it at the time but I'm glad we're on the same side now."

They each took a chair and regarded the other for a moment.

"What Gwen said about you taking it easy?" Dan prompted.

"She worries too much."

"Bullshit, Jim. Remember, I was there that night, and in the hospital, too. I've no idea what I'm getting myself into here, but I would rather spend a couple of weeks holidaying with you and her and not do a thing about Zoe Summers than have your health on my conscience."

"Listen Dan, I need some stimulation or I might just waste away. Honestly the body is a bit frail, but my mind is as sharp as ever and I think you're going to need me. Come on son, tell me what you've done so far."

Dan studied Jim's eyes and detected only a steely resolve. "On one condition and it's not negotiable. You said honestly and I'm holding you to it, okay? The moment it gets too hard or you feel it harming your health, that's it. You pull the pin and take a back seat. Deal?"

"Deal," Jim replied with a touch too much enthusiasm.

Dan wasn't done yet. "And there are no secrets from Tara and Gwen. I've already given Tara my word."

"Okay, now will you please tell me what you've been up to for the last ten months?"

Being a little more assured Dan felt a tingle of excitement as his brain scanned through the hundreds of documents and files he had studied and researched since they were last together. He took a breath then began to relate what he knew so far from the Zoe Summers police files.

In the conservatory Tara and Gwen were discussing the same matter.

"He has promised me and I have to say that since he came back from here last year, he has been altogether different," Tara said.

Gwen sat back in a chair with Bradley nestled in her lap asleep. "They had a big effect on each other. Jim's injuries have obviously taken a great deal of getting over, but he's emotionally scarred too."

"Does he know what Dan might be getting into? I know they've deliberately not discussed the details of what Dan's been doing at home. He told me it would be better to tell Jim everything in one go, rather than bits and pieces as he went along," Tara said.

"We haven't talked about it at all, either. I said while Jim was recovering, he must only concentrate on that. I'll be honest with you, I was hoping Dan might think there was enough in your lives when this little one arrived and he'd be able to leave it in the past."

Tara shook her head slowly. "That isn't his way. He won't let this thing go until he's either found out what happened to her or exhausted every avenue trying. He's promised me and himself though that he wouldn't put Jim in harm's way, and I believe him."

Gwen stroked Bradley's forehead. "The trouble is Jim will likely want to get involved boots and all too, and the truth is I just don't think he's up to it. I suppose we'll know soon enough."

"If it comes to it then we'll have to make them see sense."

"Tara, sweetheart, in all our years together I can count the times on one hand when I've told Jim no, you're not doing this or that. He didn't like it then and he definitely won't this time."

Dan started at the very beginning because it was his way and he knew Jim would appreciate it too.

"I went right back and reviewed the police files and original notes. I needed to examine what the investigating team had to work with to see if there were any gaps first. Only when I was sure of the official inquiry did I add myself to the mix and see what I could add as a witness or suspect. Sorry if it sounds like I'm blowing my trumpet a bit too loudly, but with what I know, I must be the prime suspect."

"It's okay, I get it," Jim said. He looked like he wanted to add something; instead he cleared his throat and looked at his shoes. Dan raised a sympathetic eyebrow, sensing Jim's discomfort. It had been a long time since he first started living with the concept of being a party to Zoe Summer's death; he was accustomed to the suspect tag.

"The investigation was by the numbers, although I got the impression manpower was reduced quite quickly, probably because since Zoe was a druggie, she was somehow less worthy. I'm not making any judgements, we all did it at one time or another with victims and offenders didn't we?"

Jim nodded. "Anything other than a normal upstanding member of society and you're automatically looked on as somehow less deserving. It's just the nature of things."

"Anyway, Zoe Summers' family didn't help much either. They thought she was a lost cause a couple of years before, didn't seem to make much of a fuss when she died or when the cause of death was determined. They managed to erase her from their lives before she died and were keen to maintain the status quo afterwards. No apparent pushing from them for full explanations."

Dan continued weaving the known evidence, creating a word tapestry of the case to date for Jim to gaze upon.

"I guess she fell into the scene like so many others. There's little to suggest there was a painful family situation she needed to escape. Probably tried a pill one night or shared a spliff with a friend behind the bike sheds and before she knew it, she would have been selling her mother's jewellery for a heroin hit that was mostly baking powder or brick dust rather than the real shit anyway.

"The forensics," he said, becoming more deadpan and factual, "were limited mostly by the contamination of the environment making reliable evidence impossible. A dozen different DNA identifiers, under fingernails, on clothing, in her hair, et cetera, but nothing court quality. Blood, hers on her boot lace, and hers and another unknown on both socks she was wearing." He was tempted to stop there and ask Jim for a comment as this puzzled him from the time he first read it in the documentation, but decided to continue.

"Also, unidentified human hair in the sock on her right foot, probably not hers as it was ginger and three point five centimetres long.

"The injury to her leg was nasty but superficial, nothing conclusive about the type of weapon. It wasn't a knife. Somebody described it as being like a large serrated skewer and there were traces of metal dust in the wound.

"Stomach contents were limited as she threw up on the floor immediately prior to death, traces of alcohol and bread, rice, vegetables, meat and…" he paused again, "black shoe polish. Blood was filled with hepatitis A and B, early signs of septicaemia too; the conclusion being that she wasn't a particularly careful user from the outset. Her hair follicle tests showed previous drugs use but not very recent. Bruises in the usual places but also on the inside and outside of her nose, the nostril area particularly." Dan looked up at Jim but got nothing in return and so he ploughed on.

"The room was in a shit state as you would imagine; the archetypal drugs hole. Needles, foils, cutlery, and glass. Traces of Zoe on the chair, door, and one or two discarded objects including the can of Steeltown cider, which was a supermarket home brand; fingerprints, the usual stuff. If you were writing a thesis on drugs culture in middle England, this was it."

Dan went on for several more minutes, describing the room and the rest of the house, talking as if he was reading from the back of a medicine bottle. When he was finished, he sat back in his chair and blew out his cheeks.

Like a modern Buddha Jim was still rubbing both sets of index and second fingers with respective thumbs as his arms rested on the arms of his chair. "Hm. So?" he said pushing out his bottom lip.

Dan was tired from talking and they remained quiet, a comfortable silence enveloping the room as the grim details permeated deep into them both. It was a full two minutes before Jim broke the silence.

"Names to go with the DNA?"

"Three. All have previous convictions and intelligence sheets like a film script. We'll be needing your contacts to do some more digging."

"I should have enough favours to draw on for that not to be a problem. If I play my cards right, we might even create a little rivalry for them to help. What about the cider can and that shoe polish?"

Dan nodded. "Yes, the same as I drank from, at least I think it must the same can as no others were found. There were no traces in it because it was flushed out with water. The polish, I don't know, but I think it's going to be important. Incidentally, there were traces on her clothes, in her hair, and on her skin in a couple of places."

He didn't expand; these information fragments along with many more would need exploring further but now wasn't the moment.

"When do you want to make a start?"

"As soon as. I've been waiting a long time to get going. I know we've been over this before, but I'll say it again. There's absolutely no problem if you don't want to be involved. I can't say what is likely to happen."

In the subdued light of the study the glint in Jim's eyes was all the answer required.

"So, have you boys decided on just how much trouble you're going to get into yet?" Gwen asked as Dan and Jim entered the kitchen some time later.

"No only talked about it," Jim answered, shooting a guilty look at Dan. "Want some coffee? I'm going to have some decaf fruit something or other and pretend I like it."

Dan gave him a 'poor you' look in return, smiled, and said, "Coffee's good."

"Tara and I've been talking too, about how much we might be able to help," Gwen continued as if given permission to speak on the subject in as much detail as she wanted. "I've been the wife of a policeman for more than half my life and Tara's got more sense in her head than both of you put together, so we think you would be foolish not to include us. Our perspective, if you want to call it that, plus, we both have knowledge of this matter."

Tara took on a regal air as she regarded first Dan and then Jim with a penetrating stare. She didn't speak, she didn't need to.

Jim sniffed the air as if trying to inhale Dan's coffee. "So, it seems we've a team of four. I think we're ready for our first briefing, boss," he said.

Dan pulled his chair in closer to the table, making him sit straighter.

"I'll start with the information first, set out the intentions and then go over the method, admin, and comms. I expect you will have lots of questions but don't worry too much now as the answers will come as we get into the tasking."

He got three accepting nods and continued.

"I was the covert operative in a large-scale test-purchase job in Mapperley. My role was to infiltrate the local drugs scene, find out who the main dealers were and where they were working from so other officers could then arrest and prosecute. I was given a relatively free rein and reported to a handler who was one of the officers involved in the greater operation. The operation itself was given the name Cannonball.

"My cover story was that I was moving back to the Nottingham area from London as I needed to get away from an arrest warrant for drugs supply offences and decided on Mapperley because my mother used to have family there and I knew it as a child. I was building a small network of druggies to deal to myself and therefore needed a regular supply.

"Local officers confirmed Mapperley was an area which was drugs rich but the number of day-to-day arrests for possession and supply didn't match the number of drugs in the area and therefore it was believed a sophisticated method of moving it around must exist. My job included gathering information on this. I passed on my evidence either by meets with my handler or by dead drops. I was several weeks into the job when I first went to twenty-two Powton Road."

Dan continued describing events in verbal technicolour. Tara looked much the same as she did whenever Dan talked about Zoe Summers: numb, shocked. Gwen's face was the picture of granite concentration. Jim glanced from Dan to her, his expression shifting from neutral to concern.

Fifteen minutes later Dan paused to drain the dregs of his cold coffee.

"Up until I read the files that's all I knew or remembered. My, or rather our, intention now is simple: find out who killed Zoe Summers. Our method will be to initially use the evidence from the files and my own additional information, generate new lines of enquiry and follow them until we can answer our unanswered questions and identify the killer by gathering enough evidence that would normally satisfy a court beyond reasonable doubt. I see no point in making things sound any more complicated than that. The only other thing I want to add is that all your safety is my main priority and I won't endanger you for the sake of this." He pointedly took time to stare into the eyes of Tara, Gwen, and Jim in turn before finally adding, "We can worry about admin and comms when the time comes."

The kitchen was silent, apart from the clock that ticked loudly for several seconds before Jim spoke. "I think it's about time you told us all what you really found in all that paperwork."

CHAPTER FOUR

It was well into the evening when Dan finished. In between times they stopped to eat and to attend to Bradley's needs. He was now tucked up in his new residence but still in contact via the two-way monitor Tara brought from home. The strip light burned brightly above the kitchen table, which was covered in small piles of paper Dan used during his detailed explanation.

"How can you know so much just from reading what other people have written down? It makes you wonder why they couldn't do it themselves," Tara asked incredulously, checking the monitor's battery light.

Gwen patted her knee as if to say don't worry, I'm as bemused as you. "Yes. Can you just recap the important bits again, Dan?"

"Sure, and I'm not making any comment on the investigation because of it, but to me these things are obvious, and of course I've got the extra inside knowledge of being there."

"I've got one question though," Gwen continued. "You haven't actually said if you found anything yet to confirm you didn't kill the poor girl?" The *yet* comment wasn't convincing.

Dan showed no emotion. "No, there's nothing obvious so far to make me think one way or the other. The forensic evidence was poor quality but there was a lot of it. A couple of things interested me particularly and should have been explored more. She had a lot to say even though she was dead."

Dan noticed Jim look up. Both were policemen, he sensed Jim's slight shiver as the words came out. It was for good reason. He knew when the shiver passed it would be immediately replaced by another feeling, not quite excitement but something close. Expectancy.

"You know something already, don't you?" he said very slowly. "Bloody hell, do you think you know who did it?"

Tara and Gwen looked at Jim in amazement and then followed his gaze to Dan. The corner of his mouth twitched and then settled back into its earlier non-committal appearance.

Tara cracked first. "Dan. Dan?"

He reached out and gave her hand a squeeze. "No, I don't know who, but I might have an idea of why."

Blank expressions all around encouraged him onwards.

"It came to me when we were talking earlier, Jim, and it's only a train of thought at the moment."

More empty looks and quiet consternation filled the otherwise silent room. "You said about creating a rivalry, remember?"

Jim stayed quiet.

"The night it happened, Zoe was wearing an old jacket and I only remembered there was a badge sewn onto the front of it when I noticed it wasn't in the police photos. At first, I thought it might have been removed for special examination but when you mentioned rivalry, I realised what sort of badge it was."

"Badge? There wasn't anything about a badge in the files," Jim said.

"I know and that's precisely my point. There was one the night she died but it was gone by the time the photos were taken. Of course it wouldn't have been noted if it wasn't there. When you said rivals it all made sense."

"It doesn't make any sense to me." Tara frowned.

"Sorry, T. It was a gang patch. A badge is a prized possession, signifying she was a member of a particular gang. You know as well as I do who'd want to take one off a dead body."

New Zealand's own gang culture regularly filled many column inches in the papers and minutes of television news.

"Other gangs, rival gangs!"

Dan nodded. "Well it's the only thing which makes sense to me."

"You and your Sherlock Holmes," she teased. "What is it again? When there's only one thing left it must be right regardless of how unlikely it is, it must be the truth."

"Close enough. Somebody removed the patch from the jacket before the police arrived at the scene. Can you think of another reason?"

They couldn't.

"Same thing here of course. Any gang would love the chance to take the colours from another, it's the ultimate insult," Jim said, jokingly adding, "So, I take it you being you, you can remember all the details."

On cue Dan's mouth twitched again. He laid a blank A4 sheet on the table and went to work on it with a pencil. As he drew, he described the emblem that Zoe wore the night they met and the night she died.

"A quarter of this, so around four inches by three...There was a black background with a dark green border, green like holly. The logo in the centre was the skull of an animal with horns attached, imagine a buffalo skull with those big horns in an elongated 'S' shape pointing from the centre towards the top corners. Sorry, I'm not a good artist but you get the idea. Between the tip of each horn was the word 'Stingers' in Gothic capitals. The skull and the word were either white or maybe silver originally but the thing was so dirty I'm not sure. The whole thing was embroidered. Like this." He turned the sheet so the others could see it the correct way around.

Jim spoke first. "You're right, you are no artist, but I know that design and I sure as hell know the Stingers."

"How many years ago was this? And you can remember all that?" Gwen said, sounding doubtful.

Tara grinned. "If he says he had chicken soup for lunch three days before all this happened you can guarantee he did, and he would be able to tell you what the spoon looked like as well. He's a weirdo, Gwen, but we should be very glad he's our weirdo."

"Gracious! So, what do we do now?" Gwen asked, regarding Dan curiously.

"Jim? It sounds like you've some knowledge of them."

"Yes, they were a pain in my backside for a while around that time. Sprouted up with a few other gangs when Mapperley was the centre of the Nottingham drugs scene. Mostly white kids from the council estates close by. They operated on the fringes of some of the more established groups. They never got a foothold as I remember but they caused a lot of agitation for a while. They disappeared as quickly as they appeared."

"We'll need to know all there is. Members, associates, offences attributed to them," Dan confirmed for Tara and Gwen's benefit.

"And their rivals," Jim said. "I can tell you one thing straight off the bat: they didn't allow female members."

Gwen looked crestfallen. "Oh no. Does that mean it's a dead end even before we get going?"

Dan thought for a moment, accessing the mental pictures of the scene once more, pressing play and watching the dark memory unfold. Finally, rationalising all the facts and dismissing what appeared to be impossible he said, "No not necessarily. The jacket Zoe was wearing was much too big for her, so not hers probably. Boyfriend maybe."

"Why's that?" Tara asked.

"Their patches are really important to them. The jacket didn't fit her, so it was lent to her by the owner, and who else but a boyfriend would lend his coat with his colours on. So?" he said, turning to Jim again.

"So, C1 Sheets of Stingers."

"What are they?" Tara asked.

Jim held up an apologetic hand. "Sorry, police jargon. A C1 Sheet is the document we complete when an arrested person is brought into the police station. It's the record of their time in custody and it doesn't just end with the individual, it also includes a detailed description of the clothes they're wearing at the time and the contents of their pockets, et cetera. So, if one of them was brought in wearing that sort of jacket it will be recorded. Find the jacket, find the boyfriend."

"This sounds like a good start, doesn't it, Dan?" Gwen asked.

"It does. A good line of enquiry the police didn't have access to, and there will be more to come I'm sure."

"Like what?"

"The shoe polish. That's really got me."

"I thought that. Why on earth would she have it inside her? Was it some sort of sick torture?" Tara said.

"I never heard of that one before either," Jim offered.

Dan sniffed. "Nor me, but she was literally covered in the stuff. Well, not covered, but it was on her hands and arms and in her hair so she sure as anything wasn't just cleaning her boots with it. Come to think of it, it was on the jacket too, and we now believe the jacket might not have been hers, so it must be something associated with a wider group, not just Zoe."

"Line of enquiry number two?" Gwen asked.

Dan felt this was more than enough to start with and didn't want to drown them with information on day one. However determined he was to resolve Zoe's death once and for all, he was equally determined to not destroy what he had now in the process. But being determined was one thing; achieving it was another altogether, and with that in mind he decided it was time to change the subject.

"It seems Bradley isn't suffering from jet lag, but I can't say the same for me. I don't know about you, Tara, but I'm exhausted."

Gwen's motherly instincts surfaced. "Why don't you get your-selves off to bed then? There's no mad rush for this is there? It will all still be here tomorrow."

"She's right, son. I'll make some calls tomorrow, you try to relax," Jim agreed.

Dan concurred. "I was thinking maybe we could have a drive out and explore the area a little if the weather is okay. I don't want you to get bogged down by all this."

Tara beamed. "I would love that if we could. The coast around here is supposed to be some of the best in the whole country and I would really like to wander around a couple of the little villages or towns."

"Good. I can make those calls and see what I can dig up, then when you're ready we can continue," Jim said.

They all got up from the table a few minutes later, leaving the piles of documents and pictures in situ. Gwen took a long glance back at it as she turned off the light and closed the kitch-en door. Dan saw and put his arm around her shoulder. "It'll be alright," he said knowing she'd be feeling the same oppressive sense of foreboding lodged somewhere between her throat and stomach.

The next morning was dry and bright. Dan and Tara felt much brighter too. Bradley slept through the night meaning they also managed an unbroken nine hours and, to all intents and pur-poses, felt fully recharged. When they entered the kitchen, the table was back to its usual condition and was a picture of break-fast heaven. Dan predictably took coffee on board first while Tara contemplated the various toast options before selecting a dense looking multi-grain to which she applied some of Gwen's home-made grapefruit marmalade.

Gwen took charge of Bradley's needs, spoon feeding him a mushy combination of banana, apple, and biscuit cereal. He wolfed it down in no time as he eyed up other items on the table. Tara made him drink some water first before handing him some dry white bread, which he jammed into his mouth and started to destroy by sucking and chewing with his new teeth. Conversation was pleasantly banal, Tara confirming their intention to take off after breakfast for the day and make the most of the good weather.

"Where's Jim?" Dan asked after a while.

"He wanted to make an early start," Gwen answered, not quite concealing all her true feelings.

Dan and Tara exchanged a look confirming they both heard the same thing. Dan excused himself and went out into the spacious hall. The muffled voice of his old boss directed him to the door opposite; he knocked and entered Jim's study, bringing clarity to the voice. Jim had the phone cupped to his ear with one hand and motioned for Dan to come in with the other.

"Yes, got that....Oh right....You've got to be joking." Jim spoke in short clusters of words allowing the other party to do most of the talking.

Dan sat down and looked around the room, taking in more details as he listened to one side of the phone call.

"Well that would be really useful too," Jim continued. "Listen, if you could get all that packaged up for me, I'd be very grateful. I'll give you a call again in a day or two and depending on, well you know, depending on what I'll need next, I might even come up for a visit." He signalled to Dan that the call was coming to an end. "Yes, I will....Alright and to you. See you and thanks again.

"Morning, Dan, sleep well?"

"Yes thanks. It sounds like you're busy. Have you had any breakfast yet?"

"My porridge earlier," Jim said, clearly not wanting to waste time on irrelevant details. "That was Barry Towers, I'm not sure if you remember him but he was my Family Liaison Officer after I got injured and he became a friend. He's at the Central

Intel' Department these days winding down to his own retirement in a year or two. I told him I was researching for my memoirs, which I know he didn't believe but he was good enough not to ask why."

Dan's intention when he left the breakfast table evaporated. He raised his eyebrows, wanting Jim to continue.

"He's going to sort a package out for me, sorry us. Question, Dan, did the girl's patch have a lightning bolt on it?"

"No. Why?"

"It seems like the Stingers had a sense of humour. The early patches were like the ones you described but the later ones had a lightning bolt on them because they used to carry Tasers around. Apparently one poor PC on foot patrol got zapped one day as he was trying to effect an arrest and to celebrate the occasion, they put the lightning bolt on the patches from then on."

"Nice." Dan smirked, appreciating the funny side in the way only a policeman could.

"It might help narrow down dates possibly," Jim offered. "I've got a list here of other people to call. Has Gwen sent you to check up on me?"

"Not in as many words but remember what you said to me last night. You don't have to do it all today either, you know."

"Are you and Tara off out after breakfast?" Jim asked, changing the subject.

"We are. I'm not quite sure where we're going but we'll definitely end up in some little antique shops."

"Why don't you leave Bradley with us then? You can make the most of it for the whole day and babysitting will give me something else to think about other than this."

"That would be great if you don't mind."

"Of course not. The little lad has stolen Gwen's heart away already. Come on let's go and tell them."

By lunchtime lesser mortals might have been regretting offering to babysit Bradley. Gwen, however, was maintaining her happy countenance despite his ear-piercing howls, which started moments after Dan and Tara disappeared in their hired Ford.

"It's alright, Mummy and Daddy will be back later," she soothed, shifting him from one arm to another once again as they walked around the corner of the house and into the back garden where they were sheltered from the cold breeze.

"I thought you would have worn yourself out by now. Why don't you have a sleep?" She hoped the fresh air and her steady pace might have the desired effect but after forty minutes Bradley was still stoutly refusing to comply. His cries were markedly hoarser than they were two hours before.

As they approached one of Jim's rose beds bordered by railway sleepers to keep the weeds and rabbits out, Jim straightened up from the plant he was working on.

"He's got his dad's stubborn streak, I'll say that for him. Are you still okay love?"

Gwen shifted Bradley to her other shoulder again. "Yes. He's just not used to us or being here or being away from them, that's all. He might even be suffering from the flight still," she reasoned, turning Bradley to face Jim. "I think I might go in again and see if he wants to have a drink. Are you coming in soon too?"

Jim pointed his dirty trowel at the bare rose plants. "Maybe twenty minutes."

"Right then, if you're not inside in half an hour I'll be coming to fetch you. It's cold this morning and I don't want you overdoing it. And that does not mean you will be going straight back to Dan's work when you come in either."

"Twenty minutes, promise. I love you, Gwenny."

She turned away feeling a warm glow that belied the weather.

Dan and Tara were feeling warm too. They travelled a short distance along the coast to Thurlestone, following up on Gwen's recommendation of several good, quaint shops and a very good pub for a hearty lunch.

"What do you think of this one?" Tara asked, holding up another crystal decanter. "It says Waterford and has four glasses to go with it. I really like the stopper, it's heavy, it feels nice."

Dan looked up from a rack of old newspapers. "Just what we need to carry back with us in the luggage."

"I thought if we bought enough while we're here we could send a big box back."

"Here!"

"Don't panic, not here in this shop today; here in England. I'm not going to get another chance soon am I? I love all this stuff. It has character built in."

Dan didn't understand. He liked new and clean apart from his chair at home. Tara's love for vintage covered every facet of her life, from her shop in Auckland to the things she wanted to have in their house. In a quiet moment a year or more ago he wondered if she was in some way trying to make up for her lack of family history, but as he pointed out to himself at the time, that was far healthier than the way he dealt with half of his past issues.

"Sure, great idea," he said, sidling over and placing a light hand around her waist.

She beamed. "I can just see us drinking our brandy out of it. I'll take this and the glasses and the silver coasters too," she said to the sales assistant.

Two more shops and three more purchases later they found themselves in the Lounge Bar of The Black Bear pub.

"I've got to have the steak and kidney pie with peas and gravy," Dan enthused, swirling the last third of his Winterton's Ale in the glass before swallowing it down. "And another one of these."

Tara grinned. "I'm going to have the local fish and chips."

As Dan got up, he asked, "Would you like another cider too?"

"Please."

He ordered the food and drinks at the bar and waited for the drinks to be poured before returning to their table.

"This is great," Tara said as he sat back down.

"Yes."

"No, I mean all of this. I know we came here for a reason but thank you for not getting consumed by it straight from the get-go. How are you doing really?"

"I'm alright, surprisingly. I thought about it as we were driving from the airport to Jim's but as soon as I saw him, I knew he wasn't as strong as he would have us believe. I nearly caused his death once before; I don't want to do it again."

"What do you think you'll do next?"

"If he's just making phone calls now that's fine with me. Let's see what he can generate from them and then decide after. In a perfect world we can find all we need contained in the information, and believe me, there's nothing I'd prefer."

"And your gut instinct."

"Seriously, I've not got one. Whether it's because I've been carrying this around with me for so long or maybe because I don't want to know. I really have no idea how it's going to end. Completely new territory for me in a way."

They tried to exchange a little small talk and reviewed the photos Tara had taken so far, mostly of Bradley with Jim and Gwen in different settings around their home; Dan continued not to show any outward signs of his inner feelings and their food arrived before she thought to question further. Her plate was nearly as big as their car's hubcap and yet the fish still dangled over the sides.

"What sort of fish is this! Don't they do portions in this country? I thought breakfast would keep me going all day. How I am I supposed to get through this?"

Dan broke the crust of his pie, delivered in the decorative dish it was cooked in. The plume of steam he set free dissipated into the air and he dove into it with his fork, then added a healthy number of peas before sliding it into his mouth. It was so hot he was forced to juggle it around until he could swallow.

"I'll finish whatever you can't. You've got to admit it's good though, isn't it."

Tara could only stare. "I don't know how to begin."

At times like these Dan almost forgot the main reason for their being back in England once more. When he left and moved to New Zealand, he honestly felt he would never return and yet this was the third time back in as many years. Coming the first time for the trial of Katrina Mallinder included a visit to the crematorium where he was able to say a final goodbye to his parents, which also allowed him to lay their memories to rest.

The second time was to help the daughter of his best friend, Nick. The great bonus of that trip was his reconciliation with Jim, even if it did bring Zoe Summers into stark focus.

This time felt like it was going to be the last; there were no skeletons left in the cupboard once this was over, however he couldn't think to the future because the future depended on the degree of his participation in her death. It could be over in a week or so, or it could be at the end of a long prison term. When he told Tara earlier, he was surprised he didn't add just how collected he felt. He fully expected to be a churning mass of emotions at the prospect of the impending investigation and prospect of discovery. Instead he was calm, and it was this fact that concerned him.

Previously, emotion doubled as a handbrake for his actions. Concern, worry, and fear made him evaluate what he was doing, occasionally changing his mind or at least forcing him to minimise the risk he was about to take. Here and now, the Zoe Summers investigation was an articulated monster slowly driving up a long hill. As they gathered their evidence it would begin to gain more and more momentum as it approached the crest. Dan knew when they reached the top of the hill with suspects in their sights, he would start descending the other side faster and faster with no way of stopping.

CHAPTER FIVE

When the phone rang Gwen couldn't move quickly enough to grab it and stop the noise. She felt like it was just two minutes ago the poor little soul finally sobbed himself to sleep on her shoulder. To her great relief he didn't stir.

"Hello," Gwen whispered into the handset. "No, I only got him off a little while ago. He's right here with me and he's fine. Is everything alright with you…No of course not, you two have a good time and we'll see you later. You've a key anyway, so if we're all in bed you can let yourselves in….Okay, take care. Bye. That was Tara, Jim," she said, replacing the handset. "They might be later getting back."

Jim sat in the other wicker lounge chair in the conservatory poring over his favourite reference book on roses. "I guessed from what you said. So, you'll be happy to have him all to yourself for the whole day."

"Oh, look at him? Who wouldn't want to?"

"You must have the patience of a saint. How long was he crying for before?"

"He's a baby, Jim, that's what they do but he's absolutely fine now."

"Why don't you put him down for a sleep for a while? I can make some tea."

"I will in a minute."

It had been a very long time since a child had stayed in their home. Gwen always regretted they didn't have more themselves. Their own son Bradley was the apple of her eye; when he disappeared the sorrow she experienced almost killed her. Many times she wished Jim could understand what it was like to suffer the ruin of a mother's love lost. He was terribly upset too, but he had his police family all around him, a hundred other sons. She cried when they found out Dan and Tara wanted to name their son Bradley; it brought back memories but also healed her a little too. She and Jim were incredibly touched by it. Even though it was more of a nod from Dan towards Jim and their re-connection, to Gwen it meant a lot more. She had a family again.

After lunch Dan and Tara moved inland to the old market town of Kingsbridge. It was much busier than Thurlestone but still managed to maintain its historic character. Tara wasn't disappointed with the number and variety of shops to wander through in search of "More stuff," as Dan put it. She preferred "Lifestyle enhancers."

After browsing around the third such premises in a short while, Tara pointing and picking up, Dan nodding in a I'm-really-trying-to-be-interested way, she came across a boxed silver cutlery service.

"What do you think? I love these handles and the engraving on them."

"I like the box," Dan agreed, rubbing his hand over the polished dark wood before looking at the contents.

"Feel the weight of these carving knives," Tara enthused.

Dan didn't reply, and Tara wasn't surprised. She continued extolling the qualities of the antique flatware despite thinking Dan was mentally somewhere else. After a minute or so she became uncomfortable; he was still standing silently next to her and hadn't wandered off. When she looked, she saw a scarily familiar face: Dan's eyes were boring into the box. She knew he was thinking, fitting ideas and images together into a pattern, which made factual sense considering the known information of the subject he was engrossed in.

"What is it?"

He reached a hand into the box and rested it on the knife sharpening steel.

"What's the matter?" Tara asked again.

"Zoe."

She shivered at the mention of the name again, but very much like Jim the day before it was because she knew a revelation was coming. Dan slowly pulled the tool from its worn velvet mould. The handle was made from the same off-white bone as the rest of the assorted knives, forks, and spoons. It fitted comfortably into the palm of his hand and when he wrapped his fingers around it the balanced craftsmanship was clear. Protruding from the handle, the well-used steel spike of the business end was some thirty centimetres long and a little under two in diameter. The length was a tight corrugation of the hard metal so that when a knife blade was drawn across it, it would sharpen immediately.

Dan held the steel up level with his eye line and moved it from side to side, so he could see along the whole length. A small smile widened into a grin and he held it on the same plane a little lower, so Tara could see too.

"Zoe?" she asked, not understanding.

"Here let me show you." Dan took out one of the knives and pulled the blade over the steel in a slow, high pitched squeal. "Hold your hand out."

Tara did as she was told and cupped her hand under the old tool. Dan gently tapped the body of the steel with the blunt topside of the knife and the grin she saw a moment ago returned to his face. She looked at the tiny fragments of metal flakes, no more than powder that speckled her palm. She tried to remember what Dan had told them all about Zoe, her life and death and the injuries she sustained in the process.

"Oh my God, Dan, it's what caused the horrible injury to her leg." She gasped as the details filtered into order.

"Yes, it must be, the shape of the wound and the metal dust that was inside it. There can't possibly be anything else to cause those injuries."

The feeling of rising sickness caught Tara. "That poor girl," she gasped. "I can't imagine what she must've been feeling when this was done to her."

She brushed the dust off her hand and put the steel back in the box. The need she felt a few minutes before for a cutlery service was gone, as was her enthusiasm for the rest of the day.

"So, will this be going in your big box back to NZ?" Dan asked.

"No," she said quietly.

"What's the matter? Are you okay?"

"Hey, come on, we've just realised the cause of one of her injuries. For all we know she might have been tortured with the bloody thing. It does kind of put a spoiler on the day, don't you think?"

Dan put his arm around her shoulder and pulled her close. "It's horrible as you say. I do know. Sorry to say it, but I think we'll find out a few more horrible things before this is over. The life of a druggie like Zoe Summers is so alien from anything you've ever seen or imagined; you're going to have to prepare yourself for shocks. I can't ready you for some of it because no words can. Jim and I've witnessed it multiple times and so our feelings are immune to a lot of what you might experience for the first time. I suppose it's the same with a lot of police things, to deal with it you must be desensitised to it."

"I suppose, but you have to understand that I won't be able to do in five minutes what it took you twenty years to learn. That doesn't mean I don't want to be involved. It just means you have to consider it too. An hour ago, we were joking around about the size of my fish and now we're discussing this. Maybe the same might be true for Gwen as well.

"I know how you can get caught up in the moment and when that moment's gone it's gone. We're here on a very specific mission but our life is continuing at the same time, and when we go home, I don't want there to be any damage left."

Dan held her face in his hands and kissed her. "Whatever you say, as usual you're right. So, I'm sorry for the way I said what I did but please don't let it spoil the day. It's a lovely set." He picked up the box again. "If you like it, get it, and let's enjoy it for what it is and have something great to remember the day by."

"Jim, it's for you. Barry Towers," Gwen called from the kitchen door.

The latest call in a day of substantial telephone activity was unexpected but welcome. "Barry, I wasn't expecting to hear back from you so soon."

"I wanted to call to say I've got quite a bit for you but also to ask if you're interested in Zoe Summers' previous arrests. She was nicked several times but only cautioned twice and never charged. She was interviewed once for a drunk and disorderly plus possession of a small quantity of cannabis. It's all looks pretty boring to be honest, but I thought you might want it anyway, and I would rather send you one package than a number in dribs and drabs, if you get my drift."

Jim did; Barry was sticking his neck out to help as it was.

"Thanks, I understand. If she was only ever interviewed once, I'd like to see what she said."

"Okay I'll copy what I've got onto a disc and send it out by mail tonight if that's alright then, sir."

"It's just plain Jim nowadays and a disc will be fine. I've the rest of my retirement to write down my memoirs so another day or two isn't going to make any difference," Jim replied lightly.

The untruth was entirely for Barry's benefit and Jim hoped it would make him feel less guilty about his indiscretion; an incriminating email out there in the digital ether wasn't a good idea. In his heart he knew Barry didn't believe the memoirs story; a formal request for information through the official channels was the proper avenue.

"If you ever get down this way please remember to look me up, and if I do get up there, I want to take you out for a beer and a curry."

"No problem, sir, I mean, Jim. It's great to hear from you again. Good luck with the…the memoirs."

"You look like the cat that got the cream. He must have given you some good news," Gwen noted as Jim swaggered into the kitchen and sat down heavily on one of the chairs around the pine table.

Jim gave the teapot a shake to see if there was any inside. "I can take some of the credit. It was me who got the force to computerise many of the old investigations that weren't closed. A few years ago, it would have taken weeks to accumulate what Barry's got me in a day. Not only that, but he's also pulled up a load of other non-related stuff about Zoe Summers and the Stingers."

"Did he say what he found for you?"

"No and I didn't want to ask. He will be thinking the less he knows the better."

Dan and Tara strolled back along the footpath towards Kingsbridge town centre. The water of the estuary to their left was dark and hardly moving. They walked for about two miles before turning around again and in that time the conversation roamed across a dozen different topics, from Jet back at home to the need for Dan to get his eyes tested while they were in England. Tara's hands were cold against his, although it was quite warm for the time of the year. She jammed both hands deep into her coat pockets while still linking arms with Dan.

The result was they needed to coordinate their steps as if they were participating in a three-legged race.

Now the conversation returned to another cold subject.

"I know you always said you will go to the police with whatever you discover about Zoe, but you never told me what they might do to you when you tell them you were there that night," Tara said.

"It probably depends on whether or not I'm complicit in her death, and of course on the person making the decision." Dan pulled her in even closer. "If the decision-maker was Jim at the time I left the job, there's no doubt he would've thrown the kitchen sink at me," he joked. "If he was the man he is now, I would probably be disciplined and thrown off undercover duties forever. I might even get moved back to uniform. That's best-case scenario."

"Do you know who that person is nowadays?"

"It'll be the current head of CID. It was one of the things I was going to ask Jim to take a look at. He or she will probably be someone I've never even heard of and that will be no bad thing."

As they walked, he gently swung the big brown bag in which the cutlery set and one or two other purchases were placed. After further discussion in the shop he convinced Tara that in time she could learn to disassociate herself from facts or things, and as he put it, "leave it at work."

Dan was glad she wanted to come with him to England. His regular practice of self-analysis continued to affirm his knowledge about what they were here for. He decided the night they arrived in the country he wasn't going to try and change his thought processes as it would only make the whole thing more complicated. He hoped that having Tara close would provide a welcome counterbalance to the situation.

When they got back to the car they were pleased the little remaining afternoon sun made the inside warm.

"Where to now?" she asked once they were settled.

"I thought we could just drive unless you want to do some more shopping. Pick a direction."

"I don't know, you're the expert."

Dan turned the ignition key and headed for the exit. They drove away from the coast, along country roads with high hedges towering over the narrow road, causing Tara to comment on how much wider the roads were in New Zealand. The green hills and the contrasting red brown soil occasionally visible in the bare fields made for varied conversation and they passed the time happily, discussing things in the near or far distance which caught their eye.

After half an hour Dan was still driving; he now had a destination in mind that he had visited a dozen or more times before.

"Nearly there. I wanted to come this way rather than the main road but it's only a couple of minutes now." As he spoke, they passed a 'Welcome to Totnes' sign.

"A real castle!" Tara exclaimed. "This is amazing, how old did you say?"

"It dates back to around 1070. I first came here as a child but when I was training, we used to come to Totnes regularly. I ran a couple of training lessons in the town. The castle was built by one of William the Conqueror's knights after the area was gifted to him. I only know all this because my mother told me she could trace her ancestry right back to the time of William the Conqueror and one of his knight's named Judhael. She said her family was directly descended from him, so I always liked to think this was the family home from way back. I thought you'd like to see it since you're always asking about my history."

Tara touched his face. "Thank you. So, what else can you tell me?"

"The tower and a few walls are all that's left but it used to be a fortified tower which was on top of the hill with another great stone wall surrounding it. This type of castle design was called motte-and-bailey, but don't ask me which one the tower is, and which one is the wall."

They climbed the steep steps up to the tower from where they could look out over the town and surrounding area.

"Wow what a view," Tara said, gulping in the fresh air.

Dan turned around, taking in the fantastic vista.

"You can see why they built it here overlooking the town. Anyone trying to attack would have been visible for miles before they could get anywhere near, and when they did arrive, they'd have to try to battle uphill whereas the defenders inside would have this massive advantage. They would fire arrows from the safety of the walls, and used catapults with rocks in, or sometimes they would even use dead animals."

"Yuck, that's gross."

Tara took a load of photos while Dan continued to tell her as much as he could remember. When the cold got too much for her, Dan said, "Ready for your last surprise?"

"Definitely."

"It's not so much of a surprise as a pilgrimage to the pub we used to go to every time we were here. It's the oldest pub in town."

A few minutes later Dan pulled up in the near empty car park of the Kingsbridge Inn.

"This area's called Leechwell and there used to be a leper hospital around here near to the freshwater springs, they're supposed to have special healing powers. The pub itself is over four hundred years old."

Tara stood and gazed up at the front of the building. Its stark white painted front was in sharp contrast to the black window frames and soffits which rose up to a sharp point.

"How cute is this? I bet you had a few good nights in here."

"Come on, let's go in. Wait until you see inside."

The bar was as deserted as the car park. Tara's eyes widened to the size of saucers as she took in the low beamed ceilings and ancient black timbers. The whole place exuded history, from the stone floor to the brass trimmed bar facia, and all around, the striking black and white synonymous with Elizabethan architecture.

"Nice isn't it?" Dan said as he found a table to his liking.

Tara's face glowed. "It's beautiful."

"When I first arrived in New Zealand, I always thought it was quite funny when people talked about old things being a hundred or a hundred and fifty years old. I know it's because we're a young country, but can you imagine, this place was built in the sixteenth or seventeenth century, we're talking four to five hundred years ago, and yet you can still come in any time you like and sit down with a beer just like people did when Elizabeth the First was battling the Spanish Armada. It's one of the things I realise I do miss nowadays."

Tara smiled at him and touched his knee, but the pub surroundings meant she couldn't hold any sort of concentration. After a moment she was gazing around the place again. Dan got up and went to the bar where a young man in a check shirt was polishing glasses. When he came back, he was holding two identical half-pint glasses.

"I want you to try this."

Tara put down the brochure she'd found on the adjoining table. "I was just reading more about the history of the pub and the area." Dan placed a glass in front of her. "This looks interesting what is it?"

"It's called Old Familiar. It was my beer of choice when we used to come."

Tara gave it a sniff before tasting the rusty brown liquid topped with just a hint of foam.

"Oh no, that's disgusting," she moaned, hunching her shoulders and covering her mouth with her free hand as if she might have offended the barman.

Dan laughed out loud. "It's an acquired taste. Try again."

Tara was now laughing too as she lifted the glass again. She took the smallest sip as possible and recoiled from the glass as if it was a hand grenade.

"No, oh no, I can't. It's horrible, how can you drink this stuff?"

Dan looked over his shoulder in the direction of the barman. "No go," he called. "Can I have a pear cider?"

The barman was grinning as wide as Dan. He nodded and moved towards the pump handles.

As Dan took another gulp of his Old Familiar, Tara watched him with a mixture of amazement and incredulity. His glass was empty by the time the barman brought over Tara's perry and she gladly slid her first glass over to him.

"Much better," she said after the sweetness of her new drink removed the last trace of Old Familiar. "It's a wonder you didn't kill yourself on that stuff. It's like drinking mud."

"They say it's nearly as old as the pub itself."

"You can say that again. It certainly tastes five hundred years old!"

Dan almost snorted his current mouthful all over the place. "That hurts. This is my heritage."

Tara picked up the brochure once more and finished the passage she was reading before she slipped it into her shoulder bag. "It's been a lovely day. When was the last time you were here do you think?"

"Probably around eight or nine years. Come to think of it, I probably brought Harry here at one point in time."

The reference to Harry Spiller, the Auckland detective and now close friend, was meant to be a happy thing and it was, but only for a moment. Dan suddenly felt guilty about mentioning Harry.

"I'm sorry about earlier, you know the sharpener and all that."

Tara became serious too. "It's alright. I think we must face the fact we could put a spin on anything and everything and get back to Katrina Mallinder or Zoe Summers. Until this is over it's going to be a part of all our lives, but when that day does come, when this becomes history as well, I don't want us to look back and feel unhappy. I want you to promise me that. When we go home you have to be able to look back and have good thoughts and memories. See I'm learning to separate myself already."

Dan leant across the table and kissed her. Tara smiled for a second and then her face turned into a playful grimace.

"Yuck, I can taste that foul beer again."

CHAPTER SIX

The next morning Dan and Tara came down to breakfast in good spirits. They'd stayed at the Kingsbridge Inn for the rest of the previous afternoon and evening, sharing a plate of toasted sandwiches for dinner as neither could manage a full meal after all their earlier indulgences. When they got back to Salcombe it was late and the house was quiet. To add to their contentment, Bradley slept through as well. His face was like sunshine when he opened his eyes to see them both looking into his cot and he gurgled as Tara picked him up.

Dressed casually in jeans and sweaters they were already feeling entirely at home at Jim and Gwen's. As they entered the kitchen, Gwen looked up from her newspaper.

"Here he is," she cooed towards Bradley, who responded with huge gummy smile.

Jim started to pour coffee from the filter jug and Dan gratefully picked up one of the filled mugs as he sat down.

Jim patted his shoulder. "Did you have a good day? Where did you get to?"

While Tara and Gwen caught up with how Bradley had been, Dan described the events of the day before. When it came to the sharpening steel and its importance to Zoe, they both became earnest.

"It's really unusual to have a weapon like that. I'd be amazed if it was just a random thing. My guess is that it would be a weapon of choice for whoever had it," Jim stated.

"I thought that too. A dump like that house was hardly likely to have one in the kitchen cupboard so to my mind, it was brought there. I don't remember seeing one on show though and I'm sure I would if it was there."

"Easy to conceal until it was needed. I'll need to get on to my man and see what he can find," Jim said.

"While you're at it can you ask him who the head of CID is at the moment?"

Jim looked a little surprised. "I'm not a complete bloody dinosaur yet, you know. I might be out of the job, but I keep up to date through a few mates, the Retired Officers Association, and computer sites. It's only reprobates like you who lose all contact once you leave."

Dan conceded Jim had a point.

"Detective Chief Superintendent Tom Bushell is your man," Jim said without giving anything away about his feelings towards him.

"I don't know him. What's his story?"

"Nice bloke by all accounts. He took over from Scotty Dobson about twelve months ago. Bushell is like a lot of the new heads of departments all over, brought in from another force area. He's a flyer and will be a chief constable one of these days, so I wouldn't be surprised if he was gone soon too. If I was him, I'd love to have a coup to talk about at my next interview."

Dan was glad to hear Alistair 'Scotty' Dobson was no longer in command as he was another in a long line of senior officers to have fallen foul of Dan's competency barometer in years past. He chose not to go into detail, lest he give Jim the ammunition to shoot another barrage of home truths at him, like he'd managed to do once or twice before.

As they worked through another of Gwen's hearty breakfasts, Jim told Dan the rest of what little he knew about Tom Bushell. From what Jim said it sounded like the most senior detective in Nottingham was so results orientated he would hopefully jump at any opportunity to close the lid on an unsolved murder by convicting the person responsible, even if the information did come from an unconventional source. That was the good news. The bad news was he wouldn't be content just to have the killer; anybody else criminally connected with the incident might also be in his cross hairs and he was apparently a rigid advocate of no deals or plea bargains.

Jim also explained that the intel Barry Towers was sending might still be a day or two away. "What do you want to do today?" he asked when he finished.

"I'm not sure if Tara's got plans," Dan said, looking in her direction. "I would quite like to sit and read through it all again, see if I missed where the sharpening steel could have been and maybe we could throw a few ideas around."

When Tara shrugged Jim took it as authority to continue.

"Good, yes good, I'm free all day. We can get started as soon as we've finished here."

By mid-morning Dan and Jim were fully engrossed. The study warmed by the coal-effect fire was a mass of typed documents and photographs placed in an order both could understand. Dan was still no closer to establishing who might have been carrying the steel, however.

"So much took place after my memory of the night ended. It seems obvious the steel became active in that time. Zoe didn't have the injury to her leg before I drank out of her can. The post mortem states the injury was caused prior to death and death was because of strangulation. To me the two are so distant from each other that I can't see the same person using the steel on her and then deciding to strangle her. What do you think?"

Jim thought for a moment. "No, I can't remember any job I was ever involved in where a weapon like that was accompanied by strangulation. The amount of personal physicality sets those offenders apart."

Dan agreed. "That leaves various scenarios. A strangler acting against usual signature behaviour patterns, two or more unrelated individuals, or two or more related individuals. What's your favourite?"

"Two or more related. How unlucky could she be to piss off two people in one night to the extent they both wanted to assault her? While we're talking about it, the bruising on her nose looks deliberate to me too; I'd add that into the mix as well." Jim took a breath and continued. "We all believe you're not involved, obviously, and I can't recall a single instance of you losing it so much you laid your hands on anyone. Is there anything in your history to suggest you're capable of these types of assault? And one more thing. The PM has got the sizes of all the bruising around her neck. Did you ever compare them to your hands?"

"I did, more than once. The spread meant the hands were slightly larger than an average British male and a very unscientific guess would say this male was between five feet nine and six feet three. I'm right in the middle of that."

"As are half the population," Jim offered hopefully.

"To answer your question no, I never got physical to the point I lost control. The most physical incident was one day when a colleague got jumped by a few blokes as he was about to make an arrest, one of them was the size of a house. I kicked and punched him half a dozen times without giving him the chance to hit me back. I didn't stop until he was lying on the ground.

"Regarding that night and Zoe...it's just the not knowing. I'm so unused to it. I don't know what to do with that. Under the influence of whatever shit I had inside me I can't honestly say what I was capable of. I wish to hell I could turn the clock back and do it all differently."

Jim shook his head in disbelief. "I can't say I remember you being any different when you came back to Garstone, son. Then again in those days I tried not to think about you too much anyway. You were such hard work. How did you cope carrying on doing the job as if nothing happened?"

"It's funny, all the years before, the issues with my dad, bad relationships and the other assorted crap turned out being the exact preparation I needed at that moment. I was so screwed up that this thing, this impossible thing which you couldn't even make up in your wildest dreams, was just like another part of my crazy life. If I was anything like normal, I wouldn't have been able to get out of bed in the mornings. I honestly think I would have ended up doing something stupid to myself."

The quietness in the room enveloped them. Dan picked up his coffee mug just to have something to do and when he realised it was already empty all he could think to do was laugh. It took a few minutes before they were able to continue and when they did, the change of subject within the greater topic was a welcome relief.

"Shoe polish? I've thought about that for days on end and got nowhere. I hope you're going to put me out of my misery," Jim said.

"Sorry, I've drawn a blank too. It must be important though, the amount of it, where it's located."

They cleared a space and took out all the documents that referred to it. Dan liked duplicating this type of paperwork where there was a crossover between more than one evidence strand; this way, all the different strands maintained all the relevant information, rather than having to mix and match depending on which subject they were looking at. Jim approved too, despite the fact it probably trebled the total document count.

Dan started. "I tried researching unusual uses for shoe polish but couldn't see anything in that. People use it for shining up things other than shoes, such as wood and metal, but I can't see why that helps us and it definitely doesn't explain why she would have it in her stomach.

"We can discount the obvious, that she was actually using it for cleaning her shoes, or cleaning anything else come to that, so it must have another use. What are the properties of the stuff which may be of use to a young, female druggie?"

"It comes in different colours," Jim said, beginning a list.

Dan started to write as Jim continued. "It's waxy, it smells, what else?"

"It's readily available and doesn't draw attention to itself even if bought by a drugs user." Dan continued writing as he spoke. "Does it have an ingredient in it, like cough drops with pseudoephedrine which can be distilled out?"

Jim looked hopeful. "Good one, let's check that."

Dan stood over him as Jim got to work on his computer but after several minutes of investigation, they were still at square one.

"Nothing, scrap that idea." Jim groaned.

They went back to the list Dan was writing.

"It generally comes in small tins, hey is it the tin rather than the polish?" Jim asked.

They looked blankly at each other.

"No," Jim said, answering for both. "Don't you hate this?"

"Hate it? No, these are the things I really like. The answer is here Jim, it's right here in front of us but we aren't looking at it the right way yet. Have you got any in the house?"

A minute later they each had a tin of Cherry Blossom shoe polish in their hands; Dan's was black and Jim's light tan.

"Okay what now?" Jim said peering into his open tin. "It lasts forever. I've had these for at least three years."

Dan rubbed a finger into his and then rubbed his fingers together.

"This is how Zoe got it on her hands. Prolonged contact with it to get it into her skin and it was black."

Jim loosely replaced the lid on his tin and put it on the floor behind him and they stared into the black of Dan's, willing inspiration to jump from the inky contents. They examined it from all angles for several more minutes, repeating the adjectives they'd collected already and searching for a key to unlock the mystery.

Eventually Jim's frustration surfaced. "Bugger this! It's bloody shoe polish, what else can it do? I need some fresh air."

As he got up Dan put the lid on his tin too, disappointed not to have found what they wanted and hoped for. Seeing Jim's tin, he picked it up too, dropping the insecure lid in the process. He picked it up and went to replace it properly. As he did, he saw the polish inside had started to melt from having been near the fire. The semi-liquid polish now had a glossy sheen to it that wasn't there in its solid state.

"It melts," Dan said.

"What was that, son?" Jim enquired half turning from the door.

"It melts, shoe polish melts," Dan replied, writing on the bottom of his list.

Jim looked inquisitive. "I know. So?"

Dan studied the two words on the page. "I'm not sure yet," he said, joining Jim.

As Bradley was sleeping upstairs, Tara and Gwen were taking full advantage. When Dan and Jim found them in the lounge they were sitting on the big sofa, hunched over several large photograph albums.

"Hello you two. As you were off having fun, we thought we'd do the same," Gwen explained.

"Believe it or not there are two of you in here as well," Tara said, tapping the album on Gwen's lap.

He looked at Jim in surprise.

"Department photos probably. Remember every year or so I would get you all out in the car park? I bet you look as miserable as sin in them."

Tara and Gwen laughed in unison.

"That's exactly what I said when I saw them. Posing for pictures is still not your favourite pastime, is it Dan?" Tara joked.

Dan unwisely felt the need to justify himself. "I was an undercover policeman for God's sake."

"So, what about yesterday up at the castle? You didn't want your photo taken there either."

Jim playfully punched Dan's arm, and Dan decided not to try and reason any further.

"I always took a good photo," Jim stated.

Gwen smiled knowingly. "Yes, you do dear. You're still as handsome as the day we met. I already showed Tara the wedding photos and some of our Bradley's. Have you finished what you were doing?" she said closing the album.

"Shoe polish," Jim said. "What would you use shoe polish for if you were Zoe Summers?"

Gwen had nothing. Tara thought for a moment and then asked, "Is it a craving thing for drug addicts or does it help with coming down?"

"Not that I'm aware of but we've drawn a blank," Dan replied.

"I'll check. Why don't you tell the girls what we've come up with so far?" Jim said, heading back to the study again.

Dan reeled off the list from memory. "Okay what we have is shoe polish is waxy, it smells, it generally comes in the same shaped tins, anyone can easily buy it, it's very long lasting, and finally, it melts."

Tara went to say something and stopped with an, "Uh, oh no forget that."

Gwen tried to look encouraging.

"It's not easy, we know. We also have to think it might be a complete red-herring, but something tells me it's not," Dan said.

"I take it you've Googled it?" Tara asked.

"Yes, no luck. Shoe polish is generally just for cleaning shoes, but you can also clean and shine wood and metal with it."

Tara and Gwen looked at each other for inspiration. A fruitless number of minutes later Jim came back in.

"No joy, nothing about shoe polish and drugs users I can find."

"Well there's only one thing for it," Dan said authoritatively. "Time for coffee."

Dan went back to the paperwork again later in the afternoon when Jim took Gwen, Tara, and Bradley into town to do the weekly shop. Ploughing through file after file, he tried his best to assess everything with a clean eye and open imagination.

When he came to revisit Zoe Summers' family information file, he studied the family portrait on the first page. He thought it must be one of the last pictures taken of Zoe in that environment. She looked fourteen or fifteen and stood behind a high-backed cane chair in which her mother was sitting. To Zoe's right, her father stood mirroring her position. Completing the arrangement was her younger brother Andrew; he sat with his back to the right leg of the chair, cross legged with his arms folded but relaxed. The group all wore different shades of blue and the same photographer's 'look at the bird' smiles.

He wondered if any of them could have imagined how their lives would change within a few short years.

Detailed research into the family was impossible up to this point and he still wasn't sure if he would be able to make any progress now, or if it would be even necessary. The family's disowning of Zoe was understandable to Dan. Given his own past he could easily see his father doing just the same and his mother, if she was still alive at the time, tagging along in dutiful silence.

Anthony and Elizabeth Summers, married for a year and a half when Zoe was born, Andrew two years almost to the day after that. Dan read it all again, but he could recite it without the notes. Anthony, area manager for a photocopier company, Elizabeth a teachers' aid at the school Zoe and Andrew attended.

He continued into the Summers' information, reabsorbing the text. They were normal in every sense of the word. All four of Zoe's grandparents were alive and well, the extended family included aunts, uncles, and cousins whom they visited and had visit. They had no criminal connections until Zoe became embroiled in the drugs scene. They were not active in local government, they were not members of clubs or gyms, they went on holiday for two weeks when the children were off school each year.

There was no reason in the whole world for them to become a national news item overnight and yet they did. After that nothing would ever be normal again.

At Zoe's funeral Anthony spoke for a minute exactly. He said the family were devastated they lost their daughter and sister, he said she was a lovely child who managed her early childhood issues and became a lovely teenager until she left home. He said he wished things could have been different.

Anthony and Elizabeth spoke to the police in the days after Zoe's murder; they were interviewed formally and informally, but what they said was of no use to the investigation. When the police asked if they wanted a Family Liaison Officer to stay in touch and keep them updated, they said no. When the investigation was wound down with no positive result, the Summers didn't complain and the files made no mention of them being satisfied the police did all they could. On the first anniversary of Zoe's death the current Deputy Head of Major Incidents telephoned the family as a courtesy; at the end of the short call he was asked not to call again.

Dan returned to the family photograph once more, trying to focus all his senses and experience on the image, hoping to see what he had not been able to see so far. It very soon became obvious there wasn't anything there to see, just as it always was.

It was a great relief to hear the crunch of tyres on gravel soon after and then hear familiar voices that nearly drowned out the ones in his head.

CHAPTER SEVEN

The next morning as Dan was coming downstairs the doorbell rang.

"I'll get it," he called to anybody who might be listening.

"Good morning," the courier said. "Package for J. Allen."

The brown A4 envelope was secured with clear tape at both ends. The name and address were handwritten in blue ink and the post mark was smudged but still distinct enough for Dan to easily read the city of origin. Nottingham.

Handing the envelope to Jim, who was at his usual seat at the kitchen table, he said, "Present for you."

"You mean us," Jim replied.

"Does this mean we're not going out today?" Tara asked.

"I think you can safely say I won't be. There's no need for you to stay in though. I could look through it first and then fill you in when I'm finished."

She kissed Dan's cheek. "No chance, one for all and all for one."

"She's right, son. Better for us all to keep current." Jim placed the envelope on the table where it sat invitingly.

As Dan drank his coffee, the others talked around him. He heard them, but it was if he was in another room. When Gwen and Tara finished tidying, they all moved into the lounge.

"Sorry I can't wait any longer," Dan said, ripping into envelope and emptying a stack of white A4s onto the coffee table.

"How do you want to do it, son?" Jim asked.

"Let's start by arranging it like we've done before with the rest. One, Zoe before Powton Road, two that night, three the

PM and the police investigation, and four other people before and after the night. Anything else leave until last and we can look at it then."

Jim passed out the documents. They all noticed a few photographs in among the pages. As he handed Tara her share, a CD dropped to the floor and came to rest shiny side up.

"What is it?" Tara asked. She picked it up and turned it over for them to see the other side. Much to their combined angst, the paper label was clean.

"Well there's only one way to find out. Can we use your laptop Jim?" Dan asked.

As the disc started to whirr in the CD drive, Dan's gut started to revolve too.

"It just says audio file," Jim said, looking at the screen. "Are we all ready?"

Hearing the sharp series of beeps, Dan tensed like a cat. Gwen and Tara had no idea what was coming but he and Jim knew instantly: the beeps were the unmistakable sound police tape recorders made at the start of all recorded interviews to help the tapes synchronise.

"What is it?" Tara asked.

"Someone I never thought I'd hear again."

They all jumped when a confident sounding female voice broke the silence.

"This interview is being tape recorded. I'm Detective Jelena Copich and I'm interviewing Zoe Summers. Zoe, can you tell me your full name, address, and date of birth please?"

Tara stared at Dan. He was also staring, only far into space.

"Zoe Rebecca Summers. No address. Twenty first of May 1989."

She sounded like a million other seventeen-year olds Dan spoke or listened to in his lifetime and yet she sounded like absolutely nothing he ever heard before. The voice he was hearing wasn't the same one who had been in his head for the last seven years and who he associated with the girl Summer he met all too briefly that fateful night.

Jim paused the transmission. "Are you alright, son? Do you want to do this?"

Dan didn't know what to say. He looked blankly from Jim to Tara and Gwen, who sat like conjoined twins with their hands entwined against fused knees on the same sofa from the day before when they looked through the family photo albums.

"Um, yes, it's a bit unexpected but it will be good for us all to hear what she said in her one and only police interview."

"My goodness, she sounds so normal," Gwen blurted out.

Dan tried to gather himself and concentrate on the matter in hand. "It might be useful, I mean, I think it would be a good idea if we all have a pen and paper to make notes as it goes through, then we can compare them at the end. Jim, does it say how long this lasts?"

Jim looked at the screen. "Just under ten minutes."

"Okay it shouldn't be too hard. If we can all just listen, not interrupt, and write down whatever you think of."

Jim handed out an assortment of note paper, pens, and pencils. When everybody was ready, he clicked the mouse pad again.

Despite her name Jelena Copich was unmistakably local to the Nottingham area.

"Thank you, Zoe. When you say no address, can you explain that?"

"I'm dossing down. I got kicked out of my last place."

"Okay I might need you to explain that some more later. Before we start the interview proper, I need to tell you certain things so I know you understand, and I comply with the law relating to how I must conduct this interview. Do you understand that?"

"Yeah."

The next two minutes of the recording were Jelena Copich explaining Zoe's rights and other legalities, during which Dan tried to appear composed and reassuring for Tara's benefit. Having been through the same interview process on countless occasions he was ready when the first real question was put to Zoe.

"Zoe, you were arrested in the early hours of the morning for being drunk and disorderly in a public place being Connaught Drive and for being in possession of cannabis, which is a controlled drug. I want you to tell me about the time leading up to your arrest, starting from where you came into possession of the cannabis or when you had your first drink, whichever came first. Tell me in as much detail as you can, and I will then ask you some questions about what you say. Take your time and start when you're ready."

The CD broadcast the sound of laboured breathing until Zoe's voice came through again.

"What is there to say? We were drinking all afternoon yesterday. Someone had the dak and he gave me a bit. I didn't smoke it all because I was drinking. Most of them went about midnight when the vodka ran out but then someone got some beer. Then later there was a bit of a fight, not me. When

the police came, I didn't do anything, but they put me in the van anyway. They didn't find the dak until I got searched in here. That's it."

Dan snatched a glance at Tara and Gwen. He didn't want to draw their attention away from the task, but he wanted to see they were not too transfixed by the voices to make notes. He noted both their pens were moving.

"Thank you for that, Zoe. I should tell you it's my job during the interview to try to obtain sufficient evidence to prove the offences you've been arrested for. If I can do that, I will be able to charge you if the custody sergeant believes that's appropriate. I can do that by asking you one question after another, or the other alternative is for you to give me a more detailed account. I believe I can establish all the evidence I need by asking you questions and telling you the evidence other witnesses have provided. What would you rather do?"

"Alright." Zoe sounded resigned.

"It's entirely up to you. I've statements from two police officers and one of the other people who was arrested at the same time."

"I said alright. I just want to get out of here as quick as I can."

Dan was impressed with Copich. Having a suspect describe their crimes was much better than the to and fro of question and answer.

Zoe sighed loudly and continued. "I was with Sean, Minty, Donny Ormond, Billie and...oh no that was it. We were at the Connaught Drive shops yesterday about one or two in the afternoon. Minty got some vodka which he said he bought but he probably stole it. We just sat on the benches drinking

and taking the piss out of all the people going by. We stayed there all afternoon, well past when the shops closed. Don't ask me the time, do I look like I've got a watch.

"Later we had a smoke. I was given the weed and we all had a smoke…Donny okay, Donny had the weed, he gave it to me."

Dan knew what just passed. When Zoe said "someone" and then "he gave it to me." Copich would have raised an eyebrow or opened a palm, done something to let Zoe know "someone" is not good enough, I want a name.

"It was late by then. The pubs were kicking out. Minty then got some beer and I honestly don't know where it came from. I didn't see him go and come back but suddenly it was just there, and we were all drinking it. For all I know I might have gone to sleep and woke up again. I'm not good on beer usually but I drank it anyway. What else was I going to do? There was quite a bit of it.

"Donny and Billie then got into it and at least two police vans arrived. I just wanted to go but when I told Sean I was going he got all angry because he was supposed to stay at Billie's that night, and he wanted me to go with him. He tried to grab my coat back and I gave him a big fuck off and that's when I got arrested."

Jim paused the transmission again. "Everybody okay?" he asked, clearly aiming the question at Gwen and Tara.

"Fine," Gwen replied.

Tara smiled and nodded.

Jim clicked once more.

"Thank you again for that, Zoe. You've mentioned four other people. Can you tell me their full names and addresses if you know them?"

"Sean is Sean Darcy, he's NFA too. We got kicked out together. Donny Ormond, I don't know him very well. His name is Ormond, but we call him Donny after an old school pop singer. Billie Smith or Smythe with a y, lives over in Mapperley Ridge Estate, and Minty is Callum Mintram who lives in a bedsit down on Powton Road."

"A witness has described one of the males being very short. Who was that?"

There was a significant pause. "Um. Donny."

"You don't sound very sure, Zoe. What about Sean? Are you and Sean together then? Is he your boyfriend?"

"No. He wishes."

Dan prayed for Copich to ask if she did have one.

"Where were you and Sean living?"

"Godiva Street off Powton Road. It was a squat but the owners got the police to come and move us."

"Where are you going to go now?"

"Friends I suppose. I'm not sure."

"How much did you have to drink altogether?"

"Don't know, quite a bit."

"Were you drunk when you were arrested?"

"Of course, we all were."

"You said you gave Sean a big fuck off. What does that mean?"

"When he tried to grab me, I pushed him off and screamed at him. I didn't push him too hard, but he still fell over probably because he was drunk."

"Being intoxicated and then screaming at people and pushing them, would you say that's acceptable behaviour?"

"I guess not."

"What about the cannabis, was that influencing you too at that time?"

"The few joints I had. No."

"And you were in possession of cannabis when we searched you upon your arrival at the police station. Where did that come from?"

"The same, Donny. I smoked some and kept some."

"Do you know possessing cannabis is an offence?"

"Yes."

"What were you going to do with the cannabis in your pocket?"

"Smoke it."

"Thanks for your honesty, Zoe. It seems to me you understand you were drunk and disorderly and you were in possession of an illegal drug. Is that right?"

"Yes."

"Is there anything else you want to tell me, Zoe?"

"Like what?"

"**Anything to do with this matter?**"

"**No.**"

Copich's tone changed noticeably, becoming softer. **"Can I ask you about your current circumstances, how it is a sixteen-year-old girl from a decent family ends up squatting in empty houses and drinking vodka and beer in the street at midnight?"**

"What's that got to do with this?"

"Well, it might affect how we decide to deal with you. You've admitted to two criminal offences but there are options as you've not been in any real trouble before."

Tara signalled Jim to stop the interview. "I don't understand. Is she allowed to ask questions not relating to the crimes?"

"There are rules but yes," Jim replied. "Like she said, it could be a factor in deciding to charge her or maybe just give her a caution. I knew Jelena, she's a smart operator. She could also be sounding Zoe out as an informant in the future or seeing if she knows anything about the local drug culture at that time. There are still a few minutes to go, let's see what she said next."

"My mum and dad are very straight. They don't know how to cope with anything a bit different. It's not their fault, it's all mine. I started to get into trouble at school and I just ended up like this.

"I always suffered from health problems, it makes things hard, you know. One day when I was about thirteen or fourteen, I was bunking off school with a friend because I'd had another attack. We met these boys. They gave me this pill which took the pain away and that was it. Soon I was taking pills every day and…"

Dan heard an almost imperceptible sniff and there followed a silence in which he hoped Zoe would continue and guessed Copich would have been thinking the same at the time.

Unfortunately, Zoe decided enough was enough and only silence followed.

"I'm sorry to hear that. If there was a way for me to help you now would you want me to? There are programmes for people to get off drugs and alcohol. If you got onto one of them the council might look on you more favourably for accommodation, or I could give your parents a call."

"No don't do that, please," Zoe begged. "I don't want them to see me like this. I'm a total let down to them and all I do is cause trouble for them and Andrew. They don't deserve to have this shit to deal with too."

"I'm sure they wouldn't think like that if you called and said you wanted to come home or that you needed their help."

"And all I would do is let them down again. I don't want to do that anymore. I want to move away if I can one day and go somewhere I can get clean and just be normal. I didn't want this life you know."

"Underneath that tough exterior you're a really sweet girl aren't you, Zoe. I would like to help you if I can, but you need to ask. Will you at least think about it?"

"Maybe, what was your name again?"

"Jelena, Jelena Copich. Is there anything else you want to say, Zoe?"

"No thank you."

"Alright, the time is eleven forty-two hours and I'm turning the tape recorder off."

A mechanical click, then an extended hissing noise until Jim turned off the recording.

Dan, Tara, Gwen, and Jim sat in silence. Tears welled up in Gwen's eyes. After a long moment Tara put her pen and paper down on the floor at her feet, which broke the spell cast over them all.

Gwen found a tissue in her pocket and dabbed her face while Jim made throat clearing noises. Tara guiltily looked at Dan as if in doing so she was invading something most personal and private. His face gave nothing away.

Ten minutes later Dan and Tara were walking around the garden. She wore a coat and gloves, but he was still in just a sweater.

"She wasn't another dirty druggie at all was she?" he said apologetically.

Tara squeezed his hand a little tighter. "It doesn't sound like it. I wonder if there's anything in the other paperwork to say if she and the policewoman had any more dealings."

"Yes, it's one of the things I thought of too. Can you believe it? She didn't want to be a burden to her parents and that's why she stayed away," Dan said.

His head was as downcast as his mood. After hearing the interview to the end, they all decided a break would be a good idea, which was why he and Tara were now slowly lapping the garden.

"How long was this before the night she died?"

Dan made the quick mental calculation. "Nine months, give or take."

"I don't know what else to say, Dan, I mean I wasn't expecting to actually hear her voice on a tape and I definitely didn't expect to find out she was a kid like that. I don't know how to explain it."

Dan did. "She was a girl with thoughts and feelings. She was living a shit life but hoped for better things in the future. Some people's real lives are not like you imagine or see on the TV, are they?"

They carried on around to the side of the house and into the brunt of the blustery wind coming off the sea. The smell of the salt in the air did a little to revive Dan's sense of misery for the past and how it was starting to reveal itself.

"Are you okay, darling? What do you want to do next?" Tara asked.

Dan took in a couple of deep breaths. "What I can in the only way I know how."

Jim and Gwen sat together; their conversation was deeply personal too. It seemed Zoe touched them all. By the time Dan and Tara returned, the room was quiet, as if it needed all four of them together again before it could move on. It was equally necessary for Dan to be the one to initiate the movement.

"Are you guys okay? I think we should go through the notes we made during the interview and see what there is."

Gwen and Tara readily agreed but Jim had another idea. "Can I suggest you go through your list and then if there's anything else we've got that you don't, we can add that to yours?"

"That actually makes really good sense. I've seen first-hand what you can do with a few facts," Tara said.

When they were ready Dan began.

"Zoe was an inherently decent person, traits she acquired from her parents, and even in her desperate situation they were traits she never shook off, which means hers was a very strong character, strong enough to put them first. Sean Darcy was a good friend because they lived together in at least one Godiva Street address. He wanted to be more than a friend, but Zoe wasn't interested in him in that way. He liked her so much he gave her his coat, she said he tried to take it back. Why? Maybe because he was a Stinger and his patch was on it. He didn't want to let the patch go, not Zoe. There's a history between them to investigate.

"Other associates are Callum Mintram of Powton Road, Billie Smith or Smythe of Mapperley Ridge, and Donny Ormond, Donny being a nickname.

"Mintram supplied the alcohol. He either had lawful or unlawful access to it. So, the possibilities are he works around it, can afford to buy it, has access to where he can steal it, or knows somebody who can supply it to him.

"Ormond is a drugs supplier, low-level certainly, higher levels maybe, but unlikely as he sits around all day with these other users getting drunk on cheap alcohol. That's not the behaviour of your better class dealer.

"Zoe says she's not good on beer, which could mean a number of things but as she states there were health issues as a youngster it might be connected to that. Her health issues obviously were never properly resolved because she experienced 'attacks', as she described them, which were so acute she ended up taking a pill from a stranger hoping it might help take the pain away. We don't know who she was playing truant with that day or the identities of the people who gave her the first pill. We need to know that.

"She was desperate for her family not to know how far she fell, she cared for them that much. She still loved her parents and little brother and she was embarrassed by her situation, but not completely resigned to it. She talked about getting clean, moving away, and building a future.

"At the end Copich was sounding her out as an informant, although I believe she wanted to help her too. I'm wondering whether she did talk off tape because we know Zoe wasn't charged. This probably ended up being one of her cautions. It would be very interesting to know what Jelena Copich and Zoe's relationship was like after this." Dan wasn't finished. "Did you hear her when she stopped mid-sentence as she was talking about taking the first pill?"

"No," Tara said, clearly talking for all three.

"She said she was soon taking pills every day, then she stopped mid-sentence."

"I did hear that, but she didn't say anything after. The police-woman spoke next," Gwen stated.

Dan knew what he heard and understood what it meant. "You're right Gwen, she didn't speak but she did let out a small sniffing type noise. I've heard it a hundred times, I've done it myself. Zoe was reliving that time and when she got to the part where her life changed forever, she couldn't explain it further out loud, but she was thinking it in the quiet that followed. All those memories and regrets inside a girl who should still have been at school. Instead she had already experienced more pain and suffering than most of us have in our whole lives and yet she was still thinking about her parents and her brother and trying to do what she thought was best for them. This little girl was stronger in her own way than many I've ever met."

Dan sat back, already prioritising some of the points he raised, embedding them into the jigsaw of what he knew and wondering what else there was contained in the pages of Barry Towers' package.

"Oh, my goodness," Gwen said. "That's incredible, I mean it's terrible for her but amazing you got all that."

Tara let slip a little laugh. "He does that, Gwen. If I got anything written down that he hasn't I'd be jumping around the room celebrating."

"Dan, what's the matter?" Jim asked.

"Sorry, I don't feel very celebratory. There's some good stuff there and probably more in that lot—" he indicated to the document stack "—but this has brought something else home to me." He rubbed his face with both hands and thought of the Summers family photo again.

"It's always bothered me why she said anything at all that night. I was in deep trouble with the drug dealers and she tried to help, for all I know that's why she was killed. It's a sickening thought that she was killed for me but what makes it worse is that was her preferred option. The other consideration is still that I did it.

"Having just listened to her, what she said and how she said it means one thing. She made a conscious decision to try and help me regardless of the danger she was putting herself in. Up until five minutes ago I could only guess her motivation, but I feel like I know her more now and I think she might have lost her life trying to save mine."

Several more minutes passed before they were able to continue. Tara was visibly upset by Dan's revelations. Whether or not it was because Zoe became more real wasn't clear; she excused herself and went to the bathroom to splash her face with cold water. After a minute Dan went to check on her. The door was open and he saw her looking into the mirror. He imagined her hoping for a vision of one day soon, all this being over and instead it seemed to be reflecting a fear it may never be. Unable to think of appropriate words, he quietly left her.

There were one of four neat piles waiting for Tara when she appeared back in the lounge again, and Dan looking at the floor.

"What are we going to do? Put all these in order like you said earlier?"

"Yes please, it shouldn't take too long. I don't want to look at it today though. When we've done this let's all go out for a while," Dan said gently as he looked up again.

Thirty minutes later there were seven unequal stacks of paperwork on the coffee table and four emotionally drained individuals meditating upon the contents.

Gwen stood up slowly and rested her hand on Dan's shoulder. "Come on, let's take that little boy down to the harbour to see the swans. There's a lovely tea shop. Our treat."

CHAPTER EIGHT

That evening Dan was quiet, although he managed not to be completely reclusive. He offered a comment, contributory nod or grunt here and there as Tara and Jim chatted. Gwen buzzed between lounge and kitchen, tidying the day away to keep busy.

Bedtime was a blessed relief. Dan got changed in the dark after Tara was in bed. When he finally climbed in beside her, she enveloped him in her arms and pulled him closer.

"Bad day, huh?" she said.

He could smell her orange blossom soap and skin moisturiser. "You could say that. I have to admit I wasn't expecting any of that this morning."

"It's good to know you're human after all then. Anybody with an ounce of humanity in them would've been affected by what you discovered about Zoe today. I know I've said it before, but I'm amazed at how you see so much in the smallest details. I used to doubt you now and then, but you've shown me too many times just how accurate you can be. The thing you said about her when she stopped telling the detective about her taking the pills—that was unreal."

"I used to have those exact same feelings. That poor girl."

"Will you be able to sleep tonight, is there anything you want me to do?"

Dan was out of words for the day. All he wanted was to know was that he wasn't alone. He pulled his arm and hand upwards, touching Tara's chest. "Anything?"

Hours later Tara's words became reality. He wasn't sure if he was awake before or if Bradley's grumbling woke him. In any event, Dan got out of bed and went to see his son. Bradley was wide awake in his cot and seeing his daddy, he grumbled louder. Dan scooped him up with the top blanket and quietly left the bedroom before Tara woke too.

The central heating maintained the whole house at a pleasant temperature despite the seasonal chill outside doing its worst. Even the conservatory where Dan settled was still comfortable in the middle of the night.

"What is it Baba, can't sleep either, eh?"

Bradley rolled his head deeper into the blanket and wriggled his tiny feet. Dan rocked him gently as he looked around the garden room, taking in the photographs of Jim, Gwen, other people and places all of which were transformed into black and white by the night and the moon.

"You know there's nothing your mummy and I wouldn't do for you, don't you? And there's nothing you can't tell us when you get a bit older and the world starts to screw around with you. I promise we'll always try to look after you, Baba.

"Do you know when I was young, I would have given anything to have someone to talk to about all the crap, and also to share all the good stuff. I think one day you should have a little brother or sister to tell in case I'm not around, what do you think of that?

"I want to be there to look after you but just in case I'm not, you have to know you can always tell your mummy if there's a problem. She's one of the good ones Bradley, one of the very best ones.

"If I go away it will only be because I have to. When you grow up, you'll realise that you must be true to yourself, whatever that means, and sometimes you will do things that nobody else will understand or agree with. If you take my advice you should always try your best at whatever you do and don't worry if some things don't work out because of it."

Dan looked down. Bradley's eyes were all but closed again and he was breathing in tiny innocent puffs. Despite knowing his son wasn't hearing anything he continued.

"My mummy told me once that my daddy used to sit up with me during the night and tell me stories about his work, but I don't remember that. By the time I do remember things about them it was generally bad things. When you grow up, I hope you remember all the good things. Jim and Gwen will be around too, you know. They might be a long way away and you might only see them occasionally, but they'll always be there for you. Do you know how lucky that makes you, Baba? Well let me tell you, it makes you one of the luckiest little boys in the whole world.

"I want to tell you something else too. One day you might hear stories about me and how bad I was and some of the bad things that I did. I hope mummy and Jim and Gwen will explain to you and you will understand. I never meant for a lot of those things to happen. I didn't go looking for them, but they had a way of finding me. I'd like to think that because they happened to me it saved someone else from going through it and maybe it was part of some great plan because somehow, I would be able to deal with it and find a way to carry on until the day I found your mummy and then we had you. Because you make everything worthwhile and I would go through it all again ten times over if I knew you would be there at the end. Does that make any sense to you Baba?"

Dan rocked his son in his arms until the colour began to return to the photographs as the sun came up on a new day.

CHAPTER NINE

"You started early, son."

Dan stretched his legs out from their crossed position. "Morning Jim, how are you?"

"Good, how long have you been up?"

"It was early. Bradley woke up in the night. When he went back to sleep, I was wide awake, so I thought I might as well do something useful. I've made a bit of progress actually."

Jim pulled one of the spare chairs out and readied himself for action.

"Your friend Barry has basically sent everything. A lot of it is duplication but I'm not unhappy about that. It gives me confidence there won't be important details still out there and the picture we make up will be as good as it can be.

"Zoe was cautioned for the D and D and the possession but there was no further contact between her and Jelena Copich, or any other police come to that. There are no later information sheets, no stop checks by foot or mobile patrols, nothing."

"That's a bit odd. Do you think she moved out of the area?"

"I don't know. I doubt it somehow. After all, she was dead at twenty-two Powton Road just nine months later, so her lifestyle didn't change that much. One very good thing, her friend Sean Darcy was a Stinger, and he's still in the area. He got himself arrested just over a week ago and gave an address in Nottingham. There's a load of other stuff about the Stingers which I need to trawl through properly but nothing about shoe polish. I was hoping to have more on who was occupying Powton Road at the time of her death but there doesn't seem to be anything on that either."

Jim pondered for a second. "So, are we happy or not?"

"Yes, I think so. It's going to take us forward but how far and whether it will be far enough we'll just have to wait and see."

"You must have thought about what if, at the end of the day, you can't find all the answers and have to say this is one investigation which remains unsolved."

Dan shrugged a tacit acknowledgement. "Only a million or so times. We have to give it a real go though."

"Where do you want me to start?"

"The Stingers. I need to know who they are and what their relationship was to Zoe. I want to know which one of them will be most vital to us in identifying the dealer at number twenty-two, and his gofer Vic, because they've got the answers I want."

Jim got to work as Dan continued reading and sorting.

"Will you be seeing Nick on this trip?" Jim asked after a while.

"Almost definitely. I'll have to go up to Nottingham at some point. I can't see any way this is going to get resolved from your house."

"I'd like to come along if that's okay. Unlike you, I still have friends in the job who could be useful. You burned an awful lot of bridges before you left."

Dan smirked. "On the subject, what happened to that asshole Ben Binder?"

Jim shook his head and started to chuckle, which rapidly became contagious. It wasn't long before both men were roaring with laughter. It took Dan's second effort to restore order, but not before Jim needed his handkerchief to wipe away the tears that were flooding out of him as he panted for breath.

"Hell Jim, take it easy. Are you alright?"

"Yes, son, I'm fine. You just can't help yourself can you."

As he started to laugh again Dan held up a hand like a schoolteacher. "It has been said that I will be the best friend you ever have but if you make me your enemy, well, you get the idea. He should've done some serious jail time."

Jim agreed but could only offer a senior officer's point of view. "What we know and what we can prove. It's always been that way and always will be. In a perfect world he will get his just deserts one day."

Unfortunately, the combined half century of police experience told them there was no such thing as a perfect world.

Morning coffee came and went followed by Gwen's homemade soup and bread for lunch. As Dan and Jim worked on through the day, further conversation was limited. Occasionally one would seek confirmation from the other of some small fact or pass on a nugget of unusual or interesting information. Although their surroundings were homely and comfortable, the atmosphere was all business. Throughout they played a game of taking turns in moving paper from one pile and putting it on another with or without a note or comment attached.

Jim was fully engrossed with photos and descriptions of Stinger gang members half way through the afternoon and didn't notice Dan stop what he was doing with a sheaf of medical reports detailing Zoe's death injuries. The document in his hand was a written description of the bruising around Zoe's neck and nose. When Dan read it, he almost missed the significance and would have completely if he wasn't holding an orange in his other hand. He read it again and looked at the orange, squeezing it tightly for several seconds, moving it around his palm and fingers. It took a third reading of the report before he was satisfied. The urge to shout was near impossible to squash as emotion flooded from his head to his heart and back again. As Jim continued stoically plugging away, Dan closed his eyes for a moment of contemplation. He needed to absorb this new reality before he could share it.

It was almost 6:00 p.m. when Tara came in to tell them it was time to call it quits for the day.

"Bradley has only seen you for ten minutes today. Come and spend a bit of time with him before his dinner and bed."

"I think we've done some pretty good work today," Jim said, rubbing the back of his neck.

Dan got up from the floor and reached out to hold Tara's hand. "There's still so much to add. All the investigations into the occupants of the house failed to identify three or four of the crucial bodies and we don't know any of them yet either."

Tara looked jolted. "Bodies!"

"Sorry, I mean other individuals who were there and relevant to the inquiry, not literally bodies."

Jim pointed to one of the new paper piles. "I might be able to assist. The other person Zoe was with in the kitchen when you first saw them, was it a male or a female?"

"Unfortunately, I've got no idea. I went back over that one time and again but there's just nothing up there," Dan said, tapping the side of his head.

"Have a quick look at this," Jim started to say before Tara stopped him in his tracks.

"No, it can wait. Come on both of you, out of here and turn the light off."

Dan was happy enough; the fragments of information and evidence in his head from the day required shuffling before being stored away, and there was one great discovery he needed to tell them about.

"Yes boss," he said for them both.

Gwen prepared four gin and tonics, putting ice and lemon in each and then handing them out.

"I can see you've had a good day," she said to Jim.

"That's the hardest I needed to concentrate for several hours at a time since we moved here. It takes it out of you."

"Do you still miss it?" Tara asked.

"Yes and no. If I read something in the paper or there's an item on the news about a major investigation I wonder where they're at with it, but getting up every day and going into the office to deal with budgets and complaints for ninety percent of the time? No thank you."

"And the people," Gwen added. "You do miss the friendships."

"Of course, you spend the greater part of your life with them in that environment. As a youngster in uniform it was us against the world, you know, Tara. Night shifts, punch ups in the pubs and clubs when you've got to rely on your mates to be there when you're in trouble. Then when I got onto CID, you need that professional backup, protecting the evidential integrity and having the right people around you when you're involved in some of the worst crimes. I'm sure Dan will have told you much the same."

"He has. It's what you call a dysfunctional family, isn't it?"

"But family nevertheless," Dan confirmed.

"Jim and I met when he was still a young PC in uniform and I worked in a travel agents shop in town," Gwen said. "He always wanted to join CID, didn't you? We got married when he got his first CID posting in Nottingham and we moved into a police house close to the station. Most of your friends were in the police until we started playing bridge and joined a club; then you managed to meet some different people, but it was still years later."

"That's the problem with the police. It can be very hard to meet new friends from outside the job," Dan said. "For people like me especially, for whom the police are their whole world. I hardly knew anyone who wasn't in the job."

"Not healthy that, son," Jim remarked.

"I do know that now. There was never a pressure release valve, something different to talk about or another environment to be in."

Gwen sipped her drink. "Like us and the bridge. However did you manage to do all those undercover jobs? I would have hated for Jim to do something like that."

"I mentioned it to Jim before. I was single which helped, and those jobs were my escape. Although I was still being a policeman, I was somebody different and so I suppose I felt the pressures were on that other person and not me. I reasoned it in that way then. Of course, it all caught up with me in the end."

"You must have been scared at times?" Gwen persisted.

"Do you know, I never really was. I don't know if that was bravado on my part or because I did feel in control for the vast majority of the time. What happened to Jim with being assaulted so badly, I didn't come close to anything like that in my whole career. I got the odd punch around the ears when I was younger but half the time it was probably my own fault for saying the wrong thing to the wrong person or not being aware of my surroundings enough. It teaches you to use that sixth sense people talk of the police having and develops your natural abilities."

"Some of us," Jim interjected. "You got my share and more."

"Do you want to tell us what you discovered today?" Tara enquired of the two men.

Dan nodded to Jim. "You first. I'd like to hear what you've got before I explain what I've found."

Jim put his drink down before he began and started as if he was briefing staff once again. "Dan asked me to look at the Stingers as my first task and then secondly, try to identify Vic and the dealer to whom Vic was reporting. The information Barry sent down yesterday included a lot of what we knew already as well as some new material. Given all that, I also decided to have a look at the person Zoe emerged from the kitchen with when Dan saw her for the very first time. That was three objectives in all and I believe I've some new information concerning all three.

"Firstly, the Stingers. I've a list of names who are definitely Stingers. Next to that there are a number of associates who are not gang members but connected to them. I won't go through all the names now, but I can tell you Sean Darcy figures largely as one of the gang founders.

"Second, the man Vic. He was the man who spoke to Dan and Zoe, although he knew her as Summer, and she knew him. I can't find any reference to a man called Vic. Dan, is there any chance it might be another name, maybe Nick or Rick?"

"No, she definitely called him Vic and he responded to that name."

"Alright then. The fact there's no reference to a Vic is in itself interesting and we'll have to look at that later, but I did manage to compile a list based on Dan's description of him, which might be good, because Barry also sent photographs I could check against.

"The dealer he was reporting to was my next objective. As there were no references to Vic, and therefore no references to his associates or a description from Dan to go on, I've compiled a list of known heroin dealers active in Mapperley at that time. I've put them in age order as it's more likely this dealer was in a similar age group to the occupants of the household. It's not a big list, I have some photos again and so we might get some joy there too.

"Lastly, Zoe's kitchen associate. I've two possibles. One is Sean Darcy and the other is a female called Caroline Farthing, Carly to her friends. She and Zoe were close for a time and she also has a connection to the Stingers. I think with another day or two's work and some more phone calls, we can come up with several concrete avenues to go after and positively identify some of these people."

Dan took on every word from Jim and slotted them into his mental picture of the scenario.

"Sounds good Jim, thanks. Any questions so far, ladies?" He paused. "No, okay while you've been doing all that today I've been concentrating on Zoe. I started by going through all the new material Barry sent, which included her medical records from the hospital before the PM and tried to build up a better picture of her life from the time she was cautioned by Jelena Copich to that night at Powton Road. I'm now sure the reason for her being killed must be related to her immediate past and her killer is involved in that immediate past."

Jim had known Dan for a long time, Tara for more than four years. He was a seasoned detective with an ear and an eye for facts; she lived with him day in and day out. Both knew some of Dan's nuances but despite all this, it was Gwen who heard what he said and understood its meaning.

"You know you didn't do it!" she exclaimed.

"What!?" Tara and Jim called out in unison.

"You said you now know you're sure and the murderer was involved with her in the time just before she died."

"Dan?" Tara begged.

"She's right, it wasn't me," Dan replied, allowing the words to wash over all of them.

The confusion of hugs and tears, accompanied by hows and whys were utterly lost on Dan. All he felt was absolute relief partnered with absolute grief. The next thing he heard properly was Jim.

"Let the boy explain," he was saying, but it was several more minutes before he could.

"It was in the documents Barry sent us," Dan started when they were all finally calm enough to listen. Tara was sitting on the sofa with him while Jim rested in the matching chair and

Gwen perched on its arm like a canary in her yellow cardigan. "The bruising around her neck was fully described in the hospital report."

"Didn't you say the bruising matched the size of your hands though? Don't get me wrong, I couldn't be happier, son, but what changed?" Jim queried.

"It wasn't the size. It was the bruising pattern. According to the record she was strangled with two hands around her neck and the pattern of both hands are similar but not the same on each side. On her left the bruising caused by the third finger is less than the rest, almost nil in fact."

Tara, Jim, and Gwen's blank expressions demonstrated the need for clarification. "Believe it or not I was about to eat an orange when it occurred to me. Here let me show you."

He picked up one of the big church candles from the mantelpiece and gave it to Jim. "Imagine this is my neck and you're going to strangle me. Go on."

As Tara and Gwen watched on Jim put his hands around the candle and squeezed. "Like this?"

"That's it, do you see?" Dan asked enthusiastically.

"No. What am I doing wrong?"

"Nothing, squeeze as hard as you think you need to strangle me."

"I am, I am."

"Right, now take the third finger of your right hand off without reducing the pressure of the rest of your hands and fingers."

Jim tried to do as he was told.

"And?" Dan urged.

"I'm trying, I can't. Every time I let that finger release a bit all the others do. Gwenny, you try."

Gwen shook her head in mock terror. "I don't want to, Tara you do it."

Tara tried next but couldn't either. It was impossible to allow the pressure of one finger to be released when they were squeezing hard enough to strangle the life out of the candle with all the others.

"I couldn't do it to my orange either. To strangle Zoe, the killer must have used all the force you were using on the candle. The only way to do it without exerting equal pressure with all the fingers is if one physically can't. It must be weaker than the others and there's nothing wrong with my grip. I couldn't have caused that pattern of bruising. I couldn't have strangled her. Not only that, but we now know the killer had a physical injury to that finger at the time. If we're lucky it's something permanent and he or she still has it."

The uncontained joy of the others was embarrassing to him. As they celebrated the great news Dan knew it should be more than okay for him to be happy too, just as an innocent man facing a judge and jury would be if found not guilty. He wanted to celebrate, but the black mass inside him relating to Zoe for so long was now a void of nothingness leaving him feeling empty inside and incapable of sharing their joy.

After dinner when the assorted emotions of the group had circled in closer to each other and they were able to talk for thirty seconds without becoming over excited again, Tara, Jim, and Gwen wanted to know what Dan proposed as their next plan of action.

"This changes everything," Tara enthused. "We've got a suspect now with a unique signature. Are you going to be looking for that weak hand as the number one priority?"

"Certainly, it must have a very high priority, but we mustn't put all our eggs in that basket," Jim said. "Like Dan said earlier, maybe it was a temporary injury at that time but even if that's the case there may be a police record of someone in the files having a hand injury at that time. It's the biggest break so far. Not only that, Dan's said all along he wants court quality evidence, which means beyond reasonable doubt. While this is good, great in fact, it's still not enough on its own to convict. We need more."

"Are you feeling a bit better, Dan?" Gwen asked.

"Yes thanks. It's been a big day and it will take some time to get used to the idea. Jim's right though, this is a major step forward, but we do need to keep focused on the other threads and make sure we cover them all to the end. I think we should try to finish the rest of what we identified today and maybe you can call Barry one more time, Jim, and see what he can do with a person with a damaged right hand so we've that information when we're ready to proceed."

"Whatever you want, son."

Dan was grateful for his understanding. "And then maybe we can think of going up to Nottingham after that."

Before bed a few hours later, Dan went to check on Bradley and tuck him in again under the duvet which he had wriggled free from.

"Well after all we talked about last night it looks like I'm going to be around for quite a while, Baba," he whispered while stroking Bradley's ultra-fine hair. "Between you and me I was terrified at the thought of not seeing you grow up, but everything is going to be okay now. Sleep well, Baba, I love you."

Tara appeared silently behind him. "Hey darling, what are you up to?"

"I didn't hear you come in. I was just finishing a conversation we started last night," he said as she remained in the doorway between the bedroom and the walk-in closet.

"I woke up and you were both gone. You were up a long-time last night. I can't imagine how tough this must have been. I'm glad you're talking, even if it's to our little man."

"He's a really good listener."

Tara stroked her hand along Dan's arm. "I know you can't be happy yet but I'm so happy for you. You never deserved any of this. Can you believe when we go home you won't be carrying all that guilty baggage?"

"You know it's thanks to you mostly. I wouldn't be here, not just here in England doing this now, but here in my life if I had not met you. I'll never let you down."

Tara kissed his neck. "We're a good team. Come on we need to sleep; I've got a feeling tomorrow will be another big day."

CHAPTER TEN

For the first time since Tara could remember, Dan slept through the night undisturbed and was still fast asleep at 8:00 a.m. An hour before she'd got up to attend to Bradley and then put him back down in the smaller travel cot at the end of the bed before going back to bed herself. She watched Dan's eyelids flutter, expecting them to flip open at any moment and savouring every second until they did. Bradley was awake but gurgling happily, therefore she was completely content laying very still and watching her man at peace.

His appearance in her life was a gift. They'd been introduced at a time when her world fell into a tumult and despite Dan's history—which would have destroyed most people—they somehow managed to navigate a course through death and disaster to the eventual safety of a deep loving relationship. She took a long time to come to understand some of his idiosyncrasies and there were others which were still way past her level of comprehension, but what she did know was how much he loved her. He'd also taught her what enough really meant, and she knew her life with him and Bradley was enough.

Dan woke at that moment to be greeted by Tara's beaming smile.

"Good morning, you look very happy," he said, sounding wide awake.

"I was just thinking how lucky we are. You slept well."

"I did."

"Do you have to work today? It looks like it might be a nice day."

"I really ought to after yesterday. Jim will be as keen as anything, and while we have a bit of momentum it would be good to make the most of it."

Tara was disappointed but grudgingly understood. "It was worth a go."

"Sorry, T. Look on the bright side, if we can get this sorted soon, we can have all the days out you want."

This morning Jim was indeed straining at the leash to get started and Gwen was doing her best to keep a tight grip on it.

"You must make sure you don't overdo things and if you're not going to keep a check on yourself, then I'll do it for you."

"I'm alright, Gwenny love. All we're doing now is paperwork."

"I know but just look how excited you're getting over that already. Goodness knows what you'll be like if Dan wants you to do anything else."

"He'll want to update us all this morning so if it makes you feel better, we can ask what his plans are."

There was a tangible change to the atmosphere when Gwen joined the others. Placing a tray with four cups on the spare table seemed to signal a switch into work mode. The immediate hysteria of Dan's previous day's news intensified this morning's feeling of progress. The others wouldn't say out loud, but they were far more excited about the prospect of identifying a suspect who wasn't him. For Dan, it was more about respect for Zoe and her memory. She'd hinted to Jelena Copich about reclaiming a better existence for herself and the bastard who took away her chance was still out there somewhere. The day before he was working towards an end which wasn't fully understood. Now his mission was crystal clear.

"I want to identify people today, hopefully match some descriptions with photos or names and be able to put them in place at the scene like pieces in a jigsaw. To make it easier, that's exactly what we're going to do. I will draw a sketch of the house at Powton Road and we'll attach the notes to it to build it up.

"We'll do one person at a time and it will take all four of us to do each one."

Dan described how the process would work and for the next half hour while he drew up a plan of the house the others prepared all the other associated documents and pictures.

When they were all ready the big table looked like the war room from an old movie, with Dan's sketch plan covering most of it and the pieces placed around the edge waiting to be manoeuvred into position according to the movements of key players.

He indicated to a blue square with his own photo stuck in the centre.

"This is me in the chair. Over here is the kitchen and the kitchen door where I first saw Zoe and the other person, here is the sofa where the dealer was sat and here is Vic who floated between me and the dealer. There were two other people, here and here, and another here; they were using.

"Let's start with Vic and we'll do all the descriptions in the same way. Remember what I said before; hair styles can change; young people get older and taller so don't discount anyone unless they can't be the person I'm describing. All we want now is a list of probabilities based on a description only."

Dan talked very slowly, allowing them plenty of time to complete their tasks and giving him the opportunity to see what they were doing.

"He was a white male, aged between sixteen and twenty. He was about six inches shorter than me, so around five four to five seven. He was a proportionate build for his height and had a clear complexion and dark coloured eyes, so not blue. He had a Mohawk haircut which was dyed orange and he had a small birth mark or similar on his right cheek which was crescent shaped and about the size of a ten pence piece; the points of the crescent were directed away from his nose. He wasn't wearing glasses and was clean shaven. To me he looked like a young George Best. He was wearing a combination of dirty blue denim jeans and a dark coloured sweatshirt or jumper. He wasn't wearing any jewellery I could see and didn't have any other visible marks, scars, or tattoos."

As Dan described the first of the players Gwen started sorting through all the photographs, putting to one side any that were clearly not the male Dan was describing and then putting the others in an order most likely to be the person according to the description.

Tara was looking at the list of Stingers Jim prepared the day before and like Gwen, she sorted them according to their similarity to the description of Vic. Jim's stack of documents included other individuals' information sheets, custody records, and ancillaries, courtesy of Barry Towers and the original file.

When they were finished, they placed their prioritised information on the blue square that denoted Vic.

"Good. Next, we have the dealer," Dan said, and so began the painstaking repetition of spoken description and document sorting.

It took well over two hours to go through the list and when they were finished, they were all ready for a break. Tara checked the baby monitor; Bradley had slept through the entire period and still appeared to be sound asleep.

Jim puffed out his cheeks. "It's hard to believe the level of detail, even down to the broken second hand. I wish now we'd worked together on a major incident job."

"That was fun, if fun is the right word," Gwen remarked while pouring tea from a china teapot.

"I know what you mean," Dan replied. "It does make you feel good being able to construct something which feels more real. Like doing a jigsaw, not ploughing through more sterile written lists."

"I like that you use real people in the descriptions too." Gwen said. "Much better for making a mental image."

"I always found having my mind's eye at the forefront of the work was very important. Do any of you think you've definitely got the person somewhere in the room?"

"I think I may have user number two," Tara said.

"Great, what makes you so sure?"

"His chipped front teeth and the hair. I know you said hair changes but the description I was looking at was within three months of the night and is exactly what you said, peroxide blonde with a black line from the right temple backwards past his ear. That and the teeth together can't be a coincidence."

"That certainly sounds like the boy. I'm not as sure as Tara but I might just have Vic," Jim said.

"Don't keep us in suspense then. Who?" Gwen asked.

"Adam Paul Vikkert. Eighteen at the time but described as baby faced. We need to confirm a few things, but he had a circular mark on his face a couple of months before and nothing two or three months ago. After what you told us about the bruising on Zoe's neck I was wondering if maybe he suffered an injury or something before you saw him that cleared up completely after."

"Vikkert! Adam Vikkert; I've got a picture of him," Gwen exclaimed. She dashed out of the room as the others revelled in her delight. When she came back, she was shaking. She put it down on the bench top so they could all see it clearly.

Adam Paul Vikkert. DOB 31.07.1991, the legend at the bottom of the photo stated, followed by 16.08.2013. It was a custody photograph, taken in a police station following an arrest only a few months before.

Dan studied the face. The first fraction of a second was all he needed to know this was Vic; the remainder was to indelibly imprint this newer version of him into his brain so he would never forget it again in the future. There was no Mohawk, no fresh complexion, and no crescent on the cheek. Now, or at least very recently, Adam Vikkert looked like an army recruit after initial training: mousy hair in a short back and sides, skin that showed time spent outdoors, steely brown eyes that were slightly hooded as if he was trying to look mean, and the two clean cheeks were fractionally hollow, emphasising the tough appearance.

"This is him, older but it's him," he said sternly.

"There's more on this guy. He wasn't a Stinger but there was an association to them and there's a list of other associates too. It's all there in the file," Jim confirmed.

Dan felt a volcano rising inside, one which he knew he could cap and draw energy from. The game, as his hero would say, was afoot, meaning things were about to start gathering pace exponentially and he wouldn't stop until he knew it all. "Great work. Tara, who do you think user two is?"

"Billy Mackenzie is the name I have, which is taken from a police officer stop check form and also the Stinger associates list Jim made up."

Dan remembered seeing the name but couldn't immediately connect him to Vikkert. He looked at Jim for assistance.

"Um, no, I can't put the two of them together at the moment," Jim said.

Dan nodded. "No, nor me, but if it is in there it's only a matter of time."

By mid-afternoon the known facts had grown substantially. Adam Vikkert and Billy Mackenzie gave up their secrets in the mountain of documentary evidence at their disposal and while there wasn't a direct link between the two of them, there were several indirect ones. There was also a new list of possible identities for the dealer.

Of the names Zoe mentioned to Jelena Copich only Sean Darcy seemed likely to have a connection. Dead ends were still numerous. At first when Billy Mackenzie became of interest they wondered if he and Billie Smith/Smythe were one and the same and they spent good time checking until they realised the latter was in fact a girl. Tara appeared deflated, but Dan quickly pointed out it wasn't a problem.

"Think of it this way: it's not been a waste of time, it's just another fact we didn't know before but this one happens to be irrelevant to the current investigation at this time. Who knows what it could mean in the future."

"And," Jim said, "look at your Powton Road house drawing now. There are more blue squares with identities attached to them than there are empty ones now. That's more progress in a day than the whole police investigation managed in months."

Indeed, there were. The two still eluding them were the dealer and the friend with Zoe. The earlier exercise didn't identify them but Vikkert and Mackenzie could be the stepping stones to revealing them too.

When Dan was finally content the sketch plan was as complete as it could be and all the photos and documents relevant to the blue squares were in place, he sorted everything else for archiving and ended the day's work.

"Thank you for today, we've made great strides. Tomorrow we can really get into Vikkert and Mackenzie. I'm as sure as I can be, they're going to lead us to the dealer, if not then definitely in the right direction. I think after tomorrow we should be ready for a trip north."

"To Nottingham?" Gwen enquired.

"Yes, no need to put it off anymore. We'll have pretty much done everything we can here. It's time to go and talk to a few people."

Jim rubbed his palms together.

Gwen furrowed her brow causing him to stop quickly. "I'll be honest with you Dan; I don't like the sound of it. Neither of you are in the police anymore and you're going to be looking for some pretty nasty characters. Why can't you just go to the police and tell them what you know and leave it to them?"

"It's a fair point, Gwen. All I can say is what I said before. I want to have sufficient evidence that a court will convict and at the moment there's not."

"But you can't guarantee a result no matter how much evidence there is."

Dan had to accept Gwen's logic. "True again. It's just something inside me which I've got to do."

"We'll be careful, it's not as if we're going to be kidnapping them and torturing them for information. I still have contacts and Dan's friend Nick is up there too, so we won't be on our own," Jim said.

"I understand why it is you've to go," Tara said to Dan. "I don't like it, but I understand, and I know it wouldn't be a good thing to stop you. But you, Jim, after all you've been through and the way you still are now, I'm sorry, I really am but if anyone has got to go it should be me."

Jim looked crestfallen and a little insulted too.

"She's right, love," Gwen added. "You're not up to anything physical and unless you can promise me there's no danger involved at all, I don't want you to go."

"Hey, wait a minute, who said anything about you going? I'll decide who's going. What about Bradley for one thing?" Dan said to Tara.

"Gwen said he can stay here with them," Tara countered with equal intensity.

That started a quick-fire exchange between Dan, Tara, and Gwen about who had been saying what to whom and what was going to be happening in the coming days. It seemed a three-way verbal tug-of-war was breaking out and Jim wasn't invited.

"That's enough, quiet, the lot of you," Jim bellowed. "This is my house, and this is me you're all talking about. Now just bloody calm down the lot of you."

Dan, Tara, and Gwen were silenced and did as they were told immediately. It was obvious the old adage of being able to take the man out of the police but never the police out of the man was alive and well.

"That's better. Now I want to know what the hell is going on. Right up until a minute ago I was under the impression that at some point Dan and I were going up to Nottingham to follow up on what we've been doing here all week and to see if we could solve this girl's murder. As far as I'm concerned that's still what is going to happen but if you or you—" he indicated to Gwen and Tara "—have got something to say on the matter I would appreciate being included in the conversation. And one more thing." He turned an annoyed eye on Dan "We might talk about something and come to an agreement, but you don't unilaterally decide anything for me."

Tara held out an open hand. "Sorry, I didn't mean to say it like that."

"Right now, one at a time. What have you and Gwen been discussing?"

Gwen answered hesitantly. "I'm just worried that you're not strong enough if talking to people suddenly turns into something else. You'll be no use to Dan, and I can't cope with going through a repeat of the last year, or worse."

Jim stopped his wife there. "Tara, what's this about you going and Bradley staying here with us?"

"I apologise too. Gwen did offer the other day if we needed to go anywhere at any time. I didn't say specifically about going to Nottingham with Dan and so what I said a few minutes ago is in no way Gwen's fault, I just got caught up in the moment. Having said that, I don't want to have anything happening to you on my conscience."

Jim's tone and demeanour softened. "Mm. Alright son, your turn."

"I've no intention of making your mind up for you. It was more when Tara said she was coming with me," Dan said through gritted teeth.

Tara took a breath, but Jim had more to say.

"For the record I feel absolutely fine and so if I'm more use going then I will."

It was Gwen's turn to look crestfallen as her husband laid down the law. "Unless it means upsetting you. If you don't want me to go, then I will stay here and help you look after Bradley. Just to be clear, I won't be as happy as a lamb, but you come first." Gwen gulped and began to cry.

"Come on Gwenny love, that's enough of that, we still haven't established who's going where yet. Dan, when do you think you'll want to head up there?"

"Maybe two or three days. I want to talk to Nick first to see if he's available and there will some planning to do."

"It seems I won't be coming on this particular fishing trip after all, so that gives you a couple of days to sort it out between yourselves whether or not Tara will be. If Gwen's said the lad can stay here, then take it as read."

Dan turned to Tara and felt as if the whole world was watching. "T, I can't tell you what to do, I have expectations, but I don't know what will happen for sure."

Tara bridled. "For four years I've sat on the sidelines while you've travelled around the world trying to find the most dangerous situations to throw yourself headlong into—a character trait I have to tell you is not best suited to a long and happy relationship—and while I think of it, if you've passed it on to our son then you can do the worrying in a few years' time and see how you like it."

Dan started to answer but she cut him off with a raised finger.

"Don't say a word. I'm not finished with you by a long stretch. The only thing you've got right in the last ten minutes is you can't ask me to go. You, mister, can't ask me to do anything in that sort of way, which for a genius doesn't make you very clever does it?"

Dan glanced away from Tara's tirade to Jim and Gwen. They sat together on the sofa; their warm exchange before seemed a catalyst for the more heated show Tara was putting on now.

"Don't look at them for moral support. They're not going to help you this time. This is about our future. Up until recently, you half convinced yourself you were a murderer and I was the one who got to deal with what all that meant. Now we know you're not, you're hell-bent on finding the real one, so don't for one minute expect me not to be on the outside of dealing with that too. My understanding is you're going to Nottingham to try and identify people connected with Zoe and talk to them. You're going to gather evidence and if there's enough of it when you are finished you will take it to the police. Other than meeting a few lowlifes how is it going to be any more dangerous than all that stuff you've done before?"

"It shouldn't be, but I can't guarantee it," Dan replied honestly.

"And can you guarantee I won't get run over by a bus the next time I go into town with Gwen?"

"No."

"So, this is what is going to happen. *We're* going to Nottingham and when *we've* finished there it will be the end of this. Then *we're* coming back to our son and then *we're* going to get on with our lives. And I'm not asking Dan, I'm telling you."

Dan was quiet and Tara held his gaze to keep it that way.

Gwen squeezed Jim's hand. "I do love a happy ending," he chuckled.

Tara's tough appearance dissipated although her resolve remained concrete. She cracked a smile and curled her arms around Dan's neck. "You know where this story's heading don't you?"

"Listen Tara, I was just trying to do my best, you know that right?"

"Of course, and you know despite your genius you don't always get it right. As far as I'm concerned this is either together or not at all."

"I'm sorry."

"I think you owe Jim and Gwen an apology, not me."

"Don't make him have to do that as well. The boy has suffered enough," Gwen said.

"I don't know what to say," Dan replied over Tara's shoulder.

"It sounds like you've got a new partner. It might not be such a bad thing for Tara to go with you, son," Jim admitted.

Later when they were alone Gwen cuddled up to Jim as they listened to a concert on the radio. "Are you cross with me for saying what I did about you going with Dan?"

"No love, not cross."

"What then? You've been quiet ever since."

He sighed heavily. "It's hard being told you're too old or too frail to do something you've spent your life doing. I would never do anything if it was going to upset you and so I can't be annoyed with you for saying what you did, but it's clear I need to consider myself unable to do some things any more, not out of choice but because I'm just not capable."

"It's not because you're incapable Jim, you're still recovering from that terrible beating."

"There's no difference. Face it. I'm not going to get much better than I am right now. I love it here and my gardens, but I wouldn't like to think that's all there is from now on. To be perfectly honest I think he needs me at the moment as well."

She looked puzzled. "Dan?"

"Yes, you've read his biography. All that stuff throughout his life is coming to a head and it can still go one of a few different ways. Take it from me. There are going to be some twists and turns for him before it's all over. I've known Dan longer than anyone and I knew his dad too."

"What are you getting at?"

"I might be wrong, and I hope I am, but I'm not sure however this ends he can walk away happy."

CHAPTER ELEVEN

The next morning's pile of documents was a fraction of the previous day and Dan's objectives regarding them were equally focused.

"Adam Vikkert, Sean Darcy, Billy Mackenzie. We want every connection between these three individuals and especially the names of people who are associates of all three. Apart from me I'm sure everybody there knew everybody else. The dealer's not going to behave like he did unless he was comfortable, so can each of you take one of those three and write down every name or nickname, every address, and every vehicle you can find, then we'll cross reference them and see who we end up with."

Tara picked up the pile closest to her.

"What are you going to do?"

"I'm going to give Nick a call in the other room."

"Say hello from me," Jim said.

"I will, any problems give me a shout."

"Hi, we've been expecting you. How is everything?" the familiar voice said, sounding genuinely pleased to hear from Dan.

"Amber, I thought you were still away at uni. I'm good, really good. And you?"

"Great. Are you coming to see us?"

"I hope so, that's why I was calling. Is Dad around?"

"He is, I'll get him for you. Are Tara and your baby coming too?"

"Tara is but not Bradley this time although I'm sure you will get to meet him before we go back to NZ."

"I can see Dad now, when are you coming?" Amber asked as Dan heard her walking from inside to out.

"A day or two."

"Brilliant, I can't wait. Here he is, see you soon."

"Bye Am, see you."

There was a rustle of the handset being exchanged before Nick blasted down the line, "Hey mate!"

After a brief exchange of pleasantries, the two friends got down to business with Dan describing the progress made so far. Nick was obviously delighted to hear Dan now ruled himself out as a suspect. When he also said the killer must have had a deformed, injured, or otherwise damaged third finger on their right hand, Nick tried but failed to recall a name to go with the description.

"To hope you would immediately be able to name that offender was too much to ask," Dan admitted.

"I'll ask around and do all I can to see if anyone else does though," Nick answered. "So, when can we expect you?"

"What's today, Tuesday. Let's say Friday, how does that suit you?"

"Perfect. I'm off over the weekend and the whole of next week. You're going to stay with us, aren't you?"

"If that's okay with you and Penny."

Nick laughed. "You must be joking, short of running over the dog, I don't think there's anything you could do not to be her favourite person in the world. It's going to be great to meet Tara finally as well. The girl who tamed Dan Calder."

They talked for a further thirty minutes until Dan said he should get back to the others and hung up. The mood in the other room was muted to say the least; Dan guessed the news must not be great. Jim cut to the chase.

"Bloody nothing, son. I can't believe it."

"We've been through and can find several links between Vikkert and Mackenzie, Mackenzie and Darcy, or Vikkert and

Darcy but not a single one for all three. We've looked at all the names from every angle, but no one stands out," Tara explained. "What do you make of that?"

Dan tried to assess the disappointing facts. "I wouldn't have guessed there would be none. Maybe there are none or maybe we're looking in the wrong place. How many do you mean by several?"

"Where is that sheet, Jim?" Gwen asked. She leant forward to the A4 sheet he indicated to. "Vikkert and Mackenzie three males, one female, no addresses, and one vehicle. Next is Mackenzie and Darcy one male and one female only. Then Vikkert and Darcy eleven males, one female, four address, and three vehicles."

She handed Dan the A4 so he could see for himself.

"Mm interesting," he said after a minute of head tilting and brain crunching.

"What is? Interesting good or interesting bad?" Tara asked.

Dan felt that he was just pointing out the obvious as he turned the sheet to face them. "Well if we just take the numbers as an indicator on their own, we would have to say that Mackenzie and Darcy hardly know each other at all, but Vikkert and Darcy must know each other pretty well. Also, there are only two females mentioned across all three of them and Zoe is the one who links Vikkert and Darcy."

Jim puffed out his cheeks. "So, what does that mean?"

"I'm not sure but it's interesting. Are any of these known dealers?"

"Not directly. A couple of the addresses and one of the cars were said to be places drugs were being dealt from but none of the names here were attached to those addresses or the car. The car didn't have a registered owner in fact," Tara stated.

"Interesting," Dan said for the third time.

Gwen couldn't disguise her disappointment. "Sorry Dan, but it doesn't appear interesting in the least to me. I know you're the policeman, but what is there to get excited about? Isn't it all very random and rather disconnected?"

"It does look that way," Dan admitted.

They all sat in relative silence, drumming fingers and scratching heads.

"We could go back over it again to see if we missed something," Jim said.

Dan did expect more in truth. The fact there was so little, as Jim put it, 'virtually nothing' was troubling, and it occurred to him if that was the case there might be a reason for it. "No don't do that, but can you go back and see how many of all those connections are before and how many after Zoe's death?"

Without a word Tara, Jim, and Gwen got back to work again as if they were trying to make up for their earlier failures. As they checked and cross-referenced, Dan studied the current list again. Gwen was right: it was random. He decided to go and make himself useful while the others were busy.

"Who's ready for a coffee?" Dan said cheerfully when he came back a short while later.

"Perfect timing; we've just finished." Tara sighed.

"It wasn't hard. Just two or three before the date of her death, everything else was after," Jim said, helping himself to a cup and a biscuit.

"Are you sure? Sorry I don't mean to question you."

"Yes, definitely," Gwen added. "What's so surprising about it? I wouldn't think it makes much difference."

Dan tried to explain. "Well with most organised drug dens there's always some information which leaks out and the police get to hear about it from informants. After all, it was why I was in the area in the first place. The other thing is word must get around, so the buyers know where to go. In Powton Road they weren't just buying either; some people, as you know, were actually using in there too."

Gwen held up her hands. "Okay, I understand they can't just pop up."

Dan took a sip of coffee and was going to have another when the lightning bolt struck him. When he shouted Gwen nearly spilled her drink. "You're a marvel! How could I have been so stupid?"

Jim's eyes bulged and Tara clasped her hands together. Dan knew he was about to take another big step albeit in a different than expected direction.

"All this time I've been assuming Powton Road was a well-planned and prepared location to deal from, but it wasn't, in fact it was the complete opposite. No, hold on, that's not right." He paused as another shard of truth sliced into his head. "It was, *and* it wasn't."

"Dan, what the hell are you talking about?" Tara inadvertently giggled.

"Gwen got it. Random, disconnected, pop-up, she said. My God, it was some clever bastard who conceived this. Sorry Gwen, I didn't mean to swear."

"Thank you, but will you please tell us what you're talking about?" she replied.

Dan took another deep breath and swallowed down the remainder of his brew before he was able to get the order of everything in place. "I was on that job for the best part of two months before I met John, then Stan took me to Powton Road, and I never heard of the place until that day. You checked and said there was hardly any information before her death, hold that thought, alright?

"I got there and there were people using, people buying, and the dealer running his business in a very professional manner. Hold that too.

"Gwen, you said pop-up. Think of a pop-up restaurant; they appear overnight and run for a short period of time before disappearing, but they take an awful lot of pre-planning so they can do just that. Do you see now it was a pop-up drug den?"

The glimmers of understanding were an indication they were following Dan but not getting the full implications.

Dan pressed on. "Pop-ups, I've never heard of one ever before, have you Jim?"

"No."

"That's why there are no great connections between Vikkert, Mackenzie, and Darcy or information on Powton Road. It may well have only been up and running on that day and they probably didn't know each other beforehand. I was completely wrong when I said the dealer was comfortable because he knew everybody. He was comfortable because it was so new there was no chance of details or information getting out about it and he was only going to be there for a very short period.

"Now if we know the place was a drugs den running in those circumstances then it could actually be incidental to Zoe being killed."

"I get all that, but am I still missing something? I think I am," Tara interjected.

Dan's senses were reeling as the full ramifications became blindingly obvious to him. "It's got nothing to do with the drugs as such. She was killed for another reason but as I said the other day, it was because of something immediate, something she did or said. And what she did was try to help me!"

"Why would she think you were in danger unless she knew you were undercover?" Jim asked.

"Exactly," Dan answered. "And she wasn't the only one. It has never occurred to me that my status was compromised but it makes perfect sense."

"So, who then?" Tara asked.

"Your list from before, all the connections and associates. It's not who is on it but who's not." He pointed to the discarded A4 sheet. "Discounting those who were there to buy, use or sell, who is not on it, but we know was there?"

After the seconds of silence became a lingering moment Dan put them out of their misery. "Stan. He took me there. He knew of the pop-up when there would have been little or no information about it. He and John Trew befriended me in the couple of weeks preceding and to me seemed at least minimally involved in the local drug scene, yet there's no mention of them in any document I've ever seen other than the log books I completed. They, John Trew, and Stan or Craig Matthews, whatever you want to call him; it was one or both playing me from the beginning, and I missed the whole thing until five minutes ago."

"Why would he take you to Powton Road if he knew you were a policeman?" Gwen asked in open disbelief.

Dan was sure he had it now. "I think that's one of the questions which will take us where we need to go. He felt safe, confident, if you like. Maybe because it was going to be there one day and gone the next. He knew so much more about me than I knew about him, he was controlling me and what I was doing was actually no threat to him at all."

Jim was ramrod straight in his chair once more. "So, he saw Zoe and it only started to unravel then when he realised she knew too."

"Or when he saw she was trying to help or protect me. Zoe and Craig Matthews—that's the connection we've been looking for."

"You're right. Stan or Craig Matthews aren't in anything we've seen. I find that hard to believe, in fact it's impossible. I tell you—" Jim indicated to Gwen and Tara, "—anyone who habitually occupied the places Dan was at that time would have one or two basic information entries against them at least."

"And that means what to us?" Gwen asked.

Dan answered as Jim nodded along in agreement. "It means this person, whoever he is, must have had knowledge of the

Powton Road pop-up before it came into being. Remember I met John at least two weeks before Stan took me there. I didn't find and use him; he found me, deliberately, as part of his agenda. The Cannonball operational objective was to disrupt the local supply of drugs and lock up the dealers, but this is something entirely different."

"This is sounding amazing to me," Tara said. "I understand you were looking into some fairly low to mid-level drugs supply at the time but from what you're talking about, now it sounds more like part of some big plan of which this drugs house was a very small part."

"That's exactly what I'm thinking now, T." Dan laughed, mocking himself. "Us, the so-called police experts with all the information we thought we had, knew nothing. And I was the worst of all, just stomping around in the dark believing I was secretly embedded. John was working undercover on me and he was directing my movements, showing me just what he wanted me to see and therefore controlling the flow of information I was sending back to the police. He must have been laughing his arse off at my incompetence."

Dan sat back, taking in the full extent of the uncommon feeling of utter failure.

"Until now, son," Jim replied. "What are the chances of him expecting you to resurface years later with the knowledge you have? I used to think cold cases were pretty hard to investigate because there was no momentum to start with. Look what we've gotten in a few days added to what the police originally managed. The other advantage we have at this time is whatever was happening in Mapperley then will be a matter of historical record and fact now; people will remember what happened."

Dan's eyes widened. "Of course, the local networks of druggies, criminals, and prostitutes. Between them who knows how much they will know."

Gwen shifted nervously in her seat. "I would be careful in wandering the streets of Mapperley with Tara to speak to some of those people."

"Don't worry, we'll be careful," Tara replied before Dan had a chance to comment.

CHAPTER TWELVE

The journey up to Nottingham was stress free. Aided by the pleasant powdery blue day and a good selection of music, the Ford hummed along the M5 and M1 motorways until Dan selected the more local A52 when the main road became only slightly more congested.

Over the previous two days, he spent no more than thirty minutes on making a paperwork plan of action. The remainder of the time was devoted to his family. Other than their Kingsbridge and Totnes day out, this was the first time he and Tara were going to be away from Bradley for more than an hour or two. Tara was demonstrably emotional about leaving him in Salcombe with his new surrogate grandparents, while Dan tried to be more stoic.

"Almost there," Dan said as he turned off the main road. Edwalton was no more than five miles south of the city centre but its leafy backdrop belied its proximity. As they passed the golf course Dan indicated and turned into a stubby cul-de-sac consisting of six houses with matching fronts. He pulled up by the Hetherington family's garage and killed the engine. Before they could get out, the whole of Nick's clan burst from the front door of the house like champagne corks in a flurry of waving arms and excited voices. Nick ripped open the driver's door and manhandled Dan out, while Penny and the girls enveloped Tara. Like an incoming tide of friendliness, they washed their visitors indoors and Dan was genuinely surprised at the fervour of the welcome. Despite all the phone calls and Skype conversations he'd had after the last visit when Amber was in trouble, he was still uncomfortable with the Hetherington's level of gratitude. Finally, calm was restored, and they were able to settle in the newly built garden room.

"It's so great to have you back, and to meet you in person," Amber said, flicking her attention from Dan to Tara.

Tara, Nick's wife, Penny, and all three of their daughters Amber, Rosie, and Viola only became properly acquainted via the Skype calls since Bradley was born but it was clear they loved having her and the little boy as a part of their extended family. Penny repeated how guilty she felt over how she thought of and treated Dan at times in the years when he and Nick worked together, and how she changed when he dropped everything to come back from New Zealand to assist Amber. Even when Tara tried to explain how Dan's moral compass worked, Penny still couldn't get past how much they owed Dan.

"I know I say it all the time, but you're all so grown up now," Dan said to the girls. "Even saying it makes me feel old."

"We're both driving now, and we can vote in the next election," Rosie said of herself and Viola.

"Poor old Dad. I think he can't wait for us all to leave home. Four women against one is not fair," Viola added.

Penny stood at Nick's shoulder as he reclined in one of the garden chairs.

"No, I couldn't handle just the two of us. It's bad enough when Amber is away at university."

They chatted happily as if it was a week, not a year, since they were last together and Tara showed off the latest photos of Bradley. An hour disappeared before the conversation turned away from sunny subjects. Nick had recently updated Amber with some of the history which brought Dan back to Nottingham, but the twins were deemed too young to be told. They believed Dan was helping Jim with an 'old job.'

"You sounded moderately hopeful on Tuesday," Nick said.

Dan half expected Rosie and Viola to be a little creeped out by the thought of what he was here for or maybe uncomfortably giggly. In hindsight their reaction would only confirm to him how mature they'd become.

"I think it's amazing how a girl just like us could end up like that. And it's even more amazing that some policemen still care about them years later," Viola said.

"Did you and Mr. Allen have a lot to do with the original investigation?" Rosie asked.

Dan managed half an answer. "He was the CID boss who reviewed it years after Zoe Summers was killed, but at that time it remained unsolved."

"After what happened to Amber if anyone can do it, I'm sure it will be you."

"Thanks Rosie, we'll do our best." He returned to Nick's earlier comment. "It moved on again after we finished talking on Tuesday. We think she's more likely to have been in the wrong place at the wrong time as opposed to being killed because of what was going on in the house at that precise time."

Penny flashed a look at Amber. "Will you talk to her family, Dan?"

"We'll try, but if they're going to be like they were at the time it might be a thankless task."

"If they knew how much Zoe loved them though, and why she stayed away because she didn't want to cause them distress, they might think differently now," Tara interjected.

"Oh, it makes my heart break." Penny sighed.

Amber offered Dan a limp smile. "And you're not likely to get involved in anything to scary or dangerous this time?"

"Not if I've anything to do with it," Tara replied.

"Well I can pretty much be all yours next week if I can help," Nick said.

"Sounds good. We can go over some details later but what would be good now is a drink at The Archer. Why don't we all go?"

The pub was the same as always and if Tara had been taken there blindfolded she would have known exactly where she was from Dan's description of his and Nick's favourite watering hole. At times like these Tara felt like she knew him a little better.

"That isn't the same awful stuff you made me try last week, is it?" she asked as Dan put down a tray of drinks.

"I got T to taste an Old Familiar the other day. She wasn't impressed," Dan explained. "No, this is another local from around here."

"Your man here does have an odd taste in beer," Nick said, pointing to Dan's muddy brown glass with his bottled lager. "He used to try and get me to drink the filthy stuff too."

Soon they were all laughing as stories were exchanged across the table like chess players vying for the upper hand.

"You can say whatever you like but which one of us has given evidence at the Old Bailey?" Nick goaded at one point.

The Central Criminal Court in Newgate, West London, famously known as the Old Bailey after the street, is the pinnacle of British justice, where innumerable major cases have been tried over hundreds of years. Dan often lamented his regret at never visiting, let alone giving evidence or having one of his own cases heard there.

Tara enjoyed seeing Dan like this. He was in a different state of happiness to the ones he displayed at home. Most of the time when they talked about his past in England it was a shadowy conversation, but here his memories and experiences sounded good and some so funny it made her ribs ache.

Once Dan and Nick decided to call it an honourable tie, Penny and the girls wanted to know more about Tara and Dan's life in New Zealand.

"Pretty good now. Bradley makes it perfect," Tara began. "The house is all finished, I work part time in the shop, which leaves me time to go off looking for more things to stock in it. I hope I can find lots more while we're here."

"Oh, you should definitely come with me and we can go to all sorts of places. I love all that retro stuff," Amber enthused.

"That sounds awesome. Baggage is no problem. I'll be sending a big package back separately. Where should we go?"

"Birmingham, Leeds, Sheffield, York, oh yes, York! You will love it there."

"What about you Dan, what else do you do now?" Penny asked.

"Just the consultancy stuff, all word of mouth and relatively risk free. Since I worked with the police a few years ago there hardly seems to be a week go by without someone calling. It gives us the freedom for Tara to go off whenever she wants, and I can have Bradley, as I work from home virtually all the time anyway. It works really well and we're quite lucky in that we don't have to work but we choose to."

"We want to travel, that's our next big plan," Tara continued. "I would like us to learn to sail and then get a boat and go off around the world for a year or two. You're not so keen though, are you?"

"Too much time travelling between places rather than being there and seeing it. But we'll do something soon, so we can be back in time for Bradley to start school," Dan answered.

Nick looked impressed. "That sounds like a great plan. It's good to see you guys doing so well. If anyone deserves it, it's you."

"To be honest we always wondered what you'd end up doing," Penny added. "Thankfully you found Tara."

"I think a lot of people would have shared your thoughts. When I went to New Zealand it was the right thing to do but maybe not for the right reasons at the time. I used to be your typical sceptical male cop. Since we've been together and through all we've been through, I think I'm a lot more open to the possibility of many things. A work in progress, she calls me, and being here is a part of that progression."

"I always thought you were sad, but I don't see that anymore," Viola said.

Tara smiled. "You should try living with him."

"Hey, I'm all better now."

"You know exactly what I mean. When you get miserable you could be an Olympic champion."

As Dan conceded the others happily made the most of his discomfort. Another round of drinks and conversation later they were ready to head back home again where Penny's beef casserole was working in her cavernous slow cooker.

Penny put the sponge on the draining board when the last plate was washed. She turned to Dan who'd kept time with her drying the assorted crockery and cutlery items.

"You know I will never be able to thank you enough for what you did for us last year. Amber could easily have been taken from us."

"I was glad to be able to help, Pen. She, Rosie, and Viola are fantastic girls."

"I mean it Dan, you saved us all you know."

He continued rubbing the last plate even though it was completely dry.

"I never really understood why you and Nick were such good friends. You haven't got an awful lot in common, or you certainly didn't when you worked together."

"I don't think we ever thought about it. When we were on surveillance, we were required to rely on each other so there was trust from the start. He talked about you and the girls a lot and it felt like I knew a little about your family. Somewhere along the line I started to feel a part of it. Neither of us imagined it would happen like it did."

"You know I didn't have any time for you when we first met. You were the opposite of what I thought was good for us as a family," Penny said apologetically.

"And in fairness you were right, so don't beat yourself up over it. I honestly believe it was people like Nick and you who kept me on the right side of sanity. You saved me as well."

"Tara's lovely," Penny said after a short pause.

Dan put his cloth down and his arm around Penny's shoulder. "We make each other happy and I finally know I'm entitled to be. That was one of the hardest lessons."

Penny paused again. "You will be careful, won't you? You've a family to look after now."

"Absolutely. Don't worry Pen, this is the last skeleton in my cupboard. Before we leave, we want to plan a visit for you and Nick to come out and see us. Just because I'm on the other side of the world doesn't mean I've lost the feeling of family with you. I'm like one of those rescue puppies. You've got me for life not just for Christmas."

"Okay buddy, tell me what you have," Nick said.

The evening TV schedule was no competition for his interest in Dan's latest venture. They occupied the two chairs while Tara, Penny, and Amber sat like eager contestants on the sofa. Nick had briefed the family to a point before his friend's arrival; Penny and Amber insisted they wanted to do whatever they could to help as well.

"My covert operation was compromised from an early stage and the man I thought I was using to get to the good stuff from was in fact working me. John introduced me to Stan, and he was the guy who took me to Powton Road," Dan began, dispensing with any superfluous information.

"Stan was his nickname, real name he had me believe was Craig Matthews, but I'm now positive that will be bull. He took me to the address, which was a pop-up drugs den in the same way you get pop-up restaurants. The benefit of this was it could do a load of business in a short space of time without the details of its existence filtering down to the police in time for us to act.

"We've some other names and descriptions too, but this guy Matthews is my main interest now. I doubt he's the brains of the operation though. The person who planned all this won't be close enough to risk identification easily."

"What about the other one? John Trew?" Amber asked.

"I don't know if he knew about it or was just a friend of Stan's. He never said anything that made me suspicious at the time. Having said that, I've gone from thinking yes-he-was to no-he-wasn't and back again regularly since the other day."

"What about the killer having a broken finger you mentioned?" Amber asked.

"Yes, the person who strangled Zoe must have had something wrong with the third finger on their right hand and that person is probably male because the size of the hands matches a person of my size."

Nick nodded. "What else?"

"Zoe was also injured with a knife sharpening steel just prior to being killed. We can't tell if the two attacks are related or if she was just really unlucky. Sorry to be so blunt, Penny.

"There are a couple of other issues which I know are going to be important, but I don't know why yet. There was also shoe polish, black shoe polish on her clothes, under her fingernails, and on other parts of her skin." Dan looked blankly at the others who looked blankly back at him.

"And there's a Stingers gang patch missing from the scene. It was sewn on the jacket she was wearing but the jacket belonged to someone else. I remember the patch when she was in the room with me but when the police photographed the scene it was gone. It's important too, again, I don't know why."

Amber asked the obvious question. "So, what are you going to do Dan?"

"Hopefully after last year there will be a few of the working girls in Mapperley who'll remember me. I'll start there to see if someone can help, then reassess."

"I can do some force intranet checking to begin with. Our group all have laptops now, so I can do it from home," Nick offered. "I'll deal with any questions if and when they come some other time."

"And we can do whatever you want," Amber added.

Dan took a breath. "Amber, you and your mum don't have to get involved in this."

"Oh yes we do," Penny shot back patting Amber's knee. "If you can't understand why we have to help then you're not much of a detective."

Dan looked at Nick, who nodded his agreement and approval.

"Alright then, you three will be the central hub for the information. Tara knows what I mean already but you'll be receiving everything coming in from us and Jim and you will have to examine it, weed out the rubbish, and keep us going forward. It might not sound too exciting, but it's the most important job of all and you will need to steel yourselves for some of the things you're going to see and read."

"Can I make a suggestion?" Penny asked. "I don't know about Tara or Amber but for me it would help if I could see what it is you're talking about. I drove out through Mapperley the other day and I went to Powton Road. Number twenty-two looks almost derelict so I'm sure no one lives there. I would like to see inside."

Dan looked at Tara and saw her reassessing her previous opinions of Penny, adding another layer of admiration to her character description.

"That's not such a bad idea, Dan, I think it would help me too," Tara said.

"Why don't we go first thing tomorrow?" Nick asked more as a statement of fact than a question.

He and the girls looked at Dan for confirmation. At the thought of being in the house again his stomach turned into a maelstrom and a lump developed in his throat, which he noisily cleared before able to get an answer out. "Okay, tomorrow."

Dan didn't dream that night as Tara would have bet on, but only because he couldn't sleep. He lay still, looking at the stars and the occasional plane's lights through the bedroom window, glad to find a little comfort when Tara stirred every now and then. There had not been a single day gone by since that night in 2006 when Zoe Summers and Powton Road were absent from his thinking. He could recall every detail of every moment up until the tainted cider paused the video tape in his head, and then the continuation of the macabre scene in the morning was crystal clear again. At least he knew now it wasn't his hand impressions on her neck; that filled part of the blank space, but it didn't do anything to quell the pain and hurt he felt for her.

In the morning he would step back in time to revisit the scene and try to take the steps forward necessary to finally lay the memories and Zoe to rest for good. Within him was a greater sense of duty than a career in the police ever instilled, and a fear of failure not felt since he was a boy witnessing his father's abuse of his mother without taking any action to stop it.

CHAPTER THIRTEEN

Dan thought twice before deciding to drive directly to number 22 and park immediately outside. His police training told him to park around the corner or at least drive through the area first to see what he could see. The fact was, he and his passengers were the only ones in the street, let alone the country, for whom 22 Powton Road was remotely interesting this morning.

This was Tara's introduction to Victorian style housing. She stepped from the car and looked up and down the street at the two rows of identical houses on either side of the worn tarmac road. All the front doors were recessed like sunken eyes and the postage stamp gardens, some with and some without iron railings, were the only visible colour. This moody palette of greys was a perfect accompaniment to the day.

"People live in these, it's so depressing," she said.

"I know, it looks so sad," Amber replied. "I saw photos of the streets around here when I was at school. This was still a nice place to live up until they started building the blocks of flats and estates. It was lovely until then, all the gardens were made up and the metal fences and doors were all brightly coloured, it was beautiful. I can't believe people wanted to move away from here to live on the top floor of those hideous flats."

Tara looked unconvinced. "What's around the back?"

Nick scuffed the pavement with a heavy shoe. "More of the same. They were built at the time of the industrial revolution I think, when this area and the whole of Nottinghamshire was one of the busiest in the country for coal and manufacturing. Thousands of people moved here to work and so street after street like these were built to accommodate them. There will be a narrow alleyway behind the yard and then all this in reverse again. Hey Dan, we should probably try the back. It'll be our best chance of getting in."

"No need. The front door is open," Penny said in a tone several notes below her usual voice.

They followed Penny's pointed finger to the mud brown door and needed to look hard to see the gap between its inner edge and the frame in the shadows. Suddenly it didn't seem to be the same good idea it was the night before and nobody could think of a thing to say. Dan eventually took the lead.

"Come on. Watch out though, there could be anything inside."

He pushed the door and then pushed it twice as hard to force it open with a loud, dusty scratch, instantly soaking in the atmosphere which was both familiar and alien. He was taken back a lifetime in seconds.

The hallway walls dripped aged wallpaper, complemented by the paint around the doors and skirtings, which was once white but now could be described as anything from grey to green. The carpet he remembered being there was gone, replaced by a mixture of newspaper and assorted rubbish. All the other doors along the hall were closed adding to the dark, oppressive feel and odd heavy silence.

Dan was pleased the smell he remembered and associated with the house was gone. Of all his senses, it was the smell of things that evoked the biggest emotions. The night he arrived at Powton Road the rough cannabis stink masked and consumed all others, and in the morning, it was the acidy stench of Zoe's vomit. Now there was a sweet, damp mustiness clinging to every surface and in the air. It was thin and just the top layer of several others including animals, old food, and smoke or fire.

He tiptoed towards the staircase and dog-legged around it further along the hallway. Ahead of him was the kitchen and to the right, the room where it all happened. When the house was new this would have been called the back parlour, where the occupying family would have spent most of their time. The door was ajar; having trailed Dan this far Tara, Nick, Penny, and Amber stood at the doorway allowing him a moment alone inside.

Shit, he thought, not needing to close his eyes or think hard to access his memory bank.

They were all there popping like bubbles in front of his eyes and at the same time he could hear the scene from the past—and smell, feel, and taste it too.

Like the hall, bare floorboards replaced the carpet, and the sofa where the drug dealing captain held court was gone but—he could hardly believe it.

The chair! The filthy, torn and tattered, saggy springed chair was still here. It now occupied a space in the far corner of the room as if it were hiding in shame. Dan looked to the point where it was seven years before and in his mind's eye, saw dark shadowy stains where his feet once rested and where Zoe's still body lay, though there were no marks to see now. In his head he also heard the buzz of drug dealing activity mixed like a cocktail with the sub-human noises heroin users make as the poison begins its journey around the bloodstream. As if by magic this buzzing was replaced by another; that of the flies who conspired with Zoe's greener than green sick to wake him the next morning. The air in the room pulsed slowly like a weak heartbeat. Dan dragged the chair back into position and the pulsing stopped as he slowly folded down into it. The springs that caused so much discomfort before again jabbed painfully into his backside, but nevertheless he settled down, remembering how he only noticed wetness once he sat the first time. The fabric was so worn that the woven polyester once advertised as indestructible and with a lifetime guarantee was threadbare, only held together by a combination of dirt and despair.

When he was ready, he looked up towards the doorway and the kitchen. He thought, *Zoe's not there.* But she was, in every speck of dust that floated around the room. She emerged from the doorway and slowly made her way towards him, stopping by the chair and dropping at his feet, so he could feel her against his leg. Dan was aware of the dealer and Vikkert, ignoring them this time around. He also noted but tuned out the users concentrating all his efforts on Zoe.

The moment the others allowed Dan was now an uncomfortable period where watching felt more like intruding.

"Is he alright do you think?" Penny whispered. "I can't imagine what he must be feeling right now."

Tara held up a hand. "Just wait. I've seen him like this before."

Two minutes later Amber could bear it no longer. "How much longer do we have to stand here doing nothing?"

Without meaning to sound so aggressive her father replied, "As long as it takes."

Unaware of the time and not caring, Dan rewound for a third time to see Zoe cross the room and sit down on the floor next to him. The cider in her hand moved up to her lips and tipped back; once, twice, three, four times all in quick succession before she leant back against the chair. When the ghost of Vikkert challenged him again, Dan strained to maintain his focus solely on Zoe as she moved to his lap and offered him the can. Her eyes bore into him again with such intensity his heart stopped, just as it did in 2006, but because it was just her he was watching this time, he noticed something was wrong with the picture. He froze the frame where it was with her eyes fixed on his, so he could recap until he was sure.

Oh fuck, he said to her in his head, and then he threw up on the spot where Zoe was no longer.

By contrast the air in the back yard was fresh; Dan gulped it in gratefully while Tara rubbed a concerned hand over his back and shoulders while he rested on an old wooden crate.

"You had me going there for a minute, mate. Are you okay now?" Nick asked.

"Yes, sorry."

Tara kept massaging. "There's no need to apologise to us, it stinks in there. Do you want to tell us what happened?"

Dan stood up. "No, I need to show you."

They followed him back into the house, through the kitchen to the hall and back parlour.

"I was sat here when I saw Zoe come from where you are standing. She came from the kitchen, I'm sure, which means she might have come through the back like we just did, or she was in the kitchen when I arrived," Dan said. He counted out the five steps it took to get from the doorway to the chair.

"She walked over to me slowly, deliberately, and took four sips from her can before she slouched down next to me here. When Vikkert challenged me, she crawled up onto my lap and offered me the can."

"And that's all you remember because of what she gave you," Penny stated.

"From that moment on yes, but there was more she was telling me, or rather, trying to tell me, before I took it. Let me show you again.

"I always looked at the whole scene for clues, for everything going on in the room. But I missed concentrating on what was really important."

"The dealer?" Nick asked.

"No, that was my big mistake. Zoe was trying to tell me it was me! She knew I was compromised, knew I was seriously at risk."

Nick looked lost. "I don't understand."

"She was trying to warn me, Nick. You try taking four mouthfuls from a drink between there and here."

Nick mimicked Zoe's actions, walking slowly from the door. Even going very slowly he had to rush to get the imaginary can up to his mouth four times in the few paces. "It doesn't make sense. You can't walk that slow and drink that fast."

"Unless you're trying to hide how nervous you are by going slowly. Try again, this time imagine you're literally shitting yourself with fear but still desperate to warn me I'm in danger. Remember, you must appear relaxed."

Nick repeated the short walk. Dan watched intently as he flew the can up and down while trying to calm his nerves.

Penny watched too, with a look close to horror painted on her face. "Oh my God. You can actually see it."

"Bloody difficult though. I could only get three mouthfuls in that space of time." Nick laughed.

"That's not all," Dan continued. "When she got on my lap and looked at me, she was also trying to warn me, not offer me the cider. Her look was so intense I took the can from her without a second's hesitation. I thought that's what she wanted me to do but junkies don't have the eyes that will do that to you."

Nick thrust both hands into his trouser pockets. "Hang on a minute that can't be right. We know she was; her previous cautions for possession, she admitted it, Dan. Look at her post mortem for Christ sake, the blood, the hair follicle tests."

"I know, and up until a few minutes ago you're one hundred percent accurate. She was, past tense. The blood showed hepatitis and septicaemia, the hair showed drugs, but have we ever asked how historic? There were no traces present in her blood at the PM. And her eyes, Nick, I looked into them and I'm telling you she was clean that night."

"She did tell Jelena Copich she wanted to get off the drugs and she disappeared for the previous nine months until that night with you," Penny queried.

Dan jumped on her comment. "That's right Pen, plenty of time to get clean."

Tara stood in front of him and looked deeply into his eyes. "Sorry to spoil your party but you can't be right this time, darling. You just said she drank from the can four times before you. Whatever you took from the can she did too."

Tara's comment was like a hammer blow to his theory and Dan couldn't believe or understand how he could be wrong.

Amber had been quiet until now. "Dan, are you sure there was something in the cider?"

"Yes, no question," he answered dejectedly.

"And if you were tested the next day could it work out of your system so quickly there was no trace?"

"Depending on what it was, it could quite possibly be gone in a few hours."

"A few hours? Hmm, so how does it work then if Zoe was killed? Surely her body wouldn't be able to clear itself and there would have been something on the post mortem?"

Dan looked from Amber to Nick. She was right. He battled to remember the night again; Zoe's slow walk from the door to the chair, the can, her eyes.

"I've got it!" Nick shouted, making them all jump. "I couldn't drink four times and I bet she didn't either. Dan, are you sure she drank from the can? Was she pretending?"

The can, her eyes, her mouth. The can, her eyes, her mouth. The can. The eyes, the mouth. The mouth, the mouth, Dan repeated over and over in his head, seeing it all again until he was positive.

"She never swallowed. She was just lifting the can up and down," he replied definitely.

"Bingo!" Nick shouted again. "She must've had a fit when you did."

Tara leant her hand on the back of the chair and instantly regretted it. Yet Dan was voluntarily sitting in it. "Do you really think Zoe was completely aware of what she was doing, Dan?"

"I'm convinced now. She somehow got herself clean after the Copich interview. I don't know why she was here that night but whatever the reason was she still risked everything to help me and it cost her life." He took a last look around. "Let's go. We've work to do."

When they got back to the house Dan needed a shower. Remembering the filthy chair, Tara took his clothes and put them straight in the washer, so he had to hunt out new ones before he joined the others downstairs.

Rosie and Viola must have been complaining before he came in, and Penny was clearly not having it.

"My house my rules," she chided them. "Besides, you're so busy with all your stuff you hardly have the time." As if to hammer home the point she added, "Where are you off to in a few minutes?"

"Georgina's," Viola answered sheepishly.

"Well there you go. Would you rather be there or creeping through a derelict house in Mapperley? Will you be home for dinner, or will you be busy in their pool and cinema room stuffing yourselves with popcorn like last time?"

The girls giggled in submission. "We'll call you, Mum," Viola said, kissing Penny on the cheek.

"Alright. Take care."

Dan indicated to Penny's board of sandwiches. "Remind me not to get on the wrong side of you again." He grinned. "Can I give you a hand with these?"

"And don't you forget it." She returned his smile and handed him the board.

The decibel level in the house lessened substantially the moment the twins closed the front door behind them. Dan noted Penny's satisfied sigh and followed her through to the garden room where the others were recounting the morning's events.

"What did we miss?" she asked.

"Nothing, we were waiting for you. Thanks for this," Tara said, handing a plate each to Amber, Dan, and Nick.

"You might as well go, Dan," Nick directed.

Dan finished his first bite; it felt better to have something in his stomach again. "This morning only served to prove Zoe wasn't killed because of her relationship with the drugs or the occupants of the house. She was killed because of me. We can also say now she wasn't an active drugs user at that time, but she was obviously still involved in the scene somehow.

"I want to absolutely guarantee that last bit, so can somebody check the PM again and see if there's any more in the hair testing to date her last drugs use?"

"I'll do that," Tara answered.

"Thanks. Just to clarify when I said she wasn't killed because of her relationship with the drugs or the occupants of the house, what I meant was it wouldn't have happened if I hadn't been there. It would be reasonable to guess the killer thought she was helping me, and I was investigating the drugs activity."

"It doesn't sound like the action of a Stinger. They were not violent criminals; young lads mostly who existed on the periphery, running errands for the big boys and so on," Nick said.

"Agreed," Dan confirmed. "I can't see them having the wherewithal to organise the house as a pop-up either, but it does make them prime targets for information now."

"I was thinking," Penny said. "You were out of it almost immediately after you drank the cider; what could have been in it to have such an impact on you so quickly?"

"Good question, Pen. I remember thinking that the next morning. The answer is probably quite boring. I hadn't eaten for a while before I went to Powton Road that night, I'm not a smoker or drugs user either, so I think I was just a weak, susceptible druggie virgin. I certainly did more than just have the cider that night, but I don't remember any of it."

"Oh okay. The other thing is from what you said, it makes sense to me that the killer knew Zoe would have been clean too, and when she told Vic the heroin was for both of you it would have alerted him."

"Good thinking, Mum." Amber said. "That has to be right, doesn't it?"

Dan nodded. "Very good. It might well be, or if not the killer, at least someone in the house had the influence to have her killed," Dan replied, omitting the fact he also considered the same thing in the shower a few minutes before.

Nick looked up from his empty plate. "Are you saying the killer may not be one of the named people we're aware of and you've described so far?"

"I've always been pretty sure—no, I *am* sure I was the only person of my physical stature there and because of the bruising on her neck fitting, I was also always my own best suspect. Now I can say it wasn't me, there are two other possibilities: either the killer was in the house somewhere, but I never saw him, or he arrived after I blacked out."

"I've another question. Sorry to ask, darling, but why didn't they kill you too?" Tara said.

That was another fact Dan devoted many minutes to since he became sure he wasn't Zoe's strangler. The only answers he came up with so far made him very nervous.

"Zoe was insignificant, borne out by the lack of family activity before and after her death, and the lack of effort in a protracted police investigation," he said, trying to sound humble. "They knew I was a policeman. Kill a cop and the investigation is a no limits time, money, and resources frenzy, involving every agency you can imagine and a media super story to boot.

"These bastards took all that into account and certainly expected I would report it first thing in the morning too, leading to an embarrassing confirmation of a failed undercover operation, a dead teenager, and an operative who committed the cardinal sin of taking drugs. When you add all that together it makes a scary picture of a very cool and calculating group or individual, extremely confident in their processes and security."

Tara gulped. "I wish I hadn't asked."

"Believe me, I wish that wasn't the answer either."

Later in the afternoon Dan and Nick prepared to make their second trip in the same day to Mapperley. The working girls wouldn't be out in numbers until the early evening, so they were in no rush to leave the comfort of their armchairs. As they talked, Tara sat alone at the table, studying several sheets of notes.

"I should have kept some of the phone numbers from last year," Dan said.

Nick smiled. "I'm sure they won't be too far away from the same lamp post you first met them at."

"Was there much fall out after I went home?"

"With Teddy Parker? No, with him gone it didn't take long for a few new faces to appear from what I heard. The streets of Mapperley aren't something I've got any interest in, in my job," Nick said, staring at the floor. "What do you want to do?"

For once covert operations weren't required and Dan's operation order for the evening was one sentence simple.

"Find a few people to talk to, hopefully people sympathetic to Zoe."

Tara interrupted their conversation with some confirmatory news.

"You were right about the hair follicle tests they carried out on Zoe," she said, reading from a document. "Evidence of marijuana, opiates, and amphetamines in the last twelve months blah blah.

"It says hair was tested at length of five centimetres from the scalp with nil result, ten and fifteen centimetres from the scalp with positive results. Five centimetres represents approximately the previous three months, ten represents six months, and fifteen nine months. So, she was drug free for the three months before she died in all likelihood."

Dan thought for a moment, considering carefully the implications of what he wanted to do next.

Turning to Nick first he said, "Sorry mate, change of plan, can we go tomorrow instead? There's something else I've got to do. Tara, I need to get changed into some decent clothes. Can you be ready to go out in about thirty minutes?"

CHAPTER FOURTEEN

"Darling are you sure you want to do this?"

"I have to, Tara," Dan replied.

The Ford pulled up and parked; Dan clicked up the handbrake and took the key out of the ignition. He checked himself in the rear-view mirror and within his steely reflection could find no reason to abort his current mission.

"Thanks for coming. I can't promise what sort of reception we're going to get."

Tara smiled back. "At least we probably won't be risking our lives this time. Come on, or all the neighbours' curtains will be twitching."

They opened the garden gate and walked up the pathway to an enclosed UPVC porch which contained a cactus and a welcome mat. Tara rang the doorbell.

Through the patterned glass it was impossible to say if the shape moving along the hallway towards them was a male or female until the door opened inwards. Dan recognised the face immediately; the shape of the nose and forehead were a giveaway, although the woman's eyes and cheekbones had not been passed down to her daughter.

"Mrs. Summers, Elizabeth Summers?" he asked.

"Yes, can I help you?" Zoe's mother replied.

"My name is Dan Calder, and this is my partner Tara. We were hoping to be able to talk to you for a few minutes."

She didn't respond, forcing Dan to speak again.

"I was one of the policemen involved in the investigation regarding Zoe."

Elizabeth Summers recoiled and reached out to the door frame for assistance.

"I'm very sorry for arriving unannounced. I was in the police, but I've been retired for several years now and we live in New Zealand. We've come over because I have some new information about Zoe's death, and I wanted to tell you personally. Please, could we come in?"

There was a glimmer of familiarity in the eyes but still no reply.

"It must be a terrible shock for you," Tara said. "Why don't you and Dan sit down, and he can tell you while I make a cup of tea?"

Tara took one step forward; Elizabeth Summers blinked.

"Come on," Tara said gently.

Whether she wanted to let them in or was simply unable to say no, the dumbstruck Elizabeth Summers allowed herself to be led back inside by Tara. Dan closed the door and followed. More by luck than judgement, Tara opened the first door they came to and found herself in a lounge with matching furniture, painted walls, and a large flat screen TV.

Dan sat in one of the chairs as Tara settled Elizabeth on the end of the sofa closest to him and then carefully sat next to her.

Dan leant forward catching her eye. "May I call you Elizabeth?"

Hearing her name had the effect of normalising the situation enough for Elizabeth Summers to reply. "Sorry, it was a shock after all this time. Did you say you're from New Zealand?"

"Yes, Elizabeth. I retired in 2008 and emigrated there. We live in Auckland and have a baby son called Bradley."

"But you said you've some new information."

Tara went to rest her hand on Elizabeth's shoulder but hesitated. "Are Anthony or Andrew home? Maybe it would be better if we could all speak together?" she said, drawing her hand back.

"Andrew works in Scotland."

Dan quickly scanned the room, taking in the complete lack of masculine effects, the single drinks coaster on the small table next to the other chair, and the pristine lace covers over the back of all the furniture apart from that same chair. But before he could express his condolences for her husband's passing Tara, oblivious to the fact, innocently spoke again.

"Will Anthony be home soon?"

"My husband died last year," Elizabeth replied in a gritty tone.

Tara went as white as a sheet; she looked like she'd been kicked to the ground and had fallen on Elizabeth Summers in the process.

Dan watched Elizabeth carefully. Studying the body language, he recognised the sorrow for Andrew being hundreds of miles away but indifference to her husband being gone altogether.

"Elizabeth, we're so sorry for your losses. It must be very difficult for you and now to have us arrive. I'll go and make that tea while Tara tells you a bit more about Bradley and New Zealand."

He gave Tara a 'trust me' look and headed out of the room, ignoring her horrified look. He took his time making the tea, hoping his instinct would be right about leaving the two women alone for a few minutes. It was hard not doing what came naturally and taking in his environment as he put the tray together, it was impossible to ignore the empty wine bottles on the bench and the part filled or full ones in the refrigerator. When he returned to the lounge Elizabeth was at least far more engaged, if not quite a new woman. Without wanting to break into the conversation he took his chair again and sat back.

"This is Bradley with Jim and Gwen," Tara said, flicking her eyes up to Dan and firing him the smallest smile.

"He looks just like you. You must be missing him terribly," Elizabeth said, tilting the phone to get a better look at the small screen.

"We do but they're great with him and it's really important to us that we do what we came to England for."

"Do you think you will have more? I always wanted three or four, but it wasn't meant to be."

"You must be proud of Andrew; a partner in a law firm sounds amazing for such a young man."

Dan couldn't help feeling amazing pride in Tara. She'd tapped into Elizabeth's psyche and broken down barriers he knew he couldn't.

"You gave me such a shock when you came to the door," Elizabeth said after a while and more photos.

There's no easy way, Dan thought. "If I called you out of the blue it might have been worse. At least you can see who it is asking."

Elizabeth turned directly to him for the first time since he came back into the room. "You need to tell me a few things before I even think about answering any of your questions."

"That's more than fair. Perhaps I should start at the beginning, not knowing how much Tara's told you already." He took a long, slow sip from his cup and then an equally long breath. "I was involved in the drugs investigation at Powton Road to begin with and Jim was the head of CID when the case was reviewed in 2010. I should also say I wasn't directly involved in the murder investigation but what happened to Zoe did have a profound effect on me and I was very disappointed whoever's responsible has not been found yet. Last year I got reacquainted with Jim and we thought we might be able to make more progress together than I could on my own."

"I don't understand. If you're both retired, why aren't the police involved and why are you so interested still?"

"I hope they will be soon, but I want to have some concrete evidence to take to them in order to force them into taking action. As to why I'm so interested; it's because I was there the night Zoe died."

"What! How?" she cried.

"I was an undercover drugs buyer. I was there gathering evidence."

"Drugs. Those damn things took her from me years before."

"I know, but for what it's worth I can tell you Zoe was trying to get herself off them and away from the whole scene."

Elizabeth let out a bitter laugh. "I find that hard to believe. When Zoe walked out that door, she did a lot more than leave this house. She broke us apart. I tried to get her to come home but she thought she knew better. After the first few months we never heard from her again."

"You have to believe me," Dan urged. "Zoe was clean for months before she died, and she stayed away from Mapperley too. I'm not sure what she was doing at Powton Road that night, but nine months beforehand she indicated to police that she wanted to improve her life and get it back on track again so she could come back to you and you could see she'd made the effort to turn herself around. Honestly it's the only reason she didn't contact you before; she wanted to feel she was deserving of your love before she came home."

Elizabeth looked like a woman who used all her tears up over a lifetime where hard knocks were the routine and good fortune was an infrequent visitor.

"That's easy to say but difficult to believe."

Tara sighed deeply. "We don't pretend to understand what you and your family have been through, or the lasting effects. I heard Zoe's voice when she was interviewed; I can tell you there wasn't a day that went by without her thinking about you and hoping one day she would see you all again."

Elizabeth nearly sneered. "Those are just words. Zoe killed us as a family before she killed herself. We didn't talk, we didn't laugh, we didn't live after she went."

Tara became stony faced. "She didn't kill herself; she was murdered."

"No, if it hadn't been for the drugs, she wouldn't have been there in the first place. If she had not got hooked none of this would have happened, Andrew might be closer, and I would still have my family. Do you know we can't be in the same room as each other for more than five minutes anymore without the silence becoming too awful? He's going to have children of his own one day and I pray I will be dead by then because I won't ever see them and that will be like being killed all over again." She stared hard at Dan then Tara in turn before finishing with another personal truth. "You know they say time heals, well let me tell you it does not. It just makes the scars deeper."

Dan sympathised, recognising a fellow tortured soul who discovered their own way of existing in a world they didn't want or deserve. Instead of offering kind words or feelings of pity he opted for a stance he wished he was presented with at times.

"Zoe was an imperfect person in an imperfect world, and she made some very bad decisions," he said harshly. "But she wasn't responsible for what happened between you, Anthony, and Andrew afterwards. We all make mistakes and sometimes, like Zoe, we don't get the opportunity to put them right again, but at least she started to try and I'm going to finish it for her.

"She loved you, she was sorry for what pain she caused you and like it or not, you can't take that away from her. The only question you have to answer now is, are you going to help too?"

Dan hadn't taken his eyes off Zoe's mother. Her look confirmed he had an advantage over the sad woman, and he sought to advance it further. More gently he continued, "Elizabeth, I'm a lot newer to parenthood than you and I've more to learn for sure but there's one thing I know already and that's that you can't stop being their parent ever. Even if they're in another country like Andrew or gone for good like Zoe, you're still the parent, still their mother, and the title comes with a set of rules which you don't get a say in changing or adopting only in part."

The clock on the wall seemed to be ticking a lot louder. Dan waited for a response.

"It's hard," Elizabeth said finally.

"I know. People who think humans are the most advanced species are deluded. How many animals can you think of who treat each other like people do?"

For the first time she managed a smile. "How did you become so wise?"

"Like you, I've been hurt, but fortunately enough, time has been on my side to learn and now I've got Tara and Bradley as well as good friends who tell me the truth whether I want to hear it or not."

For two and a half days Bradley had been as good as gold. The fact Tara and Dan were not there each time he woke up or needed a change didn't seem to bother him in the slightest, but today after waking early from his afternoon sleep, he cried incessantly.

"There we are, it's all alright," Gwen sung over and over as she walked and rocked him in her arms around the house, wearing a trench through the carpets and wooden floors.

"Do you think he's sick?" Jim asked.

"I don't know, love. He's been so good up till now. Maybe we got lulled into feeling it should be like it has been all the time."

"They did say he gets stomach pains now and then. Shall we give them a call?"

"No not yet, can you take him for a minute while I make him up some milk and chamomile?"

Jim lifted Bradley and remembering how he used to carry their own son when he was an infant, tipped him face down along the length of his crooked arm. Cradling Bradley's chest in his palm he started to rub his back with his free hand.

Bradley's pained cries turned to exhausted sobs and then no more than a whimper as his tiny body jerked then released its contents from both ends simultaneously.

"Bloody hell, will you look at that mess?" Jim said looking at the floor.

Gwen couldn't care less. "Oh, bless him. Just stay there and I'll clean that up. You must have the golden touch today, Jim."

"You better get new nappy and clothes too," he replied, still staring at the floor.

Ten minutes later the Allen household was calm once more. While Gwen attended to the floor, Jim changed Bradley, marvelling as only a policeman could at the spectacle contained in the nappy.

"I'll tell you one thing Gwenny, I'm glad I forgot what a filled baby's nappy looks like. It was more maroon than brown and the stink," he said returning to the room, which now smelled like a disinfected pine forest.

"I don't need all the details thank you. I'm just glad he got it all out, the poor lamb," Gwen replied, taking Bradley back into her own embrace once more. "You will have to finish the floor. I can't get all of that out."

"It doesn't even look like regular sick," Jim said almost sounding mildly impressed.

Gwen gave him a withering look. "What did I just say about details?"

Elizabeth Summers opened up and talked at length about Zoe and Andrew as children, about how normal they were. However, she never mentioned her husband by name, making Dan wonder if Zoe's death was the initiating factor in the family's implosion. He hoped it was, rather than there being other historical reasons.

When he felt the time was right Dan returned to the subject of Zoe's latter years. "Did you have any contact with her at all?"

"Not after the first month, like I said. She changed in the space of two weeks from the girl we knew into a street animal. The last thing I ever saw her do was spit on my shoes."

Dan winced, recognising what the abuse of drugs can do. "Not that it helps now but those first days and weeks can be the worst for the other people looking on. She would have fallen hard into the scene and a healthy-looking person will change into a shadow of their former self overnight depending on the drug or drugs."

Elizabeth's face darkened. "Didn't you say you were there the night she died? Did you see her?" She frowned.

"I did. Her clothes made her look worse than she was. If you just saw that you would have said she wasn't good, but I saw in her eyes she was actually okay."

"Did you talk to her?"

"No," Dan replied honestly, relieved the question wasn't, *did she talk to you?*

Elizabeth shook her head. "So what was she doing there if she wasn't involved in the drugs anymore?"

"That's one of the big questions to be answered, and I was hoping you might have some clues even if you didn't immediately realise it yourself. There was black shoe polish under her nails, on her arms, and even in her stomach. Does that mean anything to you?"

"No," she said, looking up as if he was mad to ask.

"She also became friends with a local gang called the Stingers."

"The police told me about them, they mentioned a few names, but I never heard of them before."

"Do you know who her friends were before she left home?"

"Her best friend at school was Becky Ireland. She went to the local youth club and there were a few friends there. Clare, Helen, Bronwyn are a few I remember."

"What about boyfriends, did she ever bring any home or mention one?"

She regarded him with disbelief. "I thought you said you knew about Zoe."

"I'm sorry I'm obviously missing something."

"Zoe was gay, openly. Surely you must know that if you've been investigating. It made no difference to me, but her father did have difficulty understanding. From her early teenage years she was aware of her own sexuality and she never tried to hide it, even when she got beaten up at school twice."

Dan was lost for words. How it could be that there was nothing in what he'd seen and read? And why she was wearing the Stingers jacket?

"Bullies?" Tara asked filling the space.

"Kids can be very hurtful, but she was a very strong character," Elizabeth said as a complete explanation.

Dan recovered to probe a little further. "That night in Powton Road she was wearing a boy's jacket, one of the Stinger gangs."

Elizabeth shrugged, saying but not saying *so what?*

"Did Zoe have any close friends who were male at all? Maybe not at that time but at any time you remember."

"Well only little George Zuckerman. He and his family were our next-door neighbours when the kids were young, when we lived in Ruddington. He and Zoe were inseparable for years."

Dan trawled his brain for this latest name but knew it wasn't one he was aware of up to this point. "Can you tell us about Zoe and George?" he asked while still processing.

"George was a sweetheart. He was at least a year or two older, but he was like a little pixie. Zoe was small in stature but even she looked big against him. They just hit it off from the first time they met, and they'd play together all day every day. George could make her laugh until she cried and used to make up stories about them going off on big adventures."

"You talk about him in the past tense. Did something happen?" Tara asked.

"Oh God no! At least I hope not. When we moved away, they lost touch, that's all. They were like brother and sister, only ones who never fought and always looked out for each other."

Dan and Tara spoke together; as he queried if Elizabeth knew anything current about George, Tara asked, "How old were they when you moved from Ruddington?"

"We moved here in 2001, so Zoe would have been twelve. George's family owned the same house for years, at least two generations I think because they were the local coal merchants and the house and coal yard were together. I imagine they'll still be there.

"As for what George's doing these days, I've no idea if he's not in the family business. The last time I saw him was when he and Zoe were riding his bike along the street on the day before we left Ruddington."

"It's not a common name so it should relatively easy to find out," Tara said to Dan.

"Austrian heritage," Elizabeth said absentmindedly.

"We should be going, but I really want to thank you for talking with us," Dan said. "It must be difficult, but would it be alright to call again sometime or to give you my number in case there's anything else you remember?"

He watched her study him for a second, deciding whether to answer in the affirmative. She obviously decided not yet.

"What will you do if you don't find out who killed my girl? The police never did."

Dan held out his hand to shake hers. "That's not an option. I owe it to her, and to you now."

Elizabeth kept her hands by her sides. "You can leave me your number if you want to but don't call me unless it's to tell me who murdered my Zoe."

They were almost at the door when Dan remembered one last thing.

"When Zoe was interviewed nine months before she died, she mentioned health problems growing up. Can you tell us anything about that?"

Elizabeth folded her arms defiantly. "Another irony and typical of our luck. Our family doctor was a family friend too. It was only a couple of years ago actually, another of his patients with the same condition. Zoe suffered painful bowel condition as a young girl. We tried all sorts of diets, but nothing worked. She learned to live with it."

When they were back in the haven of the car Tara felt able to talk.

"The poor woman. We should get on to George Zuckerman as soon as we get back to Nick and Penny's don't you think?"

"Yes and no. The first thing is to know how tall Donny Ormond is." Dan looked at her and winked.

Tara's jaw dropped. "What now!"

"When Jelena Copich interviewed Zoe, she listed four boys: Sean, Billy, Donny, and Minty, and she nearly named another but stopped herself. Then when Copich mentioned a very short associate being with them Zoe hesitated before she named Donny Ormond."

"Little George Zuckerman?" Tara exclaimed.

Dan nodded. "Little Georgie. Zoe's history might include trying to protect some people before me."

Despite Tara's protestations to call Nick and get him to check this new name before returning, they took a drive into Nottingham instead as Dan wanted to see what the Connaught Drive shops and near area looked like. En route they stopped at a newsagents to buy a paper serving the surrounding areas. As Dan pulled back into the traffic, Tara checked the ads. It didn't take long to find what she was looking for.

"Here it is. Zuckerman's Coal and Coke. Mill Lane, Ruddington. Phone number and email address," she said. "What's coke?"

"It's another solid fuel made from coal. We used to have it delivered to home when I was a boy."

"If George was with Zoe on the day she was arrested, what could it mean?" Tara asked, folding the paper so the ad remained visible.

Dan thought for a second. "It might not be anything at all. Realistically it's too coincidental for that just to be a one-off meeting following Zoe's family moving away."

"Absolutely, if she was protecting his identity from Jelena Copich. I mean you don't do that unless he means something to you," Tara said.

"I agree. I'm looking forward to meeting him soon. Here we are," he said pulling into a vacant parking spot. "This is the precinct."

Connaught Drive sounded more impressive than it was in reality. Tara looked aghast at the grey concrete monoliths towering overhead.

"Not what you expected? Hardly Ponsonby is it?" Dan said referring to Tara's shop in upmarket Auckland.

Identical multi-storey residential towers on three sides enclosed the paved courtyard allowing access from the vacant fourth side. Poor sodium lights failed to illuminate the area, and a state of wintry dusk covered the area like a foggy morning. Tara nearly missed the shops altogether; they constituted the ground floor of the tower blocks but were set back so there was a covered walkway around their three sides. A mixture of takeaways and less-than-a-pound shops were over represented but she also spotted a post office, hardware shop, and fresh fruit and vegetable outlet, though she doubted the validity of the fresh description.

She watched Dan soaking in the detail, adding it to his mental picture of what he knew already. His eyes fixed on a bench seat made from cast concrete with rubbish bins standing sentry on both ends. She took him by the hand, and they wandered over to sit down.

"This is where she sat," he said.

Tara didn't doubt his accuracy. "I don't imagine this place has changed much since Zoe was here."

"For sure. What does that tell you?"

"Oh no, is this a test again, Dan Calder style?"

He smiled. "Come on have think for a minute and tell me."

Tara took a deep breath. "Well I can see it would be a good place for a group of young people to come and hang out. I guess the locals aren't going to complain too much. I bet this was a regular haunt."

"Okay so far. What about Zoe and George?"

Tara's brow furrowed. "Zoe and George? Right give me a second. I've known you long enough, I should be able to do this. Zoe and George, Zoe and George…"

Dan watched as Tara paced around the bench.

"Well if they came here together that tells us they were friends, or as you would say, associates, at that time."

"Now you're thinking. And?"

"It's hardly a shopper's paradise. If George came separately, I can't see it was to come to the shops, so it was to meet Zoe here?" Tara stated as her confidence continued to build.

"Or possibly visit someone in the flats, but I would say you're more likely to be right. Anything else?"

She paused. "George came here to meet Zoe. They must've known each other reasonably well for him to come here. Also, she wanted to protect him, so more than reasonably well. After all, she named Sean Darcy and she was living with him." She wanted to give Dan more and strained to think. "Don't tell me, don't tell me. She wanted to protect George, okay I get that, they were good friends and so she wanted to. There's more, isn't there? They were friends, oh God I hate you sometimes." She was about to concede defeat when she repeated herself one more time.

"She protected him because they were friends. Ah no! Or because there was another important reason to?"

Dan punched the air. "Yes!"

CHAPTER FIFTEEN

Amber was out buying required reading material for her return to university at the end of the following week when Dan and Tara got back to the house, nonetheless Nick and Penny insisted on hearing the latest. Dan and Tara repeated what they learned before she and Penny went to check on the questions arising from the meeting with Elizabeth Summers and the visit to Connaught Drive, leaving Dan and Nick alone.

"How are you doing?" Nick asked when the duration of polite silence was over. "Remember it's me asking."

"Fine."

Nick waited patiently until Dan looked back at him. "I remember when we used to say fine stood for fucked up, insecure, neurotic and emotional," Nick said. He could see his best friend's eyes were speaking volumes; it didn't matter that at that precise moment Dan couldn't find any useful words to go with them.

"I like Tara. I can see she really cares," Nick added.

Dan sighed. "It's all for her and Bradley, all this, you know. I'd be living, but miserably so with all this still in the background if it wasn't for them."

Nick looked deeply into the facets of his whisky tumbler, catching glimpses of a thousand unidentifiable reflections. "I wish you would've told me before you left the job, at least some of it. We might have been able to do something together then."

"There was never a right time. Can you imagine what Penny would've been like? And your girls were far too young to be aware of any of it."

Nick took a turn to sigh. "Yes, but still."

Dan said no more, and Nick understood it would be useless to press. He finished his drink and set the tumbler down.

"What with this Zuckerman character to add to the list you might have to re-jig your priorities again. Have you decided what you want to do next?"

Dan looked a little concerned. "I was thinking we almost have too much going on now and starting to wonder if I might be getting off track. I'm certain the girls will be back in a minute to confirm my suspicion that George Zuckerman was there that day and we'll know Zoe deliberately kept his name from Copich."

"What's so wrong with a lot of info and leads?"

Dan's eyes narrowed. "The mind behind the pop-up is not consistent with leaving a trail of clues behind. Something's not right."

"Oh, shit no, please don't say that. You know what happens when you do."

Before Dan could answer Tara and Penny returned with the expected news.

"I still don't know how you manage to remember all these details but of course you're right. David 'Donny' Ormond was five feet five inches tall according to the custody record the day he was arrested with Zoe," Penny announced.

"Short but not so much that you would pick him out for his height," Nick said.

Tara picked up where Penny left. "Zoe was obviously quick enough to think of the next shortest in the group. George slipped through the net when the police arrived or maybe he was lucky to leave just before they got there. Having seen it today, if he was under the shop entrances he would be easy to miss don't you think, Dan?"

"Definitely."

"You didn't say, have you got a photographic memory or that other one, what is it called? Are you alright Dan?" Penny asked.

"Yes, I'm good," he lied. "Eidetic is the other type of precision total recall but no, I'm neither, in fact I have to want to remember something in order to do so, actually make a conscious effort to decide to file it away in my head, but once it's in, it seems to be there for good."

Tara continued. "I read back through Copich's interview while Penny was getting that, and I think she missed a question or two. When she asked who Zoe was with and she listed the four names, she did nearly say a fifth but held herself back. Copich sort of noted it but didn't pursue it, carrying on with a question about Sean Darcy instead. I double checked."

"I can do some digging on Zuckerman before we go to see him," Nick offered.

"That would be good, but I must get down to Mapperley next. I've already put it off twice. Why don't you do that first thing; Tara and I can go while you are?" Dan said.

Nick nodded. "No problem."

Dan turned to Tara. "You said question or two?"

"You really don't miss a trick, do you?" Penny laughed. Tara indicated her approval of Penny continuing. "In the Copich interview, she didn't mention shoe polish. Tara noticed first. Copich was good you said, and so if Zoe was covered in it, she wouldn't have failed to ask, would she? Therefore, we thought this must be a time before Zoe first encountered it. Our conclusion is the shoe polish must be in the nine-month period between the interview and the night she died."

Penny and Tara exchanged a nervously excited look, which they transferred to Dan. "Perfect," he said.

Mapperley was dry and unseasonably warm the next day. Tara felt inexplicably less comfortable than she did previously though, as if the area ought to be permanently cold, grey, and damp. Therefore, she felt compelled to wear a jacket.

Their first stop was the corner café at the end of Powton Road. It was generic in every regard; the plasticised check table cloths, heavy-duty white crockery, glass fronted food cabinets, and wall hung water heaters were all taken straight out of the international greasy spoon catalogue circa 1970. Dan selected a table in the centre of the room and after pulling the chair out for Tara he sat opposite her, so he could see the door.

The menu was generic too. He ordered the big breakfast, which Tara responded to dubiously, hoping her scrambled eggs on toast would come with less than the same fatal quantity of cholesterol. His coffee and her Earl Grey tea were delivered in matching mugs by Gloria, the owner, chef, and waitress who wore a home-made apron and comfortable shoes. Other than themselves the café's only other customer was an older man wrapped up in a heavy coat, scarf, and cheese-cutter cap. Early breakfast diners had been and gone already and the first wave of the lunchtime crowd were yet to arrive. Gloria's name tag was as old as the décor. She ignored the older man who was apparently busy with the dog racing page and nursing a near empty mug of his own.

"You're not from around here," she stated impolitely but only as a matter of fact.

"Not anymore. I used to work around here though," Dan answered.

"Oh yes, and what was that?"

"I was in the police."

If Gloria was surprised it didn't show. "Mm I see, and what about you love, you don't look like police?" she said to Tara.

"No, we're back here on holiday for a few weeks."

"I don't think so love, nobody comes to Mapperley on holiday."

Tara was concerned Gloria might think they were being obtuse.

Dan was unworried. "No, today is special. I'm hoping to run into a few people I met last year when I was here."

"Last year?" Gloria said non-committally.

Dan put his mug down with a bump. "Josie Lamas was a friend of mine. Teddy Parker definitely wasn't."

Gloria's eyes warmed. "Ah, so it was you was it?" she asked, explaining she knew all there was to know about the business which brought Dan to Mapperley the year before. "Who is it you're hoping to see?"

"Purdy and Estelle. Do they still come around?"

Tara desperately hoped Gloria's mind would be favourably made up about Dan. If her knowledge of his activities in the locality was based solely on the Mapperley grapevine, she hoped it would be sufficient.

Gloria cracked a smile to match her eyes. "Purdy took early retirement if you want to call it that. She and Josie were old mates and after what happened her heart wasn't in it any more. Estelle, is that her name did you say? Does she have a younger sister?"

"That's her," Tara answered quickly.

"They were a happy ending, which makes a nice change around here. Josie named her in her will, so she could finish her education. It was a bit of a big do I can tell you. Josie looked after a lot of the girls before and after she died."

Dan smiled. "That sounds like the Josie I knew. I remember them both talking about Estelle going back to college one day. She wanted to do politics and philosophy. I do still need some help though, Gloria. Can you recommend somebody I can contact? Or Purdy's phone number even if you have it?"

"I'll get your plates and see what I can do," she replied, showing them a wide smile.

"That was a bit risky," Tara whispered when Gloria disappeared behind the counter.

"No, not at all. Josie was loved. Anyone and everyone who lives in this area would know the story about what happened."

Tara smiled as widely as Gloria. "This must be a first for you then, feeling safe in a less than police friendly area."

When Gloria appeared next, it was with two mountains of food. Tara felt full just looking at it and guessed there must be at least six eggs atop her doorsteps of fried white bread. Dan's eyes grew as wide as the plates and he thanked Gloria, but she didn't speak, instead ghosting back behind the counter once more. The old man was taking no notice, but Tara was aware he hadn't turned the page of his paper from the moment they walked in. If she'd noticed, she was sure Dan had too. He had dug into his big breakfast with gusto; it had been a long time since he ate so wonderfully unhealthily and if Tara had anything to do with it, he knew it would be a very long time until his next.

By the time he was finished Tara's plate still looked the same as it did when Gloria set it down. She finished as much of the eggs as she could, however the fried bread defeated her completely. Gloria cleared the table, putting two more full mugs down in place of their empty ones. If Tara's eyes could have spoken, they would have groaned.

Dan flicked an eyebrow towards the old man.

"Oh, don't you mind Eric," Gloria replied. "He'll look after you. I've got him another tea."

She reached to the counter behind her and placed a third mug on the table. Tara looked bemused, but Dan understood. He picked up his and the spare and indicated for Tara to stay.

"Tea," Dan said, placing the two mugs down and taking the chair opposite the old man. Eric lowered his newspaper and slid the fresh tea under his book keeper nose.

"My name is Dan Calder; I was here last year."

"Thank you for the tea," Eric said, surprising Dan with a voice that was twenty years younger than his face and very well educated.

"I knew Josie Lamas for years and she taught me a hell of lot. She was a good friend to me. Did you know her too, Eric?"

"And now here you're back again with your good lady this time. How was your breakfast?"

Dan was happy playing Eric's game to a point as there wasn't anything for him to lose. He wanted the locals to know he was around and hopefully realise he was no threat. "It was great. A long time since I've enjoyed one of those and a shame, we can't take the time to enjoy more of our visit. Anyway, to business. Gloria sent me over here for a reason. If you can help me I'd be very grateful, if you can't then I won't waste any more of your time, or mine."

"So, what does bring you here then, lad?"

"Zoe Summers, Sean Darcy, George Zuckerman, Adam Vikkert, Craig Matthews, the Stingers, and twenty-two Powton Road." Dan spoke the list like he was reading instructions off a box.

Eric sipped his tea in a continuous up and down motion reminiscent of Zoe and the cider, giving away little of what he was thinking. Dan waited.

"Who's your lady friend?" Eric asked finally.

"My partner. I want her to know what I'm doing as this could be an unpleasant business." Dan called Tara over and introduced her. Eric removed his cap and shook her hand gently.

"Your man here is on a mission, isn't he? It must be hard for you living with him when his focus is elsewhere?"

"Not really," Tara replied uncomfortably.

Eric's face changed as if he was upset to have caused Tara's discomfort. "Sorry, I didn't mean to offend."

She smiled limply but remained quiet.

"Tara is new to all this, Eric. These are my problems from way before we met, but for her and our baby I need to resolve what happened to Zoe Summers. I'm on the right track but I can't do it without some help from the community."

"Why would you want to be telling me that?"

"It seems you've not quite made up your mind yet as to whether you're going to help me or not, so I wanted to give you all the information you need to decide."

Gloria reappeared again and squeezed between Dan's pushed out chair and the nearest table. "Purdy lives over on Topley Corner now. I talked to her a minute ago and she says to call her." She placed a small piece of yellow paper on the table.

Eric looked down at the paper and seemed to receive the confirmation he was waiting for. He undid the top two buttons of his coat and pulled on the scarf until it relented and slid clockwise around his neck revealing his black shirt complete with notched Roman collar and white band.

"I did wonder. What should I call you now?" Dan said.

"Eric is still fine, lad. Father if it makes you feel better."

"Were you Josie's priest, Eric?"

"I was. She talked about you a few days before she died, and I hoped to meet you afterwards, but we never got the opportunity, did we? I'm sorry about before but I've spent twenty years building up relationships in Mapperley and I could wreck them in twenty seconds if people like Glory and Purdy lost their trust and faith in me. How are you doing a year on, Mr. Calder?"

"Call me Dan. With Tara's help and a few other people too, I'm alright thanks. I felt, and still feel, guilty over Josie because if I hadn't asked for her help, she would probably still be here, but who knows what Teddy Parker would have done if he wasn't locked up for the rest of his life."

"Indeed, indeed. I can tell you Josie was content. She didn't fear what this life held in store for her; she made her peace with the Lord a long time ago. She even toyed with the idea of joining an order who would allow her entry, so she could spend her remaining years in prayer. I like to think we both knew His plan involved her being accessible to girls like Estelle though. If I could have told you anything it would have been that she died without guilt and there's no need for you to carry any in her name."

Dan bowed his head momentarily, allowing Tara room to speak.

"That means a lot to both of us."

Eric smiled benignly. "And so, you've returned with Dan this time in search of what I wonder? Given your list of names and the unfortunate number twenty-two Powton Road, it can't be anything good."

"Dan was at the house on the day Zoe Summers died and we feel we can find out who killed her. The other names, they're witnesses at the very least, if not to the murder then to Zoe's lifestyle in the months before. We spoke to Zoe's mother," Tara explained.

"May I ask why this means so much to you? I couldn't help overhearing what you said to Glory."

"It's complicated and sensitive," Dan replied. "Personal reasons are so I can make my own peace I guess, and because Zoe deserves it. She will still be seen as a drug taking, lost and somewhat useless person, but we know now she wasn't. Her family and friends need to see she was getting herself straightened out at the time of her death."

Eric sat back and regarded Dan with experienced eyes. "Are you a man of God, Dan? It makes no difference, but you don't look to me like you feel the Holy Spirit within you, although you do sound as if you're seeking some form of redemption."

"I'd be lying if I said yes."

"So why is it so important?"

Dan could feel Tara nodding and heard her voice in his head saying, *go on tell him.*

"I don't know how to say it without it sounding pompous, Eric. She died trying to save me. Zoe was close to returning to her family, having got herself clean, but she still made the decision to help me and I think she was conscious of the danger she was putting herself in to do so."

"I never met Zoe or heard of her, to be honest with you. She sounds remarkable."

"Before that evening I hadn't heard of her either. I suppose if you push me, I would have to say that there are some truths which are worth anything to be told."

Eric looked skywards. "That they are, and our friend Josie said the same thing."

Dan looked guiltily at the finished list several minutes later. Zoe Summers, Adam Vikkert, Sean Darcy, George Zuckerman, Craig Matthews, the Stingers, 22 Powton Road. Gloria supplied another full sheet of the yellow paper which Dan used for Eric's information and he explained the relationships between them as best he could over the next hour and another mug. By that time, he was bursting for the toilet.

"There," he said, finishing the final arrow between Zoe and George Zuckerman. "One more thing, Zoe's killer had or has a damaged third finger on his right hand. When I see Purdy, I'll tell her exactly the same and say we've given the list to you. All our contact numbers are at the bottom, including Nick and Jim. Can you excuse me for a minute?" he said, getting up.

Tara was left sitting at the table with Father Eric Lambert of Saint Paul the Apostle Catholic Church, Mapperley, as they now knew him to be.

Eric folded the sheet into four and placed it in his trouser pocket.

"Do you have to be home by a certain time or is Dan determined to stay in Nottingham for as long as it takes?"

"We've got open ended tickets, but I think we'll have to put a date on it sooner or later if we can't make enough progress to give the police a name by the end of the month. Having said that and knowing him, I can't see it happening," Tara said.

Eric let out a short laugh. "He's an interesting individual. They say we're all products of our experiences and I would imagine that's no truer than of Dan. I pray he will find peace with or without the answers he's seeking here in Mapperley."

Tara looked anxious.

"Mapperley," he continued. "People won't be falling over themselves to help you. They might have what you want, but even if you know it don't take it for granted that they will feel the same about Zoe as you do. Everybody knows the address and what happened there, everybody will have heard of her and the Stingers too, but you may become very frustrated at getting that far but no further."

When Dan came back Eric gave him a business card. "Please call me if you'd like to."

"Thanks, I will. What have you two been talking about?"

"Eric was saying we might not end up with the answers we're looking for because of the unwillingness of some people to talk," Tara said.

"Well if we don't ask then we'll never know."

"Of course, there's always the chance nobody does," Eric added.

His words struck a nerve with Dan. For a second it was annoyance and then just as quickly it became fascination. "If it does end up like that perhaps you could do me a favour, Eric?"

"That sounds interesting. Go ahead," Eric replied.

"People are so tight-knit around here. Can you honestly believe nobody knows, or has at least heard a rumour or suggestion? I can't. What would it mean if nobody knows in actuality? We'd better be going if Purdy is expecting us."

Dan and Tara left Eric at the door; he and Gloria waved them goodbye as they drove off towards Topley Corner and their next appointment.

Dan's advance warning was still not enough to prepare Tara for Purdy in real life. He immediately noted her retirement appearance was exactly the same as her working one.

"Who'd have bloody thought!" she exclaimed as she flung open her front door and flung herself around Dan. Wearing a hairy bright pink singlet top which was trying and failing to contain her bosom, white leggings and stilettos, reminding Tara of an impossibly large fairground candy-floss.

"Come in, come in. I can't bloody believe this."

"How are you, Purdy? Is it still Purdy?" Dan managed to ask as he freed himself from her furry affections.

"I can't bloody believe this," she responded again, slamming the door behind them.

The flat was compact but felt even smaller when they were ushered into the lounge crammed with oversize furniture and shelf units littered with ceramic animals and Toby jugs.

"You're looking good, retirement suits you. This is Tara," Dan said.

Tara tried not to focus on Purdy's tattooed chest, but it was very difficult. "Nice to meet you. Dan's told me quite a bit about you."

"You too, my darling. So terrible about Josie but oh we did have a few laughs, didn't we?" Purdy said, covering the whole of the previous year's dealings in ten words. "Do you want a cuppa or something stronger?"

"No thanks," Dan and Tara said in unison. The café was still too recent in their memories to contemplate more refreshment.

Without further discussion Purdy enthusiastically updated them on her year, including the eldest son's apprenticeship, youngest's latest school report, and her own new venture of

Sunday market trading in china dogs and cats. Talking as though it was a race and captivating Tara with her larger than life personality, she finished her monologue with a full stop that lasted a whole sentence.

"I never thought we would see you around here again. What brings you back? Or shouldn't I ask."

Dan was grinning. "I wish I could say it was pleasure, but it's all business again."

"And he's dragging you along for the ride this time?" she said to Tara.

"I'm a willing passenger."

"Go on then Dan, let's have it? Glory told me about the girl from Powton Road. What is it with you and that street?"

"Not by choice. If she told you what I said to her then you know as much as me. The girl Zoe was killed and I'm here to find out who and why."

"Are you sure you don't want tea? No okay. Of course, Zoe Summers, I remember it like yesterday although I had no idea they were doing drugs from the house until it all blew up."

"It's alright, it was very secret," Dan said.

"Ah right, there you are then. I didn't know her, never met her. The boy Sean I knew through the Stingers, he used to run stuff around for some of the dealers who wanted to keep their hands clean. That was the Stingers claim to fame but they were just kids really, doing other peoples' dirty work. Who were the others?"

"Craig Matthews," Dan said.

"No never heard of him."

"Adam Vikkert, maybe called Vic. He had a Mohawk haircut at the time, seemed like he was more senior than Sean Darcy and did the talking for the dealer in the house."

Purdy thought for a moment, squinting with concentration. "Was he a tall but skinny thing?" she questioned, pursing her lips.

"Yes, he reminded me of the guitarist from the band U2."

Her eyes lit up. "I know him! Yes of course, not the famous one, the other one. Vic."

"He knew Zoe. I'm very keen to meet him," Dan said slowly.

"Poor bugger. I pity him when you do then."

"Any ideas where he is now?"

"No but if he's still around I can find out by tonight."

"Do you remember anyone with a damaged or injured right hand? Third finger to be precise. That's who killed Zoe."

Purdy mewed. "Oh, that's creepy. You just sent a shiver right through me."

"Why, does it mean something?"

"No, you silly sod, you can't go around saying things like that out of the blue and not expect a bloody reaction."

"Sorry, I didn't think. The last one is George Zuckerman. He's very short. His father is the coal merchant over in Ruddington and George was friends with Zoe."

"No, definitely not," Purdy replied immediately, then bursting into a raucous laugh she added, "Not a lot of use for a coalman in a block of flats."

In the end they felt obliged to take up Purdy's next offer of tea, which she brought in with an assortment of biscuits. She showed them a photo of her eldest son Dale receiving a certificate to accompany a completed stage of his baker's apprenticeship. Conversation roamed across several subjects, but all were locally situated. Dan told her of their meeting with Eric earlier in the day.

"Not my cup of tea but each to their own," she said. "Remember Estelle? Well of course you do, she was into all that through Josie."

"He said," Tara replied.

"After that do with your detective friend we kept in touch for a while. Nice girl, I've a card from her somewhere with a phone number if you need it?"

"Great, thanks, I won't call her unless I need to though."

Dan left Purdy with a list like the one they gave Eric. On the way to the door she showed them more photos of her sons.

"Thanks again, lovely to meet you. We'll wait to hear from you," Tara said as Purdy gave her an all-enveloping hug.

She then gave Dan a kiss while clasping her hands to his cheeks, which seemed to deposit a full tube of lipstick on his mouth. He waited until she closed the door with a loud bang before wiping it off.

"What an amazing woman. I have to admit she's the first prostitute I've ever met but I'm happy to meet lots more if they're all like her." Tara giggled as Dan scrubbed off the pink passion with a tissue.

"She's a character," he said once his face was clean again. They continued back to the car. "Sometimes you find the most honest people in the most unlikely places. If you're a friend of Purdy she would do anything for you, like Josie."

"At times like these I can see what you saw in the job, I mean where else could you meet people like that?" As they reached the car, Tara grinned. "Where to now?"

CHAPTER SIXTEEN

Nick's day wasn't wasted either. The advantages of officers in his unit having their own individual laptops were never intended to include unauthorised access of the force databases but he took to the task in the same way Dan attacked his breakfast.

After dinner Dan and Tara, plus the full complement of Hetheringtons retired to the lounge to go over the events of the day. Being careful with their exact wording for benefit of the twins, Dan and Nick took turns.

"George Zuckerman is a partner in the family firm now," Nick said. "He and his dad have been running it together for a couple of years. George is a fine upstanding member of the community as far as I can see. Never come to the attention of the police, not even a parking ticket. I've got a picture taken from his drivers' licence."

Dan added to Nick's opening salvo. "My contacts didn't recognise him either. On the other hand, Sean Darcy and the Stingers do ring some bells. They used to run drugs around the area for some of the savvier dealers who didn't want to be caught hands on. That might be how Darcy came to be at the pop-up. He wasn't Zoe's boyfriend though which might open up questions about the jacket again."

Nick took over once more. "Darcy; I've a load of stuff on him and the Stingers. Lots of names and addresses. The most interesting to me was a man called Ashley Royce who was arrested and charged with assault with a weapon in 2005, the weapon being a chef's knife. He received a community service order plus compensation to the victim."

Excitement crackled around the room.

"Royce is in fact a chef, which he tried to use in mitigation. He lives and works in Leicester now. Hasn't been in trouble for three or four years."

"That's good. Did he have any previous for drugs?" Dan asked.

"Two for possession of class A."

Dan grinned. "Nice. Class A means harder things like heroin or cocaine," he said for the others' information.

As they continued going to and fro with their factual dialogue Dan began to form yet another mental schedule of priorities with a caveat being anything more relevant and immediate that could arrive courtesy of Eric and Purdy. The trait was to his mind a very good thing, although others found it to be frustrating through his career. He decided Zoe must remain the central figure to stay on track and therefore Adam Vikkert and George Zuckerman's relationship to her were his latest number one. Vikkert because he clearly knew her that night and little George because he knew her the longest; before, during, and after she became a druggie.

Next on his hit list were Ashley Royce and Craig Matthews, with Sean Darcy being relegated down the chain as he and the Stingers allure was becoming more peripheral with each passing day.

He was pleased with the quality and quantity of evidence they'd gathered since he and Tara had been in the country. Yet since meeting Eric earlier in the day, a feeling of unease had developed that couldn't be ignored any longer.

What if nobody does know? he thought over and over.

"Dan, are you okay?"

"What? Sorry, yes."

"I said are you okay?" Tara repeated. "You're miles away."

"Sorry, I was thinking."

"Nick just asked, what next?"

"Vikkert and Zuckerman. Just those two at the moment. I want to know all there is about them and I want to talk to them. Little George is easy enough to find, but what about Adam Vikkert."

Viola suddenly spoke up. "Have you thought about social media, you know Facebook, Twitter, Instagram? Everybody's on it, why shouldn't they?"

"I'm not," Nick said.

"Or me and before you say it, yes we know it says more about us than the rest of you," Dan said.

"It's a great idea though Vio, we should definitely take a look at it. What about you Rosie, any ideas?" Tara asked.

"It all sounds horrible. She must have felt like being in a night-mare. Why wouldn't her mum and brother be more interested?"

"Not all families are like yours. It makes you realise you're the exception and not the rule these days. I can tell you that from personal experience too," Tara explained.

"That's a good point actually," Dan said. "I can sort of under-stand her mother but maybe not Andrew. Can you have a quick look at him sometime, Nick?"

Dan woke in the night for no reason and woke Tara in the pro-cess.

"I told you that breakfast was trouble," she joked sleepily.

He pulled her in, feeling their shared warmth and not at all concerned her hair was tickling his face. Consciously grateful every day for what he had now, such trivialities were easy to redefine as part and parcel, and they were infinitely better than the alternative of a cold single bed.

"What did Gwen and Jim say when you called earlier?"

"Everything is fine. Our Baba is being an angel," Tara replied.

"Gwen's words?"

"Yes. Funny isn't it how many people have lost loved ones in desperate circumstances. Not just people we know but people in general," she said, pulling in closer still.

"I suppose it shows that personal tragedies are more commonplace than we think. Until we become victims too, we don't notice what happens to other people."

"What if anything ever happened to Bradley?" Tara whispered.

"Nothing will. I think we've exhausted our share of tragedies."

"I know, but what if something did?"

Dan remained quiet.

"Hey, you're supposed to have the answers to all those sorts of questions."

"I know and I don't. But we're ahead of the game in as much as we know what can happen to people through no fault of their own. I don't think there can be two parents alive who will be more alert to…to stuff."

She relaxed again. "Stuff, that's not very scientific."

"Well I couldn't think of anything else which covered it or answered the original question."

"I've got one idea: another pair of eyes would help if we're constantly going to be on the lookout."

"I don't get it. What do you mean?" Dan replied.

"I mean a little brother or sister for Bradley. We can all look out for each other then."

Dan remembered his recent late-night conversation with Bradley at Jim's house. "Are you pregnant?"

"No, I'm not, but it's not such a bad idea. You're the fittest man of your age I know and after what Elizabeth Summers said it got me thinking. Can we at least think about it?"

"It's a huge decision, T, and a huge commitment. Are you sure?"

"I really am and think of the fun we can have training for the big pregnancy event. Remember how much you enjoyed your marathon training?"

"I've not been for a run for a while," he said cryptically.

Tara breathed in heavily and moved over on top of him. "No time like the present."

"Morning, sleep okay?" Nick asked looking up from the newspaper.

Tara smirked. "Great thanks."

She and Dan took their seats and he reached for the coffee pot. When the telephone rang, Dan checked his watch. Even years after leaving the police some things were so ingrained they were automatic responses. 8:00 a.m. was a little early. He heard footsteps pad along the hall and stop, then a female voice he recognised as Rosie.

"Hello." Pause. "Yes, that's right." Pause. "Sure, I'll get him for you." Pause, pad, pad.

Rosie opened the kitchen door. "Hey Dan, there's a man on the phone for you."

Like tumblers in a slot-machine the permutations of who and why whirred around Dan's brain. *Jim could be good or bad news if it was about Zoe, bad if it was concerning Bradley. If it was Eric it could be useful or useless information. This time of day it could even be a call from home.* He registered five other names before he got to the phone.

"Hello, this is Dan Calder,"

A voice he didn't recognise as one from his list spoke. "Hello. My name is Robert Zuckerman. Zoe Summers' mother called me. What's going on?"

The call from little George's father was brief; Dan's slurp of coffee and explanation he was going out even briefer. Thirty minutes later, Dan pulled into the yard of Robert Zuckerman and Son. Father and son were waiting for him on the step of the office door as he parked the Ford.

"Hi," he said, reaching out a hand towards George Zuckerman. Fully twelve inches shorter than his elder, George remained still.

Dan changed the angle of his arm towards the older man. "Mr. Zuckerman, I'm Dan Calder. Thanks for seeing me."

Robert Zuckerman extended his hand obviously as a courtesy rather than willingness. "You better come in."

The office was cramped; sheets of paper topped with titles such as Ruddington, Bradmore, and Bridgford were taped onto wall mounted clipboards. Robert pointed Dan to the one wooden chair as he and George sat on the edge of the worn desk opposite.

"Perhaps I should just explain and maybe that way I will answer your questions along the way," Dan said.

Robert and George's stone-faced response gave nothing away and Dan had no choice but to continue.

"I was a policeman involved in Zoe's murder investigation. Even after I left the police it's always bothered me that the offender was never caught. Recently I've started to go over the case again and I think with the help of some people I might be able to identify the person or people responsible.

"Elizabeth Summers gave me your name. I had no idea she was going to contact you though. She did tell me that you and Zoe were best friends growing up and I hoped to meet you and see if you had any information which might help me."

"I don't know anything about how she died," George said almost too quickly. His legs swung nervously in the air while his father's remained firmly planted on the floor.

Dan held out open palms. "Look, I'm not suggesting you did. Before talking to Elizabeth Summers, I had no idea you even existed."

"Zoe got messed up with all the drugs. George was never interested in things like that," Robert said.

Dan spent the drive from Nick's considering how much of what he knew to put to George in the hope of eliciting more valuable information. He was reluctant to use his jewel of knowing George was with Zoe the day she was arrested unless it was offered or there was no choice but having spent just a minute or two with him he was convinced George was an innocent. Robert's defence of his son was touched with genuine pride too, so as to highlight his regard for the young man.

"Mr. Zuckerman, I assure you George has got nothing to worry about from me. I only want to find out what happened to Zoe. George is there anything you can think of?"

Robert would not be placated. He folded his Popeye forearms and glared at Dan. "He doesn't have to say a word to you. I've got a good mind to call the police. What you're doing must be wrong."

"If you want to call them, I've no problem with that. I always intended taking my information to them when I got enough. Look, I've travelled from the other side of the world because this means so much to me. The only person who has got anything to worry about is the man who killed her. George, if she was your friend surely you would want to help me."

George's swinging legs stopped.

Put a fishing rod in his hands and he could do a good impression of a garden gnome, Dan thought but noticed at the same time how muscular George was. His upper body was as wide as it was long, and his arms were like sides of ham. Clearly humping bags of coal around for a living produced one or two advantages.

"Zoe and I was best friends because we had something in common," George said after a while. "I tried to tell her not to get into all that, but it was too late, so quick. Do you know what I mean?"

"Yes, I do. I've seen it a thousand times."

Robert seemed to mellow after his son decided to say more than two words. "George is a good lad. He told us Zoe died at the time."

"Did you stay in touch with her after they moved away from Ruddington?"

"Not at first. But when we got a bit older and we could go out without our mums and dads it was easier to meet up again," George replied.

Dan was sure he was being utterly truthful. Although he was a better judge of character than most, he believed anyone would see the same. George Zuckerman was one of life's good souls.

"Did you stay in touch with Zoe right up until the time she died?"

George had to think for a moment. "No, it was at least a few months before I last talked to her. Longer probably."

Dan decided to take a punt. "Connaught Drive shops?" he asked.

Impressed or concerned, it was difficult to say. "How did you know that?" George exclaimed.

"Zoe didn't want you to get in trouble when the police came that day. Did you go before they arrived or were you able to slip away?"

"She told me to make myself scarce just as they arrived. I wanted her to come with me, but she had to stay, she said. Do you think if she'd come with me she might not have died?"

"I don't know George; I don't think any of us will ever know that. Are you alright to try and answer a few more questions?"

George looked to his father who gave a confirmatory nod.

"You said you and Zoe had things in common?"

"Because we were different. My height, and she had bad health issues and because she was gay. I was the first person she ever told. We were just friends. We were such good friends without loving each other that way."

"I see," Dan said, and he did.

"We didn't have to pretend or feel like we had to be different to who we were when we were together. We even gave funny names to each other. I called her Sunny because her name was Summers and she was always happy. She called me Dog because she said I was so loyal. I was gutted when she got involved with that lot and then the drugs stuff, but she was in pain a lot. She said at first it was just to stop it hurting."

"I've heard from her mum and she mentioned it to the police during an interview about her health issues. Do you know exactly what it was?"

"Bad cramps since she was really young. She said nobody knew what it was, and nothing worked until the drugs, that is."

"I'm sorry George, sorry you lost your friend. Can you tell me anything else? Why did she have to stay there that day you last saw her?"

"I don't know. She called me in the morning, she wanted to see me because she was going away for a while. When I got to Connaught shops they were already arguing and fighting so she never told me what she was doing or where she was going. She just said she had to stay. She did keep looking at Sean Darcy though, sort of nervously."

Dan thought for a second, remembering other names or place George might know. "Do you know an Adam Vikkert? Zoe called him Vic."

The name clearly meant something, but Dan could see George was struggling to put it into context. "Vic? I heard of him but not from Zoe. I'm not sure but that might have been who the others were fighting about when I got to the shops. It definitely wasn't Zoe. Come to think of it, she looked really scared when they said Vic's name." George looked genuinely surprised to have remembered such an odd fact. "Yeah, I'm sure that was right."

"Thanks George, that's a big help. Did you know Sean or any of the others very well?"

"No, not at all. Zoe didn't want me to meet them. She was embarrassed by the way she'd got."

"One last thing. Did you hear anything after she died about who or why?"

George sighed and looked deeply unhappy. "No."

Dan moved to get up, but George wasn't finished.

"I didn't go to the funeral or anything. I only went down to Mapperley to see her. Like I said before, we were different. There's no way I would ever have become friends with the likes of Sean Darcy, more likely they would have beaten the crap out of me for a joke. I miss her though."

"You're not the only one George."

"You could have fooled me. It was like no one cared at all when she died. I thought the police would call me eventually, but they didn't. It was in the papers and on TV for a while, then nothing. No one talked about it. You know how people are in the pubs and so on, well it didn't happen at all and not once did I ever hear someone say, oh remember that Zoe Summers, I reckon it was so and so."

When Dan left, he gave the Zuckermans the same list of contact numbers he gave to Eric and Purdy. They shook his hand because they wanted to, and George even said thank you for Dan not forgetting his best friend. Driving out of the yard he couldn't help feeling a little happier for Zoe, that she found at least one good friend like little George in her tragically short life.

His priority schedule was shuffled again too. He was now determined to find out as soon as possible why Zoe had to stay at Connaught Drive that day and where she was going to for so long that she wanted to say goodbye to her best friend.

"Sean Darcy," Dan spat as he walked in to the garden room where Tara, Nick, and Penny were sitting.

"Sean bloody Darcy. Did you say he was arrested recently and gave a local address?"

"Fenwick Street I think it was, I'll have to check the number. Why?" Nick answered.

"Little George and Zoe were best friends. The day Zoe was arrested she told him she had to stay at the shops, and she kept looking towards Darcy. Within no time she disappears for nine months. I don't know Darcy, but I know I don't like him, and I want to find out why."

"Well, no need to ask you if you had a productive morning is there," Tara said. "Tell us what happened."

Dan related the visit, apologising again for not doing it first. By the time he was finished the others were sharing his renewed interest in Sean Darcy, with Nick verbalising his concern for Darcy's well-being by the time Dan was finished with him.

The sound of the side gate being opened stopped them all momentarily, until Amber appeared.

"Hello you lot. Have I missed something?" she asked taking a seat.

"More of the same," Penny answered, and Amber seemed to understand.

She directed her gaze at Dan. "What have you been doing?"

"I just talked to George Zuckerman, he was Zoe's best friend when they were young, and they stayed close. She told him she was going away somewhere; I think maybe with Sean Darcy on the day she was arrested at Connaught Drive."

"Right, so you're going to go after him next. I pity him." She smiled broadly, reflecting her father's earlier comment. It seemed Penny's more of the same line was a family joke regarding Dan's ability to seek and destroy like some sort of human guided missile.

"As soon as I can," Dan said.

"Did you get all you needed?" Penny asked Amber, changing the subject and taking note of all the bags around her.

"Most of it. I'm a little disappointed to be going back when things are starting to get interesting here." She paused for a moment and then continued. "Will you be going to see Darcy on your own?"

"I hadn't thought that far yet," Dan said suspiciously.

"Darcy is twenty-eight or nine, now isn't he?" she asked, looking for the pages she'd read at some point over the last days.

"That's right."

"Well even though you're lovely and charming, I think having a female more his own age might be something of an advantage when you see him. Why don't I come with you?"

Penny bristled. "Now hold on right there, Amber."

"Think about it, Mum. It's a good idea for several reasons. Dan would keep me safe."

At the mention of his name Dan prepared to give his opinion.

"It's not such a bad idea. I was about to say I should go but it makes more sense for Amber to be there," Tara said, beating him to it.

"I was okay last year when we went out Mum, wasn't I Dad, Dan?"

Dan agreed. "Having her there might take the nervous edge off any feeling of confrontation or interrogation Darcy may feel, so it's fine with me," he said, passing the buck back to Nick and Penny.

A few minutes later and with negotiations completed, Dan and Amber got themselves ready to go out again.

"You don't really envisage any problems, do you?" Amber queried as Dan got back into the driver's seat, having made a quick stop at a corner shop. He started the engine and moved off.

"No. If we find him and if he will talk to us, all we want is information. I find it hard to think he was complicit in what happened to Zoe the night she was killed."

Before they left Nick's, Dan assured Penny he only wanted to talk to Sean Darcy. In the circumstances there wasn't a lot else he could do anyway.

"And the Stingers are no longer active from what we know, are they?"

"Your dad said Darcy was arrested a week or two back for shoplifting and at the time he was taken into custody he was in a pretty bad condition. I'm thinking his fifteen minutes of fame as a gang member is long gone."

The Fenwick Street address was a bail hostel where otherwise homeless people got an opportunity to get themselves back on their feet if they wanted to or could be bothered. It was a large red brick building that in its heyday was undoubtedly occupied by a wealthy family complete with servants' quarters below stairs. Now the layout satisfied the requirements of mass feeding, washing, and sleeping. Dan had visited many similar locations previously and knew the drill; he didn't think to ring the doorbell and walked straight through the open, imposing front door into a cavernous hallway. The reception-come-office was situated immediately to the right, a three-metre square nook with reinforced glass, kitchen bench top partitions, and a heavy-duty fire door with three sturdy locks. The glass slide was open, and a full-length fluorescent strip indicated the office was occupied. Two steps later Dan could see a middle-aged male with a checked cotton shirt and glasses on a cord around his neck sat at a desk with a laptop.

"Afternoon," Dan said casually above the noise of a score of people, all doing a dozen different things at once, which was the way in these places.

The man with a plastic name tag looked up.

"Can I help?" he said, looking suspiciously at Amber.

"I hope so, Duncan. My name is Dan Calder. I'd like to speak to Sean Darcy if he's in."

"And you are?" Duncan replied, his tone aimed at Dan but with his gaze still on Amber.

"I'm just Mr. Calder these days and this is a friend of mine, Miss Hetherington. He doesn't know us. We're hoping he might be able to help with some information."

Duncan peeled his eyes away from Amber, who maintained her appearance of calm.

"So not police or probation then. This is just a social visit?" Duncan probed.

Dan didn't answer.

Duncan looked across the office to an area Dan couldn't see but knew would be a board with the residents' names on and a method of stating whether they were in or out. After another cursory look at them he picked up a tannoy microphone on the desk and clicked the black button below the mouthpiece.

"Sean Darcy, Sean Darcy can you come down to reception, you've got some visitors."

The cacophonous noise from every direction melded into a buzz, likely leaving everybody with a headache at the end of the day. Dan tried to listen for footsteps, but it was impossible even though the lack of carpeting initially gave him hope.

A minute passed during which Dan looked around; Amber focused on him and Duncan watched her. Dan was about to ask if he would try again when a pair of feet, then a body, and finally a face he recognised from the recent weeks' information gathering appeared halfway down the stairs. Darcy continued down.

Sean Darcy made being disinterested a complete description, from the way he physically appeared to his disposition and bearing, as if he were a human battery that had lost ninety-nine percent of its capacity.

It was all he could do to summon the energy to say, "Yeah what?"

"Sean, my name is Dan Calder, and this is Amber Hetherington. We would like to ask you a few questions."

Duncan went back to his laptop, although his head stayed tilted towards the glass opening.

Darcy looked no higher than their knees, showing a premature bald spot on the crown of his head.

"I don't know you. What do you want?"

"It's about the Stingers," Dan said. "About the time you were in that group."

With his head bowed it was difficult to read any response, but the shaking of Darcy's hands stopped momentarily. "Nah fuck off. I ain't interested."

"It won't take long, Sean. I've brought you a few things if you will," Amber said in her best steady voice.

"Not interested," he said, sounding slightly more interested.

Dan rustled the bag he brought in from the car, opening the top under Darcy's nose so he could see inside.

"Just a few minutes. Have you got anything better to do?" Dan said.

Darcy straightened a little and reached for the bag, but Dan drew it back.

Darcy considered his options for a few seconds before he motioned towards a closed door. "Come in the day room."

The room was big with two sets of French doors leading out to a garden patio area. Set with a large table in the centre and an assortment of sofas and chairs that didn't match and a large aged TV in one corner and a notice board in another, it was as typical of its type as Gloria's café was. Fortunately, it was devoid of other residents. Dan took a seat at the table and Amber followed suit. He put the bag on the table top and waited for Darcy to give in to temptation and take the seat nearest to it. Holding the bag at the bottom Dan emptied the contents, making sure they stayed within his reach and control to begin with. Four packets of Benson & Hedges, two Mars Bars, a large bottle of

Pepsi, chewing gum, a Cornish pasty, and several packets of fla-
voured crisps tumbled out like a heart attack waiting to happen.
Dan pulled a twenty-pound note from his pocket and put that
on the table too.

Darcy understood the rules of the game without words from
Dan; he didn't move towards the items.

"You were in the Stingers?" Dan asked in a business-like manner.

Darcy sat back in his chair, but he was at least looking up, so
he could see them, and they could see him.

"So? Common knowledge."

"You used to run stuff around Mapperley for a few of the
dealers," Dan stated.

Sean Darcy's conflict over the goodies on the table versus the
conversation was clear.

"You're not police so who are you? It's ancient history now."

"Why don't you just concentrate on answers and let us worry
about questions."

Slowly Darcy reached out, hooked bony fingers around one
of the cigarette packets and slid it back across the table. He
found a box of matches in his shirt pocket and lit up, after
dumping the cellophane and foil packaging straight onto the
floor. Dan allowed him to inhale deeply and exhale before he
continued.

"You were friends with Zoe Summers too."

Darcy stopped mid second drag. He struggled to say something and in the end could only come up with. "So?"

"I want to know about you and Zoe, you and the Stingers
too?"

Dan enjoyed watching Darcy thinking of a way to answer
with no more than three words and took the time to silently
reassure Amber all was well.

After another long pull on his cigarette Darcy said, "Me and Zoe were mates, that's it. She did a bit of stuff and I helped her out."

Dan resisted the temptation to lean across the table at him.

"Come on Sean, how'd you meet her, how often did you see her, what else did you do?"

"I don't remember all that. We met in a pub; I think she wanted some pills."

Dan feigned irritation and went to put the Pepsi back in the bag. For the first time Darcy responded with something like urgency.

"Alright, alright. We met in a pub. I liked her. She started coming in regular and I would sort her out. When she wanted H or ice, I could get it."

Amber narrowed her eyes. "So how did you get from being her supplier to living with her?"

Noting Darcy growing more agitated with each question, Dan bet he was down to a few useless pence in his jeans pocket and his last cigarette before the present one was ten agonising hours before.

"She needed a place. I told you I liked her. I had a room in a house, and she asked if she could share with me."

"So, was she your girlfriend then?" Amber said, knowing better.

Darcy showed a modicum of confidence. "Sort of."

"How long was that for? Right up until when she died?"

"No way. I mean no, me and her split up ages before. I had to take care of business and she was holding me back."

Dan reached his tolerance level with the cockroach. The few minutes spent in his company, plus the information he had on him already was more than enough to measure the few qualities he was equipped with. He decided it was time to assert his dominance and start asking some more pertinent questions to really make him squirm.

"That's enough of the bullshit, Sean," he said, maintaining his flat tone and Darcy's stare with his own. "She was no more your girlfriend than she was mine. Zoe was gay so don't waste my time with any more of your crap. I'll leave you all this, but you're going to tell me what I want to know, or I'll make a few phone calls and the shoplifting charge which got you in here will be the least of your problems.

"I know you haven't spent any time inside yet and we both know you're far too chickenshit to last five minutes in prison, so first, who did you and your Stinger mates run around for? And second, the day you and Zoe got arrested at Connaught Drive, where was she going later?"

Darcy visibly quivered. Amber contained her surprise.

"Fuck man just hold on, I mean shit, come on. I was telling you. I didn't say she was my girlfriend, I said sort of," Darcy blurted out.

"And which of my two questions does that answer, Sean?" Dan's tone remained hard, but he became a note or two quieter. It appeared Sean Darcy was even weaker than he thought.

Living down to Dan's expectations, Darcy crumpled like a wet weekend. "I was gutted when Zoe got killed. I didn't even know she was back in Mapperley."

Dan's internal antenna shrieked, picking up on Darcy's statement.

"Back from where? Where did she go?" Amber demanded.

"You said Connaught Drive shops—that was the last day I saw her. She was getting picked up," he said.

"To go where," Amber persisted.

"I don't know and that's the honest truth. Someone got her a job, well not a job but doing something way out in the country somewhere."

"Details, Sean," Dan hissed.

"Fuck, it was ages ago. I don't know. All I know is she was going to get paid but she had to go away, and it was all really secret." He looked at Dan and then at Amber. Changing tack, he tried again. "When I was in the Stingers, I met a bloke called Matt, Matt Craig."

Dan's antenna shrieked again as Darcy continued.

"He said he knew someone that needed a few people to do some work for him."

"And," Dan insisted.

"Fuck, I don't know, I told you it was secret, Matt never told me, and Zoe never told me. It must have been drugs because everything was. Matt was like an arranger."

"Who for?"

"I told you I don't fuckin' know!"

Dan knew he was close to Darcy's popping point, but he pressed for a little more. "There's no such thing as a secret in Mapperley, Sean. You must know something else."

"I don't, I promise. Zoe wanted to get away, this was her chance and I swear to God I never knew she was back."

He did indeed look like he was about to burst into flames as he desperately fought for something to end the questioning.

"What about your friend Vikkert. Tell us about him."

Darcy's eyes almost bulged out of his head. "No way. I stayed right away from that mad fucker," he shouted.

He went to get up but Dan put a hand on his wrist, pinning it to the table. Darcy began to shake uncontrollably as if he was having a fit and then as if he pulled the word out of fresh air he blurted out, "Stromboli."

Such was the bizarre nature of Darcy's choice of word, Dan and Amber were both taken aback.

Seeing it temporarily cause his unwanted visitors to baulk he repeated it and at the same time regained some self-control. "Stromboli. I heard it once or twice."

"Heard it where, what does it mean?" Dan asked.

"In the pub, I don't know. I don't know what it means but I heard it around when Zoe was going away."

Dan could tell he wasn't going to get anything more from Darcy, but they stayed long enough for Darcy to chain-smoke two more from the packet before leaving. During that time, he didn't say anything else which Dan thought useful.

"Alright then?" Duncan asked as they passed the office on their way out.

"Thanks yes, maybe see you again," Dan replied, expecting never to have to revisit.

He and Amber resisted the urge to run down the path to the car, so keen were they to get in the quiet refuge.

"Stromboli." They both said at the same time.

"What the hell is stromboli? Apart from an Italian food," Amber gushed.

Dan was excited as she was. "No idea, is it a name?"

"Did you see him? He was so freaked out."

"Sean Darcy is a bottom feeder, Amber. I can see what he saw in Zoe, but God knows what she ever saw in him. He was a hanger on to the coat tails of some of the more important players. I guess he never got close to anything really important, that's why he doesn't know much either. But when he said stromboli it was genuine. Like he said, he doesn't know what it means but it did mean something."

Amber beamed. "I can't wait to get home and tell the others."

CHAPTER SEVENTEEN

"A small island in the Tyrrhenian Sea, off the north coast of Sicily?" Penny said, making it sound like a question.

Tara countered with, "A type of turnover filled with cheeses, meats, and or vegetables."

"Or a 1950 film starring Ingrid Bergman about a woman who marries an Italian prisoner of war and when she moves to the island, she finds it and the locals cold and harsh," Nick added. "Take your pick Dan."

Google, it seemed, wasn't the font of all knowledge after all. Dan dismissed the rolled-up pizza without another thought and looked at the others. Penny and Nick were sharing a sofa, Tara knelt on the floor, and Amber was curled up on one of the lounge chairs.

"Volcanic Italian island or Ingrid Bergman movie set on the island?" he said, thinking, *they're expecting me to have an answer. No, the answer!* But he had nothing.

Unintentionally, he burst into laughter. "I don't bloody know!" he roared, causing the others to recoil then join in his hysterics.

The release of tension made any more useful thought momentarily impossible. Over the next ten minutes they all relaxed, taking turns reviewing the Google descriptions on the first four or five pages and getting the same each time.

"The island looks quite nice for a week away," Nick said unhelpfully.

Tara caused more laughs when she added, "But the movie looks like hard work."

"Are you sure he wasn't just bullshitting mate?" Nick said to Dan.

"No, he definitely meant it," Amber replied.

Dan was sure too. "She's right. There's no way he said that accidentally. It was important to what we were asking. He believed it meant something to Zoe then. It means something to us now."

"Perhaps we should ask Eric and Purdy? They might have a better idea because they were and are in the area," Tara offered.

"Good thinking, I'll give them a call."

A few moments of hope swiftly disappeared: neither Eric nor Purdy recognised stromboli, although Eric did say the movie was quite good. When Dan terminated the second call, he couldn't disguise his disappointment.

"Have I missed something?" he said to Tara as they stood on opposite sides of the kitchen table.

She finished pouring the hot water into the coffee pot. "You're asking me? If you don't know my love, then we certainly don't. Remember, not everything is going to be in your evidence and information. If it was in there you'd know."

"But stromboli. You could go your whole life without hearing or saying that word. In Mapperley you're probably more likely not to, and a scumbag like Sean Darcy even more so."

"Maybe he misheard it? You did also say he was freaking out by that stage."

Dan thought about it and went back over that part of Darcy's questioning in his head. "No, he heard it correctly I'm certain. It's not as if it rhymes with a hundred other possibilities."

He took the tray for Tara as they headed back to the lounge where an air of despondency hung. Taking their seats again, they joined the others in looking around for inspiration, but the only sounds were that of Rosie and Viola noisily announcing their arrival from the front door.

"In here," Penny called back.

"Hi, did you have a good time?" Nick asked as the twins joined them.

"It was okay. We saw your friend Colin in town, Dad. He says hi," Viola chirped.

Rosie followed up her sister. "What have you all been doing?" she said looking at the sheets of A4 and open laptops.

"Getting frustrated. Any idea what stromboli means?" Tara replied.

"Strom…what?"

"That's exactly what we've been thinking," Dan said. "Stromboli?"

"Never heard of it, what does it mean?" Rosie giggled.

"It's a little Italian island or a type of rolled-up pizza but we're trying to work out what it's got to do with drug dealing in Mapperley," said Nick wistfully.

"No, it isn't," Viola said. "Sorry, I mean it might be that, but it's someone else too."

"Someone?" Penny, Tara, and Nick said together.

"Hold on I'll show you," Viola called over her shoulder as she shot out of the room.

The sound of her stomping up the stairs and then banging cupboard doors in her room continued for a minute or two before she clattered back down again.

"Here," she said triumphantly. "He used to scare me when I was little."

She carried a DVD box with a brightly coloured picture on the case. Even though it was upside down in her hand the name was instantly recognisable.

"Pinocchio?" Penny exclaimed. "We've got all the Disney films and watched them a hundred times…"

"I remember," Rosie interrupted. "You used to hide behind the cushions."

"Why that one, Vio sweetheart?" Penny asked, finishing her sentence.

Disney cartoons didn't feature in Dan's growing up and he was still completely lost but consciousness was dawning on the others.

"The scary puppet master," Nick said.

Dan stared at him. "What!"

"Stromboli is the puppet master who buys Pinocchio and keeps him locked in a cage to perform in the circus."

Though they didn't know why, everybody was charged with electric excitement at the thought of what this could mean. Dan was desperate for more information.

"Here, let me Google it," Amber said, grabbing his computer.

She tapped the keys and entered *Stromboli Pinocchio*. A few seconds later seven pairs of eyes were staring at the screen.

Whereas stromboli on its own gave them the shortlist of three items they spent an age studying with no joy, including the name of the long nosed wooden toy resulted in something quite different. As Dan read the description of the character several words and lines stuck out like they were on fire.

Stromboli is one of the five antagonists…He's a puppeteer, a showman, and a gypsy, his primary concern is making money…Buys Pinocchio from a villainous fox called Honest John…He locks Pinocchio in a cage to ensure that his star attraction doesn't return home…His name in the original Italian story literally means 'Fire-eater'…Stromboli is a threatening and imposing villain; for this reason, he's often cited as one of Disney's greatest villains. He's named after Stromboli, the Italian volcanic island.

Unbelievable, he thought.

"Unbelievable," he said.

While several colourful pages printed off, Dan sipped his coffee quietly. Even Rosie and Viola realised it was the time for a break in noisy activity. During the hiatus Amber busied herself on the computer.

"What are you up to?" Tara queried at one point.

"Pinocchio was originally a fairy-tale and the Disney film is very different from the story. Stromboli only figures in the film. In the book the same character is called Mangiafuoco which literally means fire-eater. I wanted to check we didn't go off in the wrong direction, but it does look like the film is the reference point we should concentrate on for Stromboli."

Nick kissed the top of his daughter's head. "Genius."

Dan was glad too; it confirmed what he was thinking but nevertheless he drank two more cups before he was ready to explain.

"Powton Road was a pop-up which took a lot of planning and imagination to design and even more to run with so little information getting out, except to those who the designer wanted to know, of course. Craig Matthews was so professional he had me on a string. Matt Craig was an arranger, Darcy said. Zoe went away for nine months. These are all facts we know.

"Stromboli the character in the story was a puppeteer who bought Pinocchio from another devious character called Honest John; a puppeteer is behind the scene controlling things, literally pulling the strings. All Stromboli's actions were designed to make him rich and he kept Pinocchio locked up to stop him returning home. Who does that make you think of?"

"Zoe," they replied universally.

"Nick, do a search for Stromboli on the force database will you?"

"What?"

"Humour me, please?"

Nick silently did as Dan requested, turning the machine so his friend could see.

"What the…" he said as the result returned a screen. "I've only seen this once before and it scared the shit out of me then."

Dan smiled grimly.

"What is it?" Penny begged.

Nick turned the computer again so the rest of them could see. UNAUTHORISED SEARCH. PLEASE LEAVE PAGE, it read in the central box.

"What does that mean?" Tara asked.

Nick answered incredulously, "Stromboli is a person, operation, or other police reference which only the highest ranked officers are able to access. This is too weird."

He closed the lid of his computer as if leaving it open might be the cause of an immediate raid on the house. Looking at Dan they wordlessly shared a conversation the likes of which was as serious as any they ever had.

"Nick?" Penny implored. Not getting an answer she tried again. "Dan, what is it?"

Nick responded. "I know I'm repeating myself from other occasions, but what the hell are we going to do?"

"I think I need to make another call," Dan said.

As the others watched on, he took out his phone and dialled. After an excruciating number of rings, the recipient picked up.

"Hello."

"Hi, it's me, how are you doing?"

"Good, good this is a bit early; I was expecting you to call later. Is everything alright son?"

"Fine thanks Jim. I've got a question for you. What would you say if I asked you who or what Stromboli is? You're on speakerphone by the way."

He heard and felt Jim's sharp intake of breath through the phone.

"Where on earth did you hear that?"

"Part of the Mapperley grapevine. What does it mean?"

In his study the old detective went from standing to sitting heavily in the guest chair as beads of sweat appeared on his forehead.

"It was so far over my head and pay grade I wasn't permitted to know more than basic details when I oversaw CID. Stromboli is, or was, a myth, at least I always hoped he was. What on earth are you mixed up in this time?"

"That sounds ominous," Dan replied, casting his gaze around the room full of shocked faces.

"Sorry son, but you really caught me on the hop. I don't think I ever mentioned it to anybody, including my immediate seconds-in-command. As far as I know if he, she, or it existed at all, Stromboli was a person, the single biggest distributor of heroin in the country with massive secret caches hidden in remote areas."

"Jim, I don't understand. How can some Mapperley low life pull that name out of thin air? What were you told?"

Jim cleared his throat. "This is Official Secrets territory, Dan. I was told there was a file in existence on this Stromboli and I might be granted access one day if and when there was enough information to do anything with it. I was only told that much because it was put into our system and they had to."

"They?"

"Home Office, SIS, who knows, it's the bloody Government."

"When? Sorry to press you," Dan asked.

"I'm not sure, I'd have to check. Are you sure this is not some horrible unlikely coincidence?"

"Bear with me for a minute okay."

Dan related the Stromboli puppeteer facts before asking Jim an apparently innocent question. "Do you know the Pinocchio story?"

"I remember Gwen and I taking our Bradley to see it when he was a boy," Jim answered.

"Do you know the name of the character who sold Pinocchio to Stromboli?"

"Do me a favour Dan, we're talking about a cartoon from bloody decades ago," Jim spluttered.

Dan stifled a laugh. "Sorry, it was a fox named Honest John."

"Alright. So what?"

"Take a look in the file at the name of the person I met and introduced me to Craig Matthews. Matthews was the one who later took me to Powton Road."

"Yes, I remember him, hold on. I've got it right here."

While the Hetherington household looked blankly at each other and listened to the sound of Jim thumbing through paper, Dan concentrated on the deafening sound of his heartbeat banging out a tune in his head.

A long minute passed then Jim cleared his throat again. "You're bloody kidding me?"

Dan grabbed Tara's hand. "We're all listening, Jim, go ahead."

"John Trew," he said in a hushed voice.

Dan smiled unhappily. "Honest John and John Trew. Still think it's a coincidence?"

"Holy shit," Nick said, unable to prevent releasing the mild expletive in the presence of his wife and children.

"I don't know what to say and I'm not sure I can actually do anything either. We should both take a while to think about this and maybe talk again tomorrow," Jim said deliberately.

"Yes, good idea. Sorry to drop this on you, I had no way of knowing. I'll speak to you again sometime tomorrow afternoon." He looked up to see Tara mouthing words at him. "Oh Jim, are you still there? How're Bradley and Gwen?"

"Fine son, fine."

"Tara says she'll call again in a while," Dan said apologetically.

"Right ho, Gwen'll look forward to that. I'll tell her. See you, try to take it easy, son."

Dan switched off and dropped the phone on the floor before he noticed he and Tara were still gripping each other's hands.

After casting a cautionary look at the twins, who'd been amused by Nick's accidental outburst, Penny said, "I know we spend a lot of time with a tea or coffee in our hands doing this, but I could really do with another drink now, and I mean something a bit stronger than coffee."

Dan was drinking brandy. Nick cupped his favourite whisky in one of his tumblers. They were still unmoved from their respective seats long after wives, partners, and children had gone to bed. Having covered every detail of the current situation, and their past careers to a much lesser extent, all that remained to finish discussing was the future, especially the immediate future.

How he could have stumbled so helplessly and hopelessly into a scenario where government departments and agencies such as the Special Intelligence Service were at the centre of things was at the very farthest corner of even Dan's imagination.

"What else can I do but pull the pin? I can't risk you, Jim, and who knows who else. It must stop right here, right now. Can you imagine what we might blunder into if we carry on with nothing else to go on?"

Nick drained his glass. "This is big."

"Too big for the likes of us," Dan replied.

CHAPTER EIGHTEEN

The next morning was brilliantly bright, which seemed like an insult to the way Dan was feeling. After breakfast he sat in the garden room watching a few puffy clouds barely moving across the sky, slowly bubbling into patterns that failed to materialise into anything recognisable.

The vast amount of information he and his unlikely team accrued to this point was still far too insufficient to risk the attention of unknown parties at opposite ends of the legal and criminal spectrums.

"Who can tell if I haven't already alerted the good guys or the bad ones to the fact we're either looking at them, or at least in their direction?" he whined.

Tara was sitting next to him. *Frozen Summer was never meant to end this way,* she thought. When she re-focused on Dan he was still talking.

"I should tell Elizabeth at least, and I'm thinking George too. I owe them an explanation so soon after saying I was going to stop at nothing to find Zoe's killer. What do you think?"

"Sure, darling whatever you think is best."

"I should tell her in person, but I'll give George a call in a minute. I suppose we can think about going home now too."

Nick and Amber entered the room, exchanging muted good mornings with their house guests. They all knew there was little else to say and there was a definite feeling of depression around the whole house. Tara started thinking of seeing Bradley, which gave her comfort, but Dan's best effort was brooding silence.

"Why don't you go and call George now, and later we can go back to Elizabeth Summers' house? We might as well get on with it," Tara offered five minutes later.

Dan sighed, half-smiled, and pulled himself out of the chair with great effort.

"Hi George, it's Dan Calder here. How are you doing?"

"Oh hello. We have to be out in a few minutes so," George said, explaining his imminent departure from the depot but managing to sound guilty in the process.

"No problem. I wanted to call you just because there has been a bit of a change of plan at my end and I wanted to tell you personally."

"Okay, I was going to call you. Dad said I should when he reminded me of something."

"What was that?" Dan asked, although he was really thinking, *don't bother, George, I've let you down.*

"It was before Zoe went away for all those months. One day Dad took us out in the car, and we went up to the Peaks, you know the Peak District."

Dan sat a little straighter. "Yes, I know it. Who do you mean when you say us?"

"Me and my mum and brother went out for the day, Zoe came too. We were driving around, and Zoe said that one day soon she'd be up here doing some work. Dad asked her why because we were in the middle of nowhere. I forgot but Dad said about it yesterday."

"Do you remember when your dad told you? Do you remember the area now?"

"It was a long time ago and me and Zoe were still quite young, but yeah I think so."

Dan was ramrod straight now. "Could you or he take me to that spot again, where you actually were when Zoe said it?"

"I don't know about that Mr. Calder, it was a long time ago like I say."

"Call me Dan. Is your dad there, George?"

Dan went to grab the road atlas from the car. He passed the twins on the driveway on the way back to the house. They had another movie date with friends.

He bounced into the garden room reinvigorated. Tara's jaw dropped open.

"Oh God, what now?"

"Who'd like to go for a drive in the country? Nick, we'll need boots, binos, and backpacks."

The phrase the friends used on surveillance operations was their light-hearted way of saying it was a kit intensive operation. Later it also became a phrase used in both households to describe something requiring a lot of equipment or stuff in general. Nobody was in any doubt about what was happening.

Before they left the house an hour or so later Dan explained in more detail.

"George said that after Zoe mentioned working in that area, she got embarrassed, as if she'd let out a secret by mistake, and she didn't explain it any further. Robert said they were on the A515, somewhere either side of Fenny Bentley. He remembered that because he always pointed out where one of the early Zuckerman ancestors lived and worked when they went for days to the Peaks."

"What are you thinking Dan?" Amber asked as she tugged on the boots he and Nick got her the year before when they went on their 'special op' to Jim Allen's house.

"Zoe was going away to work for a long time, Stromboli had dumps of heroin in secret locations."

Tara and Penny shared a disbelieving look.

"So, we're going out to look for where a huge hidden stash of heroin used to be? I'm only asking," Tara said incredulously.

"I don't know what we're looking for to be honest. After everything that's happened, I'm a bit reluctant to say I know anything anymore."

"So? Oh, forget it." Penny laughed. "Look at you three with your stormtrooper boots. I'm coming along just to see what you do."

Dan drove. As arranged, they met up with Robert and George Zuckerman part way through their day's round a few miles out of town. Robert indicated as best he could on Nick's detailed Ordnance Survey map the location he thought it was they'd been when Zoe let slip her work plan. Five minutes later they were properly on their way.

"Just like old times for you two is it?" Tara said, interrupting Dan and Nick's schoolboy-like conversation ten minutes later.

"Sorry, is it that obvious?" Nick replied.

Penny nudged the back of his neck. "Just a lot."

Nick sat in the front passenger seat with the map and another road map across his knees. He and Dan had been jabbering non-stop from the moment they departed about roads, the Peak District National Park, and the weather affecting potential search areas.

"It'll be getting dark within a few hours of us getting there I imagine, but it'll be good just to see it and decide if there's something we can do another day. There are bound to be a good number of country pubs we can get dinner in afterwards. My treat for the sudden about turn," Dan remarked.

Tara crossed her arms. "So long as you're not building your hopes up just to have them dashed again like yesterday."

Dan checked her in the rear-view mirror and gave her an encouraging smile.

Bypassing the city of Derby, they continued out in a westerly direction towards the market town of Ashbourne at the southern perimeter of the national park, widely known as the gateway to the Peak District.

It was 2:00 p.m. when they arrived, and the blue-sky morning had given way to darker clouds. Dan parked outside the old limestone Town Hall and killed the engine.

"Robert said Fenny Bentley, which is only a couple of miles north from here along the A515. It really is like a needle in a haystack, but I thought we could find out a little more about the area here and then take a drive up as far as Buxton, which is twenty miles."

"So, what exactly are we looking for here?" Penny asked.

"Pretty much find the local information centre, grab some literature, and ask what the local landmarks are going up the A515," Nick answered. His and Dan's partnership over the years meant they were almost always on the same page work wise. "Maybe also ask if there's ever been stories about unusual happenings, if the person or people look like they would be into gossip and rumours."

Tara, Penny, and Amber all looked similarly aghast.

"You mean little old ladies with nothing better to do?" Tara laughed.

Nick shrugged. "Well."

"Nicholas Hetherington, you chauvinist pig," Penny huffed.

All Nick could do was shrug again. Dan tried to come to his friend's rescue. "It's a tried and tested police intelligence gathering technique."

After the immediate hilarity subsided Penny made a proposal. "Why don't you two fascists drive up to Buxton and leave us here to gather your intelligence. We'll do our best in our limited female way."

Dan thought about a retort but decided against it. "Thanks Pen that's a great idea. Shall we meet you back here in say, two hours?"

Tara shook her head. "Make it three. We can keep ourselves occupied until then and you two can go tramping around the country."

"Okay, see you here at five," Dan replied.

Tara, Penny, and Amber didn't need to search hard for the Visitor Information Centre; it was six steps away from the car in the Town Hall entrance foyer. As they walked in Amber stifled a laugh. Behind the desk marked Visitor Information and Services sat two ladies of a certain age. They faced each other, leaning inwards so close their foreheads were almost touching and they were engaged in a secretive looking conversation. A sharp beep sounded; the noise activated by an alarm on the floor under the welcome mat brought the ladies up from their huddle in unison.

"Good afternoon," Lady number one said as if it was her turn. "Welcome to Ashbourne."

"Hello," Tara and Penny answered together.

"Can we help?" Lady number two chirped.

While Amber faced the other way feigning interest in a landscape photo, Tara and Penny approached the desk.

Penny took the lead. "I hope so. We'd like some information on the local area and maybe some of the most interesting landmarks at this end of the national park."

Number one replied confirming the thought they were indeed taking it in turns. "Lovely. Are you staying in town here for a while?"

"Not today but maybe over the next few days as we're travelling around," Tara said.

Soon a pile of pamphlets, brochures, and flyers were stacked on the desk as the ladies gave a practiced information soundbite to go with each one.

"Do you walk or bicycle? Are you here for the bird watching?"

"We'd certainly like to see some of the countryside, the Peaks sound beautiful," Tara said, grateful her New Zealand accent was of some use. "If we had two or three days in the area where would you suggest?"

Both ladies were delighted to be asked the open question and have the opportunity to demonstrate their knowledge. Over the next ten minutes they took Tara and Penny on a verbal whistle-stop tour of the Standedge Canal Tunnel, Heage Windmill, The National Stone Centre, Chatsworth House, and Poole's Cavern among a barrage of other interesting sites as they described the five hundred and fifty square miles of the first national park in the UK. They also included details of nearly two thousand miles of Rights of Way and sixty miles of cycle trails as well geological facts about the gritstone and limestone make-up of the peaks. By the end Tara felt she knew this part of the country like a native.

Tara purchased a traveller's guide and put all the handouts in a plastic bag with it. Feeling sure she had the confidence of the ladies now, she decided to test Dan and Nick's theory.

"While we're here, could you help me with something else?" she asked.

"Certainly, if we can."

"I've got this thing for the history of the country. Coming from New Zealand there just aren't the same number of historical references. Are there any stories of unusual or interesting events?"

For the first time the ladies appeared at a complete loss. Tara reminded herself to let Dan know what she thought of his intelligence gathering technique.

"What do you mean, dear? Ghost stories and haunted houses?" Number one asked.

"Oh yes! And you know, anywhere I could go and see and wonder what may have happened here."

"Well we've all sorts of ghosts and ghouls across the area and there are enough myths to fill a hundred books. Let me see.

There was the Christmas Eve murder in Hassop, the potty murder of Matlock just for starters," Number two said.

"That's right, then there's Margaret Vernon who lost her lover and rode off to Hazel Badge where she died of grief. Robin Hood used to visit often, and his accomplice Little John was supposedly a giant of a man who was born in the Peaks. Is that the sort of thing you meant?" Number one added.

Penny enthusiastically joined in. "And maybe unsolved crimes or rumours of criminal activity?"

The ladies looked at Penny and then at each other. This wasn't the gentile conversation they were usually accustomed to with visitors. However, it was just the sort of thing which pepped up quiet days or filled coffee breaks.

"Well of course there's poor Wendy Sewell," Number one said as if she and poor Wendy Sewell were blood relatives. "The newspapers called her the 'Bakewell Tart' because she came from there and she had a reputation."

Number two took up the story. "She was bashed to death in a graveyard in Bakewell. They thought they caught the killer, but he was innocent and released from prison after serving years for it. 1970 something was it?"

"Mm 1972 or 1973 I think," One said.

"Bakewell, that's some way north isn't it? Is there anything closer or more recent?" Tara enquired.

"I thought you said historical. Well that horrible Yorkshire Ripper was supposed to have buried some of those girls, but who knows where. Oh, there was the couple who killed themselves with an overdose up on the trail a few years ago," Two said somewhat cautiously.

Amber swung her head around much too enthusiastically in her haste to join her mother and Tara, nearly knocking over a stand of postcards, which caused the women to take a half step back.

Tara remained calm, rubbed her forehead, and pushed back some hair which wasn't in the way. "Trail?"

"The Tissington Trail, it's the bridleway and cycle path from here in town up to Parsley Hay near Hartington. You've got the brochure," Two said slowly.

Much as they wanted to, they were not brave enough to ask for more. Tara, Penny, and Amber managed to stay a minute or two longer before they gave their thanks and said their farewells. They hoped more than they believed that it was a normal end to their visit.

Outside on the pavement and out of sight of the ladies who by now had a new subject to dissect head to head, they jumped up and down with excitement.

"Don't tell me Mum, you need a drink?" Amber squealed.

"We all do. Come on," Penny answered striding off towards the nearest pub.

Dan and Nick drove the route first without stopping just to get a feel for the road between Ashbourne and Buxton. On the return route they stopped multiple times to make notes, take photos, and seek inspiration.

"Small needle, very big haystack," Nick said as he looked out across the landscape from the car park of The Duke of York on the outskirts of the village of Flagg.

"We've found smaller ones in the past," Dan replied, trying to sound encouraging and confident. "Seen enough here?"

"Yes, more than enough."

The routine was to walk out for about seventy-five metres and then circle around in a clockwise three-sixty to be able to view the surrounding area without trespassing too far into farmers' fields. Back at the car Nick completed his notations, cross referencing them to his map descriptions and coordinates. As they moved off the concrete and back onto the tarmac Nick looked left and right out of habit too.

Dan stopped in the middle of the road. There was no traffic in either direction.

"What's that over there?" he said pointing.

"I'm not sure. Hold on, it could be the railway line," Nick said, consulting his Ordnance Survey map again. "Um no, bridleway and cycle path, I think. Right, where to now?"

"You tell me, you've got the map."

"Okay, one kilometre, the Tagg Lane crossroads."

"What's there?"

Nick laughed. "Bugger all from what I can see. Like I said, very big haystack."

He was right. The junction of the A515 and B5055 at Tagg Lane was just that, a crossroads with a coppice of trees on the right and empty fields on the left. Nevertheless, Dan parked up and they got out to repeat the procedure of a general surveil, note taking, and photos.

Although they had no idea what it was they were looking for, one thing was certain. Dan would know if they happened on it by accident.

By 4:30 p.m. they'd worked their way back down to Fenny Bentley, which Nick informed Dan was the southernmost village in the whole of the Peak District. Dan swung the car right off the main road for a quick tour as they wouldn't have time for a more detailed look if they were going to be back in Ashbourne by the agreed time. The village was made up of pleasant houses surrounded by pasture. There was a lack of shopping amenities and from what they could see, only one nice looking black and white pub and restaurant combination similar in age and appearance to the one Dan took Tara to in Devon.

Dan didn't stop the car, but they did have to complete a couple of U-turns at the end of cul-de-sacs before they considered Fenny Bentley done.

"Ready to head back? We might have to do a little more another day but I'm not sure we'll make much progress based on what we've seen this afternoon," Dan said, pulling onto the main road once more.

Nick had seen enough too. "Yes, I can't honestly say I saw anything that got me excited. I hope the girls haven't been bored."

CHAPTER NINETEEN

Tara, Penny, and Amber's delight was only slightly tempered by the fact it was also a told-you-so moment for Dan and Nick.

"So, what do you make of that?" Amber asked them after Penny repeated the Visitor Centre discussions.

"There are no coincidences," Dan said.

Nick managed a confirmatory grunt as he drained his bottle.

"Why didn't you ask them exactly where they were found or what else they knew?"

"It was sort of embarrassing. We didn't know how far we could take it. I think it took us all by surprise," Tara said, speaking for all three.

"It'll be searchable on the internet," Amber added. "We thought it would be better to do it at home later though. I do know the Tissington Trail is the old railway line between Ashbourne and Buxton for cyclists, walkers, horse riders and so on."

"That must be what you asked about as we left that pub near Flagg. A lot of old disused lines converted into cycle paths. The map is so new it didn't show the railway," Nick said to Dan.

Dan looked at Tara, who was smiling with eyebrows raised.

"We were just using the car park," Dan said. "But talking of pubs, we might as well eat here now, and we can check this alleged suicide when we get back."

"If you can contain yourself that long. We've all seen that particular look in your eye before," she replied, kissing his cheek.

Amber had the article in front of her. "I'll just read what it says. 'Coroner reports on the Tragedy Trail', is the headline. 'The bodies of Gary Knowles, twenty, and his twenty-two-year-old girlfriend Susie Watt were discovered by hikers at about 8:30 a.m. on Friday 14 December…last year…'" she said, checking the date at the top of the page. "'…about a mile south of Alsop on the Tissington Cycle Trail near Scriveners Hollow. Knowles and Watt, both from Leicester, were known to the police and had previous convictions for possession of drugs.'"

Nick looked down to consult his OS map and quickly identi-fied the area, if not the exact spot, his daughter was describing as she continued.

"'Early indications were that they both died of an overdose as a syringe and other items were found next to their bodies by a group of holidaying walkers. One of the group, a retired police officer from the Isle of Man, secured the immediate area and called the local police. By mid-morning the scene was cordoned off and expert forensic and photographic teams were working. The bodies of the two lovers were removed in the early after-noon and it was believed post-mortems would be required to confirm the cause of death.

"'At the time Detective Sergeant Gordon Grieg of Ashbourne Police Station said, "While it's too early to say for sure what happened it is always a tragedy when young peoples' lives are cut short." He appealed for anybody on the Tissington Trail the previous day who saw Knowles or Watt or might have infor-mation to contact Ashbourne Police Station on the 0800 Crime Beaters number. The trail was re-opened to the public the next morning.

"'Subsequent post-mortems on Knowles and Watt did con-firm both died from such massive overdoses of heroin that the Coroner, Julianne Beckwith, stated in her findings that while she couldn't record a verdict of suicide, she was inclined to believe that may well have been the case. She therefore recorded a verdict of death by misadventure.

"'The 13-mile Tissington Trail was opened in 1971 and forms part of the National Cycle Network running from Parsley Hay to Ashbourne.'

"That's it," Amber said looking up. "There are other articles, but this is the last one and it says it all really. When they decided it was a suicide pact interest soon faded away. Probably not newsworthy enough because they didn't come to a much more gruesome end."

"Knowles and Watt," Dan said to Nick, pointing out the spot on the map.

Dan turned the map around so Penny and Tara could see while Nick got to work on the database checks.

"What am I looking at? You know what I'm like with maps," Tara protested.

"Nick is the expert, but this is what's here," Dan answered.

He explained the markings for cycle path and bridleway among others and some of the other map features so they could get an idea of what was there, and then flipped through Nick's notes from earlier in the day to find the nearest spot they stopped at.

Nick quickly found both Gary Knowles and Susie Watt in the force system. While they came from Leicester, which was the adjacent police area, they also came to the attention of police in Nottingham.

"Junkies, shoplifters. He was drunk and incapable once as well," Nick said to the group while scrolling through Knowles' short history as they pored over the map and other written pages.

"Hold on, this is more like it. He has one association with guess who. Sean Darcy."

Dan grinned. "That's good enough for me."

"If this is all open fields and countryside how are you going to find whatever it is you're looking for, presuming you know what that is in the first place?" Tara asked.

He grinned again but this time a lot more ironically. "That's a very good question, T, and not one I have an answer to. I'm open to all suggestions."

"You need to Winthrop that," Penny stated.

They all looked at her in surprise by what she said and how she said it.

"Winthrop that, what does that even mean?" Tara asked.

Dan looked blankly at her too.

"Captain Winthrop, at least I think he was a captain, was in the British Army while working in Northern Ireland during the time of The Troubles there. He came up with a search technique to find dumps of guns and so on that were hidden out in remote areas. Oh yes," Penny continued, savouring the moment. "He was aware the republicans had large dumps which would be either buried or concealed in a way that could only be found by using landmarks to guide the finder in. That's because the person concealing the stuff was very unlikely to be the person who went to dig it up. The process was to use trees or telegraph poles, or maybe stone walls as a starting point and then have other lesser landmarks to guide the finder to the exact spot the things were buried or hidden. No maps, nothing written down." She looked away nonchalantly. "But I'm sure we all knew that."

It took several minutes of confused at first and then admiring and jovial conversation before she finally put Tara and Dan out of their misery.

"Last year when you sent us away to Wales, your friend Martin set up a treasure hunt for Rosie and Viola. He taught them the Winthrop search so they could go off and find all sorts of things he buried. They had a great time, told me all about it when they got back."

"Pen you're amazing." Tara giggled. "But you're not seriously thinking about getting the girls to go out on Tissington Trail, are you?"

"No, if there's one thing these two have taught me it's about using the experts if you can, like them, and surveillance. We need to call Martin. If you like Tarzan and Gladiator you're going to love him," she swooned.

While Penny told Dan and Tara a little more about Martin Foster, Nick went to place the call which he knew would be very short and succinct.

The phone was picked up on the first ring.

"Hello Outback Enterprises, Martin speaking."

"Hi Martin, Nick Hetherington."

"Nick, how are you? It's been a while."

"Good. You?"

"Grand. A bit quiet this time of year but that's not a bad thing after a busy year. What's up?"

"Winthroping. Penny has just been telling us about you and the twins last year."

"Oh yes. Are you pissing in someone's pond?" Martin asked.

"Dan Calder is here. It's a murder hunt, properly serious."

"I see. Do you want advice or practical assistance?"

"What would you suggest for a Winthrop search over a large open area?"

"Let me think for a minute as you tell me a bit more. Go ahead."

Nick gave him the thirty second briefing during which Martin remained silent. When he was finished, he waited, thinking how their call must sound like a covert radio conversation.

"I can't get to you until the day after tomorrow if that suits. What about a briefing at zero eight hundred on Saturday? I can bring all the shit I need," Martin said.

Nick knew his friend wouldn't make the offer unless he wanted to and felt no need to say something like 'Are you sure?' or 'If it's not too much trouble.'

Their association began on a joint army/police course and was solidified some time later when he helped recover two of Martin's stolen dogs, apprehend the culprit who took them and killed another. As Martin's dogs were as important to him as any family member, Nick instantly became a member of his do-anything-for-this-person inner circle.

"For your info the objective could be a drugs cache or the location of a distribution centre," Nick said, completing his micro briefing.

"Roger that. I'll give you a call if anything changes but it won't so see you on Saturday. Say hi to all your girls. Till Saturday."

And with that Martin was gone leaving Nick holding his receiver and listening to the dial tone.

When he got back Dan was still describing the area around Gills Tor, which was the closest point to Scriveners Hollow he and Nick surveilled. He stopped when Nick appeared.

"Martin will come up on Saturday morning, so I think we'll have to put Rosie and Viola in together for a few nights unless you want to share with one of them Amber?" Nick said, cutting to the domestic chase.

"Which gives us a day to do more digging into Stromboli. Talking about that, I thought Jim would have called by now," Dan said checking his watch.

Instead of spending the afternoon on Stromboli after a morning in the garden, Jim and Gwen took turns trying to comfort and placate a very unhappy little boy. At 4:00 p.m. Bradley was still screaming; in desperation they took him to the Accident and Emergency Centre in Salcombe. Unfortunately, the rest of the town's population seemed to have the same idea and it was a couple of hours before he was initially assessed and then another lengthy wait before he was seen by the house paediatrician.

Even though it was almost 10:45 p.m. when they got home the only thing Gwen wanted to do was call Tara.

"It's me Tara, sorry to call you so late and there's nothing to worry about, but I wanted to call you straight away."

"Gwen is everything okay? Is it Bradley? Or Jim?"

"Yes, we're all fine now but we've been at the A and E with Bradley because he was crying so much and obviously in pain."

Tara gasped.

"He's fine, honestly he's fine, Tara. They say it was another episode of his tummy trouble you told us about. They gave him a magnesium muscle relaxant which seemed to help, and we're home again now and he's sound asleep. He must have absolutely worn himself out."

"Gwen, I'm so sorry."

"Don't be silly sweetheart. The main thing is he's fine now, but I did want to tell you. We mothers have all been there and I know exactly what you must be thinking."

"Should I come back?"

"Look, that's precisely what I would say in your place too but there's no need. Jim and I are more than capable."

It took more questions and more re-assurances before the call could be terminated. Gwen passed on the message from Jim that he couldn't do what he said to Dan, but he would get to it tomorrow.

Later in bed Tara found it impossible to settle without discussing Bradley again. They went over hers and Gwen's phone call once more and Dan cursed the failure of the doctors at home to properly diagnose the problem.

"Perhaps we should take tomorrow off rather than spend it all on this stuff. Gwen's call put things in perspective," he said.

Tara cuddled closer. "Can we? It would be lovely to do nothing, or at least not feel like we have to do something," she said. "Will Nick be alright about it?"

"Of course. Why wouldn't he be?"

"He has to go back to work soon, remember?"

Dan thought for a moment. "I'll talk to him tomorrow but he's fine."

"Missing out on your fun and games, I don't think so. We've all seen how you two behave together when you're, in quotes, 'working'."

One of the many reasons Dan loved Tara so much was because she was able to think in the round, with equal empathy for all the different parties, whether they be in agreement or conflict to her position. It was a quality Dan recognised as a very good thing, but one he didn't possess. It had been knocked out of him in no uncertain terms by his father and his career.

Reassessing his last comment, he tried to make good. "You're right of course. I will talk to him tomorrow."

While Dan and Tara slept in the heart of the country others at opposite ends were very active.

Jim had not been able to think of much else since Dan introduced Stromboli back into his consciousness. He hadn't told Dan, but one other incident did come to mind at the mention of the subject. However, he wanted all the facts before mentioning it. Gwen was as exhausted as Bradley and went to bed soon after finishing her call to Tara, telling him not to stay up too late but Jim knew he wouldn't be able to sleep until he got what he wanted. That was why he was still riffling through a few old diaries and files well past 1:00 a.m.

The lights were also burning brightly behind the thick stone walls of Martin Foster's secluded house. His friend Nick said Winthrop search, drugs cache, murder hunt, and properly serious. The decorated Special Forces veteran didn't do anything by halves and knew only one way to do things and that was the right way.

P.P.P.P.P.P. was etched into the grain of the open lid of the heavy wooden trunk he was leaning over. As he selected from the mint condition clothing and equipment inside, memories of the first time he heard the phrase from an instructor during selection to the regiment came back to him. 'Proper preparation prevents piss poor performance.'

He lowered the lid when he was finished and clicked the pad-lock back in place.

CHAPTER TWENTY

"What time did you come to bed, love? I didn't hear a thing," Gwen asked as she held up a delighted Bradley so he could see the birds on the lawn through the kitchen window.

"It was late, but I needed to try and find what I was looking for," Jim said, returning Bradley's beaming smile. "He looks like a different baby today. Here let me take him for a minute."

Fortunately for them all Bradley was a hundred percent better than the day before, his current healthy glow resulting from a long sleep and a recently filled belly.

"I would like to give Tara another call. Do you think it's too early?" Gwen said as she handed him over.

"Maybe another half hour. What would you like to do today? How about we take a drive up to Dartmoor so he can see the ponies?"

They finalised plans over another cup of tea as Bradley went from Jim's arms to the floor and then began exploring the low-level cupboards. They never considered the need to child-proof the kitchen, but the inquisitive youngster soon had Gwen questioning their future requirements. Jim remedied the situation by giving him a saucepan and wooden spoon to play with in the centre of the floor.

"Never fails. Who needs all these modern toys?" He chuckled over the tinny racket a few minutes later.

Dan's first thoughts of the morning were a continuation of his last ones the night before. He sloshed a large sponge over Nick's car in the driveway as his best friend and partner was carrying out his weekly ritual of vehicle maintenance. Nick was using the sponge's twin on his side, cleaning off the grime before he would dry and wax.

"It's a bugger you have to go back to work so soon," Dan said.

"I know. I thought we'd ground to a halt, then this Stromboli thing happened. It's too much to believe Zoe wasn't connected. Don't forget to do the rubber seals around the windows."

Dan smiled and did as he was told. If maps were one of Nick's babies, so were work vehicles, and the obsession transferred over to his personal cars as well. "Got it. Zoe went away to be involved in whatever Stromboli was doing."

"So, do you agree with Jim that he or she's a person?"

"Probably, but it could also be the name for the operation, for want of a better term. I'm a bit concerned there may be a greater number of people involved, confusing the whole thing for us."

Nick stopped for a second. "How so?"

"The thing I read about the Disney story of Pinocchio says there are five different villains. Stromboli and Honest John were two, so who's to say the other three won't make an appearance?"

"Just what we need. Actually, you should watch the film."

"I told T we would have today off, but we might be able to get away with that. Seriously though, are you okay about going back to the office before we've finished?"

"I have to be, don't I? This is very unlike you. The job dictates the job, why are you so concerned about me all of a sudden?"

"This is the new improved Calder; caring and sharing," Dan said with as much conviction as he could muster.

Nick looked nervous and unsure how to answer. "Well stop it. It's not you and it doesn't help. Make sure you do the roof-rack slides," he said as a full stop to his sentence and the entire conversation.

Dan noted Nick's over aggressive use of the sponge and the pursed lips. Wondering if Tara would choose to say more if she was in his place, he kept his head down and his mouth shut.

It took Jim most of the morning to finally locate the right diary. The police required retiring officers hand back all their notebooks because at some time in the future the contents may be required as evidence. In court and with permission of the judge, officers may refer to their notebooks in order to refresh their memories of an incident, but it was common practice for lawyers to also ask to see them in that situation. Since becoming a detective Jim routinely kept a diary as well as his police issue notebooks; he could write freely in these without having to consider what an ambitious defence lawyer would make of his thoughts and descriptions, which would have been relevant to him at the time but not necessarily make great reading to others in a court room six months or a year later.

The hard-covered exercise books were also a legacy of sorts; he would love one day to have given them to his son as an account of his working life and a source of never-ending stories or anecdotes. That was a lost dream now, however their value to him was beyond words.

On Monday 17 December 2006 the first entry read, *Tide times for 24 April are different to indications given by Bryn Talbot. Statement from Coastguard/Expert evidence.*

The second was underlined. *Anniversary Flowers.*

The third read, *Call from Adrian Bullmar SIS 01 656 6111 xt243. STROMBOLI. MIR +10. Confirm Tues 18?*

He flicked past two more handwritten pages to the next day's entries but there wasn't anything about Stromboli. To be sure he also checked the next weeks' worth too, but again there wasn't anything else. He was sure there were never any others after that time.

He was pleased and relieved finding it after having a few self-doubts about committing it to paper so many years before. He made a copy on his desktop machine and put the book back in the stack it came from after marking the page with a folded tissue.

"About time," Gwen chided him when he walked back into the kitchen.

"I'm sorry love; I really wanted to find this thing. I haven't forgotten, let me make a sandwich and we can take it with us and find somewhere to watch the ponies. Is Bradley still okay?"

"He is. Use the ham in the fridge and maybe some lettuce and tomato. I'll get the little chap ready."

Amber was a little disappointed not to be able to report a new revelation of her own or even expand much on the detail contained in the newspaper article. So far as the internet was concerned the results for Gary Knowles and Susie Watt were painfully small, in fact bordering on non-existent.

"Sorry Dad, I'm sure I've looked at everything. I checked different spellings of the names as well, but this is it," she said, waving a sheet of paper with a few handwritten lines on it.

"You can't blame yourself for something which isn't there Amber," said Penny, putting a consoling arm around her shoulder.

"Really, that's it?" Nick said.

Penny glared at him. "Nick please!"

"No, not you Amber. Really, is that all? You can do a search on any two random names and come up with more than that. Dan would say there was a reason for there being so little. As if someone had made a concerted effort to prevent more detail being available. Go and show him."

Dan and Tara were cuddled up watching Pinocchio; it made strange viewing to see he was making notes. When Amber asked if she could interrupt Tara paused the DVD.

"Dad asked me to show you this. It's all there is on the internet about Knowles and Watt."

She handed over the page and waited as Dan quickly read the lines, flipped the page over in case he had missed something and then back again to look at what she had compiled.

"Is that it?"

"Everything, I promise."

Dan held the note in front of Tara's nose.

"A bit odd don't you think. So little."

"Oh, right yes," Tara answered.

Amber felt exponentially better. "He said that's what you would say."

"Good work. This all adds to the no-such-thing-as-a-coincidence vibe I'm getting. What do you think?"

"I was disappointed but now I can see what you mean. How's the film?"

Dan was non-committal; Tara on the other hand was enjoying every minute. "Oh, it's so lovely." She sniffed. "I'm even singing along to the songs. I forgot how lovely it was."

When Amber grinned and sat down in a chair across from them Tara pressed play again.

It was 8:00 p.m. when Tara called for her daily chat with Gwen about Bradley. The fact he was sleeping peacefully after a good day, which included getting to see his first Dartmoor ponies, eating his first sausage roll—or rather, "just a small piece of Jim's before I could stop them," as Gwen put it—and giving Gwen her first ever kiss without her pleading for one was both calming and also a reminder of how much Tara was missing him.

They talked happily for another twenty minutes without mentioning Zoe Summers or the myriad of sub-plots surrounding her. When the time came to address the subject, both were disappointed.

"Jim wants to talk to Dan; is he there?"

"Right here and a little too keen to get the phone off me," Tara replied, flicking him a dismissive look.

"We better go then and let them get on with it. Jim is panting like an old dog as well. Take care Tara love, see you soon."

Gwen and Tara passed their respective handsets over like relay race batons.

"Dan?"

"Jim, hi."

"How've you been, son?"

"Alright, we made a bit of progress on Stromboli yesterday. It turns out a young couple apparently killed themselves in a heroin overdose up here in the Peak District National Park the year before Zoe died. By itself that would've made my nose twitch but there was so little coverage of it, I can't help thinking it was deliberately kept on the QT."

"I've something else for you too on that subject. Tell me though, when did they off themselves?" Jim asked, looking at the printed page on his lap.

"December fourteen, 2006," Dan replied.

"Well, son, I'm happy to tell you your instincts are still very much on song. I had to check first but there was another time I was contacted by SIS about Stromboli. One of their agents, no idea of rank, called me on Monday the seventeenth to tell me I might need to prepare a Major Incident Room with ten staff. He was going to call me back the next day if it was a go, but he didn't and there was no other contact from them at any time after. Whatever they thought may eventuate requiring an MIR didn't. You know what that means?"

"Yes of course. Stromboli was a very real heroin supply network which SIS knew about but not enough to mount an operation against. Jim, this couple were called Knowles and Watt. I can only think of two possibilities to explain what happened to them. One, they got their hands on some of the stuff Stromboli was moving and decided to have a party for two which went as wrong as it could. Or two, Stromboli needed to get rid of them and this was an easy and effective way."

"Hell's teeth, son. What would they be doing to be mixed up with something like Stromboli?"

"They were both known to police but no stops or incidents in several months before they died, just like Zoe Summers. What if they were working for Stromboli, Zoe too? It would explain the disappearances from their home areas before their deaths and provide a plausible link between them, i.e., their death scenes and the connection to the drugs."

"Could be, son. When SIS heard about Knowles and the other one, they could have thought they were getting closer, hence the call to me on the Monday after, but it either didn't pan out at that time or they did something else that I didn't need to know."

"Have you got any contacts at all who could just give you the heads up on Stromboli?" Dan asked.

"No, not a chance. I never moved in those circles."

Dan thought desperately for anything else but drew a blank. After tentatively suggesting a number of other vague what ifs but dismissing them as soon as they were aired, they called it a night.

Dan came off the phone feeling frustrated and hoping the arrival of Martin the next morning might also herald the arrival of some actual progression rather than a continuation of what was happening lately. Gathering information and evidence was always good if you were moving forward with it; if you weren't, the weight could bury you forever.

Martin was in pain; he was nine minutes late and that was unacceptable to him.

Banging the door closed on the Land Rover and swinging his backpack over one shoulder, he strode up to the house.

Viola opened the door before the doorbell's echoey chime evaporated. The enthusiastic welcome of the Hetherington females left Martin feeling uncomfortable. He dumped his bag as he was ushered through to where Nick, Dan, and Tara were. Formal introductions were completed before he apologised for his late arrival, but Penny waved it away.

It didn't take a Dan Calder mind to see Martin was less than happy in situations such as these—not social, but family focused. He forced smiles as Rosie and Viola eulogised about the stay at his centre and when they kept pushing Penny to confirm how great one thing after another was. He sat militarily polite: bolt upright on a hardback chair with his hands on his knees as if he were about to have his photo taken for a group course. It was with some relief when the topic of conversation finally turned to the matter in hand.

"It's probably best if Dan tells you what we've got and what we want to do next. In fact, why don't the rest of us leave you two to it for a while?" Nick said, handing the stage over.

When they were alone Dan introduced himself again properly, adding, "Thanks again for last year."

They briefly discussed the links from that time to what was happening now and paid courteous respect to the fallen, Zoe and Josie Lamas, which provided the type of genuine context both understood. It was for Martin a proper introduction; justification was born from history and context.

Dan then provided greater detail. Martin pulled out a notebook and pencil from a thigh pocket. Dan went through his IIMAC—information, intention, method, admin, and comms—briefing spiel as Martin made notes in concentrated silence. When he was finished, they both took up their coffee cups for the first time.

"Questions?" Dan asked.

Martin consulted his notebook. "No comment on your info. Intentions so far as I'm concerned are to search for and identify

ex-dumps or caches and also areas or buildings which might
have been distribution centres; all relating to a person or operation known as Stromboli."

"Yes."

"There's nothing to suggest any of these are still active?"

"Correct."

"You mentioned the OS map and your recce notes; can I see
them?"

Dan found and opened the map, placing Nick's notes along-
side it on the table. While Martin studied Dan stood back. After
a few minutes Martin pulled out a multi-tool from another
pocket and folded out a small magnifying glass. He leant back
over the map with the glass so he could see particular contours
and features in even greater detail and then wrote a series of
eight figure numbers in his book, locking down the precise location down to a few square metres.

"Okay," Martin said when he was finished without explaining
further.

"I deliberately left the method vague as you're far better
placed to decide that," Dan said.

"Mm yes; Winthrop's the way to go to begin with."

"But I'm happy to give any assistance I can."

Martin displayed the faintest eyebrow twitch indicating Dan
might not like what was coming next.

"Is Nick available to support?" Martin asked directly.

"Unless he can get some more time off then no. He goes back
to work early next week."

"What's your search experience?"

"None. Nick and I worked together on the surveillance team
for several years. He was the one who did things like rural ob-
servations, I went in other directions."

"Maybe Nick and I can get things rolling today and tomorrow
then. No offence but I would rather work alone than have to

worry about inexperience around me. By the sounds of it, the risk assessment is very low but that's not the point."

When they were finished and joined the others, Martin had formulated two action plans; the first included Nick, the second didn't. Amber and the twins had already abandoned their elders in favour of another day in town since Amber was due back at university in a few days' time.

"All good?" Nick asked as Dan and Martin took vacant seats around the kitchen table.

"Yes. Are you free to go up on Tissington Trail with Martin today? Back up duties," Dan answered with a question of his own.

Nick hesitated for a second before responding. "Sure. When do you want to go?"

"ASAP. You're on the clock I'm told," Martin said.

"Oh, right okay. You better tell me what you want and what I'll need then."

"A mountain bike and kit for a day out. You'll be hiding in plain sight, with eyes out for me. No great dramas. Just to give me a heads up on approaches while I'm doing my thing. I can then decide to either get out of the way or go completely covert depending on where I am and what I'm doing."

"Anything else?"

Without missing a beat and to the surprise of all Martin said, "Expect an eighteen to twenty-four hour shift."

"Why so long?" Dan asked.

As if to confirm in Martin's mind his work-only-with-suitable-staff rule, he addressed the room with an important fact regarding Winthrop searching.

"Winthrop is reliant on landmarks. Some are clearly visible during the day but disappear after dark and by the same token, night may throw up one or two you'd otherwise disregard in daylight. I want to do the route in daytime and at night. Get all the intel the first time and not give you half the story."

Martin's timely lesson showed Dan he was truly out of his depth and confirmed Martin's expertise.

Tara and Penny kept their own counsel during the conversations over Dan's lack of usefulness but they were thinking the same thing. When Nick and Martin went off to make final preparations, Tara asked Dan the obvious question.

"Why aren't you going with them, darling?"

He smiled back wryly. "Martin's a pro, an expert. He only works with experienced people too and I don't make the grade on this."

"Ooh that must sting a little."

"I don't have to like it to get it."

"I think this must be the first time since I've known you that you're taking a backseat."

"You're not helping."

Tara rested her hand on the top of his. "Sorry, just thinking out loud."

"What exactly are they going to do then?" Penny asked.

"What you suggested, Pen. Martin's going to Winthrop the trail. There's a possibility he could identify a building Stromboli was using. That would be our ultimate goal; after that, old and empty caches could still offer clues."

"Aren't you getting a bit too far off topic? How does that help you find out who killed Zoe?" Penny persisted.

"A building can often lead to a name, be it an owner or tenant. Whoever or whatever Stromboli was, is responsible for an integral part of her death. The reason he wants Nick there is because it's in his nature to do things properly; better to be over prepared than not prepared enough, and Nick's search experience is miles better than mine. Unfortunately for Nick, it might not be a picnic. I'm not just saying it because I'm not going, but he could be in for quite an uneventful time and we know what his patience level is like."

CHAPTER TWENTY-ONE

Nick and Martin chugged along in the latter's Land Rover, the GPS on his mobile phone providing directions. Nick's original backpack was deemed too garish and his gear was now stowed in an old grey spare Martin brought along. Their bikes were attached to the tow bar carrier, brakes and tyres checked.

In the company of someone more like a kindred spirit, Martin's usual bullish persona allowed his humorous side a little air. They joked about people and courses, which was the other thing they had in common and generally the ice-breaker subject of their meetings.

Martin's solitary existence, after a career of life or death, sculpted him into what he was now. Nick would never say he thought it strange Martin was in a customer-based business where he was required to deal with people all the time. Fortunately for him and more by happy accident than original design, the customers loved the oppressive Sergeant Major style of Martin's adventure courses and team building exercises because they were made to think and feel more like 'proper weekend warriors'. There was hardly a soul who after attending for a half-day or full weekend, didn't go home battered, bruised but keen to tell their friends what a great time they had.

"I thought you might bring the dogs with you," Nick said as they rattled over a cattle grid.

"I did think about it but for the sake of a day…" Martin clipped his sentence before starting a new one. "Floss has been a right shit lately; she's in season for the first time," he explained.

"Are you still going to breed from them?"

"That's the plan. Specialist search dogs for the MOD. Good money in it and they've already signed up to six pups in the first two years; paid in advance."

Nick laughed. "Bloody hell mate, you've become a right entrepreneur. How did you swing money up front?"

"I told them if they wanted to secure the lineage they would have to. Oh yeah, I'm all about the money these days, at least I am when it comes to them. I thought about naming all the pups from the first litter after world currencies as a nice little salute; you know Buck, Rand or Euro."

As Nick cracked up, Martin gave him his best innocent look. "What? They have to have names." He laughed.

Nick tried to look serious. "I knew you were army, but I didn't realise you were such a mercenary."

In Ashbourne they found the long stay car park in the town centre, paid, and unloaded their gear.

"First things first: café, tea, and fill the thermoses," Martin said, pointing to a blue sign on the other side of the car park advertising all day breakfasts.

The café was quiet, but they still selected the table in the farthest corner so Martin could run through a few things for his new sidekick.

"You'll be between eight hundred and twelve hundred metres behind me, bird watching if anyone asks; I've got a couple of books, a camera, and binos for you. I can't say how often I'll be stopping or how long each stop will last. Let me give you the short lesson."

"No need, I trust you," Nick said.

"There is. You might just see something I miss and so I want to know you know what to be looking for, okay?"

"Okay," Nick repeated, feeling slightly chastised.

"Winthrop puts you in the head of the person who made the cache," Martin emphasised. "Therefore it's an excellent way to actually locate it. Bear in mind the vast majority of the time items will be retrieved by someone other than the person who hid them, so it must be well hidden, easily accessible, and able to be quickly retrieved. It also has to be easily located with basic verbal instructions on where it's located.

"It relies on permanent landmarks to guide the finder to the exact spot where the cache is. Lone trees, pylons, telegraph poles, stone walls."

"I'm with you," Nick replied.

"It won't be the first landmark; that's always the starting point. From there you will be able to see the next one which wouldn't have been obviously apparent until you got to it. In Ireland you might go through a half dozen before you hit the jackpot.

"To be honest with you, it's much more like an art than a science; every Winthroper has their own idiosyncrasies. What is it?" Martin asked as Nick grunted.

"That's what Dan says about surveillance—more art than science."

"Yeah, he's right. Anyway, I want you to record a list of landmarks you see along the route; description and coordinates, got that?"

"Okay."

"Remember the first one is generally the biggest and most obvious. If they couldn't find the first one, they were fucked, so they made that one relatively easy for themselves. It's a good lesson for us. I'll compare what I've done with your list at the end, in case I've missed something."

"Okay," Nick repeated again.

"My routine is to search in circles radiating out from the landmark. One, two, five, and ten metres. Metal detector and digging. I'll do the landmark, clear it, and when it's clear, then look for the next landmark from that point. Metal detect to the next landmark also using my feet to feel the ground in case the cache's so many steps from landmark in the direction of the next I identify.

"Remember, there may be more than one landmark visible from where you are; if that's the case, do them all but go back to the first landmark in between so you can detect and feel the route."

"Got that," Nick replied, understanding his role more clearly.

"I'll tell you where I am and what I'm doing. If my actions are too unusual that's when I want you to be eyes out so you can give me a heads up on movement towards me from your direction."

"Okay."

"Any questions?"

"No, I'm good."

"All your gear and comms are in your bag. Batts are good for twelve to sixteen hours depending on use and temperature; keep your spare batt in your pocket. Comms check me every thirty minutes. That's it. No need to prevaricate."

They finished their tea and got the flasks filled for a nominal fee before Martin visited the bathroom. As they left the sun came out; for two mountain bikers about to tackle the trail it was a great day.

Dan didn't expect to have another free day so soon; with no other plans the prospect of going through all the same paperwork again just for the sake of it wasn't a pleasurable one. Instead, at Tara's suggestion he made a few calls and arranged to meet up with Father Eric and Purdy at Eric's parish home adjacent to the church. At first glance they made a very unlikely couple, but they actually had more in common than just their connections with Josie. Purdy was a stranger to Eric's house but not the church, regularly supplying the kitchen with bread and pastries her son Dale brought home from work or college.

Eric's work in the community involved near daily contact with the prostitutes and several of them were committed church goers. They were both also avid supporters of Notts County Football Club, the city's perennial second soccer team. Eric quipped being a man of faith was extremely useful when it came to following the Magpies.

The other thing they had in common was neither had any information.

"Do you know, I'm not actually surprised?" Dan remarked when first Purdy then Eric finished what they had to say. "Since we talked, I've come to realise Zoe was mixed up with something none of us knew about; a heroin supply network, possibly centred around an area at the southern end of the Peaks National Park. Those names I gave you were all very small pieces in a much bigger puzzle and Stromboli was a person or reference to the same thing.

"Twenty-two Powton Road was probably the place it was distributed from for Nottingham but only for a very short period. Do you remember a time when large amounts of heroin became very easy to obtain suddenly in early 2006?"

Eric and Purdy looked at each other and shook their heads.

"I don't think I would have been one of those to come to hear that sort of thing at that time," Eric said. "Plus, it's nearly ten years ago now."

"I do understand that, sorry."

"The sad thing is Josie would have been the person to go to for anything like that," Purdy said honestly but unhelpfully.

"Can you think of anyone else or anything else I could try?"

"Without wishing to sound obvious or condescending, if what you say is true wouldn't the police be your best bet?" Eric asked.

"That's a dead end. The Stromboli thing was at an investigative level way above the police, our equivalent to the Secret Service," Dan explained. "The operation I was part of, which led me to Powton Road, was completely ignorant of Stromboli. We thought we were identifying your quintessential local area dealers."

"But they were using some local teenagers in the process?" Eric asked. "Was it just like this before?"

"Yes. Zoe, Sean Darcy and the couple from Leicester, Knowles and Watt, are the ones we know of."

"And Powton Road was a very temporary address?"

"Yes."

"Surely there would be other addresses then which would have done the same before and after Powton Road was active. If you could somehow identify them, it might provide you with the leads you need."

Dan wasn't convinced and thought even if his confidence was higher, he would still have no immediate ideas on how to realise Eric's suggestion. "Maybe, but I wouldn't know where to start."

"With me," said Purdy assuredly.

"Great, but how?"

"All the girls and all the kids from that time remember Powton Road; how could any of us ever forget? And it wasn't as if it was the one and only place available. I could ask around to see what other houses they used at that time."

"Purdy's right, Dan. Just like they still do today. There will be a dozen or more empty or disused houses, flats, and buildings in constant use at any one time," Eric said a little more hopefully.

Dan was grateful for the help. "Again, thank you. I suppose we don't have anything to lose, do we?"

Martin consulted with his notebook again.

"The information is somewhere either side of Fenny Bentley and then one mile south of Alsop near to Scriveners Hollow, is that right?" he confirmed.

"Correct from the Zuckermans, according to what they re-member Zoe Summers saying and then the newspaper report of the Knowles-Watt story," Nick said.

"Mm, it's four miles from Fenny Bentley to Scriveners Hollow on the road and six, give or take, on the trail. The National Park begins north of Ashbourne and south of Fenny Bentley. I'm thinking we start where the park starts and go as far north as Quarry Farm on the other side of Alsop."

"Okay."

"I'm discounting the road to begin with; the trail is likely to be where any treasure is and not just because it's where the two kids were found. Take my word for it."

Nick nodded. "Let's get going then."

The Tissington Trail's formal entrance to the Peak District Na-tional Park was marked with a wooden sign and a stile; as Martin pedalled through, he looked down to his own OS map attached to the handlebars in a clear plastic sleeve so he could read it and keep it protected from the elements at the same time. His mind wandered back to previous searches and his own training.

He stopped just before a cattle grid and waited for Nick to join him. "The question is, suppose you're an insurgent and you want to position a weapons cache in a rural district. What con-siderations would you make when placing it? Security, accessi-bility, and distribution." When Nick nodded he continued. "The general location or outer markers are easily recognised features, for example a lone tree, specified telephone pole, or derelict building, and then the precise location by some smaller local mark on that or another inner feature like a scratch on a tree or a rock. This system enables a searcher to locate the cache with-in a micro-terrain by following usually verbal instructions and without the need for X-marks-the-spot style maps or sketches." Nick was still nodding. "For a long time back in the day, it was a virtually infallible technique until the army started thinking like the opposition. With the right sort of training and a little time, a group of guys emerged with the talent to comfortably put themselves in their shoes." He smiled, reminiscing. "The code word 'Jackpot' became a regular radio transmission."

"This is it then," Nick said.

"Yes mate, stay here and give me a couple of minutes. I'll do a comms check and you can start your follow, okay."

Almost to the second, two minutes later, Nick heard, "Martin to Nick. Comms check?"

He pressed a covert button. "Ten from ten."

"Likewise. Out," Martin replied.

Martin's bike computer was linked to his smartphone; at the completion of this exercise he could produce a comprehensive distance chart and map overlay to show all the places he stopped to search. Save for pressing a few buttons and keys, he could concentrate on the search itself and it didn't take long before he found his first potential marker.

About two hundred metres along the trail he spotted a rock which looked like the head and fin of a whale breaking the water's surface no more than fifty metres to his left.

"Nick from Martin; stopping now."

Nick looked at his bike computer, it was a clone of Martin's. "Roger that."

Martin rested the bike against a tree and pulled out a metal detector and spade from his backpack. They were both folded into three parts for ease of transport. The detector beeped into life when he switched it on and he tested it against the bike, adjusting the depth identifier. He then set off from the point he first saw the rock in a straight line towards it. The technique relied on straight lines between two markers, which made his life easy, so long as he started from the correct position.

In the enemy's shoes, it meant a conversation or description like, 'You go along the trail for two hundred metres and you'll see a rock which looks like a whale on your left.' Therefore, if the cache was X number of steps towards the whale, it must be from where it was first seen. It couldn't work otherwise.

The initial search out to the rock resulted in no indication from the detector, which wasn't a surprise. In case the rock was the location of the cache, Martin carefully checked it for a scratch, mark, or other signature first, to show him where to dig but there wasn't anything visible. Next, he detected around a metre from the rock's base. Nothing. He took the spade and started to dig the same radius looking for disturbances in the soil, an indication it had been dug before. This process took twenty-five minutes and when he was finished, he had a reasonable sweat going.

He stopped for a drink from his water bottle and then repeated the detecting process, this time two metres out from the rock.

Behind Martin, Nick found his spot and settled down for the wait. He was content with his good view of the trail's start and knew he didn't look too conspicuous. To complete his cover appearance, he rested his bird-watchers bible and notebook next to him and slung the binoculars around his neck.

Thirty minutes in he did a comms check, which was ten from ten. After two more checks and no other trail users to report, he knew all he ever wanted to about Pied Wagtails and was about to make his next call to Martin when to his relief, he was beaten to it.

"Nick from Martin; moving on. Nothing here."

"Roger that," Nick replied.

When he passed the spot where he could see the whale rock a couple of minutes later, he said out loud, "Two hundred metres in two and half hours. Shit, only another twelve k's to go."

He was expecting a call to stop at any moment, followed by another several hours waiting, and wished he could swap places with Dan, who through their surveillance history together was always the patient one when it came to operational tasks.

He was so busy feeling miserable at the prospect he was pleasantly surprised to note it was the best part of two miles before Martin called the next stop, which was a small bridge.

The whale rock was a complete blow out. Martin detected and dug nothing of interest. When he was finished with the other searches at five, then ten metres, he climbed on top of the rock to see if there were other markers visible from it that could have led him to a new marker and another repeat of the last few hours' activity. There wasn't anything to see though, and he had no idea how relieved Nick would have been to know that. Winthrop searches were by definition time and effort intensive. Martin gave no thought to being disappointed; there were likely to be a score of similar search opportunities before this job finished.

The small bridge was over a stream that bubbled along at a good pace. He input the details into the computer and set the bike down before he pulled out his detector and spade.

He smirked, imagining Nick three minutes behind and about to stop; maybe pulling a muesli or chocolate bar from his backpack and no doubt berating himself for not bringing more food.

The bridge was made of stone and obviously pre-dated the time in question. As with the whale rock, Martin examined it first for a marker; satisfied there wasn't one, he dropped down to the nearest bank and detected along one side of the stream at a distance of a metre for ten metres. He then vaulted across to the other side and repeated the process back to the bridge; the detector remained silent throughout. Content to follow his tried and tested methodology, he got to work with his spade. An hour later he was finished and ready to move on.

After the fourth unsuccessful stop and search, Martin and Nick liaised for refreshments and a debrief at one of the trail's designated spots, which was equipped with a wooden picnic bench seat and table combination, water fountain, and photo opportunity.

"It's been quiet; good for us. How many, three?" Martin said referring to the lack of other trail users.

"I guess it's not the most popular time of the year to be doing this," Nick concluded.

Martin ate slowly as he updated Nick with the news, or rather lack of news, in his own inimitable style. "It's a good source. Security, accessibility, and distribution all available. Making good time."

"Really?" Nick replied.

Martin looked surprised by Nick's doubtful tone. "Shit yeah. We might get over halfway before dark and then we've got all night to do the entire route, leaving plenty of time tomorrow to finish where we call the daytime halt in a few hours."

"Whatever you say." Nick grimaced.

Martin was too focused on the task in hand to worry about Nick's feelings.

"As it's been a long time since these caches were active, I was worried about the growth of the trees causing obstruction and making the search pretty difficult, but as the trail is an old railway, it's elevated. Back when it was constructed, they must have cleared a hell of a lot because trees aren't causing too many issues; in fact, this is a relatively easy search so far. Five minutes and then we go, okay?"

In exactly five minutes Martin climbed aboard his bike again.

"Give me three minutes unless you hear from me before. Comms check?"

Nick depressed his covert microphone activator. "Ten from ten."

It was a full ten minutes before Martin did call to halt their latest progress, by which time he was almost a kilometre south of Tissington Hall, the seventeenth century mansion house. Nick would have to find somewhere and prepare himself for another lengthy wait.

The slow procession of stop, wait, and move on continued through the day.

When it started to get too dark for Martin to rely on naked eyesight alone, he knew it was the time to stop this phase and switch to night mode.

"Nick from Martin. Stopping here; on me."

"Okay, see you in a minute," Nick replied.

When he arrived at Martin's location, they shared a flask of tea and another catch up on the state of progress.

"We're well past halfway so we go to the far end at Quarry Farm and then work south back to Fenny Bentley," Martin said.

He finished marking their exact position by placing a white stone on a tree-stump and entering coordinates into his computer, ensuring he could return to it again in the light and then they set of at a brisk speed to maximise the work time. It also made a very welcome change of pace.

Quarry Farm may have been an actual farm at some point in the past but now it was no more than a name on the map. Martin considered the intelligence and the more or less nil risk attached to what they were doing.

"We might as well stick together from now on; I can't see us being compromised and having an extra pair of hands will help with lighting up our search areas. I still need you to be looking in case I miss something," Martin said as they set off.

It soon became apparent to Nick that any initial identification markers were relative to the time of day and hours of darkness searches made them much less frequent and much more obvious. As they passed several he might have stopped at, Martin explained his reasons not to, which ranged from just being plain wrong to a more detailed rationale of mitigating factors.

Their first stop at his direction was on the southern side of Alsop, at a place the map didn't give a name to.

Having not been with Martin throughout the day, Nick couldn't gauge his first reaction. Martin went through the routine of logging the map reference and preparing his kit.

What he neglected to tell Nick before was that at night, geographical features figured at the top of any list. They had stopped on a sharp incline, no more than a pimple on the landscape, but higher by far than anything within a half mile radius. Nick noted straight away that Martin liked this one. As they set their bikes down, Nick followed Martin's gaze; he was looking out over a vista which offered an unobstructed three-sixty-degree view.

"I can see why this would be a good start off," he said, taking in the countryside, which was eerily clear under the moonlit sky. His watch read 6:27 p.m.

"Whereabouts were the Knowles and Watt couple found?" Martin asked.

Nick checked his notebook. "Close to a place called Scriveners Hollow the local rag said."

Martin switched on the lamp attached to his helmet and consulted the OS map once again, holding it flat so Nick could see.

"Which is here," he indicated after a moment.

"And we're here; that's close," Nick said quietly.

Martin looked at him, so his light shone into Nick's face. "Less than two hundred metres. We might be getting a bit excited about this one, mate."

"Are we?"

"Tell me what you see?"

Nick looked around their immediate vicinity, but the pimple was featureless. "Bugger all from what I can see."

Martin confirmed what he thought. "Yes, the wind and weather has kept this spot clear over the years; hundreds if not thousands."

"And I'm taking it that's good for us because?"

"Because it will stick out like a dog's dick from all directions. Now get your head up a bit more and tell me again what you see," Martin said flatly.

Nick did as he was told. The old rail line went around one side of the base of their vantage point; other than that, there wasn't anything but wispy grass and small rocks for the first several metres. He gazed out into the near distance, slowly allowing his eyes to take in more and more of the countryside. There were a few copses of trees in the mid-distance, which in the dark terrain looked like colonies of giant penguins huddling together against the winds in an Attenborough documentary.

"It's pretty bleak and barren," he said after a minute.

"When we were in the Province, they had habit of placing a cache in the line of sight of a friendly house, so they could keep an eye on it from a distance if they wanted to. There were a number of advantages until we caught on."

Nick understood Martin was giving him a clue. He looked again and then used his binos for an even better look. Three quarters through another rotation he saw something: a squat, black object, he guessed six hundred metres away to the west. His eyes scanned it more closely until he identified a door and then a window on the side facing them. It was a small cottage built from stone and old enough it now appeared a natural part of the land it sat in, not an obvious manmade addition. When he lowered the glasses and looked at Martin. "So, what do we do?"

"From my point of view there are no other features between us and the house. I can't tell if the house is occupied so we ought to take some care. I suggest we check it out first; if it's empty, we can move around more freely."

Nick felt a little uncomfortable. "Isn't it a bit too obvious though?"

"It is, but only because it's dark and we're looking for something to be a marker or a hiding place. If we were just two blokes riding along, we wouldn't see a thing. Even in daylight you would ride over the little hump here without a second thought."

As soon as they stowed their bikes, they set off in a straight line towards the house, moving in single file with Martin taking the lead. He dismissed the idea to use the detector in favour of getting to the house in the most efficient way. The route was relatively easy to navigate; other than a few rocks, bushes, or tufts of long grass the terrain was smoother than it was undulating, causing Nick to comment halfway across that it looked more difficult than it was in reality.

From eighty or so metres out from the post and wire fence perimeter the house appeared unoccupied. They could see a window on the northern side was broken. A tattered curtain flapped out of it occasionally like a loose tongue. There was no sign of lights on inside, no parked vehicles outside. They were convinced well before they got to the front door, which itself put the exclamation mark on the vacant nature of the property, it being nailed into position at the top and bottom.

"No need to go in now. Let's clear the outside, see what there is to see and then detect back to the high point. We can review the situation there," Martin proposed.

"Just tell me this, is it as good as I think you think this could be?" Nick asked cryptically.

"Never say never, always say maybe," Martin replied, unfolding the detector.

The cottage was a perfect square, two stories, two windows on each with a back door that mirrored the front positionally but was half the size. The rear also sported a small central window just below the eaves, indicating an attic space. The overgrown outside further demonstrated the house must have been empty for many years; there were two outbuildings, both stone boxes with corrugated iron roofs and wooden slat doors. Nick took some photos of the buildings from all sides.

"The six hundred metre distance back to the hump is going to be a six-kilometre walk," Martin said.

Nick's eyes widened. "Why so long?"

Waving the detector Martin said, "I'm going to sweep this five metres either side of the straight line all the way back to give us a ten-metre corridor. If there's a cache, we need a bit of leeway to hit it."

"Are you really expecting to find evidence of an old dump?"

"No, you never expect to. Let's get on with it. Front door to the centre of the hump's base. You go ahead of me on that line and I'll sweep behind you. Don't get too far ahead though, okay."

As they moved off, the clearish evening darkened as clouds scudded across the sky like theatre curtains. The detector beeped several times before they were clear of the garden area; "Just a Coke can." Martin said, as Nick looked to see the first time. A minute later Martin held up a horseshoe which was buried close to the surface.

"Bound to be household crap here. Don't worry. At least the kit's operating well."

The twenty metres beyond the garden gate were silent. Nick kept looking ahead to keep on track with the hump, which was surprisingly easy to see even in the gathering.

"There's a low post here, watch your knees," he said over his shoulder as he caught the top of a pole in his helmet light.

"Thanks," Martin replied without looking up or altering his sideways steps.

Nick continued onwards at what felt like a snail's pace, conscious his friend was covering ten times the distance.

When the detector beeped, Nick froze and held his breath.

Martin bent down; the detector was indicating the source of the beep was either on the surface or very close to it. The light didn't immediately reveal anything and so he ran the detector across the area again, causing another beep. Nick saw when he rubbed his hand over the grass, Martin's fingers caught in something.

"Just a bit of wire on the ground," he said to Nick. "Carry on."

Nick stepped off with his right foot, put his left down, and by the time his right was about to hit the ground again the detector beeped once more.

"Wire again. Can you give me a hand?" Martin asked.

Nick retraced his steps. "What?"

"I think it's part of the same length of wire but there's no fence here. Can you help me pull it up without breaking it? Careful, it's rusty as hell."

Nick curled the fingers of both hands around the wire, cradling it gently like spiders' silk.

"You lift and pull as I clear the ground. We're going back towards the first contact," Martin directed.

He used both hands to untangle the grass as Nick gently put upwards pressure on the wire. The first couple of metres were slow going but suddenly the wire sprung up like a jack-in-the-box as it became free. They both looked up and followed the rusty vein to the low post Nick indicated just a few minutes before.

"What the fuck?" Martin said involuntarily.

Nick was less impressed. "So, it's a fence post."

"Don't be an arse, Nick. What fence do you know that's only knee high? Look, there's only the one strand of wire; no other staples or nails in the post."

"So?"

Martin huffed loudly. "Stand here." He indicated for Nick to straddle the small post.

"Now hold on a minute while I find the other end of the wire again."

Nick watched as Martin followed the wire to the point it disappeared into the grass again. He pulled it taught and looked along its length back to Nick.

"What do you see?"

It took a moment for Nick to realise how to look. Martin's helmet light was directly above the wire and aimed at him. The twenty-five or so metres of wire being tight therefore must be in a straight line between him and Martin, he reasoned. His gaze went up, past Martin's head, and in a laser-straight line behind him in the distance was the dead centre of the hump.

"Shit!" he exclaimed.

"It's a bloody guideline," Martin said.

He was soon back in search mode; instructing Nick to follow the wire, freeing it as he went. Having the wire to follow, Nick proceeded much more swiftly.

It still took forty-five minutes before Nick arrived at the hump, locating another low post no more than a spit from its base. As instructed, he then trekked back to Martin who was about halfway across the total distance, on his hands and knees with his spade.

Nick held up a light so Martin could see a little better; after a few seconds he liberated an old fifty pence piece that must have been dropped there years before. Martin rubbed the soil and green slime off the coin's surface. Nick leant forward so he could see the silhouette of the Queen. Squinting at it he still couldn't make out the date.

"1988," Martin said. I can't see anybody accidentally dropping it here unless they were going to or from the house. The most enthusiastic walker wouldn't come this far off the trail. Let's keep going." He handed the spade to Nick rather than stowing it in his backpack again.

It was another hour and twenty minutes before they approached the hump.

"What's next?" Nick asked.

Martin's detector was mostly quiet since the fifty pence piece discovery, although it did pick up something Martin thought was a musket ball possibly dating back to the Civil War.

Just as Nick was going to suggest another cup of tea, the detector sounded off close to the base of the post.

"That's not the wire," Martin confirmed. He wafted the detector again and it beeped an arm's length away from the post and wire.

"It's buried, whatever it is," he said. "I'll hold the light and you dig; slow and careful."

A grassy tuft seemed to be directly over the source of the detection. Nick got the spade under the roots and pulled it up in one large clump. While he held it out Martin scanned it with no response. Nick threw it aside and watched as Martin laid the detector over the bare patch of earth. It beeped again.

"Really careful mate," he said, intensifying Nick's nervousness.

Nick put the spade in the soil again and pushed down with his foot; it disappeared below ground. He angled the shaft back towards himself, so the blade lifted a mound of soggy, black dirt. Martin shone his light while Nick continued shaking the spade gently as the soil fell off in small clumps onto a section of already cleared ground just behind them.

"There. Stop," Martin directed.

Nick held the half-loaded spade still while Martin reached down and picked up a small round lump. It looked like dirt to Nick but when Martin ran the detector over it, it beeped.

"It's very light," Martin said as if it would make things clear to Nick. "What the hell is it?"

Nick put the spade down and peered at the object in Martin's open palm. It still looked like a lump of soil.

"Get the water bottle out of my bag?" Martin said.

Nick found the bottle and squirted some water onto the object. The caked-on soil washed off, leaving Martin holding what looked like a dull grey walnut.

Nick picked it up and was surprised at how just light it was. A moment of uncertainty then crystallised. "It's tin foil. Maybe somebody's ancient sandwich wrapper."

"You could have had me going there for a minute." Martin chuckled.

Nick handed it over for Martin to examine. After a moment rolling it in his fingers Martin nodded. "I suppose if we come back, we don't want to find it all over again. What we find we take back and chuck away at home. Even this."

It was nearly 11:00 p.m. and they still had a distance to go to complete the searching of the trail during the hours of darkness. Rather than rest on the laurels of their recent activity, which was very interesting but of unknown importance, what mattered right now was getting on because once this current phase was done, they still had to complete the daylight search.

Dan resisted the temptation to call for updates all day. After his visit with Eric and Purdy he and Tara drove down to Warwick Castle where they spent the remainder of the day exploring the medieval fortress originally built by William the Conqueror.

"Are you okay? You've been pretty quiet," Tara asked as they looked out from one of the southern ramparts towards the River Avon that curled away below them. "Is it Nick and Martin?"

"Sorry," Dan replied, burying his hands deeper into his pockets.

"No need to be sorry. What's up?"

"Of course, I'd like to be involved, and I do understand why I'm not."

"I feel a 'but' in there somewhere?"

Dan snatched a glance behind them; they were alone.

"I have a feeling we might never know why Zoe died. I've been thinking it for a few days now."

"She was mixed up in a world of drugs and drug dealers, Dan. The other couple who died too. Doesn't that go to show how horrible and dangerous the whole situation was?"

Dan slowly pulled one hand out and slid his arm around her shoulder.

"T, all that does is go towards how she died, not why."

"I don't really understand what the difference is then?"

"The more we've found out recently the less we seem to know. This Stromboli thing for instance. Can you imagine Jim, as the most senior detective in the whole force, was basically told it was a need to know and he didn't! If Zoe was somehow a piece of that sort of puzzle, do you really think we've got a hope in hell of putting it all together eight or nine years later?"

"We're all doing our best. No one could ask more."

"I know," he sighed. "But will it all have been worth it? Not just Zoe; everything."

They decided to have dinner out, arriving back at Nick's as the late-night news on TV was starting. Penny and Amber were sitting arm in arm on the sofa.

"Look at you two. I hope I'm still cuddling up with Bradley when he's your age," Tara said by way of hello.

Amber smiled. "What did you think of Warwick?"

"Lovely! Very chocolate-box cover."

Dan dropped into a chair and tried to focus on the latest headlines, which seemed to involve more trouble for Britain's railway system. "Have you heard anything from Nick, Pen?"

"He called much earlier to say he was sitting around not doing much at all, but I've not heard from him since this afternoon."

Dan checked his watch. "I might go and have a shower," he said, excusing himself.

"Is he alright?" Penny asked after a minute.

Tara smiled. "I think it's all starting to catch up. He's spent close to the last four years trying to clear out all the skeletons in his cupboard and find some way to make peace with them. I know there are times he wishes he hadn't even started."

"It must be exhausting," Amber said.

"Even I can only guess. I know he feels terribly guilty still with things like my brother and Josephine Lamas. He said today he didn't know if any of it would have been worth it if this last part remains unresolved."

CHAPTER TWENTY-TWO

Nick and Martin were nearing the end. Their Winthrop through the night finished hours before the sun came up. They made an executive decision to ride back to Ashbourne at 4:30 a.m. to hopefully find an all-night café where they could relax and wait before going back again to complete the daylight search. After the highs and lows of the stone house, guide wire, and tin foil, they searched three other locations all with negative results. Nick was very tired although assisting Martin rather than sitting around did help.

The Pit Stop café was perfect; clearly a local taxi driver haunt, they were able to refuel themselves with hot food and drink and were left in peace by the lone disinterested staff member, who still had a couple of hours until the end of his shift.

Feeling revitalised at first light, the ride back to where they called a halt the previous dusk was no hardship.

It was now 11:45 a.m. and they'd searched another four locations, making a grand total of thirteen over the twenty-five-hour sortie.

"Good fun eh? And it stayed dry," Martin said as they started back from Quarry Farm for the last time.

"Thanks. We couldn't have done this," Nick replied, patting his friend on the back as they continued along, side by side.

"When will you come back to that stone cottage again do you think?"

"Dan will be chomping at the bit, but I need to sleep for a while. Tomorrow maybe. Can you stay? You're more than welcome."

Martin took in another deep breath of fresh air. "Cheers. Can I let you know when I've checked to see if there have been any calls or enquiries for the business?"

Nick pushed down on the pedals increasing his speed. "Come on, let's get this done."

A few seconds later he was regretting his moment of enthusiasm as Martin sped past him, leaving him struggling to catch up, and then keep up.

"Welcome back. You look knackered," Dan said as Nick walked in through the back door, followed by Martin, who was carrying two backpacks.

"Hello. I bet you managed a good, comfy sleep, though did you?" Nick replied. "Can someone put the kettle on please?"

"Hi Martin. How are you?" Tara said, getting up from the table and switching the kettle on, which was full in readiness.

"Fine thanks. It was nice to get out and rattle the old brain cells again."

"How did you get on?" Dan asked.

Tara tapped his head. "Hey, give them a minute to sit down."

"Thank you, Tara. I'm glad someone appreciates our efforts." Nick grinned.

Tea and toast for Nick and Martin was followed by an agonising half hour wait for Dan as they were then pushed out by Penny to get cleaned up and changed out of their dirty gear.

When they returned looking and smelling a great deal better Dan finally got to hear what happened on Tissington Trail.

Martin debriefed the exercise as a whole, including the general details of the overall usefulness and number of searches completed. He then explained that in his opinion the only search worthy of further investigation was at the stone house and elevated trail hump.

"From what you said regarding a distribution site and potential sites for caches, it was the only search venue I thought covered all your bases."

Nick uploaded the information from the bike computers and Martin's smartphone onto Dan's laptop so everybody could see a map of the area, the sites of their searches, and other relevant distance information. On his machine, he then brought up an Ordnance Survey map of the area.

"This is the cottage, here is the hump, and this red line denotes the guide wire we found. Now if I put in the coordinates of where Gary Knowles and his girlfriend were found you can see that it's no more than two hundred metres from the hump; one hundred and sixty-four to be precise.

"We didn't think to go into the house as it was dark, we were limited by time, and you're not going to lose anything by going back to it over the next day or so when you've made a plan," Nick said to Dan.

"There was no sign of a cache, although if there was one between the house and the hump along the line of the wire, I do honestly think we would have come across it," Martin said.

"We did make one find though; a fifty pence piece minted in 1988. It was here." Nick pointed to a yellow dot on the laptop again.

"Unlikely to have got there from somebody using the trail isn't it?" Dan asked.

"That's what we said," Martin concurred. "More likely dropped by someone going along the wire to or from the house."

Nick produced a small snap-lock bag and placed it on the table. Dan opened it and held it so the coin dropped out along with two grey balls, one larger than the other.

"What are they?" Penny asked.

"Martin reckons this is a musket ball," Nick said, holding up the smaller sphere and rolling it between his thumb and index finger.

"And this?" Penny said again, picking up the other.

Nick laughed. "It's an old bit of tin foil. We brought it back to throw away here rather than leaving it to find again if we have to do another search of the same area."

Penny dropped it back on the table. "Yuck." She wiped her hand on her jeans.

"So, we're thinking about going back tomorrow morning and have a proper look around the stone house. Martin can stay another day at least. What do you think?" Nick asked.

Everybody looked at Dan, but he didn't reply. He was fully engrossed with the tin foil ball.

"You alright, what is it?" Nick asked.

Dan heard the question but was too focused to answer.

"Can someone get me a clean sheet of paper?" he whispered.

A few moments later Nick, Martin, Tara, and Penny were lost in pensive silence as they watched Dan slowly trying to prise the foil open without breaking it. He started with his bare fingers, but it soon became clear the structure of the foil was so degraded something more delicate was required. Penny found two cocktail sticks which Dan rubbed on the palm of his hand to blunt the sharp points. He immediately got more success in finding an edge that just about stayed intact as he pulled it away from the body of the fragile ball.

It took several more minutes before the foil was halfway flat. As Dan worked, flecks of brown and black dropped onto the paper; even though there was no physical effort involved he found himself breathing hard and was careful not to blow them away by exhaling too heavily.

The near silence was broken by Nick after a slightly larger piece of black matter dropped onto the paper.

"Will you please tell us what the hell you're playing at?"

"Did you say this was by your guide wire?"

"Right by the post, at the trail end."

"And Gary Knowles and Susie Watt's bodies were discovered a hundred and sixty metres away?"

Nick gulped. "Yes. One, six, four."

Dan finally got the foil fully open and flat. It was about thirty centimetres square and save for the half dozen puncture holes he put in it over the past few minutes, was in one piece. One side was predominantly gunmetal grey and the other was combination of grey and black. The paper was covered with hundreds of tiny specs.

Dan leant forward and carefully sniffed at both sides of the foil, but he couldn't make out anything.

"Dan?" Tara asked.

He was still yet to touch it with his hands and was almost too scared to do so in case he was wrong. Or in case he was right.

"I'm not sure. What do you think this stuff is?" he said prodding the bits of black with one of the cocktail sticks.

"It just looks like dirt. It's been lying on the ground for God knows how long, remember," Penny said.

"No, look." Dan bent the foil gently and more tiny black shards fell away onto the paper.

"This black stuff is not discoloured foil; it's stuck to the foil."

The time had come to test his theory. Dan dabbed a finger onto some of the black particles so they stuck. As the others watched on, he rubbed his thumb like Nick did with the musket ball earlier and then smeared his finger across the edge of the paper. The heat generated by his rubbing was enough for his needs; his digit left a streaky smudge on the paper and a waxy residue on the tip of his finger.

"It's shoe polish," he said.

Dan next spent a short while describing a scenario that was both unlikely and unarguable.

"Knowles and Watt were working for Stromboli in the same way Zoe was a while later. The drugs get wrapped in foil and then dipped into melted shoe polish which protects it and helps make it undetectable to smell. Probably, and this is a guess, it got further wrapped with more foil or plastic."

Nick took up the story again. "So poor old Gary and Susie nicked some and decided to make a run for it by going back to the trail from the house. They unwrap it when they get to the hump and chuck the foil away."

"Maybe they didn't realise how pure the heroin was or maybe they were just stupid or unlucky. Anyway, their party ends very quickly and unhappily," Dan said.

Nick grinned. "I suppose that answers the question of what we're going to do next. Well, I need my bed first but tomorrow morning? We can go early."

"Yes definitely. Thank you, really, thanks both of you," Dan said.

A while later when Nick and Martin were sleeping their previous day and night's adventures away, Dan was in the garden room. The foil was now safely folded in half and put inside a clear plastic document holder. He was thinking about his recent update to Jim when Tara joined him. They studied the flimsy square.

"Didn't see that coming, did we?" she said as Dan held it up to the light.

"You can say that again."

"I bet you can't wait to get to that old house, can you?"

"Need you ask?"

"If it was the distribution point, what do you think you might find?"

"Quite possibly nothing. Knowles and Watt may not have been too clever, but Stromboli certainly was. The place should have been cleared and cleaned up when they left. The best I can tell is the house was part of a farm called Dell Farm according to some post-war maps and documents. The main farmhouse burned down in 1951 and was never rebuilt. I'm not sure who owned it after that, or who owns it today."

Tara clicked her tongue. "That's a shame, you said if there was an owner or a tenant..."

"I know now this is just more of what I was worried about yesterday. It tells us a little more about how Zoe died but still not why."

"You mean the shoe polish?"

"Exactly. She was in contact with it all the time either melting it down or dipping the wrapped heroin in it, or both. It explains her absence from Mapperley, the shoe polish on her and in her, and maybe what she was doing at Powton Road."

"How's that?"

Dan put the plastic document holder down.

"She might have been making a delivery to the pop-up at the time. I'm only guessing."

Tara thought for a minute as Dan watched the clouds. "If Zoe was visiting number twenty-two, how would she have known about you or why try to help or warn you? Why kill her if she was working for them?"

"She was killed because they knew or suspected she was trying to help me. I still can't get past that but in reality, I don't know T, I've no idea."

Martin was back up and looking completely refreshed in two hours, however it was another three before Nick reappeared, still looking the worse for wear. After a large orange juice, he felt ready enough for a talk about what Dan proposed for the next day.

It was more an exchange of views than a briefing. Dan hadn't been there and although the photos and written information was good, it was no substitute for personal knowledge. By the same token, Nick and Martin wanted to defer to his wishes regarding the objectives.

"The easiest thing is to treat it as a crime scene; look first and don't contaminate it. Next, search, identify, preserve, and seize anything evidential," Dan said. He turned to Martin. "Is it worth a further search for old caches between the house and the hump?"

Martin considered the idea. "I would say no but there's no harm in taking the kit if you change your mind when we get there. I'll just need to re-charge my detector."

"That sounds fair enough. On that note, what tools or equipment will we need?"

"Leave that to me," Nick said thinking his toolbox in the garage would have all they might require, including a large crowbar for the nailed up front door.

"Do you have any idea about how we can find out who is the owner or was previously? All this intel and hardly a name is giving me a major headache," Dan said as an aside.

"It would have to be a local authority thing. I'm not sure if being within the boundaries of the national park has something to do with it as well. I don't know anyone myself, but I can ask," Nick answered.

"What about estate agents?"

"It's worth a try. I'll ask Pen to ring some to see."

Sometime later when the house was in an unusual period of quiet, Dan and Amber found themselves alone in the garden room.

"Tara said you were a bit frustrated with the lack of names to go with all the information. Is that suspects about Zoe Summers death?"

Dan folded the newspaper he was holding but not reading. "It's all very odd. Normally, and especially in a small area like Mapperley, a few names would come up. Adam Vikkert was at

Powton Road that night, Craig Matthews was there for a minute or two, and the other one we think was Billy McKenzie. Vikkert and McKenzie are small-fry and from what we know of them neither can be genuine suspects. Craig Matthews or Matt Craig, whoever he really is, doesn't match up to the physical description either. He might well be involved with Stromboli and be connected to Zoe that way, but I don't think he killed her."

Amber shook her head. "But Sean Darcy. When you asked him about Adam Vikkert, his reaction. He said he stayed right away from him because he was mad."

"And then he went on about Stromboli," Dan continued. "I know, but he's not the killer, trust me."

"Is it worth going back to Darcy again to see if he will tell us any more?" Amber queried.

"No chance. I don't think he'd talk to us if we turned up with a mountain of cigarettes and chocolate."

"So, what did he mean about Vikkert then?"

Dan mimicked her head shake.

"Come on Dan, this is your specialty."

"What do you mean?"

"I mean, maybe we missed something in what he did say."

"He was already getting agitated before I asked about Adam Vikkert. Stromboli was a reaction to that. He really didn't want to think about Vikkert did he? 'I stay away from that mad fucker,' he said."

"So, what does that mean? Why does he think Adam Vikkert is so mad?"

Dan thought back to the hostel's day room. It took a moment to bring the picture of the scene back into the front of his mind and then put the soundtrack to it.

"I said 'there's no such thing as a secret in Mapperley, Sean. You must know something else.' He said 'I don't. Zoe wanted to get away and this was her chance.' He promised he didn't know she was back. I then said, 'what about your friend Vikkert. Tell us about him?' And that's when he blew his top. His exact words were, 'no way; I stayed right away from that mad fucker.' He almost shouted it out and then without us saying anything else he said 'Stromboli.'" He looked at Amber. "That was it."

"You're right, that doesn't explain why he would get so crazy about Adam Vikkert."

"No, I said 'your friend Vikkert?'" Dan corrected her.

Amber's eyes narrowed. "Are you sure?" Before he could reply she went on. "No sorry of course you're sure. But if you said your friend Vikkert…" She hesitated for a second and Dan leant forward, dropping the newspaper on the floor.

"What if he wasn't thinking Adam Vikkert? What if he was thinking of another Vikkert?"

He re-ran the scene again and again, playing the fractious exchange over while Amber watched with bated breath.

She was right. Dan leapt to his feet and hugged her so hard she thought he might break her ribs.

"Amber you're going to make a fantastic detective one day."

For the next few minutes they revelled in their delight before calling the others to arms. Dan was sure all the checks he, Nick, and Jim had completed so far were on Adam Vikkert; they had never searched just the surname for other Vikkerts.

When Nick entered an asterisk where a first name was usually placed, thereby instructing the computer to search for all Vikkerts on the system, their optimism was rewarded and joy unconfined.

"Edward Daniel Vikkert," Nick read from the screen. "Date of birth 06.11.69. Sixteen, no, seventeen previous convictions for dishonesty, violence, and drugs. I'm printing it now."

Edward Vikkert was Adam Vikkert's uncle but other than the blood relation there were no links between the two on the police's databases, which wasn't wholly surprising. They were a generation apart with no common associates and they clearly operated in very different circles. Adam was a pathetic amateur in comparison to his uncle's history.

Edward was a career criminal and was, it seemed, currently serving an eight-year prison sentence for a serious assault. He had been in Leicester Prison for the last two and half years. According to his history though, he wasn't incarcerated in 2006. Dan called Jim with this latest update in case his studies and knowledge revealed something more than he and Nick harvested. After dinner they and Martin remained at the table with Edward Vikkert's printouts.

"I can definitely say I didn't see him at Powton Road, or at all during the whole operation when I was undercover, come to that," Dan said, propping up a 2004 custody photograph of Vikkert against his water glass.

"It's not a face you forget quickly," Martin added.

It was true; Edward Vikkert wasn't an attractive man. His badly broken nose was nearly flat against his face and he had a lazy left eye, all of which made him look like an elderly, tired pug dog. In the colour photo he wore a number one skinhead haircut that showed a long white scar across the top of his head, adding to the overall unpleasant appearance. There was little or no family resemblance to his nephew for which the latter must have been very grateful.

"He has the size and character to have done it," Nick said.

Dan agreed. "But there's nothing about an injured hand in the files. That's not to say he hasn't. I wonder if there's a way of finding out. What are the references to him at that time again?" He roamed through the printouts while Nick consulted with his laptop in a meaningless race to see who could find the details first.

"Here it is," Nick said. "Arrested but not charged with glassing someone in a pub in Mapperley two weeks before Zoe died. No complaint by the victim who was taken to hospital with a gashed face."

Nick tapped more keys to bring up the custody record relating to the incident.

"He was taken to Nottingham North. Nothing on here about a hand injury. Because of his drunken state he wasn't interviewed and the following morning he was released due to the non-complaint."

"Who was the victim?" Dan asked.

"Hold on, it's right here. Ashley Royce. That rings a bell. Where do we know him from?"

Dan knew straight away. "Ashley Royce is the chef with the knife. Remember Darcy's associate from the intel reports? He got community service for an assault."

They grinned at each other as two more puzzle pieces clicked together.

As Nick found Vikkert's incident report preceding Zoe's murder, Dan began to look for the next one after. It didn't take too long to find.

"The day after she was killed, he's a passenger in a fail-to-stop stolen car. The car crashed, and he made a run for it before getting caught; then he assaulted police during the arrest. This guy is a real charmer. Again, nothing about a hand injury on this custody record either."

They went over both incidents twice more but there wasn't anything more apparent on closer inspection.

As Dan stacked up the paperwork Martin said, "What's indisputable is that when you mentioned the Vikkert name to Sean Darcy the first thing he said was Stromboli. You're the cops but if you ask me, Darcy at least must have thought there was something between the two of them."

"Agreed," Nick said.

"Even with his drugs history Vikkert doesn't strike me as the type to be able to conceive and implement this Stromboli supply structure. But he's absolutely associate material or handy muscle to have around."

"Well you know where he is. Visiting days are Monday and Tuesday," Nick said as he closed the laptop.

Dan rubbed his hands together. "I was just thinking the same thing."

CHAPTER TWENTY-THREE

Dan didn't mind in the slightest being on Penny's basic weekender bike. As they approached the hump, how he might appear to other trail users on the ladies' sky-blue machine was a distant second to what he hoped was waiting to be discovered in and around the stone house.

Martin's backpack contained an array of equipment, while his and Nicks were empty; a premature and optimistic consideration that they may have to carry evidential material home afterwards.

They slowed a short distance before the hump and allowed two minutes for anyone coming up behind them to pass before they dismounted and carried their bikes off the hump and into the scrubland between it and the house. Martin led them on an easy ten-minute walk, scanning the ground as he went to make best use of the daylight for what he couldn't see or may have missed two nights before.

They leaned the bikes against the back of the house where they couldn't be seen from the trail, but Martin still insisted on covering them with an old gate which was lying on the grass.

"Over to you two," he said.

Nick pulled out his crowbar from the top of Martin's backpack. "Let's get inside and out of sight."

The aged wood of both door and frame submitted easily, leaving several rusted four-inch nails sticking out like thin fingers pointing at them accusingly. They opened the door wide enough to squeeze inside and then Nick pulled it back as closed as best he could.

It was dark inside, the type of dark that has a taste and texture. The windows were all so dirty and covered with ivy; no useful light penetrated into the room. Martin opened his bag and produced several cubes the size of egg cartons that were hooked together. He disentangled one and clicked a switch that caused it to burst into light. Seeing around the room a lot better, he put the cube on a table in the centre of the room.

"They're called Ice-Lights. A German friend donated them to me during a certain European conflict."

Dan and Nick laughed.

"Impressive. What else have you got in your bag?" Nick asked.

There was enough light to see they were in a room that made up the entire ground floor and the part they were in was the kitchen. The table, two broken chairs, a sink unit, various ramshackle cupboards and drawers, and solid fuel range set into a wall recess completed the witches' hovel look. To the far right, a bare wooden staircase disappeared up into blacker darkness. There was no other furniture at all.

They clicked on their helmet lights, enabling them all to see in greater detail.

"How do you want to do this?" Nick asked.

Dan looked around the room again, making a snap decision. "Can you do the cupboards and drawers, Martin check the range, and I will sweep the remainder of the room. If you find anything, anything at all, put it on the table."

While the others got to work on their prescribed tasks, Dan took a few photos of the room from all angles. He noticed several graffiti tags on the walls, an assortment of crude spray-paints and marker pen. He didn't recognise anything in particular but photographed each one individually anyway.

The windowsills were bare, as were two wall hung shelves and a plastic rubbish bin in the corner, opposite the stairs. As he worked his way around, he became certain they wouldn't find Stromboli's secret in this room. There was a door under the stairs, presumably to a small cupboard. The door was stuck fast, and he needed to retrieve Nick's trusty crowbar to persuade it to open. As it did a cloud of dust billowed out followed by a scuttling noise and a rat the size of a kitten ran over his foot heading for the front door.

"Jesus Christ! Did you see that?" He shivered.

Martin was quick enough to follow the noise and see the rat disappear into a hole in the skirting board. "That was a good one. I can't say I've a tried a British one but Asian rats taste like chicken."

"You dirty bastard." Nick laughed.

"Look mate, you'd be fighting me for it after three weeks in the jungle when you only brought supplies for one."

The cupboard was as Dan expected; wedge shaped and stinking of rat. As he scanned around, his helmet light found nothing but a pile of old magazines, which had become the nest by the look of things. He was glad to be wearing rubber gloves, otherwise he would have thought twice about reaching in for the once glossy books. As he pulled the compacted mass out into the main room, pieces fell away, leaving a trail of chewed or soggy confetti on the floor before he dropped the clump onto the table.

"You can forget about asking me to carry that," Nick said, turning his nose up at the repulsive odour.

"Don't worry about that. I just wanted to see if I could see a date on any of them," Dan explained to his friend's great relief.

He peeled several pages away like layers of skin trying to find something that may have survived sufficiently to give him what he wanted. On the third try he got lucky; it was an edition of Cosmopolitan dated May 2006.

He photographed it and then the entire pile together and was about to chuck the whole lot back under the stairs again when he had second thoughts.

"Have you got those plastic bags Martin?"

"Blue storage box in my bag," he replied with his head still in the wood burner box of the range.

Dan found the bags and put the degraded Cosmo' inside, sealing it closed. He then put that bag in another.

When Nick and Martin were finished, they all stood around the table to discuss the search so far.

"This mag is dated May 2006 which is in our arena. I couldn't see anything else," Dan said.

"Cupboards all negative. Not so much as a plastic spoon," Nick said.

Martin had gone through all sections of the range; only the wood burner box contained anything at all and that was ashes. He used his spade to extract a sample which was now spread out on the table.

"I know what wood ash looks like compared to other fuels and this is virtually all wood but there are some bits in it I don't recognise. This here might be melted plastic and this I thought could be foil. After yesterday I thought it best for you to see."

Dan and Nick weren't sure either.

"I say take a sample just in case," Nick offered.

Dan took out another plastic bag and scooped some of the ash into, it making sure he included the unidentified material.

"Okay time to see what there is upstairs. If the cupboard door was anything to go by, mind your footing."

Martin sparked up another two Ice-Lights and handed one to Dan.

Going up first Dan didn't know what to expect but he would never have guessed what he did see as he illuminated the space when he reached to top. Nick, then Martin got to the top before Dan spoke.

"Go on, explain this?"

The whole of the upstairs was one large space, just like downstairs. All the walls from what would have been two bedrooms and a bathroom had been removed, just leaving architectural scars on the floor. Even the bathroom toilet, sink, and bath or shower were gone, as were the ceilings, giving the effect of a church's vaulted roof above them.

All that was in the space was a single, huge purpose-built table and attached bench-seating assembly. It looked like a giant's picnic table. It was at least nine metres long and made from timbers twice the thickness of conventional floorboards.

"What the bloody hell," Martin said.

"Well there's no need to say who's searching what," Nick said. "If this was Stromboli's distribution site, all the action happened right here."

Dan saw similar tags on the walls as he'd witnessed and photographed downstairs. When he looked up, he found the small square they previously recognised outside as the attic window. He squinted to see it but was unable to get a clear view, even with the Ice-Lights.

"I need to get a closer look at the little window up there."

Nick stared at him with unconcealed consternation. "You do?"

"There's no holes or gaps in the roof. If it was a significant operation, they must've needed ventilation. It's the only possibility and might be a confirmation."

Martin headed back to the stairs. "Let me see if I can find a ladder or something outside."

When his footsteps faded Nick turned to Dan. "This is it, isn't it? What SIS couldn't find or weren't even sure existed. Do you realise what we've done?"

"I don't want to think about it, Nick."

Nick wiped his hand across the dusty bench seat.

"She sat here at this table, wrapping up blocks of smack, dipping it into melted down shoe polish."

"Maybe," Dan replied.

He sat down on the end of the bench and swung his legs under so he was resting his arms on the table top and tried to imagine the scene in 2006. The table was big enough to easily accommodate fifteen to twenty people on either side.

"It would have been some business if they could fill all these seats?"

Nick sat down opposite him and placed his gloved palms down on the table top. "Dead right. Do you think it's too much to hope there would be any forensic left?" he said, wiping a finger over the dusty surface.

"I can't see it."

Nick's finger caught on an indentation. "Shit, this is rough. I've got splinters in my finger," he said, picking the tiny wooden needles out of his glove while cursing the table but then stopped. "Hey look at that. I thought it was just a hole."

Dan came around to Nick's side. Placing an Ice-Light in the middle of the table and with their helmet lights focused on the spot where Nick's finger swipe came to an abrupt halt, the dust covered table could be seen in detail. They both stared.

"It looks like the letter M," Nick said.

Dan looked at it straight on and then tilted his head at an angle. "Or a W if you look at it the other way. It's been done with a knife or something."

It was impossible to see if there were other similar markings due to the thick layer across the whole of the table and bench seat. They both had the same idea though.

"I'll find something to clean this crap off with," Dan said.

He rooted around in Martin's backpack until he found a spare fleece top. He threw it to Nick who started wiping the table top while Dan tried to find something else.

When Martin came back upstairs, he was carrying the gate which they used to conceal the bikes. Dan was down to his tee-shirt, using his sweater like a cleaning cloth while Nick was doing the same with a fleece.

"Thought you'd do some housework with my top? What happened to preserving the scene?"

Nick shrugged. "It's all I could find."

Dan wiped his sweaty brow. "Cheers Martin. Leave it against the wall under the window and we can do it when we've finished here."

"What are you doing?"

"Can you get photos of all of these?" Nick said touching another small gouged pattern he'd uncovered.

"Sure." Martin replied.

"The next best thing to signatures of the people who were sat here at one time or another," Nick added.

"Really? Why not other kids who have found this place over the years?" Martin asked.

"The even layer of dust—I don't think anyone has set foot in here since Stromboli was here in 2006," Dan said.

Nick looked up. "I was being optimistic but that's a big assumption don't you think?"

Dan pointed to the edge of the table he had just cleared. "Not anymore."

Nick stopped what he was doing and came around; he and Martin peered over Dan's shoulder. In clear capitals was cut SWGK06.

"Susie Watt and Gary Knowles," Dan said.

The size of the table meant it took another ten minutes to clear off the whole thing and the bench seats as well. Dan and Nick revealed at least twenty different sets of initials or other markings, including a stick man and fish, but there was one that was most important to them; it was also the one which made Dan wipe away a tear.

Another two metres along from Watt's and Knowles' moniker was a crude round shape carved into a smiley face. Dan's thoughts went to George Zuckerman's personal nickname for his best friend and then to Powton Road. The only hint of colour Zoe wore was her old bandana, which had a smiley sun pattern all over it.

Dan didn't ask George about the bandana before, but he made a mental note now to ask him next time if he gave Zoe her bandana. He hoped it might be a happier reminder that she always kept it with her, right up to the end.

Although there was no doubt Zoe spent time here and that this was also where Gary Knowles and Susie Watt were shortly before they died, Dan wanted to cross every T and dot every I before they left.

When they were finished with the table, he got up to the attic window. The old gate wasn't enough on its own, so Martin dragged the table from downstairs up and put the gate on top of it. While Nick tried to hold everything still, Martin scaled the gate and Dan clambered on top of his shoulders so he could reach the small window. The wobbly assent was worth it when he saw a couple of tell-tale identifiers.

"There's a ring of sticky, cruddy dust and what looks like heat damage to the paintwork on the sill. It has to be an extractor."

Dan carefully took the camera out of his pocket and snapped a few images before climbing down again.

They were glad to be outside a few minutes later; the musty atmosphere inside the house had a clawing effect on their respiratory systems, making them sound like old men. The first lungful of fresh Peak District air tasted like wine and they basked in the non-existing sunshine as if they were stretched out on a Mediterranean beach.

Dan could be excused for feeling very happy with what the house gave up, but it wasn't the adjective he chose when Nick asked him.

"Satisfied. We can be more than satisfied with the evidential lode. It puts Zoe here and the initials all over the table might finally give us few more names we've been struggling for recently."

"And the more names the greater the chance of one of them knowing what happened to her," Nick said. "We should do these outbuildings while we're here."

Martin leant up on his elbows.

"I did have a quick scout around while I was looking for a ladder but didn't see anything obvious. Having said that, you know better than me what you're looking for."

Dan selected the smaller of the two shacks for himself and asked Nick and Martin to do the slightly larger one. "You take the camera; I'll call if I need it."

Martin's earlier evaluation quickly proved to be accurate; in less than twenty minutes they were packing up and getting ready to head back to the trail and home.

This was Jim's third or fourth final ever call to Barry Towers, begging for another favour.

"What can I tell you Barry, if you weren't so useful, I wouldn't have to keep calling," he jested.

"I hope you remember that when I'm hauled in front of the chief. What is it this time?" Towers chuckled down the line.

"Edward Daniel Vikkert; 06.11.69. A real nasty bugger, extremely violent. He's currently doing an eight stretch in Leicester. I have the police intel reports, but I need the court records if you can."

He heard Barry's light fingers tapping on a keypad as he continued talking. Barry seemed to stop as he finished his sentence.

"You're not wrong Jim, I mean sir."

"Barry, Jim is absolutely fine, don't you worry about that."

"Okay Jim. He was convicted of a Section Eighteen GBH and he's done a bit under three years of the eight you mentioned. There are dozens of pages if you want all his court records. I might as well put them in a file and email the lot. Is that okay with you?"

"Of course," Jim said gratefully. "While I've got you can you just check two other things? Has he got an injury listed to his right hand and is there anything there about weapons?"

"Hold on, that's easy. I can do a quick cross reference on both those against all his files."

Jim could hear more rapid clicking of computer keys behind Barry's contemporaneous commentary of what he was doing.

"Hold on, nearly there. Do that…no, do that…click here and this and this…Here we are, no nothing about an injured hand, either hand in fact. Weapons?" He let the *s* drift into a buzz as he played for a moment more time. "Yes weapons, there's a list. Glass bottle, pick-axe handle, beer glass, chef's sharpening tool, tyre lever, another glass bottle, and last but not least, a section of a street sign. Your friend doesn't like guns or bladed weapons, Jim, but he loves a blunt instrument. I'll put these lists in the file with the court records for you."

Jim punched the air with joy. "You're a diamond, Barry. Thank you again."

"You look pleased with yourself," Gwen said as Jim rolled into the kitchen.

"I certainly am Gwenny. Put me a tea on would you please? Dan's going to be very happy with me, very happy indeed."

By the time the nightly phone calls were finished, everybody in the Hetherington household was happy and excited for one reason or another, as were Jim and Gwen in Salcombe.

Dan's exchange of news with Jim over the stone house and then Jim's thunder clap about Edward Vikkert's choice of sharpening steel to inflict damage on an adversary were as welcome in their own way, as was the arrangement for Jim and Gwen to drive up to Nottingham the next day with Bradley.

CHAPTER TWENTY-FOUR

Dan slept a lot better than Tara for a change. She was so looking forward to having her baby back in her arms again that her mind was going at a hundred miles per hour well into the night. It was therefore an agonising wait the next morning and she bobbed up and down from her chair with every passing car even though Dan told her it could be hours before they'd arrive.

Martin headed off home after breakfast, visibly embarrassed by the depth of gratitude displayed by one and all as they prevented him from getting to the Land Rover, even though he thought he'd said goodbye for the last time indoors.

Dan and Nick took themselves into the garden room but thought it only right and proper to leave further investigation until Jim arrived. All the material collected and collated in the previous week was therefore left in tantalising and neat piles. They left the room again, closing the door with the reverence of the Sistine Chapel being closed for a Papal Conclave.

Morning coffee came and went as did lunchtime. Tara was a nervous wreck by the time Jim's white Vauxhall pulled up at the gate shortly before 2:00 p.m.

"You've grown, look at you!" Tara enthused.

Bradley's gurgling smile was enough to light up the dull afternoon. Seeing his parents again caused his whole body to shake with happiness. She didn't want to let him go but Dan demanded a turn with his son too. Bradley gummed at his face with sloppy kisses.

Nick introduced the whole family while Tara wiped tears away from her eyes and Dan cuddled Bradley as if his life depended on it. When the twins started buzzing around Bradley too, Dan and Tara realised they had unintentionally ignored Jim and Gwen.

"Hey good to see you. Sorry, I didn't realise how much I missed him until I saw him," Tara said, hugging Gwen like her own mother.

"Of course, he's obviously missed you both too. Look at him with his daddy."

Dan's happiness was clear for all to see too. "Jim, Gwen. Hi, how are you?" he said, wiping away a tear.

"Well, son. I could murder a cup of tea though. We didn't stop because he was sleeping."

"Come on everybody, let's go inside." Penny said.

Bradley seemed happy to be passed from one adoring Hetherington female to another for a while. He kept turning his head so he could see Tara's beaming face following his progress but as soon as she took her eye off him for a minute to talk with Gwen he began to whine, ensuring he was quickly back in his mother's embrace.

For Gwen and Penny this was their first ever meeting but there was no awkwardness; shared interest superseded convention. Bradley was another mutual interest, and both also realised the circumstances which brought them together were too important for anything but a united front.

It wasn't long before Dan, Nick, and Jim's itching to move the conversation along became the proverbial elephant in the room. Though there had been differences between the trio in the past, they were now a tight-knit group with a single desire to get a result.

They were eventually excused further frustration by their partners, who were glad to release them so they could discuss the more emotional aspects of the subject in peace.

"This is what I have," Jim said, setting down a sheaf of loose paperwork and two bulging ring binders.

Nick's eyes widened. "You've been busy."

Jim tapped the loose documents. "This lot is just Edward Vikkert's court records. He might not have an injured finger but is it impossible for him not to be Zoe Summers' murderer?" he said, cutting directly to the heart of the matter.

Dan scowled. "I wish he was. I'd like him to be, but no. He caused the injury to her leg with the sharpening steel or provided it to the person who did. That sounds right up his street to me, but not him strangling her with his bare hands."

Jim's shoulders slumped a touch. "He does use weapons all the time. The bar fight three years ago which led to him being currently locked up was with a beer glass. None of his previous violence convictions involved a physical assault only."

Dan stared at the papers covering the table.

"So, we now have all this and where does that put us exactly?" Nick asked.

Dan cleared his throat. "Zoe Summers was working for Stromboli in the stone house for several months before her death. She would have known Edward Vikkert at that time. It's possible he introduced her into the network.

"The night she was killed, she was also attacked with a sharpening steel that's got Edward Vikkert written all over it. Her being there begs a few questions we've not answered yet. One, why did she want or have to be there? Was it part of her working for Stromboli? Two, what did she do or say to make Vikkert attack her and then somebody kill her? Three, if Vikkert didn't kill her, who did?"

"And what of the other players?" Jim asked.

"Sean Darcy knew of Stromboli but wanted nothing to do with Edward Vikkert. Adam Vikkert was at Powton Road the night she died. Billy McKenzie was there too but he was off his face when I last remember seeing him. Matt Craig or Craig

Matthews took me there but didn't stay. He's certainly involved with Stromboli; he knew far more about me than I knew about him. There was the unidentified dealer and possibly one or two other unidentified individuals.

"Then there's John Trew; he's also heavily involved, but Stromboli is key. I can't see how her being killed is not linked to Stromboli. Have I missed anything?"

"No, that's as tight as a drum. What have we got to help answer those questions?" Jim asked, taking a seat by the door.

Dan and Nick both sat too, so the three men surrounded the table.

"The old house has given us quite a bit," Dan started again. "It was Stromboli's distribution centre for a period of time in 2006. The workers seem to have a tradition of carving their initials into the table where they worked packing the heroin. Those initials included the dead couple Knowles and his girl-friend Susie Watt, and Zoe's smiley sun. They're the ones we know. The ones we don't are RL, AB, LF, GB, TA, TT, DC, DN, HR, RB, HY, DK, GW, LK, CV, FR, CA, TE, PL, JJ, and then a couple which could be letters or numbers such as GO or zero, OB or zero B, and lastly TS or T five.

"What sticks out to me here is the fact there's no SD for Darcy, EV for Edward Vikkert, or AV for Adam Vikkert. To me that says they weren't there or didn't take part in the manual labour all the other packers did. With all those other initials we must be able to use them, but I don't know how at the moment."

"I was thinking that too. We must be able to use them some-how?" Nick agreed.

Jim crossed his arms and unfolded them again. "If we could put names to the initials, Dan, and if there are police photos to match, could you put the names to the unidentified faces at Powton Road?"

"The only face I wouldn't remember is the person who was right behind Zoe when she came in from the kitchen; that person's always been a blur."

"You're not suggesting we look at everyone with those initials? There would be thousands," Nick queried.

"He's right Jim. How can you narrow it down enough to be worthwhile?" Dan asked.

The older dog seemed pleased he found an idea his younger pups couldn't fathom. "Summers, Knowles, and Watt were all druggies, all within a few years of each other and they all disappeared off the police radar for weeks or months before they died. I say start with those parameters."

Dan was impressed. Jim wrote down the list of initials for himself.

"I owe Barry for all he's done so far. I'm meeting him when he finishes work today. I'll take this with me and run it past him. As for the Vikkerts and Darcy, you ought to think about talking to them."

Nick smiled. "We said the same. Edward is in HMP Leicester and Darcy is at the bail hostel. I don't think we know where Adam Vikkert is though, do we?"

In the other room, Bradley was smiling again. Viola and Rosie sat him on the floor, rolling a tennis ball between them to his delight.

Penny and Gwen were listening with concerned attention to Tara.

"He's been telling me there's a possibility they will never find out who strangled Zoe."

"But there's only so much he can do, even with Jim and Nick's help," Gwen said.

"I think it's only just started to really hit home that if they have to give up—"

"He'll always feel like he failed and all the other things he has achieved will have been for nothing," Penny said.

"Exactly."

"On the plus side, they've got all this new information from the search of the derelict house. It might be just what they need," Gwen said, offering some hope.

Dan ended the call to Purdy.

"She's going to see where Adam is these days. If anyone can find out quickly, it will be her. So Nick, you're going to go with Jim to see Barry and I'll go and make another house call on Sean Darcy. Please tell him again thanks from me."

"No problem," Nick replied. "If you want to meet him at four thirty, we better make a move soon Jim, the traffic can be a pain at times; we can take my car."

Dan didn't offer an explanation as to why he was going on his own this time. He, Jim, and Nick parted on the driveway with an exchange of stern nods rather than wishing each other luck.

The hostel reception was unmanned so Dan rang the bell once, as instructed by the sign hanging on the inside of the closed glass. He waited patiently for three or four minutes without seeing or hearing another human being before the temptation to explore a little overcame him.

The day room was empty although the TV was on; the French door out onto the patio was open. Crossing the room, he saw four young men in the garden playing with a Frisbee.

"Hi, I was looking for Sean Darcy," he said in the first break in play.

The quartet looked at him blankly.

"Hello, can I help you?"

Dan spun around to see a middle-aged man, not Duncan, in the doorway.

"Hi. I did ring the bell and waited."

"Do you want to come back inside? What is it you said you wanted?"

Dan followed the man back to the reception foyer. He wasn't wearing an ID badge, but he was clearly a worker and not a resident.

Dan offered his hand. "My name is Dan Calder. I was here the other day talking to Sean Darcy and I was hoping to talk to him again."

The man didn't reciprocate with his hand or with his name.

"What do you want to see him about? Is it hostel or courts business?"

"No, neither. Is he here?"

They'd reached a stalemate and Dan knew he would have to be the one to give a little if he was going to get any joy.

"I'm ex-police. Darcy was answering a few questions the other day. It won't take long."

The man didn't seem impressed with Dan's olive branch. "Well you're out of luck. He did a runner the day before yesterday. He was due in court this morning so I imagine there will be a warrant out for him by now."

Dan was surprised. "It was only a poxy shoplifting wasn't it? Hardly worth taking off for. Did he take all his stuff?"

The man stiffened at the police style question, knowing full well what the next one would be if he said no.

"I'm not at liberty to say."

Dan had got as far as he was going to with Mr. Helpful.

"Is it okay with you if I just ask the kids outside if they know where he went?"

"Be my guest. I've got stuff to do though, so you'll have to see yourself out," the man replied, obviously thinking Dan was wasting his time.

The Frisbee game had ended and there was no sign of the green disc; a better than even chance it disappeared over the neighbour's fence, Dan thought.

"Hi again."

Acknowledgements were in short supply and so Dan pressed on. "I wanted to see Sean Darcy, but he's gone apparently."

Smirks and looks between the four.

"I don't suppose you know where he went or why?"

"Nope," said the stumpy, overweight youth nearest him. He looked like a Hobbit from the Lord of the Rings movie.

"That's a shame. And I don't suppose you know if he took all his stuff or not?"

No answer again, not even from the Baggins kid.

Dan only had one throw of the dice left. "Lost your Frisbee? And you looked like you were really having a good time. What if I gave you the money to buy a new one? They must be expensive nowadays, maybe even forty pounds for a four-man game replacement."

"You were here the other day. Sean said you scared the shit out of him," Baggins said eagerly at the mention of cold hard cash.

"Oh yes. Why's that?"

"Our Frisbee?" One of the others said.

Dan found a twenty and two tens in his wallet and held them out in his hand very much like he did with the marked money in Powton Road.

"He didn't say why. He's a bit of a pussy anyway but you really scared him properly." Baggins licked his lips clearly anxious to please and get his hands on the notes in Dan's clenched fist. "He packed his bag the same day and was going to go then but didn't. I'm not sure why. He went the next day after breakfast. Told us not to say where he was going or anything."

"And did he say where he was going then?"

"No." As if to prove he was telling the truth Baggins repeated himself three times. "No, he didn't, honest to God he didn't."

Dan handed over the cash and turned back to the building.

"One last thing boys. Does anyone know Zoe Summers, Adam Vikkert, or Stromboli?"

They all looked blankly at him again and he was sure it was due to complete ignorance.

Before going back to Nick's house, Dan took another drive down to Mapperley. Purdy's was empty, so he walked along to Saint Paul the Apostle's. Eric was collecting hymn books from the wooden pews and placing them on low tables at the end of each row. When he saw Dan, he stretched his back and indicated for Dan to join him on the front row.

"What brings you here? Not that you're not welcome at any time."

"I was just passing."

"And wondered if I had news? Have you been to see Purdy or are you going there next?"

Dan smiled. "I'm that easy to read?"

"You look troubled. I take it it's this business with Zoe Summers."

"Yes, I've been worrying we won't find her killer, not for lack of trying but simply because they've covered their tracks so well."

Eric rested his eyes on the figure of Saint Paul above the altar.

"Do you pray, Dan?"

"I'm not a believer."

"But still, do you pray? Do you make silent wishes?"

"I suppose so, but they'd be about Tara and Bradley or people I'm close to."

Eric adjusted his spectacles; Dan noticed he hadn't seen him wearing glasses before.

"If it's just them who move you to think so deeply and not others, why not focus solely on them?"

"I'm sorry, I don't understand."

"Do you know Saint Paul? I suppose not. He taught through the middle part of the first century and was said to be both a Jew and a Roman citizen, meaning he was able to communicate to both audiences trying to advance his ministry. He was converted on the road to Damascus when Jesus appeared to him. He was blinded for three days until he was baptised by Ananias. Before this conversion he openly criticised Christianity."

Dan knew Eric had a point but couldn't figure out what it could be. "You'll have to put it in simpler terms for me I'm afraid."

"Paul only started preaching the gospel of Christ after his conversion and was only able to do it because the Christ revealed himself."

"Yes, that makes sense."

"And because he was a Roman and a Jew, he spoke to both."

"Okay."

"Dan, in order to do what he did, he needed to be all three things; he had to be a Jew, he had to be a Roman, and he had to have the Holy Spirit within him."

The clouds of misunderstanding that blocked Dan's vision slowly parted.

"What are you saying, I'm too one dimensional? I don't have the capacity to have the same depth of feeling for Zoe as I do Tara? I shouldn't hope to resolve more than is beyond me? It can't be as simple as that."

"You say you're troubled by the thought of Zoe's death remaining unresolved, yet it's only your girl and your son whom you care about so much you pray for them, even though you don't believe. Why not go home and live your life with them and forget about Zoe Summers? It doesn't have to be your crusade and it's not going to harm you to say you did your best, but it wasn't quite enough.

"If Paul wasn't brought into the light, he would probably have continued to be at odds with the church all his life and wouldn't have achieved all he did. That does not mean he would have been unhappy though; he was perfectly content with his life before conversion. What I'm saying to you is you can only be the best of who you are given the tools you have."

Dan stayed. They talked for another half hour before Eric needed to get ready for Vespers, the sunset prayer service. When he left Dan was feeling different; not better or worse, just different. He tried calling Purdy and left a voicemail message.

On the way to Nick's he stopped and purchased three bunches of flowers for Tara, Penny, and Gwen.

Jim and Nick's appointment with Barry Towers took them to one of the multitude of city centre pubs. The Honest Lawyer was one of a national chain, whose choice of brand new to look olde-world décor and furnishings didn't fill Jim with much hope of an authentic ale on tap.

Barry Towers' latest role of desk jockey took a heavy toll on his waistline; he flowed out over his belt like a Yorkshire pudding and was out of breath after the two-minute walk from his office to the pub. Still, he ordered a plate of fried potato wedges to go with his beer, saying it would save cooking when he got home. The barman knew him by name.

Nick and Barry needed to make their introductions as their paths had never crossed before but once that was done and with Jim sat between them there was a no secrets air to the discussion. Before his wedges arrived, Barry needed a second pint to replace the one that hardly touched the sides of his throat on the way down to his voluminous belly.

"So, memoirs then Jim," Barry chortled as he supped a third of his second pint in one go. "Don't worry, I don't need any details, but something's got you interested all of a sudden."

"You're a good man Barry. It's for a good cause."

Towers' face opened into a glowing smile, but only because his plate of deep-fried carbs appeared. The server put the chunky china bowl in the middle of the table but only Barry made a move for them.

"I love these things," he said, smearing a crispy potato with ketchup and sour cream. It was so hot he couldn't easily keep it in his mouth but still reached for a second before swallowing the first.

Jim and Nick sipped their beers, both deciding to leave the food to Barry lest they risk losing their fingers.

"I'm glad we're able to catch up so I could say thanks again in person. How is life treating you?" Jim asked when Barry paused for air.

"I can't complain, and it wouldn't do me any good if I did, you know what I mean? Since Jeannie left, I try not to go home straight from the office. It's too quiet there without her, which is why I spend far too much time in here. The beer and chips will probably be the end of me but so what I say. Jeannie and I were meant to have a long retirement together and that's not going to happen now, so I might as well enjoy myself and not worry about anything."

Jim modified his opinion.

"Honestly, Jim don't worry, what can they do to me? On the subject, have you got something else for me?"

Suddenly Jim felt very awkward. Barry Towers may have given up in some respects, but he was uneasy thinking his requests for information were cementing Barry's what-the-hell attitude to life. Barry seemed to read his mind.

"Jim, I want to help. Nick, what do you need?"

"It's a search. We've got a list of people's initials, we think likely to be aged between eighteen and thirty, male and female. We're hoping we can filter the search somewhat," Nick said.

Barry wiped his greasy fingers on a paper napkin and immediately picked up another wedge. "Oh yes, how's that?"

"From the main cities or populous areas around the Peaks National Park, drugs activity, known to police, but then several weeks or months of no reports or stop checks in the period from June 2005 to December 2006."

Barry stopped eating and drinking. Such was his metronomic consumption to that point that it took Jim and Nick by surprise; they could do no more than sit nervously as Barry leant back and looked carefully at them. His diet was undoubtedly clogging up his veins and arteries, but his mind was as sharp as ever.

"Interesting," he said finally. "I was tempted to ask why there for a minute but on second thoughts, I don't think I want to know. I might as well finish these if you two are watching what you eat."

Jim produced the list from inside his jacket. Dan suggested they also add ZS to act as a test. Given the search parameters, they believed Zoe should come up. If she did then it was reasonable to think others would too, if they were right.

Barry looked at the list as if he was memorising it and then folded it into his shirt pocket.

"It might take me a day or two chaps."

"It's greatly appreciated," Jim answered and without thinking he might be adding to Barry's impending heart attack he said, "Can I get you another? Same again?"

They stayed with Barry for long enough that Jim had to drive back. His own health concerns were enough reason to let him off with tomato juice after his one alcoholic drink, but Nick wasn't quite so fortunate. He kept Barry company drinking one pint for every two Barry had until the pub started to fill with pre-nightclub patrons loading up before, rather than having to pay the inflated club prices later.

"I feel old after that," Nick said as they drove along.

"Barry was always a straight up and down good bloke. I think he was as skinny as a rake when he was a junior PC. Shame about his wife and what's happened to him."

Nick sighed due to his beery buzz. "I was actually talking about the kids who filled up the pub before we were finished. I remember being able to do that a long time ago, but I do take your point about Barry. Do you know what happened?"

"I'm not a hundred percent sure but I think it might have been a younger man at work."

Nick sniffed, "Poor bloke. Barry that is. It might have been better if she died. Oh, sorry, I forgot. It's the beer talking Jim. My apologies."

"It's alright, son. I don't think there's a finger of fate pointing at any of us. I got lucky because Dan and you got to me in time."

Nick rubbed his face. "That's funny isn't it? I'm with you but I think Dan has got a very strong fatalistic bent; he would tell us the exact opposite."

"Gwen said the same thing to me a while ago when I was in the hospital. You know Dan got to tell me about his past, don't you?"

"Of course, we spent years crewed together so I got some of it then, and the rest in the last year like you."

"She thinks it's a defence mechanism. If things are meant to be despite all your efforts and all the things life throws at you then at least it's an answer of sorts. I tell you this; if there's one person who deserves a little peace and happiness, it's Dan."

"I think he's doing alright now. Tara and Bradley and being in New Zealand."

"I hope so Nick, son, I hope so."

Gwen looked at her husband suspiciously when he and Nick came back in.

"Where have you been all this time?"

"We had to stop with Barry for a while. Don't worry love, I had one beer and then tomato juice."

"And what did you have?" Penny asked Nick.

"Penny, Jim and I should get going; the hotel will think we're not coming," Gwen said.

"Are you really sure? We can make room. You don't have to go to a hotel."

"No, you're fine. We said yesterday, didn't we. It's easier for all of us and we can come back tomorrow morning so these boys can get back to work again."

Penny kissed Gwen's cheek. "Alright, though by the look of my boy he may not be in the best shape."

"I'm fine, Pen," Nick said looking anything but. "Where's Dan?"

"He and Tara went out after they put Bradley to bed," Gwen replied.

When Dan finished telling Tara about his meeting with Eric at Saint Paul's he remained quiet and waited on her answer.

"I like him. I've never talked to a priest before but regardless of that, he seems like a very nice man," she said.

"Do you believe I'd be okay if we went home without discovering Zoe's killer?"

"Of course, I do. The biggest issue for me has always been you thinking it might have been you, but that's one thing we've solved, isn't it? You can have a clear conscience; it was never your case to solve then and it still isn't."

"So, you don't think we owe it to her, to her mother, and George Zuckerman to give them some answers?"

"If they knew about your involvement before and they approached you, then maybe. But you went to them, Dan. You put yourself up for them to shoot at," Tara mulled.

"Absolutely, and I said the same to Eric. So that leaves one more thing."

"What's that?"

"That night at Powton Road, she put herself in harm's way for me and she paid the ultimate price. How far should I go before I say I've tried hard enough? How far would you go for someone who saved your life Tara?"

CHAPTER TWENTY-FIVE

Tara opened her eyes and rolled over. Dan was on the flat of his back with his eyes wide open.

"Did you sleep at all?" she whispered.

"Morning. Not much."

She nuzzled under his arm and they lay still together as Tara became fully awake. Bradley was awake as well; they could hear him moving around in his travel cot at the end of the bed and it sounded like he was having a conversation with his bed toys.

"Shall I get him?" Dan asked quietly.

"No, not for a minute. I'm worried about you darling."

He shifted so he could see her face. "There's no need."

Whether it was the movement or the change in his tone to be more urgent, Bradley stopped his baby chatting and began to whimper, preparing himself for the first cry of the day. Dan pulled his arm free then crawled like a commando down the bed and peered into the cot. Bradley was looking the other way, towards the door but when Dan blew on the back of his neck he lolled onto his side and looked up.

"Dada," he said well enough to be understood and not be mistaken for another random sound.

"There's my boy," Dan cooed. "T, did you hear that?"

In a split second she was at the end of the bed too. "Oh, wow I did, he said dada!"

Dan lifted him up and out and lay him between them, so they could both wonder at his perfectness.

"He did, he said dada, that's his first proper word, right?"

"Yes, I'm sure it is. What a clever boy," Tara said though she was choked by a big lump in her throat.

It was one of those most rare moments of shared bliss. For a few seconds they were both completely happy and content.

When they were changing him a short time later, the reflected glory of the moment was still tangible. As Dan changed his nappy and wiped a sweet-smelling disposable cloth across Bradley's bottom, Tara looked in a case for the appropriate outfit for him to wear on the day of his first spoken word.

"What about his green jeans and the black top?"

"Sure, whatever you want. I was just thinking," Dan replied to the back of her head.

"Thinking what?"

"Would you like to go back to Salcombe with him and Jim and Gwen tomorrow? You've hated being apart from him and imagine if we had both missed out on him talking for the first time."

"Dan—"

"Let me finish. I was going to say if you do, I'll stay here until the end of the week and then come and join you."

"You've lost me. How do you know you will have finished the case by then?"

Dan lifted Bradley up, complete with new nappy so he could see his mother. Tara was holding the proposed outfit loosely in one hand, but her attention was fully on Dan.

"That's what I mean, T. Wherever we're at the end of the week, it's the end for me."

"But Dan?"

He smiled at their son who was wriggling his naked legs as if he were trying to run across the space between them to Tara.

"Hey, you're not going to try and talk me out of it are you? It's time. Time to move on, time for us to be whatever we're going to be. Can you do me a favour though? Don't tell the others anything. I'll do it when I'm ready."

Tara's face painted a picture of her feelings. Her day just became all the more special.

"You look like shit," Dan said to Nick when they were alone for a moment.

"It was a sacrifice for you. Pass the coffee please. I need to wake up before Jim gets here."

Twenty minutes later was too soon and in stark contrast Jim was in fine form. A good night's sleep in a comfortable bed and a breakfast made for them by someone else was the perfect start to his and Gwen's day.

"You have my sympathy if you're feeling as rough as you look, son."

"Thank you for that. I just need a few more minutes."

"And how are you Dan? I missed you when we got back last night."

"Good, Jim. Tara and I went out."

Jim clapped his hands together. "Gwen is happy with Bradley and the girls, so what have we got first?"

As always Dan started. "Sean Darcy has done a runner. It seems he was so spooked after my last visit he packed his bags the next day. What do you make of that?"

"Not a coincidence?" Jim asked.

"Definitely not. A couple of little birds told me he was scared shitless."

Jim twitched his nose. "Why would he still be like that now?"

"Search me. I was hoping you might have an idea."

"Sorry son, nothing springs to mind."

Although quiet, Nick was still paying attention. The coffee he hoped would help his head was having a counter-productive effect on his stomach and sitting still was the order of the day so far. "What if his worries aren't historical? What if they're more current?" he said.

Dan and Jim stopped what they were doing; the three men let Nick's comment percolate like the coffee for a moment.

When Jim was ready, he said, "Without knowing exactly what you said to him, who and what did you mention?"

Dan easily accessed the information he needed. "Zoe, the Stingers, Powton Road, and Connaught Drive. Then there was Vikkert, Matt Craig, and at the end he came up with Stromboli."

"Zoe's dead; the Stingers are long gone too," Nick said, as he started to show a little more zeal for the matter at hand.

Dan continued the train of thought. "Powton Road and Connaught Drive can't have any more hidden secrets, can they?"

"Which leaves Matt Craig, Vikkert, and Stromboli," Jim added letting the names hang in the air.

"Edward Vikkert is safely locked away. Adam we've not looked into, although we know he was nicked a couple of months ago."

"Matt Craig and Stromboli?" Jim said. "Surely not?"

Nick was now sitting fully upright and suddenly feeling a whole lot better. "Have we even thought if Stromboli could still be active?"

"Your intranet access, or rather block, suggests it might be," Dan said bluntly.

Another minute of private reflection passed before Dan commented again. "We have to put that in the too hard basket for now. The last thing I need is to get involved in a national heroin trafficking job. Let's concentrate on Edward Vikkert; he has to be our shortest route to Zoe's killer, and he took to her with that sharpening steel for a reason. How are we going to find out what that reason was?"

"Officially, I can go and visit him. Unofficially you can. I'm back to work tomorrow," Nick said.

Jim paused for a moment. "How do you want to play it, son? It's probably fair to say you'll only get one shot at him."

Nick could plainly see the thought of getting up close and personal with Edward Vikkert, the man responsible for one of Zoe's last injuries, filled Dan with rage.

"You should go, Nick. I'd love to get in there and fuck him up good and proper but there's other considerations," he said bitterly.

"Are you sure?"

"Don't tempt me. No, you go."

Nick hoped he was displaying the degree of understanding of Dan's inner conflict. "I won't let you down mate, but a bit of your special schooling is always welcome if you want to."

"I don't think there's much I can teach you."

Nick looked across to his best friend with open suspicion. "That doesn't sound like you. What's up?"

"You do seem to have been a bit pre-occupied this morning," Jim said, adding to Nick's surety.

"No, I'm good. If it's okay with you and Gwen, can Tara come back to yours tomorrow when you go? She's missed being with Bradley."

"Of course, son, there's plenty of room in the car. Will you and she be alright though? Is there anything wrong now?"

"No, we're completely fine, there are no hidden agendas. Come on. We've got a lot to do."

They worked through the rest of the morning by which time Nick was feeling a part of the real world again. Adam Vikkert's whereabouts were still a mystery and no amount of checking located an address for him. The arrest in August was the last report of any descriptions; he told police then he was of no fixed abode and due to insufficient evidence, he was released the same day after giving a no comment interview.

When they broke for lunch the sum total of their efforts had been to tie up a number of loose ends and only make them surer of what they didn't know. Matt Craig and Stromboli remained painfully remote.

"I'm going to call Barry and see if he's got anything yet," Jim said, holding the door open for Dan and Nick. "But I'll have a tea thanks."

"No problem come on through when you're ready," Nick replied.

"We thought it would be about that time for you," Penny said as she put the finishing touches to a large plate of cut sandwiches.

"What have you been up to?" Nick kissed her cheek and grabbed the top most wedge of crusty bread.

"Actually, we've been planning how to spend your pension. How does a long holiday in New Zealand sound?"

Dan replied positively as Nick's full mouth prevented him from saying anything. "Great idea. Is that a whole family thing or just you two?"

Penny offered him the plate. "That depends. We'll need to have some pretty big discussions before we can say. Where is Jim?"

"Just making a call, he won't be long."

Tara walked behind Dan and put her arms around his neck. "What do you think? They could use us as a base, or we could do a bit of travelling with them? I suggested even you and Nick going off and doing some tramping through the South Island, like you've talked about before."

"What would you and Penny do?"

"We could do the spas in Rotorua or Taupo possibly," she replied with a twinkle in her eye.

"We've got it all worked out in our heads anyway," Penny added.

Nick finally managed to swallow the great hunk of bread and cheese he was in the middle of when the conversation started.

"It sounds like it."

"It sounds like I've been missing something," Jim said as he appeared in the doorway. "Who's planning a trip?"

"The girls are planning how to spend my pension," Nick said in mock indignation.

"*Our* pension my love," Penny laughed.

After lunch and the details of Nick's post retirement antipodean trek had been gone over and seemingly finalised, Jim started talking shop once more.

"Good and bad news. Barry's done what he can but only came up with one possible hit. HY. Fortunately for us though, Zoe Summers did also come back."

Dan wasn't too disappointed. If HY was the one and only from the list, then that was fine; it meant concentrating their full attention on him or her. The fact Zoe also appeared lent credibility to Barry Towers' search. The downside was also obvious: if HY turned out to be a dead end so could the whole thing. "Don't keep us in suspense. Who is HY?" he asked.

"Howard Young. Howard Peter Young. I called Barry before he could do any more, so we'll have to use your laptop Nick."

"Fine. Let's finish here and get back to it."

Nick read from several different lines on his screen to build up the story.

"Young, Howard Peter; born 01.02.1989 in Loughborough. No arrests. Mm, only two incident reports in total. This sounds pretty bad already."

"Go on, what does it say?" Dan asked.

"Police called to his school when he was found in possession of a small quantity of cannabis in the toilets. This was in November 2004. Interviewed at the school by the attending officer and then cautioned at home the next day in the presence of his parents."

"I think it's safe to say Howard is not Stromboli," Jim joked.

Dan sighed. "You might as well finish, Nick."

"August 2006; he was in a group believed to be dealing. Unluckily for him when they were approached by a couple of plain clothes police and did a starburst, he was the one who got caught. He didn't have anything on him and wouldn't tell them who the others were. They told him his fortune and had to let him go."

"It was always going to be a fishing expedition, son," Jim said looking at Dan.

Nick looked up from his computer. "And we've caught nothing."

Dan shrugged. "August 2006 is about the time when Zoe would have been at the house; maybe they were there at the same time. But what does that tell us? Probably nothing."

Jim looked at his watch; it seemed their day may be ending prematurely. "Can you see if he's still local Nick?"

Nick entered a new search via the national driver's licence database. "He lives in London according to his licence. Notting Hill."

"I think I need some fresh air," Dan said.

Dan pushed the stroller along the gravelly path which wound its way around the large pond. He and Tara wrapped Bradley up against the cold before taking a walk to the park ten minutes from Nick's house, however Bradley was fast asleep before they reached the end of the road and was oblivious to the hundreds of ducks on the water and central island.

"I really think this is it, T. Nick's going to visit Edward Vikkert in prison, but I can just imagine the response he's going to get."

"Why don't you come with me tomorrow then? If Nick's got the last job, just leave him to it."

Dan was tempted; he was feeling tired, he was feeling disconsolate, and he was feeling like every moment with Tara and

Bradley was too precious to waste. However, a nagging aware-ness of his duty to Zoe stopped him from saying yes.

"Remember I said the other day about seeing Elizabeth Summers and talking to George Zuckerman and then I got side-tracked? Well I still need to do those things. Perhaps I will see them and maybe Eric and Purdy too; say goodbye properly."

"Sure, I think it's a good idea to feel you've done it the way you want to. Promise me though, as soon as you can, you'll come down to us."

He stopped and kissed her on the lips. "I promise."

CHAPTER TWENTY-SIX

The next morning Nick left for work before the rest of the household got up. The breakfast table felt oddly strange with no prospect of Dan's investigation team setting up camp again in the garden room or lounge with endless rounds of refreshments punctuating the day.

Jim and Gwen arrived to collect Tara and Bradley shortly before 10:00 a.m. and they stayed to chat for another half an hour before Jim started making noises about traffic and meal times. Bradley was happy to be going on another car journey and even happier when Tara fastened her seat belt next to him. Before closing the door, Dan leant in and kissed them both.

"See you soon but I'll call you tonight."

Tara touched his face. "Say hi to Purdy and Eric from me, tell them thanks for everything."

"I will. Have a good trip. Jim, Gwen, thank you so much once more. I'll see you in a few days."

"Alright son, don't worry we'll take good care of them and good luck."

Dan met Purdy at the café on Powton Road as Eric wouldn't be free until after midday. They ordered coffee and sat by the window watching passers-by until the steaming mugs arrived.

"See her there, the woman with the red shoes. You wouldn't think but she used to be who you'd go to if you needed a cheque book. I saw her once with at least three hundred in a bag, all the different banks, any one you wanted."

Dan took in the woman's details but stopped short of committing her to memory. "It's probably a shame but I'm not in the least surprised. How much would a full book set you back these days?"

Purdy pulled a non-committal face. "A hundred, like everything else it's always a nice round figure."

"Best to keep it simple," Dan agreed.

"You said on the phone you're going home soon?"

"Yes. I wanted to see you and Eric and one or two other people to say bye and thanks before I went."

"Aw, aren't you a sweetheart. We haven't been much helping this time around though, have we?"

"Look, I'm grateful, really grateful you even gave me the time of day and I know you did what you could." Dan blew on his coffee and took a sip. It tasted like diesel oil.

"So, no luck about the girl then?" Purdy asked.

"We've got one name; Edward Vikkert, he's Adam Vikkert's uncle. He has previous for assault with the same weapon Zoe was attacked with before she was strangled. My friend is going to visit him in Leicester Prison and try to rattle his cage. I think he will probably laugh in his face. The best we can hope for is the weapon that the police seized from him is still stored somewhere and it can be compared against Zoe's injury."

Purdy's upturned nose response could have been about Zoe or the coffee. "I didn't realise they could do that."

"It's just like bullets fired from a gun; they have unique marks on them, their own signature if you like."

"Well that's something at least, you know, getting him done for that."

"There's a big difference in him having possession of a weapon in 2008 and it being used in an attack in 2006. Certainly not enough to charge him. Anyway, what have you got planned for yourself Purdy?" he said, changing the subject.

"More of the same I expect, doll. I'll keep doing the markets and in another year Dale will probably get his certificates and move out which will make life a bit easier."

"I'm glad you're okay."

"Thanks Dan."

They finished their coffee and walked out onto the street together.

"Well you know where to find me?" Purdy said planting a kiss on his cheek.

"I do, although I think this could be it for me coming back to the UK."

"Never say never. I might need to call a superhero one day and you're the only one we know around here."

As Dan started to laugh Purdy took his hand.

"No, I mean it. Last year, the girls, that bent copper. We don't forget things like that in Mapperley."

He felt his face flush. "I'll miss you Purdy. You take care."

As he walked away, he heard Purdy's stilettos tapping a busy tune in the other direction. It was people like her he would miss the most. Genuine, real, and with their own multi-faceted stories.

It was still way too early to contemplate making his way to Saint Paul's, so instead Dan drove up to Garstone where his police career ended. He parked the Ford in the multi-storey car park close to the main shopping area and walked up and down the streets for an hour or so.

He thought he'd be able to pick out a few faces from the past and put them with the job or case he came into contact with, but after a while gave up. Outside the office of the Garstone Record newspaper he stopped. The latest edition was pinned up in the window; he skimmed a number of pages looking for the crime related stories but found nothing to tweak any memories and soon realised he didn't identify with the town or the people in it anymore. Garstone was another book he could close now.

In the end he decided not even to bother walking up as far as the police station as it wouldn't be relevant anymore either.

Eric opened the door wide. "Dan, good to see you. Please come in."

"I hope I'm not too early. I've been struggling to find things to do since saying bye to Purdy earlier after thinking I would run out of time to do things before I leave."

"So, you're soon to be off then?"

"Yes, Tara and Bradley left this morning. I said I would stay until the end of the week."

"You're a fortunate man to have a woman like her."

"Believe me, I do know it."

They sat in Eric's lounge, on couches opposite each other.

"So, how are you feeling since we last talked?"

Dan sat with crossed arms and legs. "Alright I suppose. Resigned to not being able to achieve what I set out to do. Mostly okay that there's probably not a lot more I could have done and still pissed off, sorry, still finding it hard."

"Don't worry, I hear much worse every day, even in confession as well as outside these four walls. There are some things which will always be out of our control. Is it because you feel with Zoe Summers it's personal?"

Doing his best to remain relaxed, Dan stretched his legs out. "Of course, how could it not be? She probably died because of me, Eric."

"What she did or didn't do was personal to her. What you've done by carrying this guilt with you is personal to you."

"But I'm the only one who can provide the answers to her mother."

"My son, you went to her. You offered yourself to her as the vehicle to provide the reasons Zoe was killed, when the fact is you didn't have the information or ability to make good on your offer. All you can say is you were wrong."

Dan sighed but didn't reply. It was hard to argue with plain and simple truth.

"Did you say you were here until the end of the week?"

"Yes, and I'm already thinking that may be a few days too long."

Eric looked a little disappointed. "After we talked the other day, I started to think about my next gospel reading; that's for this Sunday. Would it be too much to ask if you'd come?"

"I'm not a churchy type, remember. No offence."

"Please? I'm not asking you to take Communion." Eric smiled. "If you're at a loss for things to do at the moment, think of it as a way of spending an hour you would otherwise be trying to waste away."

"I can't promise, not after what you just said."

"That's fair. So, tell me about New Zealand. I'm like lots of other people who have always thought about going but never have."

The call to Elizabeth Summers later was short and not at all sweet. When Dan asked if he could come to see her, she immediately and bluntly wanted to know what for.

"I'm sorry, but as things stand, I don't think we can prove who killed Zoe," Dan said.

He told her about Edward Vikkert, but it sounded lame even as he heard the words.

Elizabeth Summers snorted a derisive exclamation. "So, you want to come to my house and tell me what I already know. I'm sorry Mr. Calder, but I've no interest in making you feel better about things."

"Elizabeth, it's not like that," he replied thinking it probably was.

"Didn't you hear me? I don't care. Look after your own family because one is more than enough. Please just leave me alone."

She put down the telephone.

Dan kept the phone to his ear even though there was no sound. Regardless of what Eric said he couldn't shake the guilty feeling.

Nick was home when he got back to the house.

"Hi. How was your day?" Dan asked, flopping down into a chair.

"First day back syndrome. I lost count of the emails I had and a pile of paperwork you could climb over. I called HMP Leicester and got a visiting order for next Monday."

Dan didn't react. That would be the day after he was leaving for Salcombe.

Nick continued. "It's the first available date. Did Tara and the others get away okay?"

"Yes, fine. I got a text a while ago to say they were back safe and sound."

Nick changed the subject. "Did you get much done today?"

"I saw Purdy this morning and Eric this afternoon."

Dan then described the painful call to Elizabeth Summers and finished with her barb for him to take care of his own.

"Ouch. That must have stung," Nick said.

"She's right, though isn't she? Tara initially, and now Tara and Bradley have taken second place for too long."

"I'm sure she doesn't think of it like that," Nick offered but Dan wasn't ready to forgive himself.

"How sure? Would you bet your life on it?" Dan snapped.

"Hey steady on. I thought we were friends," Nick replied.

Dan sat back and took on the look of a sulking child. Today turned out being the beginning of several different endings and he wasn't coping. Usually such times in his life could be marked with a full stop but today had been a series of open brackets and question marks.

"Sorry. That was out of order."

Nick took a moment. "I'm telling Pen we're going to The Archer tonight; they do an okay curry. Be ready in an hour."

The pub, the beer, the curry, and the company all helped. Dan cursed and swore, as well as talking in depth about how his hopes came to naught. In doing so he purged a lot of the poisonous feelings that had built up inside like a pressure cooker.

He could not fail to notice that throughout, Nick did little more than ask the right questions, allowing him to vent out the steamy answers.

When the barmaid called last orders, Nick elected to choose another subject to talk about.

"One more before we go. By the way I've a favour to ask you and Tara," he said rising.

"Go on then, I might as well make sure I sleep well tonight. What favour?"

Dan waited for Nick to return from the bar with two fresh pints before he got his answer.

"Here you go. Yes, I wanted to ask you about Amber. She has a chance on her course to do a year at an international university and one of the options is Auckland. How would you feel about her coming over? I don't know if that means she would want to stay with you or in the uni-provided accommodation, just have you close by, you know. I'm only asking since it seems Pen and I will be coming over for a lengthy stay in about eighteen months' time. If Amber's there then too, it would be a good way of seeing her while she was away from home for a year."

"Brilliant, yes. I'm sure Tara will say the same."

"After last year and all that crap with her getting arrested she sees you as much more than my best friend; we all do. If we knew you were close by to look out for her...well like I said, you know."

It was a well-chosen way to end the evening.

Dan did sleep well all things considered. When the following morning came around and he was faced with another day of kicking his heels, Penny made his mind up for him and he spent the time running errands for her, then pushed her shopping trolley around the supermarket while she did the weekly shop.

They also touched on the idea of Amber going to Auckland for twelve months and he reassured her of the good sense it made. Twenty-four hours on Dan was in an entirely better mood as he heaved the loaded trolley towards Penny's car, so it was fortunate for Eric he chose that moment to call.

"Sorry to bother you; it was just to see if you had made up your mind about Sunday?"

"Mass on Sunday morning," Dan said, answering Eric and explaining the call to Penny at the same time. She made a knowing smile and opened the car's boot.

"Sure, why not. What time do you start?"

"That's great Dan, thank you. A quarter to ten. There are no reserved seats so you can sit anywhere."

"Okay, I'd better go, I'm meant to be loading a car and it's nearly all done. I don't suppose thank you for the invite is the correct terminology, but I'll be there on Sunday."

"Alright Dan. Bless you, see you then."

Dan explained the call after the car was loaded.

"Mass? As in Catholic church?" Penny asked.

"Yes, he asked me the other day."

"And you're going? Be careful you don't burst into flames."

He grinned. "I'm having similar thoughts already."

Penny belted herself in and started the engine. "Nick will be home early today as it's Friday. I think Amber's around this evening as well; we could talk about her Auckland idea?"

"Definitely."

"It sounds like a perfect idea," Tara said after Dan explained the general idea later in the evening. "Even if she does want to stay at ours, she's a lovely girl and I can't see there being any problems; and she's as good as family. Hey, she'd be a brilliant babysitter for Bradley too. This is sounding better and better all the time."

He updated her on the news of the day, or rather lack of it, and then remembered about his promise to Eric.

"I talked to Eric earlier and he asked me to go to his Sunday Mass this weekend. I said I would."

"You're full of surprises. I never put you down as a convert."

"He got me at an unguarded moment. Anyway, that means I won't be leaving here until probably the afternoon and I just wanted to let you know."

"Okay darling," she said and then paused. "Didn't you say Nick was doing his prison visit on Monday morning?"

"Yes. So what?"

"Well I know you'd be a nightmare here, waiting for him to call you. Why don't you stay until he's done that and then you can talk to him face to face? I can just about cope with not having you here with us for one more day than planned."

She was right. Dan didn't even think about offering her a 'well if you're sure' or 'if you don't mind.'

"Thanks, I would. I'll be with you by Monday early evening then and from then on, nothing will keep us apart again."

CHAPTER TWENTY-SEVEN

Dan had not been to a church service in many years and never to a Catholic one. He was surprised by how well patronised Saint Paul's was, although he had no barometer to know if this was the norm or not. He followed behind an elderly couple, climbing a half dozen steps and entering. Dan paused as the couple dipped fingers into a bowl of water and crossed themselves before proceeding inside.

Bypassing the bowl, he deliberately searched for a seat midway in and midway along the range of pews. Being a face in the middle of hundreds of others felt better than being on the end by the aisle and somehow more on view, even though he reminded himself this wasn't another covert surveillance mission.

The church was cold but in Dan's experience they all were, as if it was all part of the deal. He absentmindedly considered the possibility it was because hell was so very hot that any house of God should be the opposite. Eric's invitation caught him at a loss for a reason to say no thank you, but as he sat, he started regretting not being able to think quicker.

A man similar in age to himself was to his left when Dan sat; as people do, they looked at each other and offered neighbourly smiles.

"Morning," Dan said.

"Good morning," the man replied and immediately went back to a whispered conversation with the woman next to him, obviously his wife.

Within seconds, a family of four slid into the pew after him. First and next to him, the wife and mother followed by the teenage son, slightly older teenage daughter and then the husband and father. Wife and mother smiled the smile.

"Morning."

"Good morning," Dan said as she turned back to her son and placed a hand on both of his knees to keep them still.

"Is your phone off?" she said to the boy.

He nodded a silent reply.

Dan was glad of the reminder; he reached into his pocket and switched his off too. All around him, the smiles and good mornings continued until it seemed everybody had greeted somebody else. In that time Dan picked up, read, and put back down the Hymnal and Missalette, which were in the pew rack in front of him. He expected to see a Bible but there weren't any. The Hymnal was self-explanatory; it was headed with today's date and indicated he was going to be singing two hymns before the end. He was glad of the Missalette for another reason; Catholic services could be quite long and the Missalette was clearly the operation order for this Sunday Mass.

At precisely 9:45 a.m. movement behind and to the right was the catalyst for much throat clearing, back straightening, and spectacle adjusting. Dan followed his immediate neighbours who both turned gently to their right as several robed figures entered their field of vision. Eric walked slowly down the aisle behind a boy carrying a tall cross made of polished metal. Dressed in a white cassock trimmed with a yellow and green stole, his vestments made him look much taller than he really was. Eric's head swayed to the left and right as he picked out faces in the congregation, acknowledging them. Behind him, two rows of two younger men, similarly dressed in mainly white, completed the priestly procession. As he passed Dan's pew, Dan was pleased Eric's head was turned the other way; it took them thirty more seconds to reach the altar at the front where they split into a practiced pattern, taking their pre-determined positions. Eric went behind the altar where he kissed it and then made his way to the front again.

"In the name of the Father and of the Son, and the Holy Spirit." Eric's voice carried to all corners of Saint Paul's, powered by his hidden microphone and several well positioned speakers.

Everyone crossed themselves as they'd done with the Holy Water earlier and said "Amen."

Dan felt like a human on an alien planet; it was another world, filled by inhabitants with customs he didn't understand. The Missalette was in easy reach but he knew even if he read it, he would be too far behind the rest of the congregation to try and keep up effectively and therefore decided to sit and do his best impression of the invisible man.

"Grace to you and peace from God our Father and the Lord Jesus Christ," Eric said with feeling.

"And with your spirit," came the unanimous reply.

Dan looked directly ahead and wasn't aware of those around him doing anything else. Eric then raised both arms to take in the whole church.

"Brothers and sisters let us acknowledge our sins, and so prepare ourselves to celebrate the sacred mysteries."

There followed a moment's silence where everybody bowed their heads. Dan's instinct was to take this opportunity to quickly look around, but he reminded himself he wasn't here to gather evidence.

Eric then led a series of prayers which initiated the necessary weekly responses. Towards the end of the prayers, Dan noticed the teenage boy sneak a peek at him; he was clearly wondering who the quiet stranger was but was quickly brought to heel by his mother's hand on his knee again.

Dan lost count of the number of Amen's he didn't say before Eric briefly stepped off the universal script path.

"Welcome one and all to our Sunday Mass," he said gently and friendly. "My heart is filled with joy to see some unfamiliar faces in our midst."

In the sea of bodies his gaze fell upon Dan; how he managed to know where he was to Dan's mind wasn't anything short of a miracle and he now felt exposed. Unless Eric had eyes in the back of his head, he couldn't have seen him when he made his way into the church. Dan thought Eric was more than his match in their notional surveillance battle.

Eric got back onto the Mass script, followed by another prayer and the first reading. Dan finally got some respite with the first hymn; he was never so happy to sing.

When everybody was asked to sit down, the relative exuberance of the singing was overtaken again by more prayer and another reading. Dan saw the boy barely conceal a yawn. After another amen, Eric stepped to one side and mounted a wooden dais where a lectern held a large open Bible in its carved hand.

He adjusted his glasses and for the briefest second Dan was sure he looked at him.

"A reading from the holy gospel; Book of Acts, Chapter thirteen," Eric began.

"'In the church at Antioch the following were prophets and teachers: Barnabas, Simeon called Niger, Lucius of Cyrene, Manaen, who had been brought up with Herod the tetrarch, and Saul.'"

Dan felt the names and places wash through his mind like watching fish in a fast running stream; entering his consciousness and then disappearing in a second. He tried his best to pay attention to Eric's story of Paul preaching his way through countries by land and sea; meeting all sorts of people including believers, doubters, and others scheming for their own interests. Eric made the story seem contemporary even though it was two thousand years old. He couldn't help noticing similarities between Eric's characters and the people in his life currently;

Tara, Bradley, Nick, Jim, and those closest, as well as his own supporting cast like Purdy, Eric himself, and even Sean Darcy and little George Zuckerman.

Having come so close to finding who killed Zoe but failing, he acknowledged he'd tried his best; now it was time to close this chapter and move on.

He fully reconnected with Eric again and watched him go about his work, appreciating the professionalism of the delivery to his congregation for several more minutes. It was a surprise when Eric took a deep breath in as he finished, soaking in the words he just read. "The gospel of the Lord," he said, removing his glasses.

As one, the congregation said, "Praise to you Lord Jesus Christ."

Dan checked his watch as surreptitiously as he could; he'd placed the Missalette upright, to keep up with the progress of the service; next up was the Homily. In brackets it simply said, 'An explanation of the reading.'

Eric's voice brought his head upright again. "We read the Book of Acts and the Gospel of Luke together do we not? The words of Luke's account of Jesus' life and the Acts of the Apostles from the man himself and who better to tell us about Paul, who we take our name from, than his closest friend and ally.

"Through the writings of Luke we know what sort of man Paul was, and what a man. Paul was brave, fearless in his dedication to spread the true word of God and so erudite."

He looked up at a mostly understanding and agreeing audience. "I had to go to the dictionary for erudite." He smiled gently at the ripple of congregational amusement.

"Learned, scholarly, well educated, knowledgeable, well read, well versed, well informed, cultured, cultivated, civilised, intellectual, intelligent, clever, academic, literary, studious, wise, discerning, enlightened, illuminated, and sophisticated it says in the dictionary. My goodness that's quite a list of qualities isn't it?

"If we look at Paul in Paphos and Perga and what he says, it would be hard to argue he's not all of those things. He speaks to believers and non-believers; he talks with Jews and Greeks and Gentiles and has the ability to somehow communicate to them all no matter how friendly or unfriendly they are."

Dan shivered; the hairs on his neck bristled the more he listened. The boy and his mother were as attentive as he was. The message was surely aimed at the whole congregation; it still felt like it was to him in particular.

"Looking at Paul's life we know that he wasn't always like he was in Paphos and Perga. No, our patron had quite a journey to become as erudite as he was."

The congregation sniggered again.

"Some say that the conversion of Paul on the road to Damascus is second only to the life, death, and resurrection of Jesus himself in importance to human history. He was a Jew but also possessed Roman citizenship. He was born in Tarsus, at the eastern end of the Mediterranean Sea and he was a strict Pharisee preaching Judaism.

"He even says, 'I was zealous in the traditions of my forefathers as a young man', which means he spoke out loudly and strongly against the church of God confessing that beyond measure, 'I persecuted the church of God.'

"So, his conversion explains in part how he went from being a young man with certain views to a man with entirely different ones and we must be most grateful because without Paul we would be missing half of the books of the Old Testament.

"Yet I also believe there must be more. As we get older, we all have many and different experiences every day which mould us into the people we are. Paul's conversion was a major experience wasn't it? But he had others and they all contributed to him becoming the man he was. I'm speaking to you as a late middle-aged man who when he was a young boy believed in fairies in my parents' garden; as a young man I believed cigarettes were not harmful and made me cool. Until the Lord God came to me when I was twenty years old, I believed when my physical body died, so did the rest of me.

"When I was a young man, I was also very shy; the thought of standing in front of a room full of people like you would have terrified me, let alone speaking to you all as I'm doing now."

Dan shifted in his seat; he was no longer feeling cold; in fact, he was feeling uncomfortably warm.

"So, my message to you today and the message Luke and Paul have for us all this morning is this. What you think and feel today might not be what you think and feel tomorrow. What you believe you can achieve in your life on Earth today is only limited by your experiences up to today. Tomorrow your experiences and your faith might mean you can achieve much more.

"Don't close your eyes to the possibilities that your experiences reveal. Have faith and seek to deepen your faith every day." Eric paused, taking in a few deep breaths. "Let us pray."

Eric bowed his head and his room followed suit, apart from Dan. He remained with his head up, transfixed and watching Eric as he began to recite the next prayer.

The first lines of the prayer were lost on him; he heard the noises of Eric's words and the congregation's responses, but they were all ambient. Suddenly Eric looked up mid-sentence and without breaking stride their eyes met and remained together as he carried on to the end of the prayer.

The Mass service continued on its perennial course, but it was lost on Dan. Eric's words fizzed like electricity through his head.

It wasn't until more physical activities surrounding the Communion started that he was able to draw his focus away from the words of the Homily.

Recognising the first line of the Lord's Prayer, Dan joined in with the rest although he said the words without reflecting on their meaning. Another prayer followed straight on by which time he lost his position on the Missalette. He was therefore taken by surprise when his female neighbour turned to him with her hand extended and said, "Peace be with you." His reflex was to shake her hand.

"And you," he replied as if he were speaking a foreign language.

All around him, people were doing the same and for a moment the whole church seemed to be in a polite uproar.

When the head of the man in the pew in front of him turned to face him, Dan was ready. "Peace be with you," the man said.

Dan shook hands with more authority, as if he knew what he was doing this time.

"And to you," he replied.

He didn't know how many more offers of handshakes to expect and it was somewhat of a surprise when there were none. Soon after Eric said more prayers in preparation for the Communion.

When people started filing along the pews and towards the altar to partake of the body and blood of Christ Dan stayed firm, bunching his knees so others could pass. The procession to receive the bread and wine reminded him of ants on a stem going to and from a food source. Eric's earlier words kept him company throughout and what he thought may be a lengthy spell was over in no time at all.

As everybody made their way back in their seats, the atmosphere in the church changed and became more relaxed; Dan felt like things were ending.

"May almighty God bless you, the Father, and of the Son, and the Holy Spirit," Eric announced with pleasure.

Once more his people responded together and with gusto. "Amen."

"Go in peace, glorifying the Lord by your life."

"Thanks be to God," everyone replied, and they began to stand; some stretching, some taking the chance to speak to another for the first time in over an hour.

Eric waited at the doors, thanking people for coming and for their thanks for his service. He shook older hands and patted young heads, giving time to all who wanted a word or two before they funnelled out into the late dull grey morning.

Dan joined the slow-moving queue; he seemed to be the only party of one in the whole church and found himself concentrating on his shoes or the ceiling to avoid eye contact and conversation.

"Thank you, Father, it was a lovely service this morning," the lady in front of Dan said.

"Thanks Eunice. How is your leg this week?"

"Oh, you know the cold weather makes it worse. I shall be putting it up when I get home."

"Well you take good care of yourself. See you soon."

"I will Father. Goodbye."

Eunice shuffled along a little quicker after her exchange with Eric and used the central brass handrail to assist her down the steps to the pavement.

"Dan, I'm so glad you made it," Eric said, planting one hand on Dan's shoulder as the other reached out and grabbed his hand.

For once Dan couldn't think of a thing to say and he became very conscious of the people behind him waiting to have a personal moment with their conduit to God and the fact he was holding them up.

"Thank you. Thanks for everything," he managed to get out.

Eric looked like he had more to say but had his duties to attend to. "When are you planning on leaving?"

"Probably first thing tomorrow. We're not finished but I made a promise to Tara and I'm okay with it."

"That's good to hear. I hope you find your peace."

They released each other's hand but as Dan made his way out, he couldn't help feeling Eric's eyes were still on his back. He stopped on the top step and glanced back only to see Eric was now engrossed with a young couple who had been sitting two rows in front of him. And yet he still felt Eric's eyes on him.

It wasn't until he was back at the car that he remembered to switch his phone on again. As it invisibly connected to the army of satellites hundreds of miles above him Dan fastened his seat belt and put the key in the ignition.

His phone beeped. He looked at the screen to see he had missed calls—nine missed calls.

Instinctively he auto dialled the last one.

"It's me, what is it?"

"Bloody church services, we've been trying to get you for an hour," Nick said.

Dan checked the car's clock; the Mass had lasted for an hour and a quarter.

"Just tell me," he begged as a gut-wrenching feeling of sickness overcame him.

"Tara called us when she couldn't get you. It's Bradley."

CHAPTER TWENTY-EIGHT

It was just as well Nick was driving; if Dan had been, no motorist including himself would have been safe. He'd almost collapsed at the wheel of his car when Nick told him Bradley was rushed into hospital; being sat already saved him.

When he burst through the front door of Nick's house, they were ready for him.

"Pen has chucked your stuff in a bag. I'm driving you, no arguments," Nick said before Dan had a chance to say anything at all.

Penny was close to tears; it was all she could do to hug him tightly for a second and then push him away.

"I'm keeping in touch with Gwen and Jim to keep your phone free for Tara." She turned to Nick. "Just go carefully."

"I will love, try not to worry. I'll call you when I can."

Nick hugged and kissed her, then he and Dan were out the door as if the house was on fire.

"Tell me again what they said?" Dan demanded before they got to the end of the road.

Nick obeyed without question; it was much better than the awful silence alternative.

"He had a bad night last night. Tara was up with him at least a couple of times. When she woke up this morning and went to see him he was asleep and seemed fine, so she went and had breakfast thinking she would get him up afterwards.

"When she did go back, he was having some sort of fit; there was sick and blood-filled shit everywhere and he couldn't cry or make much sound at all. Jim called the ambulance."

"How long did the ambulance take?"

"Dan, it was just a few minutes. I don't know exactly how long but they got there as quickly as they could."

While talking, Dan didn't take his eyes off his phone. "Why the fuck won't she answer?" he shouted as his latest call to Tara's mobile went straight to voicemail again.

"She's probably in the hospital with him, can't use her phone," Nick said.

"What hospital? Did she say?"

"She didn't know. Gwen said she was in pieces. Why don't you try Jim or her again?"

As Dan dialled, Nick threw his car onto the roundabout and then joined the motorway where he immediately got up to and past the national speed limit.

Jim's mobile was also off, lending credibility to the feeling he was still with Tara and there was a genuine reason for the lack of communication. Gwen picked up on the first ring.

"Oh, Dan it's you."

"Gwen we're on our way. All I know is the ambulance came and took them."

"Jim called me when they got to the hospital, Dan. They were diverted straight to the Children's Hospital in Plymouth."

Dan covered the mouthpiece. "Plymouth," he said to Nick who just nodded and put his foot down a little harder.

"I've not heard from him for a while," Gwen was saying.

Dan tried to calm his frayed nerve ends. "What happened?"

Gwen repeated what she told Nick earlier. Dan noted his friend had remembered every detail.

"We'll go straight to the hospital, Gwen. If you hear from Tara or Jim before us, please get them to call me?" He took a breath. "Are you alright, what are you going to do?" he asked.

"I was just going to clean up in your room. The poor mite made such a mess. Oh, Dan I pray he'll be alright."

Dan wasn't in the mood to pray; it was God's fault he was busy when Tara was desperately trying to contact him. He said goodbye and dropped the phone in his lap.

They didn't need maps; Nick's road knowledge was as good as ever.

"It's motorway most of the way and a Sunday; we should make good time," Nick said.

"I've left a message and a text for her to call me as soon as," Dan replied.

"Dan?"

Dan turned, for the first time showing Nick his ashen face and red rimmed eyes.

"What?"

"It's going to be alright."

Jim's arm was soaking wet. For as long as it remained around Tara's shoulder, her tears ensured its soggy state.

"He's in the best place possible," he said for at least the third time.

"Why did I leave him?" Tara sobbed.

"Now you stop that. He was asleep and you had no way of knowing what was going to happen. The doctor said he would be back soon so let's just wait and see what happens."

"What about Dan?" The mention of his name started her crying harder.

"I can go and try him again, but I don't want to leave you here like this."

The prefabricated seats they were perched on made sitting side by side impossible. The best Jim could do was to lean uncomfortably across to be able to reach around with his arm, allowing Tara to rest her head on his shoulder.

Further discussion was halted when as if on cue the doctor appeared again at the far end of the corridor. He walked towards them with a clipboard and a poorly disguised look of concern.

"Ms. Danes, I'm sorry to have kept you. I need to ask you some questions about Bradley."

The doctor sat down on a twin seat arrangement on the other side of the corridor, so he was opposite Tara, no more than two steps apart.

"You mentioned to the ambulance staff Bradley has a pre-existing condition. What can you tell me about that?"

Tara told him what she could. "Our specialist has called it a bowel or stomach condition, but they don't know exactly what it is. He said Bradley might grow out of it."

The doctor wrote down what she said. "When was the last time he was seen?"

"Two or three weeks before we came to England; so, six weeks at the most. He had an episode about ten days ago at your house, didn't he Jim?"

"Yes, Doctor. He was crying for a few hours when he was suddenly violently sick and filled his nappy at the same time. He settled down after that but a few days later we took him to the local A and E because he seemed to be having stomach trouble, cramps or something similar. They gave us a magnesium muscle relaxant which he took for the next two days. He has been completely fine since then until today."

The doctor nodded and added to his notes. "Do you know the name of the medication?"

"I can call my wife and find out. We still have it in the kitchen cupboard."

"That would be helpful. Now Tara; may I call you Tara?"

"Yes of course."

"Tara, Bradley is stable now. We've given him something to make him sleep."

She looked hopefully at Jim, but her hopes were short lived.

"However, I must tell you he's very unwell," the doctor continued.

Jim saw Tara's lips tremble; although the doctor had given them so little information, he believed they were being told to fear the worst.

"You must be able to tell us something?" he asked.

"He's dehydrated, and he's also lost a significant amount of blood, which is not a good combination. Currently, we're trying to get his fluids up before we think about giving him blood or plasma too. He's very weak."

Jim could only look on as Tara began to weep silent tears. He understood she was unable to fathom what they were being told. Her baby boy was perfectly fine when she went to have breakfast. By the time she finished an egg and a piece of bread he was fighting for his life. As he was with her, she didn't have to think, which was just as well; her competence to function seemed to be closing down with every passing second.

"What can we do now?" Jim asked as Tara and the doctor looked blankly at each other.

"If you find out the name of that medication it would help us greatly, just in case he has reacted to it. Other than that, if you do think of anything you believe might help, tell the nurses at the station over there and they'll contact me. I must get back now, but I'll come and see you again as soon as I can."

When he was gone Jim stood and pulled Tara up straight.

"Let's go and call Gwen about that medication and you can try calling Dan too."

She looked at him as if he were mad. "Are you stupid? I can't leave now! What if they need me?"

He understood how she was feeling and how traumatic events could make people say and act differently to how they were normally. Tara's words were a reaction to Bradley's situation, nothing more.

"If they need you, we'll tell the nurses where we'll be. You will feel better if you can talk to Dan and I know he must be waiting on a call from you. We'll only be a few minutes."

Jim's sensible reaction to her overreaction calmed her; he led her away from the doctors and Bradley. Jim told the duty nurse they would be back soon, and they continued out to the more public areas.

As soon as they switched their phones on, they both beeped impatiently.

"I'll be right over here," Jim said noting Tara's anxious look as he took a step away from her.

He dialled home and updated Gwen as best he could, until he heard Tara sobbing.

"Sorry love I have to go. Tara needs me."

He closed his phone and went back to Tara. She stood in front of him like a schoolchild being reprimanded by the head teacher. He took the phone from her limp hand.

"Dan is that you? It's me, son."

"Thank God you're there. What's going on?"

Jim's mind went straight to the facts. "We're at the hospital and have come outside for a minute so Tara could call you. Bradley's sedated and they're treating him for dehydration and blood loss. They don't know what caused him to become so ill so quickly." Dan listened and processed the simply put information. "Is there anything you can tell me that I can pass on to them, Dan?"

"Bradley was at the specialist's two weeks before we came away. As usual he said he couldn't diagnose the trouble but said he hoped Bradley might grow out of it in time. All his major organs have been checked and are perfectly normal for his age." Dan wracked his brain for more.

"When he has attacks, he always curls his legs up, obviously a reaction to the location of the pain and maybe it helps him a bit but because he can't tell us, we don't know that for sure."

Dan's cool exterior was hiding a desperate churning inside. Bizarrely but helpfully, as long as he could concentrate on the facts, he could control his emotions.

"Jim, what happened?"

"You know I told you about what happened at the beginning of last week when he was unwell at ours; I think this could be a more severe version of that. At that time we thought he might be teething or something like that. Tara ate a bit of breakfast and then went straight back to see him again and that's when she found him. She'd only have been gone for ten minutes."

"Go on, I'm listening."

"She went upstairs, and we heard her scream. When I got there, she was holding him out of the cot. We just called 999 and she held him until they arrived. He was breathing but not crying."

"Did Tara say anything to you about what she found before she screamed and you came running?"

"No, son. She was just talking to the boy. Holding him and telling him he was going to be okay. Where are you now?"

Dan looked up, but they were at a point between road signs. Nick read his mind.

"Ten miles to the M5."

"We're ten miles from the M5. So, what's that, at least a hundred and fifty left."

"Alright son, we won't be going anywhere. He's in the intensive care unit now. I'll call again if there's any change. Do you want Tara again?"

"Yes, thanks."

When Tara came back on the line, she was no longer crying but she did sound terribly frightened.

"Dan."

"Hey."

"Dan, what's going to happen?" she begged.

"We'll be there as soon as we can. T, we both have to think."

"What about? I don't understand."

"If the doctors don't know what's wrong with him yet, there might be something we can remember which will help them to decide. I've been doing nothing else, but you've spent more time with him since he was born.

"What we have to do is try and think of anything which we've not told our doctors in Auckland because we didn't think it was relevant or we just forgot. Can you do that too?"

"Yes, I guess so."

Dan became even more serious. "You can do this, T. You can help Bradley. Remember what we've done before and how we do it? Tell me."

"I remember. Put myself there at the time and place; use my senses to remember all the details including taste and smell. I can get Jim to write it down for me."

"Good Tara. I know you can do it."

Dan kept their goodbye short; he couldn't allow Tara to start crying again or she wouldn't be able to concentrate well enough.

Nick hurtled onwards, looking out for traffic police cars that might slow their progress. "How are they doing?"

"I don't know what to think. Apparently he's dehydrated, and he's also lost blood," Dan replied, looking at his best friend whose eyes were focused on the road ahead.

"I heard what you told her about remembering stuff. Is it possible? I mean do you think you can tell the doctors anything for him to be diagnosed?"

"Honestly, I seriously doubt it. If there'd been something wrong with him, she would have seen it; she's an amazing mother. But I needed to give her something else to think about and make her feel like she's doing something worthwhile."

Nick acknowledged Dan's smart thinking with a grunt and then used his index finger to point without taking his hands off the steering wheel. Dan looked and saw the blue sign above the road for the M5 South West.

"Dan must have done his evidence gathering exercise for you a hundred times. I just need you to write down what I say," Tara said.

Tara and Jim took up station on the uncomfortable seats again which wasn't ideal, but it was quiet and that suited her. The nurses obliged with a pen and some paper.

Jim looked a little embarrassed. "I'm ashamed to say no; we weren't on good terms in those days. I didn't give him or his unusual techniques the attention they deserved."

Tara patted his knee. "I know; he's an acquired taste. Just write."

They both managed to smile but it was brief and seemed wrong.

Gwen finished her latest harrowing clean-up project for now; the second such time in as many years. She had nothing but love and concern for Bradley however what came out of him was an entirely different matter. Washing the bedding achieved only limited success, so she left it to soak in a strong solution, gladly closing the door of the utility room.

Jim and Tara were at the hospital and Dan was on his way to join them. She picked up the landline.

"Hello Penny, dear, it's me Gwen. I thought I'd give you a call."

"Hi, is there any news?"

"I haven't heard anything else from Jim in the last hour. It reminds me of when he used to go off working in the middle of the night."

"I gave up counting years ago how many times Nick's run out of the house and I've not known when I'd see him next."

The simple act of speaking to someone with a shared interest was cathartic. Although neither had real news to give the other, after five minutes of mundane talk they both felt better. When Gwen came off the phone again and replaced the handset, she looked at the utility room door. She scowled and came very close to swearing.

These days Jim knew better than to question any suggestion Dan made regarding information gathering. Tara had a job to do and so did he. As she relaxed into a near meditative state, he sat very still so as not to make any disturbing noise. It was several minutes before Tara started talking in short bursts of a few words or longer descriptions of times and places she was with Bradley.

He wrote it all down.

The concrete and tarmac snake-pit known to all as spaghetti junction thankfully treated them kindly. From the air it was easy to see why the conjoined M1, M5, and M6 motorways intersection in the heart of the England was dubbed the most intimidating road in the country. Today it more resembled a dragstrip, causing Nick to quietly thank the automotive gods.

Miles later, Nick listened as Dan continued going through every aspect of the last ten months, recalling anything that might offer insight into Bradley's condition. Nick started to pick his fingernails as he drove. Thanks to the straight road, the job of steering was no more than holding the wheel and that led to idle hands.

"It's bloody useless," Dan spat. "Where are we now?"

It was a rhetorical question; Nick knew Dan would be able to take a quick look around and realise in seconds exactly where they were as this was one of the motorways they trawled up and down a thousand times on surveillance jobs in the past.

"We've done this a few times haven't we?" Dan said a few moments later.

"I'll say."

Nick was tempted to add to his comment along the lines of remembering a particular incident, but it wasn't the time or place. In all the operations over all the years he and Dan worked together, there had never been a life or death consideration, yet in the space of the last year they had raced to Jim Allen's aid and found him almost beaten to death, and now this.

"We're making good time now. I'll have you there soon."

After an hour Tara was exhausted but she was also disappointed. Like Dan she was sure what she remembered wouldn't provide them with the clue they needed.

Jim looked at the pages he wrote and then handed them to her to review.

"Shall I get us a drink? Maybe just some water; I saw a fountain as we came back."

He got up and left Tara looking at the papers.

"Do you see anything, Tara?" he asked when he returned carrying two plastic cups.

She looked up and tears started to stream down her cheeks again; there was no need to answer.

Nick didn't slow the car as the motorway became the minor A38. The good news was the dual carriageway continued for the entire journey ahead, but the bad news was there were still another sixty miles to go.

Dan continued to look at his phone as if it might make it ring. He barely acknowledged the location.

Nick gave it another fifteen minutes before he asked for help. "I'll need directions to the hospital once we hit town. We know there will be signposts but there might be more than one. I don't want to deliver you to the wrong one."

Dan forced a smile remembering the unfortunate hotel incident when they sent the entire surveillance unit of eight cars and two motor cycles to the wrong Sheraton in Newcastle because he didn't think to check if there was more than one in the city. Fortunately, that error didn't cost the operation, but it did cost him a significant amount in the bar at the end of a successful bust later the same day.

He used Nick's phone to find the address and an accompanying map and then wrote the details down. He handed Nick's phone back and stared out of the window willing the road to end.

It took another twenty minutes before his wish became true. 'Welcome to Plymouth. Britain's Ocean City,' the sign read, but it was a cold welcome for them.

"Follow the signs for city centre and possibly Devonport," Dan said.

He reached out and patted Nick's back; it was wet through. The drive had been relatively straightforward, the roads jam free and other motorists obliging when they came up behind to overtake. The greater circumstances however were nerve shredding and it was showing.

Dan's directions were abrupt, which was fine; Nick followed them without question. They still scanned both sides of the road for a signpost to the Children's Hospital.

"Next right, then second left which should be traffic lights, Queens Terrace," Dan said, putting the paper in the door pocket.

"Plymouth Children's Hospital, Admissions and Visitors," Nick said, pointing to the sign on a lamp post two minutes later.

"That will do."

"I'll drop you at the door and come and find you once I've parked. I'll also call Pen to let her know we're here."

Two minutes later Dan had the door open as the car came to a stop. Without a word he was out and gone.

Nick groaned but resisted the chance to rub his neck until he found somewhere to park and turn the engine off.

CHAPTER TWENTY-NINE

"Tara," Dan exclaimed as he pushed open the double doors.

She ran to him and they wrapped their arms around each other.

Jim decided to go for another short walk. A minute later he was on the phone to Gwen.

"He's just got here. I'll stay if he wants me to, but it's probably best for me to come home soon. I know it's the best part of an hour, but can you come and get me, love?" As he was talking he saw Nick appear around a corner. "Hold on love, I've just seen Nick. Let me call you back in a minute."

Nick saw him too and they exchanged a warm handshake.

"Are you alright son? You look drained."

"Not so bad. Have you seen Dan?"

"He's with Tara now. I thought I would give them a few minutes alone."

"Oh right of course. Is there any news?"

"No. We last saw a doctor just before Dan talked to us, when you were on the road." Jim said, checking his watch.

Nick shook his head. "She must be going out of her mind. I've never seen Dan like this either."

"I don't think we can do anything more than wait. What are your plans?"

"I've not made any. I'll have to be home by morning though because of that visit to Vikkert. I don't want to cancel and make another appointment."

While Jim and Nick were discussing one subject Dan and Tara's only thoughts were for their son.

"I don't understand. I was only out of the room for a few minutes," Tara repeated over and over.

"Please, no one's blaming you. He's obviously got something seriously wrong with him so there's nothing you could have done to prevent this fit or attack or whatever it was."

"You should have seen him. I thought he was dead."

"And the doctors haven't said any more?"

"I've not even seen one again since he was last here and that was just before we talked. Should we try and speak to someone again now?"

They sat down and held each other's hands. When Jim and Nick wandered into view along the corridor they sat too before anyone could think of a thing to say. It was a short time before Dan remembered Jim was still recovering from serious injury.

"Jim."

"Yes."

"You must be knackered too. Are you feeling alright?"

"Don't worry about me, son."

"Thank you for bringing him to me," Tara said to Nick.

"Of course. I couldn't let him drive on his own. How are you? How is he?"

"I'm alright," Tara replied. "I was saying to Dan, we've not heard any more about Bradley."

"Let's go and see about that right now," Dan said.

They crossed to the nurse's station and had to wait for the frazzled looking staffer to come off the telephone.

"This is my partner, Bradley's father," Tara said to the nurse.

"We wanted to know when someone could tell us more," Dan pleaded.

The nurse picked up the phone again. "Let me see if I can find Doctor Ripton for you."

The promise of a few minutes strained the definition to breaking point and Dan was ready to go and ask again when the doctor appeared. He didn't question the presence of the two others with Tara and Jim since he saw them last.

"Please forgive me; it has been an extremely busy afternoon. I've just come from Bradley's room. Unfortunately, I can't tell you any more than we discussed earlier; his situation has not altered."

"This is Dan, Bradley's father. Can you tell him what you told me?" Tara asked, as if hearing it from a man in a white coat would somehow make it better.

Dr. Ripton explained everything again without showing any sign of impatience. Dan listened carefully but wasn't struck by anything he could use to help his son.

"So, what do we do? Can we see him?"

"Honestly now there's nothing any of us can do until we know more. Bradley is sedated as I said and he's in a unit where visitors are not permitted, so regrettably I have to say no."

While Dan and Tara consoled each other, Dr. Ripton turned to Jim and checked his clipboard again. "Did you find out the name of that medication, sir?"

"Novoflixil. Do you need to see it? I can have the bottle brought here."

Dan looked even more confused. Tara explained as Dr. Ripton told Jim to hold fast for the time being.

With no more he could say at that time, the doctor apologised once more for the long waits between updates and suggested they go home as the next report wouldn't be for several more hours, or even the following morning.

"I really believe it will be in your best interest to come back in the morning when you've had time to rest. All we'll be doing for the rest of the day is keeping Bradley stable. I can't see how much can change but if it does, we can call you."

It was the logical thing to do and yet Dan and Tara thought it utterly ridiculous; their baby boy was fighting for his life in a lonely room somewhere close by, so not being there was inconceivable. It took the combined efforts of Dan's brother and father in all but name to change their minds.

"You can't just sit here all night, son. Look, it's nearly five and I bet none of us has eaten. It's going to be another long day tomorrow and if you want to be here early you must get some rest."

"He's right. Jim must get home somehow as well, and we only have my car between us," Nick said.

"I can drive us all back to ours so Nick can rest and shower before he heads back. You can be here in under an hour whenever they call. We can leave all our details like the doctor said," Jim explained.

"What do you think, T?"

"Please don't ask me to decide, Dan. I'm not capable at the moment."

It was her words that convinced him she needed the rest; looking into her eyes Dan could see she was close to breaking.

"Alright, let's go."

They left every possible contact number and address, confirming they would be back at 8:00 a.m.

Dan committed the journey back to Jim's to memory so they could return to the hospital in the morning without problem. He sat in the back seat with Tara slumped against him and quiet, as if leaving the hospital had drained her of all remaining strength.

Gwen's welcome was as tired as they were; Tara and Dan collapsed onto the big lounge sofa, their exhaustion becoming clearer with every second. Jim looked grey with worry and tiredness.

"Sit. Don't do anything," Gwen directed, putting him in a chair. "Let me sort out Nick and I'll be back in a few minutes."

She showed Nick to the bathroom and provided him with towels and soap. "I'll make you something too. Take your time."

All conversation was difficult and muted when they were all together again sometime later. Despite having something to eat and drink nobody felt satisfied in any way and it wasn't until Nick's time to leave came that their movements got past first gear.

Tara hugged and kissed him.

"I don't know what to say. Just take care and let us know when you know something," Nick said, sniffing.

He and Dan looked at each other. Normally they would have a comment or two about him seeing Edward Vikkert the next day, but it didn't occur to either one of them.

"Drive safe. Give our love to Penny and the girls," Dan said.

"I will. I'll talk to you tomorrow."

They didn't hug; neither was prepared to take the risk of what would happen if they did.

Dan stayed in the doorway long after Nick's tail lights disappeared. He was utterly drained mentally and physically, to the point of knowing any more thinking would result in a massive headache. When he got back to the lounge Tara and Jim were looking at the pages they produced at the hospital earlier.

"Can you look at these darling?" Tara asked.

"Of course, how did you do?" he replied without hesitation, sitting next to her.

Considering the futility of what he asked her to do, Dan was amazed at the quality and quantity she recalled. As he found when he'd questioned himself, there wasn't anything in what she said and Jim wrote that screamed a message to him, yet he found two or three things to talk about and get Tara to expand on to make her feel the whole effort wasn't wasted.

While they were talking, Jim rested in his chair and Gwen made herself busy tidying away the remnants of the day; Dan offered to help, to take his mind off darker thoughts. As they were putting trays away in the utility room, he saw Bradley's bed sheets still soaking in the sink, causing even darker thoughts to rise.

When Gwen was finally finished, she joined the others in the lounge and touched Jim's shoulder. He opened his eyes with a start.

"Sorry love, I must have dropped off for a minute."

"It's alright. You should get off to bed."

"I think we all should," Jim replied loud enough for Dan and Tara to respond too.

"Is it okay for us to take the car in the morning?" Tara asked. "We have to be at the hospital for eight a.m."

"Whatever you need. We can sort out getting your rental back here tomorrow. You might even be able to call the company and get them to pick it up from Nick's and rent another one down here."

Dan stifled a yawn. "That's a good idea."

Reviewing the events of the day for the last time Gwen remembered Bradley's sheets. "Sorry to mention it now, Jim," she said, holding his hand as he lifted himself out of the chair, "But what did you do to get the last of the stain out of the carpet the other day? I've washed and soaked Bradley's things and I still can't shift it."

"I mixed a bit of bicarb with some soda water and left it for a minute. I've seen a lot in my time but nothing like that bright yellowy green. Come on bed time."

He allowed Dan and Tara to leave the room first and then he turned the lights off.

As they were climbing the stairs Dan suddenly stopped, grabbing the handrail.

"Dan, whatever's the matter?" Gwen asked as they bunched up behind him.

He didn't know, but he knew there was something he saw or heard in the last five minutes that was now jabbing a hot iron into his brain.

Tara stared at him; throughout the day, throughout the last days, weeks, months, and years he'd never shown real physical frailty until now. He slumped down to sit halfway between floors.

"Dan, son, talk to us," Jim begged.

"No, I—hold on, just wait a minute," Dan mumbled as he began to think again despite the pain in his head.

His thoughts became words.

"Your notes T; we were going through what you remembered. Is that it?" he asked himself out loud, dragging the memory to the forefront of his mind so he could see the words on the pages again and read them as fast as he could.

"No, nothing," he continued. "I was thinking about him and the way he curls up his legs when he's in pain. You were asleep Jim and you snored once. Tara, no, you weren't doing anything. We were holding hands and your ring was digging in my finger, but I didn't care. Gwen came back in then; I heard you close a door in the hall and then you came, and you talked to Jim. You woke him up. No, no that's not it. You said Jim should go to bed and asked him about getting the stains out of Bradley's sheet."

Dan's eyes flickered as he recalled every detail. His head was pounding.

"Wait. You said get the stains out of his sheet. His sheet was stained, it was stained this morning when you found him, Tara, after he was sick and bled all over his cot."

Another agonising moment passed as he battled to think and understand. "Blood, blood in the cot and blood on the sheet," Dan said as if he were chanting a spell.

"No. What next? Jim said bicarb and soda water to get the stain out of the carpet after he was sick before. Bicarbonate of soda? No. Soda water? No, not that. Stain in the carpet? Bradley was sick on the carpet and you had never seen anything like it before."

In his head Dan saw it and visualised the scene.

"It was yellowy green; yellowy green you said, and you never saw anything like it before. Bradley was sick on the floor; he was sick on the carpet. Bradley's sick was yellow, it was green," Dan went on.

He knew that was it, but he still could remember what 'it' was. Instead he kept repeating, "It was yellow, it was green. Yellow and green."

When the flash struck it was almost blinding. He glared at Gwen. "Show me the sheets! Where are his sheets?"

Gwen didn't reply but spun on her heels and shot down the stairs defying her age and physical ability. Dan followed with Tara and Jim behind.

Gwen almost knocked the door off its hinges as she burst into the utility room and hit the lights. She pointed to the sink.

The white cotton was heavy, and no one minded as Dan yanked it out, splashing the bleach and washing powder infusion all over himself and the tiled floor. It took no time to see where his precious son had been ill such was the extent of the mess. Dan stared at the unnatural colour.

When he turned to face them Dan's eyes were filled with tears that had nothing to do with the pungent ammonia smell. "Was it just like this before?" he yelled.

"No, it was much brighter, almost fluorescent," Jim replied.

"Yes, yes, yes," Dan bellowed but he was still not quite there.

"Bright yellow sick, bright green." He only needed to say it out loud once. "Oh God Zoe, thank you."

Five minutes later Tara was hanging onto Dan's arm as he dialled, with Jim and Gwen standing by in close attendance.

"Pick up, pick up," Dan begged.

"Hello," Elizabeth Summers said doubtfully at the other end.

"Elizabeth, it's Dan Calder here, I'm so sorry to call you so late, but I need to ask you something."

"Mr. Calder if this is your idea of a joke—do you know what the time is?"

"I'm sorry, really I am but I had to call. My son is in hospital and he might be dying but I think you can help him; you can help us."

"You must be mad. I've a good mind to call the police." She sounded a little drunk.

"No please Elizabeth, one question I promise."

Zoe's mother hesitated, and Dan didn't waste the chance to go on before she said no.

"My son is in hospital with an unknown stomach or bowl condition. When he woke up this morning, he was violently sick and lost a lot of blood when he filled his nappy. He's in intensive care right now."

Elizabeth Summers remained quiet.

"His vomit was a very unusual colour and I've just remembered I saw it once before, when Zoe died. Elizabeth, Zoe was sick in the same way. You told me a week or so ago that her condition was never diagnosed while she was alive but in recent years your doctor told you what it was. Please tell me what it was?"

"Really? Are you serious?"

"Elizabeth, I swear to you, Zoe saved my life that night in Powton Road and you can save my baby son's life tonight."

"Diverticulitis. He said she probably had diverticulitis."

"Thank you so much. I will never be able to thank you enough. I've got to go now," Dan said as he began to cry uncontrollably.

"I hope your boy gets better Mr. Calder. Will you let me know?

"I will, I will. Thank you again. Goodbye." Dan ended the call and punched in the hospital number he knew by heart.

"Diverticulitis," he said to Tara before the hospital switchboard operator answered.

By the time Dan finished his call Jim had done a Google search. He read the first paragraph straight off the screen while the others sat and listened.

"'Inflammation or infection of pouches called diverticula that develop on the walls of the intestines. The formation of the pouches is relatively benign; this condition is called diverticulosis. The more serious diverticulitis can involve anything from abscesses in the pouches to much larger infections or perforation of the bowel.'"

Tara gasped and put both hands to her mouth.

They waited until the printer finished its short run before Jim read more.

"I'm paraphrasing. Diverticulosis is rarely painful, and you may not even be aware if you have it. Symptoms include cramps which subside when you pass wind or have a bowel movement.

"Diverticulitis symptoms are much more acute and noticeable. Severe abdominal pain, inflammation causing bowel obstruction, severe bleeding, and vomiting. Fistulas may develop if an infected diverticulum reaches an adjoining organ and makes a connection. The organ can then become infected. If the infection reaches and passes through the intestinal wall it may result in another condition called peritonitis, which in turn may lead to serious blood poisoning."

Tara crumbled and Gwen held her tightly. Dan in contrast became stern and straight. He took the paper from Jim and read through it again. Knowing, or believing he knew what was wrong with Bradley now had the effect of galvanising his emotions. He started to think and rationalise.

"We can go back now, T. There's a chance they will need to operate, and we'll have to give our consent. They said he was the same as when we left."

Tara said yes but it was an unconscious reaction.

Dan was already computing the route to Plymouth when Jim spoke next.

"I'll get the car; Gwen, make sure you set the alarm before you leave."

"No, wait, you're done in Jim. There's no need for you to come," Dan said.

Jim snorted. "Try telling that to Gwen while I get the car. Good luck with that by the way."

When Dan looked at Gwen, he knew it would be a waste of time and effort.

It was midnight when they arrived at the hospital. The duty head-nurse showed them into an office adjacent to the nurse's station as soon as they got to the ICU and they didn't have to wait long before a new doctor came in wearing the same harried look on his face Dr. Ripton wore earlier.

"Mr. Calder?"

"Hello that's me. This is my partner Tara."

"Hello, good evening. I'm Rowan Sinclair. I've a message here to say you called in to say you believe Bradley is suffering from diverticulitis."

Dan explained, leaving a lot of the superfluous and historical details out, while the doctor listened attentively and looked between Tara, Jim, and Gwen, who made confirming noises and gestures as if it might somehow help.

"None of us are doctors like you or have any experience to say it must be diverticulitis," Dan finished. "But we thought it may just help."

"Mr. Calder, from what I've seen of Bradley and what you've just described I would say diverticulitis is a better than even chance of being the correct diagnosis. My colleague is running tests now. If it is, then it's a very severe case; the most severe I've ever come across in such a young child."

Tara grimaced and Gwen reached out for her.

Dan kept his gaze on the physician. "What does that mean?"

"I can't say for sure, but I would imagine surgery and soon."

"Peritonitis?" Tara whispered.

"It's much too early to say," Sinclair replied.

"How long will it take for you to know one way or the other?"

"That really depends on Bradley, on how he responds to the tests and how strong he is to undergo them in the first place. But we won't know much with me standing here, so if you will forgive me? There's one last thing. If surgery is required, then we'll need your authority. If I leave you these forms, can you have a good look and return them to the nurse when you're done?"

Tara leant against Dan for support as well as comfort.

The decision to sign the consent forms only took a moment, but the rest of the night was hellishly long.

CHAPTER THIRTY

Nick looked at his phone; there were no missed calls or messages. His night's sleep was short and restless; having to tell Penny every detail of what happened and then repeat most of it again when the girls came in, he was feeling less then fantastic about his early start.

He was due at the prison to see Vikkert at 10:00 a.m. but also had work to do in the office before he could go.

Jim and Gwen returned at 7:30 a.m. from a break to stretch their legs and find the cafeteria. Tara was lying across the seats and on Dan's lap. When he saw them, he smiled limply.

Jim handed him a plastic cup with an apology for the coffee inside. "It was this or nothing."

When Dan tried it, he was tempted to agree that nothing probably tasted better, but it was warm and wet and took the taste of hospital corridors away for a short time. Tara stirred and woke up realising where they were.

"Any news?" she said sleepily.

"No. You've only been asleep for thirty minutes," Dan replied, allowing her to sit up.

Their vigil had been undisturbed since Dr. Sinclair first spoke to them. A couple of times during the night a passing nurse smiled and shook her head to acknowledge their presence, conveying a message of nothing new to report. She said goodbye an hour before, at the end of her shift, and since then they saw the morning shift replacements arrive but didn't speak to them.

Dan offered Tara his cup, which she looked at and sniffed before turning her nose up at it.

"How much longer?" she said to nobody.

"This is always the worst part. I remember last year all the waiting for news about Jim and look at him now," Gwen said hopefully.

Tara smiled wanly. "He's so small."

"But he's half you and half Dan. That's a great combination."

Jim put an arm around Dan's shoulder. "How are you holding up?"

"I can tell you I'm fine, but it wouldn't be the truth."

"If only I had told you about Bradley being sick last week. We might have been able to avoid this somehow."

Dan shook his head. "Don't even go there. I'm just glad you noticed it at all, and that Gwen couldn't clean his bedding yesterday."

"How on earth did you remember Zoe being ill like that? I'm sure it wasn't in the paperwork anywhere."

"No, it wasn't. I think I wrote it in my book but never in the more official documentation or the stuff we've prepared over the last months. But Zoe being there like she was when I woke up the next morning and how she vomited all over the floor at my feet is something I will take to my grave."

"It's hard to believe." Jim sighed.

Dan looked over to Tara and Gwen. "Honestly, I don't know what to believe anymore."

Footsteps and then the sight of yet another doctor prevented Dan from having to ponder his last comment for a while at least.

"Tara and Dan?" she asked as she approached.

"Yes," they replied together.

While Doctors Ripton and Sinclair were duplicates in uniform white coats and a look of cowboys after a long day in the saddle, the early morning brought them a new vision. One in pale blue surgical scrubs from head to toe.

"Hello, I'm Sarah McDonnell. I'm one of the surgical team here."

Gwen clasped her hands together, before pulling Jim down onto the plastic seats. Dan and Tara stood like statues.

"I won't waste your time because I need to explain what's happening to Bradley. Dan you were absolutely correct about him. He has a complicated diverticulitis which we need to do something about this morning. I and one of my senior colleagues are going into theatre in a few minutes but I wanted to see you first."

"You're operating?" Tara whispered.

Dan heard the same words too, but he was concentrated on another. "Complicated; what does that mean?"

"Yes," she replied to Tara. "Bradley's diagnosis is rather serious. His diverticulitis has affected his colon too and we believe it has led to the onset of peritonitis. We won't know until we can see but at this time, I think we'll be performing the first of two operations today.

"If I can explain a little. His colon is damaged, and we need to remove that affected part and rejoin the remaining sections today. This surgery, called partial colectomy, will hopefully prevent complications and future diverticulitis.

"He also requires surgery for other complications caused by the diverticulitis. There's a perforation in there somewhere, probably fistulas and a large intestinal obstruction. One or a combination of these things caused all the bleeding.

"Two surgeries will be required because it's not safe to rejoin the colon right away. His waste will be collected in a pouch attached to the stoma—that's the name for the abdominal opening.

"In the second surgery we'll rejoin the ends of the colon and close the stoma. But that's for another time. I'm sorry to dump all this on you without warning but our schedule was busy already. We need to do this as a matter of urgency and so he will be in first. I wanted to tell you in person."

Tara looked to Dan; she was in no condition to reply. He was almost at a loss too; he couldn't function properly as a father at that moment and so he reverted to what he knew best. He just wanted cold, hard facts.

"Right. How long and what are the dangers, if any?"

McDonnell studied the wall clock. "It really depends on the severity of his abdominal condition. We need to go carefully because he's such a very small person and so all his body parts are small too. I hope if we begin at eight a.m., we'll be finished before eleven. Of course, there are dangers associated with all surgery but we've a fine team here. While Bradley is at the extreme end of what we've seen before, you can be confident it's not the first time.

"I must go now, or we'll miss our time slot. Either I or one of my colleagues will come and see you as soon as we get through."

As she disappeared from where she came from Tara started to cry again.

"Hey, come here. It's going to be okay," Dan said. He checked his watch; it was seven minutes before 8:00 a.m.

Nick arrived at the prison later than he wanted. With only ten minutes before his appointment time, he was made to rush through the admin duties associated with a police officer meeting a prisoner.

He held up his ID badge. "Nick Hetherington to see Edward Vikkert. Sorry I'm late," he said to the fresh-faced constable who was the duty police liaison officer.

He dumped his briefcase and outer coat and signed for a police visitor pass as on similar occasions before. He was about to head out again when the constable called him back.

"You have to sign in here as well."

"What?"

"The general register too. Home Office rules."

Nick decided against telling him what he thought of the new rules as it would undoubtedly only result in a further delay. He blew out his cheeks as a token gesture. "Show me where."

The constable pointed to a list of names and numbers that filled the latest page of a great volume the size of a wallpaper samples book.

"Alphabetical order; find your man and put your details in. As you're police, don't put your name in, just your ID number; you don't want the next ones to see your name."

Great. Trust me to get a V, Nick thought as he pulled over a stack of heavy pages until he found the second of two sheets with Edward Vikkert's name and prisoner number halfway down.

He pulled his pen from the inside of his jacket but didn't write. Instead he looked in utter amazement.

After an awkward minute the constable said, "Is there something wrong? Just write your ID number."

Nick tried to think and decide what to do. He wanted to call Dan but that was impossible. He thought about trying Jim instead but realised he would invariably say 'speak to Dan.' He waved vaguely at the young man.

He heard the constable say again, "You can't see him unless you sign in," and made up his mind what he was going to do.

Five minutes later he was back in his car and driving towards the police headquarters building in Nottingham.

Dan was telling the others more about diverticulitis when Sarah McDonnell appeared once again with another theatre-ready colleague.

"Hello again. How are you doing?"

Tara snapped to attention. "You tell us. How is Bradley? Is it over?"

"Yes, I just got out of theatre two minutes ago. It went well. Too early to talk about recovery obviously but considering the amount of internal damage, he did very well indeed. He'll go back to the ICU shortly but as soon as the anaesthetic has worn off and he's awake he can go to a room where you can see him."

McDonnell's colleague cleared his throat.

"I'm sorry, I have to go again, another emergency. Give the nurses, say ten minutes, and then they will tell you about seeing Bradley," McDonnell said.

"Thank you. Thanks very much," Dan replied as the two blue figures retreated once more.

"I'm glad it's good news. Hopefully see you again in the next day or so," McDonnell said over her shoulder without breaking stride.

Nick squirmed on the anteroom sofa outside the office of the force's most senior detective. The wooden plaque on the closed door was engraved 'Detective Chief Superintendent T. G. Bushell' and up until this second, Nick was almost proud to say he had never been this close to the room before.

Mr. Bushell's PA, Sue, looked over her glasses again and gave him a knowing smile. A nervous junior officer waiting to see the boss was a regular occurrence in her working day, however Nick's arrival and request was unusual. Fortunately for him, Mr. Bushell could give him fifteen minutes Sue said when he arrived unannounced; he'd been waiting for ten minutes since then.

He looked up like a startled cat when Sue's telephone buzzed.

"Yes, right away," she said non-committally. "You can go in now Mr. Hetherington."

Her polite directive made Nick even more uncomfortable. The title of 'Mr' brought on feelings of him soon being out of the job.

"Nick, do come in. I don't think I've had the pleasure before," Tom Bushell said, rising from his high-backed swivel chair.

Bushell extended his hand, which Nick shook. "Have a seat."

"Thanks sir, and thanks for seeing me without any notice."

Nick only knew Tom Bushell by reputation, which was that he was a good bloke who had not lost his common sense en route to the top.

"So, what have you done? Or worse, what have I done? I'm not used to requests for meetings like this," Bushell asked, raising his eyebrows.

Nick spent the journey from Leicester back to Nottingham swaying like a pendulum. Call Dan or don't call Dan? Report what he knew or say nothing? Even in the anteroom he was still undecided, so he was somewhat surprised to find himself sitting in front of the head of CID and still not one hundred percent sure what to say.

He cleared his throat. "Sir, I know this is very unorthodox, but can I ask you a question?"

"You can ask," Bushell replied, making it clear it didn't mean he would answer.

Nick cleared his throat again. "Does Stromboli mean anything to you?"

He saw Bushell's eyes bulge. "Why do you ask, Nick?" Bushell croaked.

It wasn't the answer he was hoping for and Nick had to think of what to say next. "Sir, because if you do know anything, I think I know a whole lot more and I'm in way over my head but not so far as to have caused a major fuck up."

The vein on the side of Bushell's temple pulsed and Nick managed to congratulate himself on noticing although he didn't have a clue if it was a good sign or not.

After an eternity Bushell held up a hand and pressed a button on his phone console with the other.

"Sue, no calls. Cancel Peter Timmins and apologise for not telling him sooner."

Tom Bushell pushed his chair back and came around to Nick's side of the desk and took the other vacant visitor's chair.

"What the bloody hell have you been doing?"

Nick began at a beginning he invented that very second. "For the past few weeks and more I've been doing a bit of extra-curricular work with an ex-job friend on a cold case, a girl called Zoe Summers. In working the intelligence we've stumbled on Stromboli and today I realised we're much closer to it than we thought. If we do any more, I don't know where it will lead."

Tom Bushell leant closer. "What do you know about Stromboli?"

Death or glory, Nick thought. "It's either the name of a person or the reference name to a massive heroin supply network. Stromboli distributed heroin from a derelict farmhouse in the Peaks National Park in 2006. Locals were used to pack the stuff using shoe polish to conceal and protect it. Our girl Zoe was one of those packers.

"She was killed in a house in Powton Road, Mapperley, in late 2006. We know the names of some of the players and I've discovered another one today. That's how I know it's time to stop before we go too far."

Bushell stared in disbelief and took some time to assimilate Nick's information deluge. "Nick, have you broken the law to your knowledge?"

All his bridges were well and truly alight. Honesty wasn't going to be Nick's best policy; it was his only one.

"I've used my job laptop to conduct so many data searches I've lost count and shared the information with my friend."

"How much more do you have on Stromboli and the Summers girl?"

"A lot."

"I'll need it Nick, all of it."

"Yes sir."

"And your friend. You've not mentioned his name."

"No sir, he doesn't know I'm here."

"Well you had better call and tell him because I want to see him in this office in the next twenty-four hours."

"That might be a problem, sir."

"I wasn't asking you Nick. Use the phone over there. I have to make a call too."

When Dan answered Nick made sure he was facing away from his boss.

"Hi it's me. I'm really sorry to call you now with everything that's going on, but we need to talk."

"Hi, I was going to call you. Bradley has just got out of surgery. We're waiting to go and see him."

"Surgery!"

"Yes, I can't explain now, it looks like we're going," Dan said.

"Okay, um, can you and Jim call me as soon as you can after?"

"Yes sure. Is everything alright with you, Nick?"

"Yes, fine. Call me when you can. I've to go too. See you."

Nick clicked off and turned to see Tom Bushell was waiting on the phone.

"Well?" Bushell said without looking at him.

"He has medical problems and he's going to call me back," Nick said.

Bushell held up his hand again like before. "Good morning this is Detective Chief Superintendent Tom Bushell of Nottinghamshire Police. I would like to talk to someone about Stromboli, code number six."

Nick watched Bushell nodding as he listened to a voice at the other end of the line.

"Yes, that's correct….I believe so….What time…Yes of course. Who should we ask for…Thank you. Until tomorrow." Bushell put the folder back in the drawer. "Nick, come and sit down."

Nick sat.

"We have an appointment at ten a.m. tomorrow in Birmingham. You, me, and your friend."

Nick went back to his office but didn't stay. By the time he got there, his immediate supervisor had received the call from the Tom Bushell to say Nick was being seconded as of today for an unspecified amount of time.

Nick went home to tell Penny what happened and wait for a call from Dan. He and Dan always joked about there not being any such thing as a coincidence in police work. What he'd seen in the visitor's book at the prison was no coincidence and it sure as hell wasn't a joke. It wasn't close to midday when he poured himself a large whisky. Penny didn't say a word. Dan finally called at 2:00 p.m.

"How's Bradley?" he made himself ask first.

"Better than us. He's out of immediate danger and is sleeping off the anaesthetic."

"That's good to hear. What was it?"

"Diverticulitis. It's a bowel and abdominal condition."

Dan explained a little more and Nick relayed the salient parts to Penny who was hanging on every word.

"You sounded a bit off earlier?" Dan said when he was finished.

Not for the first time that day, Nick cleared his throat. "I wasn't sure what to do. I had to make a decision, so I hope you'll understand when I tell you."

"Look whatever it is, it's all good Nick. We're all here, and I've put you on speaker."

Nick began. "When I was signing in to see Vikkert I saw the names of his previous visitors. Every two months since he's been in there, Howard Young and John Trew have come to see him." Silence at the other end gave him no clue to what Dan and the others were thinking. Nick felt that he had no option but to plough on.

"After I saw that, I decided not to do the visit. Do you know how close this puts us to Stromboli? With you there with Bradley I decided to make a call."

"What did you decide?" Dan asked.

Nick's stomach was in knots, still unable to tell what Dan was feeling. "I went to see Tom Bushell, Det Chief Superintendent Bushell. Dan, Stromboli is not just still active; it has a top priority label with SIS. Unlimited budget and unlimited resources."

The sickening silence made him examine his phone. "Dan. Are you still there mate? I had to do something."

"Yes, still here. You must have near had a coronary."

"That's putting it mildly. Are we okay? I mean is what I did okay?'

"Yes sure. Anything else?"

Nick let out a long, relieved breath. "From what Tom Bushell told me, and it wasn't a lot, I think we must currently be the pre-eminent knowledge base for one of the biggest and most secret criminal investigations this country's ever known."

"Are you in trouble?" Dan asked.

Nick groaned. "I don't think I can answer that until tomorrow and that's the other reason for calling. Hold on to your arses but tomorrow at ten a.m. we, that's you and me, have to be in Birmingham with Tom Bushell to explain all this to the head of SIS and God knows who else."

"Both of us!" Dan exploded.

"Dan, I had to tell him about my ex-job friend who put it all together in the first place, but I do have an idea."

CHAPTER THIRTY-ONE

Nick declined Tom Bushell's invitation to drive down to Birmingham together, explaining he wanted to meet his friend first and they would bring all the information with them to the meeting.

The address looked like any other city office block but once inside and past the lifts for the general public they could tell this was no normal office suite. A swipe card lock protected every door and CCTV monitored each corner. A silent, business suited male with no obvious ID escorted them through three corridors to an internal conference room with no windows. Bushell was already there, as were at least twelve other men and women aged between twenty-five and sixty.

Tom Bushell's jaw dropped when they entered the room. Staring at Nick's accomplice, he didn't speak.

"Come in. Put your things down there and have a seat," one of the older men said.

After they sat in the only two vacant seats the same man instructed the suited escort to leave and close the door.

"Right introductions," he said. "My name is Kenneth Watters and I'm the Deputy Head of our nation's Special Intelligence Service."

He indicated to others on his flanks and read out a list of names and job titles like a shopping list; the various men and women responded with nods or business-like hellos. When Watters was finished, he put his hands on the vast mahogany table and entwined his fingers.

"Now Mr. Hetherington, your turn."

"Thank you, sir," Nick began, sounding a lot more confident than he felt. "I'm Detective Constable Nick Hetherington, currently attached to Nottinghamshire Vehicular Crime Task Force and this is James Allen; Jim was the head of Nottinghamshire CID until he retired last year."

"Mr. Allen, welcome. We've been wondering who Mr. Hetherington's secret associate was," Watters said, flicking a nod to a younger colleague who started typing on a laptop at phenomenal speed.

"Stromboli. You have our undivided attention gentlemen."

Nick turned to Jim and nodded before sitting back. Jim cleared his throat and began as he, Nick, and Dan agreed the previous evening.

Nick listened intently despite his exhaustion from travelling up and down between home and Salcombe for the second time in three days and spending half the night rehearsing this meeting, before he and Jim drove back up first thing.

"In November 2006 a seventeen-year-old girl called Zoe Summers died, murdered at twenty-two Powton Road, Mapperley in Nottingham. I didn't become fully aware of the circumstances for several years until I was directed to review the cold case soon after I became the Detective Chief Superintendent.

"At that time there was insufficient information to progress the matter and it was filed again. I'm not able to explain to you why, but for some reason the manner of Zoe Summers' death had a profound effect on me. I never forgot the case.

"Last year Nick came to my assistance when I was attacked in my home. That incident caused my slightly early retirement and we've remained in close contact since then. I decided several months ago to do some more investigation into the Zoe Summers case, and I asked Nick to help me."

Jim took a breath, allowing Nick to continue.

"Jim did a lot of work on the existing information before he asked me to assist." He saw Watters go to speak but he paused and waved Nick on.

"We have the written intelligence here, but the details are as follows. Zoe was strangled by an unknown person, probably male who at the time had an injured third finger on his right hand. Immediately prior to being strangled she was attacked with a chef's sharpening steel tool and stabbed in the upper leg. We believe that assailant was Edward Vikkert, who is in Leicester Prison currently doing time for another violent crime.

"We identified a number of other people who were present at Powton Road on the night Zoe Summers died. By following their information stream, we were initially told of Stromboli.

"By following other evidence trails we also located and identified an old stone building a few hundred metres off the Tissington Cycle Path at the southern end of the Peak District National Park. The building and surrounding area gave us more detail, including the confirmation that Stromboli is a person or a reference to the network which was distributing large quantities of heroin. Powton Road was in fact one of those distribution points.

"I'm sorry if I'm telling you what you already know." Nick looked up and was sure they didn't know any of this.

"Stromboli got its or his name from the Disney animated film Pinocchio. At least one of the involved parties has taken an alias from the film, a male we know as John Trew."

One of the other older males to Watters' immediate left sighed deeply and muttered, "Walt Disney cartoons. Oh shit."

Watters glared at him and he looked suitably admonished.

Nick continued. "I was going to Leicester Prison yesterday to see Edward Vikkert and put the allegation to him about the attack on Zoe, but when I was signing in, I noticed he has been getting regular visits from John Trew and another name we've come across, Howard Young. It was only then I realised how close we were getting to Stromboli, so I went to see Mr. Bushell."

"Nick called me yesterday from Mr. Bushell's office to say we must stop given Trew and Young's association to Edward Vikkert," Jim explained.

Watters looked across to Tom Bushell who acknowledged the last sentence as being correct.

"You gentlemen will have to excuse us for a few minutes. Can you wait outside? Someone will get you coffee if you'd like some."

Nick and Jim were ushered into the outer office. They wanted to talk but neither knew if they were about to be arrested. Nick accepted the offer of coffee and drank two before the door opened again and they were invited to return.

"Detective Barry Towers?" Watters asked as soon as they were seated again.

"I've asked him to use the police databases to research intelligence for us," Jim replied honestly.

"Hmm I see. And John Calder? Better known to you as Daniel Calder?"

Nick tried to remember what they practiced. He pinched the nail of his index finger into his thumb as hard as he could to induce his body to react to the pain rather than the question and not give anything away in non-verbal communication.

"Dan is one of my best friends; he was even with me last year when I got the call to help Jim. He and his family are over here on holiday from New Zealand at the moment. I've been picking his brains about certain aspects and he has been a help in that way."

"Dan Calder was also an undercover operative at the time Zoe Summers died. As luck would have it, he's been able to give me quite a lot of background information about what Mapperley was like at the time," Jim added.

Watters looked around the table, but Nick couldn't read what was going on. It was as if Dan had trained this group too.

"You've put us in a rather difficult position gentlemen. Unauthorised use of police computer systems is a serious matter."

"You're right, we've no defence," Jim said bluntly.

"This could cost you your job, Nick."

"I became a policeman to serve. We're close to solving a murder which would otherwise never have been solved and I don't believe we've harmed the public or the force in the process. I'll be able to sleep easily whatever the decision is, but I would prefer not to be prosecuted and still have my job this time tomorrow."

A hint of a smile played on Watters lips. He turned to Tom Bushell.

"He's your officer Mr. Bushell. What do you recommend?"

"He's clearly good and conscientious. Unfortunately for Nottinghamshire, in the light of what's been discussed I can't see any way in which we can keep him though."

Nick's heart sank. Jim looked at him in desperation.

"Please, Nick's only been assisting me," Jim said.

"Mr. Allen. You signed the Official Secrets Act in relation to Stromboli when you were put in post. We have some control over what you can say and do," Watters said.

"Yes, but I can guarantee Nick is no threat to your security."

"Definitely," Nick said in confirmation but still in shock.

Watters grinned unexpectedly. "Well this is much more how I like things, with me having the upper hand. As I was about to say, and Mr. Bushell agrees with me, for the time being you're far more important to SIS than you are to Nottingham and you will be seconded to us as of today. It's going to cause you some travel difficulties, but we'll have to find a way around it."

"That was bloody exciting," Tom Bushell said once he ordered the drinks and joined Nick and Jim at the table.

"Speak for yourself. I think you just about had Nick convinced he was being sacked." Jim laughed.

"SIS then, Nick. How about that?"

"Sir, I don't know what to say. I'm sorry if you feel I let you or the department down. It was never a case of that."

"I'm glad you came to me when you did. We could all have been up to our necks in it otherwise."

"I should phone my wife and tell her she doesn't have to put the house up for sale. Jim has to go south when we finish. Can I get that lift back to Nottingham with you please?"

When they parted company, Jim watched Tom Bushell's car disappear around the corner before he called Dan with the good news.

After the trials of the previous two and a half days the mood was joyous as Dan, Tara, Gwen, and the recently returned Jim sat around the table.

He described the events of the day in as much detail as he could remember. The whole experience was other worldly due to the circle he and Nick found themselves moving in. The fact they knew so much more than the so-called experts surrounding them was intimidating.

When they thought Nick was about to be carted away in handcuffs one moment and then discovered he was in fact the SIS's latest recruit the next, Jim confessed he was close to collapsing.

"So, what next?" Tara asked.

"I think the Stromboli thing will take whatever course they decide," Jim said. "Nick's going to have to separate all that stuff from Zoe Summers, which will go back to Nottingham; Tom Bushell will directly take charge of the case. I imagine he'll still have to get clearance at every step.

"Just as well we went through everything last night. When this Watters chap mentioned your name Dan, Nick and I both thought the game was up."

"So, they really believed you were doing all the investigations into Zoe Summers and you roped Nick in over the last few weeks?" Gwen asked.

"Luckily for us it does fit in with all the information we could give them," Jim confirmed. "All the printing you and Tara did while Dan was teaching us our lines made it look like I produced every scrap. There wasn't anything to link it to him, so you got to spend all day with your boy. How is he?"

Dan sipped his wine. "He's not out of the woods yet but he's not in immediate danger anymore. They said he must have been born with the diverticulitis and his insides were a mess."

"He'll be in there for a couple of weeks probably," Tara added.

Dan touched her cheek. "And then a second operation at home to seal his colon in six to twelve months."

Jim allowed himself a broad smile. The ultra-stressful beginning to the day was, if not a distant memory now, at least relegated in priority in the close company of those he valued most.

CHAPTER THIRTY-TWO

Early the next morning Dan and Tara began their new daily routine of travelling between Salcombe and Plymouth for the near future at least. Jim and Gwen happily stated they wouldn't be going any further than the end of the garden and would be available to assist anytime.

In contrast, Nick had a very busy day starting with a meeting with Tom Bushell and his hurriedly brought together team who'd be continuing Operation Frozen Summer.

He finally got to Birmingham at midday and after several hours of administration, in which he was formally inducted into the SIS and signed his life away, he gave his first briefing to his new squad. Their sole purpose was to bring down the Stromboli organisation. The squad was named K and comprised of twenty hand-picked officers from all corners of the country. They'd been together since 2007 when the service first became aware of several highly complex heroin importation and distribution networks, one of which was in the Midlands.

Over the years they worked long and hard, with most success being in the south and south east. Their very limited joy with Stromboli didn't even include discovering the true nature of the name's animated history. When Nick dropped this information on them it was as if they were hit by a bomb. The subsequent conversation explosion focused on how they'd managed to miss something so apparently simple.

The next morning Nick went to see Tom Bushell first thing to give him the latest before driving the fifty miles to Birmingham.

With no time to rest, he presided over the first proper daily briefing and tasking session. He felt like he'd completed a full day's work before lunch. He was also astounded by the resources that now surrounded him; within seconds of any request being made, the answer magically appeared.

Less than an hour after dishing out the first directives he was approached by one of the team.

"I thought you'd like to see this. We wouldn't normally bring every result back to you, but the boss asked me to show you."

"Thanks, sorry I've forgotten your name already. There's so many of you."

"Rob," the man said, acknowledging how fried Nick's brain must be.

"Rob. Yes, sorry. Thanks, what am I looking at?"

"I got Howard Young. Look on the next page."

Nick turned the sheet over and read what appeared to be a handwritten addendum to another document it was referring to.

Howard Peter Young: Application for officer entry into the British Army was rejected because of his acute colour blindness. At the time Young expressed great annoyance and became abusive to the selection panel. His anger issue wasn't previously picked up during the process, which led Dr. Moss to suppose he either deliberately concealed his propensity for aggressive outbursts or has no control over such outbursts. Young argued that his colour blindness was less of a hindrance than his other listed injury but that wasn't a concern to the army. Major Tyler stated the fact Young was missing a portion of the third finger of his right hand wouldn't affect his ability to perform the duties required whereas his colour blindness would. Young made verbal threats towards members of the panel and had to be escorted from the premises.

Nick's first thought was to call Dan but then he remembered where he was. He stared at Rob with admiration and shock.

"Listen Nick. There are no secrets from us here once we've got a name. This Stromboli has been doing our heads in for years because it was so well concealed, but there's a real feeling we can crack it now."

Nick couldn't wait to take this new information to Bushell the next morning.

At the end of the day when he got into his car, he closed his eyes, enjoying the serenity of doing nothing for a minute before starting the drive home. His head still buzzed from the day's non-stop activity. K had the capacity to suck in information, analyse it, and produce results quicker than he could invent a task from the previous result. Nick was worried he was creating a bottle neck, such was the imbalance already between the incoming tray on one side of his desk and the outgoing on the other, but he simply couldn't go any faster. It was an intense introduction, and this was just the first full day.

When he reached Junction 11 of the M42 he pulled off the road and parked in the car park of the Appleby Hotel. The cheap mobile in the glove box was one Viola used months before and discarded when a newer and better model caught her eye; the pre-pay SIM card inside was one Dan gave him the day before.

He called the only number saved in the memory and waited for Dan to pick up.

"Hey superstar, how was your day?"

"Hell, Dan you wouldn't believe what I've been doing."

"Where are you now?"

"A hotel car park halfway between Birmingham and home. I thought you were being a bit dramatic when we got these pre-pays to talk on, but I take it all back."

Dan laughed. "How's that?"

"I hope you're sitting down. In less than an hour this morning we identified Zoe Summers' killer."

"You're fucking joking me!"

Nick glowed with pride. "I could hardly believe it myself. This SIS is like nothing I ever imagined. Yesterday I was a city cop playing at vehicle crime and doing a bit of unauthorised computer work. Today I'm a secret agent and by talking to you I'm probably committing treason."

"Tell me. Shit, Nick, tell me now."

"One of the guys here was tasked with Howard Young, remember him the HY from the old house?"

"Yes, I remember."

"He was only rejected from the army for being colour blind but at his interview he went ballistic at the panel because they refused him for that and not his injured finger on his right hand. In an hour! One hour and they got this," Nick enthused.

"You did the right thing in taking it to Bushell."

"I know and he's like my best mate all of a sudden. I can't wait to see the look on his face when I give him Young on a plate in the morning."

"Hold on Nick, Tara's here. T, Nick's found Zoe's killer.... She's rather pleased, mate."

Nick scanned around the car park as they talked, half expecting an elite group of masked commandos to appear and shoot him through the head.

"There's more Dan, but we shouldn't speak for too long as you said. I'll catch you again tomorrow about this time."

"Yes alright. Thanks again for calling."

"I'll call Jim's number later. Speak to you then."

Nick clicked off and put the mobile back in the glove box. There was a need for him and Jim to be in regular contact to maintain the story they'd given Watters and Bushell. However, after the series of warnings they were both given regarding the penalties for breaching the Official Secrets Act, neither was prepared to risk their known telephones being tapped and so those regular conversations needed to be carefully managed.

As promised, Nick called after he finished dinner.

"Hi, Jim, it's me. How are things with you today?"

"Nick! Good of you to call. I'm well, son. Gwen and I have been in the garden most of the day, but she's been making sure I take it easy. I know you can't say too much but how have things been with you?"

"Good, very good. I think it will take me a while to get up to speed with the new job, but you'll be very pleased with the results even at this early stage. It would be nice if Tom Bushell keeps you updated but that's something for him."

"Have you heard from Dan today or is he still at the hospital?"

"No, he and Tara are back here now. I'll let him tell you. So, there's good news about Zoe Summers is there?"

"Great in fact, but obviously I can't tell you what."

"No son, I understand."

"Look, Jim, you take it steady. I'll try and call you again at the weekend and maybe we can arrange a meet up at some point, although I've no idea when I'm going to have my next day off."

"That will be grand, Nick. Give our best to the family. I'll hand you over to Dan now."

"Love to Gwen too Jim, see you."

Dan took the handset. "Nick."

"Hi, how's Bradley doing? Jim told me he was taken into hospital the other day?"

"He was yes. It gave me and Tara a real fright, but they operated on him yesterday and he's much better today. He'll probably stay in there for a couple of weeks at least."

Their bland exchange continued; neither really believed the conversation was being monitored but they weren't sure enough to take chances. Eventually Dan started to wrap things up.

"You sound tired."

Nick didn't make the next part up. "I am. What with the travelling and the level of the work, I won't have any trouble sleeping for the foreseeable future. Silver linings and all that."

Dan grinned. "I better let you go then. Take care, talk again soon." He said knowing their next conversation would be more secretive and more worthwhile.

Nick was dead right about sleeping easily. That night he went to bed happy and very relieved. The next morning, he was in Tom Bushell's office at 7:30 a.m. with a broad smile and a briefcase full of treasure for Operation Frozen Summer. Martin would have called it the jackpot.

Bushell read through the summary, periodically glancing at Nick. When he was finished Nick said, "The directives are at the rear."

"Directives?"

"Stromboli is going to be proceeding at an ever-increasing pace. They think we should coordinate your arrest phase just in case Vikkert and Young being taken in for Zoe Summers compromises them."

"They?" Bushell said, clearly struggling for more than one word at a time.

Nick shrugged. "I couldn't tell you. I report to a guy called Rob who refers to his boss. I get the feeling my pay grade doesn't warrant knowing who he is."

Bushell nodded. "So, this is a bit of a luxury for us then is it? You give me all the intelligence and I can take my time in planning the interview strategy for these two characters. I'm hoping to get the reports on the sharpening steel by tomorrow and know for sure if the one Vikkert had in 2008 caused her injuries in 2006."

Nick reached for his briefcase. "I should be going sir. See you same time tomorrow."

As Nick was leaving Bushell's office, Dan and Tara were arriving at the hospital in Plymouth for another day of sitting and watching Bradley sleep, all so they could be sure to be there each time he woke.

They understood today would be another where they were prevented from picking him up, which was proving to be another ordeal. If Bradley had been strong enough to cry and remonstrate the day before it would have ripped at their heartstrings, but the best he managed was a gurgled "dada" and that still had them close to tears. They were a little better prepared today.

He was already awake in his tiny plastic bed, which better resembled a washing bowl; he beamed when they bent down over him. Tara kissed his forehead and stroked his face while he blew bubbles and cooed. Dan was happy to stand and watch. After ten minutes the exertion was too much, and Bradley fell asleep again.

Dan and Tara squeezed onto a single visitor's armchair where they could maintain their watching brief and settled down for another long wait.

"I'm so glad you're here," Tara said after a minute.

"Where else would I be?"

"You know, with Nick and Zoe you could be forgiven for wanting to be in Nottingham or sat in front of a computer somewhere doing your own thing."

"In that case I should be saying sorry to you for doing things in the past that would make you think like that now. When I was at the church on Sunday and you were trying to contact me, Eric read a lesson or a passage from the Bible and then said something called a Homily, which is an explanation of the reading."

Tara looked at him doubtfully.

Dan raised an eyebrow and laughed. "I've not been converted or anything like that, but what he said made sense. It put things in perspective."

He told her about Saint Paul and Saint Luke. While she listened and watched him, Dan didn't take his eyes off Bradley.

CHAPTER THIRTY-THREE

8 February. 0600 hours. Nottingham Police Headquarters.

"Take your seats quickly please," Tom Bushell said into the microphone as several dozen assorted uniformed and plain clothes officers filed into headquarters' largest conference room.

"Thank you," he said five minutes later, bringing the room to an immediate hush.

"We're running a bit late so let's get on. This is the briefing for arrest day, Operation Frozen Summer. The op orders on your seats when you came in are colour coded and so if you're not on the team which corresponds to your document, move and find the right seat now."

Nobody moved.

"Good. I'm Detective Chief Superintendent Tom Bushell, Nottinghamshire. Welcome to those of you from London and Birmingham, as well as my Notts colleagues.

"Frozen Summer relates to the unlawful killing of Zoe Summers, a seventeen-year-old girl who was murdered in Mapperley, Nottingham, in 2006. Relatively new information has resulted in two suspects being identified to us and today our intention is to effect the arrest of those two individuals and secure them for interview.

"The arrests will take place in two locations; suspect one in London and suspect two in Leicester. Both suspects will then be conveyed to Nottingham Central Police Station for interview.

"Questions? No? Good. I'll hand you over now to the Operational Commander for the day who will conduct this briefing. Ladies and gentlemen, Detective Nick Hetherington."

8 February. 1226 hours. Ash Hill Road, Notting Hill, London.

It had been a long time since Nick was last in a surveillance car. Although Dan wasn't sitting next to him on this occasion, all his best memories of days like this included him. Nevertheless, he felt quite at home.

"This is Op Comm to all units, listen up," Nick said into his covert microphone. "Front of house arrest team, are you in position?"

"Front of house arrest team to Op Comm; yes, yes."

"Rear of house arrest team, are you in position?"

"Rear of house arrest team to Op Comm; yes, yes."

Tom Bushell reached over from the back seat and touched Nick on the shoulder. "Well done. Great job."

"Thanks sir."

Nick depressed his mic button. "Op Comm to all units; strike! Strike! Strike!"

Bushell put his phone to his ear. "They're going in now. Detain Vikkert."

9 February. 0945 hours. Interview room 19, Nottingham Central Police Station.

Jelena Copich was very pleased to have been asked to be involved. Although she wanted to lean across the table and punch him, she concentrated on the matter in hand.

"This is your one and only opportunity to talk to us. I've explained the evidence we have and our ability to use force if necessary to examine your hand, Howard."

Young snarled like a caged animal. "You can try."

Copich didn't flinch. Instead, she slammed her clenched fists down on the table to assist her standing up and leant over towards her suspect. "I've waited a long time for this moment and waiting a couple more minutes would be my absolute pleasure. Get six blokes in here now," she barked at her colleague sat by the door without taking her eyes off Young.

She sat back down to wait for the reinforcements. Young was the first to avert his eyes.

"I've got friends," he said.

"The things found in your house at the time you were arrested are another matter entirely. Other officers will undoubtedly talk to you about how you came to have several kilos of heroin packed in foil and shoe polish in your bedroom. So, let's you and me just concentrate on Zoe Summers for now."

"Jim?" Dan answered the phone quickly. He was in the entrance-lobby café, which he'd long since established made the best coffee out of all the hospital's options.

"It's done, son. Nick called me a short while ago. Howard Young admitted strangling Zoe in interview and put Edward Vikkert right there next to him when he did it."

Dan sat down on the nearest available seat and rubbed his eyes. "I don't know what to say."

"Vikkert went no comment which was expected, but Young apparently sang like a bird after trying it on to begin with."

"Why'd he do it?"

"He said he lost his calm when Zoe threw up. Vikkert had just stabbed her with the steel because she wouldn't explain how she knew you were police."

"So how did she know about me then?"

"I don't think any of us will ever know that, son. It put the interviewers in a spin when Young said there was an undercover cop in the house. It wasn't something they or SIS knew. Nick said he nearly pissed himself about that bit because in months of working there, it was one of the few things they didn't know. As he's in charge of the tasking, I think it's safe to say they never will now." Jim paused to think. "How's the little man?"

"He's good. Did Young say anything about Stromboli?"

Jim sighed. "That's another interview for another day. Nick said they're still some way off identifying Stromboli if he or she is a person, but they're getting closer to Craig Matthews and John Trew. I wouldn't hold your breath, but Nick might surprise us one of these days."

"How was he?"

"Tired still, but they've given him a new car and he's got the leave booked for his and Penny's trip to see you. So, he'll effectively retire next November and pick up his last two or three pay cheques while they're with you in New Zealand."

Minutes later and back in position Dan related the news to Tara. When he finished, she went to reply but Bradley woke up and started calling "mama." Dan smiled and nodded; it, like lots of other things, could wait for another day.

CHAPTER THIRTY-FOUR

Next morning Tara proclaimed she needed one final visit to the shops with Gwen. English Marmite and some of the chocolate bars available in the local supermarket left her salivating for more from her first try and the selection of baby clothes for Bradley was mind-boggling in diversity and quality. Gwen didn't need to be asked twice; when they departed the house an hour before the shops opened, they were in vocally high spirits. Gwen promised to meet Dan and Jim at the hospital later on without specifying a precise time.

The two men sat comfortably at the kitchen table enjoying the silence with a coffee and green tea in front of them—Dan being the happier of the two in that regard. It seemed a very long time since he felt comfortable with silence, both outward and more importantly, inward. Bradley remained in hospital but despite his current status life was good. There were no more unknowns except for positive future anticipations. Over the last few days he'd definitely let his guard down; he was more relaxed than he had been in years. After breakfast they'd call the hospital to see how Bradley was overnight, confirm if he was or wasn't having a procedure today, and then probably head on in for the daily vigil.

The overnight fog started to lift at first light, but some still hung stubbornly in the lower branches of trees along the lanes and narrow roads at the base of Beadon Road. Tara smiled as she thought of the similarity to the net curtains all the English houses seemed to have in the road facing windows.

As Gwen's new little hatchback zipped along, they chatted about its versatility and ease of parking. With some of the worst times imaginable finally behind them, Tara could talk freely and was thinking more than the next day ahead.

"Really, why don't you come out to us next summer too when Nick and Penny are over?" It wasn't the first time she and Dan extended the open invitation to Gwen and Jim. "We could take six weeks and do the whole country together."

Gwen slowed the car a touch. "It's very tempting, all that sunshine, but it's such a long way and Jim would have to be cleared to travel by his doctors. You know despite all he says he's still not his old self."

Tara saw Gwen was thinking back as she spoke yet couldn't help herself planning the extended road trip as Gwen continued talking. The Allens were the family she'd craved for longer than she'd known one was craved. They were the only 'grandparents' Bradley would ever know and certainly one of the major reasons for Dan's new-found state of well-being. She closed her eyes for a moment before an intake of breath to her right, so small and brief it couldn't be described as a gasp, drew her attention forward once more. Her vision was overwhelmed by fast moving scarlet. The oncoming red postal truck seemed to fill the entire windscreen.

Dan and Jim sauntered through the hospital's main entrance after finding a great parking spot and better still, the pay machine inoperative, meaning a free stay. They found the first lift ready and waiting to make their way up to Bradley's floor. Little victories like those automatically made the whole day better.

Bradley was still asleep, or rather, asleep again. Having had his breakfast, the effort of which was still debilitating to his small body, he'd lapsed back to dreamland just a few minutes before they arrived according to Samantha, his dedicated carer for the early shift.

"No problem, we know the drill," Dan replied. "Shall we?" he said, looking at Jim.

They took up station in the two chairs on opposite sides of a little table that enabled both to see through the clear plastic side of Bradley's bed.

"He looks a bit better, a bit rosier in the face," Jim said. His last visit was a couple of days before.

The constant room temperature meant no concerns for Bradley getting cold and so the fact he was laid on top of his bedding was a non-issue. There was a fresh empty bag by his side, attached to his chest by a stitched in tube supported by gauze and tape. It too was an ordinary part of his overall appearance now and didn't factor in their minds as they assessed his condition.

Jim took a pack of cards out of his jacket pocket and placed it on the table for later, when a natural break in conversation could put them to use.

"Coffee?" Dan asked.

"Already? We've only just got here, son. Oh, go on then, but a milky one for me so I can pretend I'm being good."

Before Dan got up, Samantha's head appeared around the door as if any more would be an intrusion.

"Mr. Allen...Mr. Calder...I mean...it's the...they um....The Police....You both."

The 'You both' was said with disbelief.

She took a deep breath and got her self-control back enough to string a whole sentence together. "The police are here. They need to talk to you both in the day room. Can you come this way?"

Dan's gut tightened involuntarily, as if he'd been grabbed by a boa constrictor. He shot a glance at Jim who seemed to have lost the colour in his face he'd been complimenting Bradley on a few minutes before. Neither spoke. They'd been in the position of the un-seen officers a dozen times before, of being the cop to request a relative, nurse, or co-worker to ask an individual to step outside to receive some news. The news was never good.

The day room was no more than ten steps from Bradley's. Dan noticed the young male officer through the reinforced glass panel busily consulting his notebook and mouthing a few words as if practicing. The coils of his inner boa constricted further.

When Jim pushed the door open, the officer stood up as he looked up.

"Mr Allen?" he said deliberately.

Jim nodded.

"And Mr…"

"Calder," Dan replied before the young man had a chance.

"My name is Oakley, Mark Oakley. I'm afraid I have some bad news for you about a road traffic crash which happened earlier this morning."

Dear Reader,

Thank you so much for taking this journey with me and especially so if you've been with Dan and me from the start.

I am constantly thinking of delivering the best product I can to you and hope you won't be too outraged by the 'second ending' of this book. For a while I've wondered *what next* for Dan and as the feedback I get from readers is always inspirational, I've decided to leave that decision to you, the readers.

So please tell me…what's happened to Tara? Is she alive or dead?

Alive means Dan's happy family lifestyle will continue into his next adventure, to begin with at least. If Tara didn't make it then Dan will be back in the area of square one but now as a single parent to Bradley as he continues his recovery.

The next book is already planned, and there are two scenarios that can play out depending on Tara's well-being or demise. I can't wait to be told how you'd prefer it to be.

Contact me with your thoughts through my website www.ianaustin.org or via my Ian Austin Author Facebook page. There's also ianaustinauthor on Instagram too, or you can even stop me in the street or send a message in a bottle!

Best regards,

Ian

The Agency

Dan Calder is an ex Brit and ex policeman looking for a fresh start in a new country but still carrying the baggage of failed relationships and a depressed, repressed past. He chose New Zealand because it was as far as he could get from his old life but did not take into account the universal six degrees of separation is no more than two or three in the land of the long white cloud.

The Agency provides a service like no other and New Zealand is the ideal location to find a new client. When Calder first encounters it by sheer chance, his life instantly changes and before long others are depending on him too.

Engaged in a deadly game with an unknown foe; this was not the new life Dan Calder planned for himself but now at stake is the ultimate reward; his own salvation.

The Second Grave

Dan Calder is back.
Back in his native England once again to help his best friend and ex-partner Nick Hetherington. Nick's daughter has been arrested in connection with the death of a Nottingham prostitute.

Back to face his darkest moment as old acquaintances and old enemies set his cupboard full of skeletons rattling once more. 'The Second Grave' has Calder facing the battle of his life to fulfil a solemn promise to his dearest friend.

New foes including a local gangster are prepared to do anything to prevent the truth being revealed. Left at home in New Zealand, Calder's girlfriend Tara senses he also views this return as an opportunity to settle old scores.

Time and the odds are against him; incredibly so too the upholders of law itself, his beloved police force. Rushing headlong towards the past; whoever coined the phrase you couldn't even make this stuff up was very wrong.